FINDING WINGS

A CHANDLER SISTERS NOVEL

FINDING WINGS

DEBORAH RANEY

THORNDIKE PRESS
A part of Gale, a Cengage Company

Scripture quotations are from the ESV Bible® (The Holy Bible, English Standard Version®), copyright © 2001 by Crossway, a publishing ministry of Good News Publishers. Used by permission. All rights reserved.
Thorndike Press, a part of Gale, a Cengage Company.

Thorndike Press® Large Print Christian Fiction.
The text of this Large Print edition is unabridged.
Other aspects of the book may vary from the original edition.
Set in 16 pt. Plantin.

LIBRARY OF CONGRESS CIP DATA ON FILE.
CATALOGUING IN PUBLICATION FOR THIS BOOK
IS AVAILABLE FROM THE LIBRARY OF CONGRESS.

ISBN-13: 978-1-4328-9568-6 (hardcover alk. paper)

Published in 2022 by arrangement with Kregel Publications, a division of Kregel Inc.

Printed in Mexico
Print Number: 01   Print Year: 2022

To my sweet sisters,
who were my first friends
and remain my very dearest friends.

Therefore the LORD waits to be gracious to you, and therefore he exalts himself to show mercy to you. For the LORD is a God of justice; blessed are all those who wait for him.

Isaiah 30:18

CHAPTER 1

November

Britt Chandler couldn't help the smile that came as she approached the freshly installed sign near the entrance to their long driveway. She tapped the brakes. The Cottages on Poplar Brook Road, the ornate wooden sign read. Billboard was more like it, the curlicue letters holding their own beneath painted silhouettes of poplar trees. The massive sign had cost a small fortune and even more to have it — and its smaller counterpart at the highway turnoff — installed. But Britt and her sisters agreed it was worth it, given the rather remote wooded acreage where they lived. More than one of their Airbnb customers had gotten lost trying to find the way on the curvy Missouri road.

Her phone chirped, and seeing her brother-in-law's name on the Caller ID, Britt pressed the button on the steering wheel to answer. "Hey, Quinn, what's up?"

"Not much. Are you home right now?"

"I will be in about two minutes. Why?"

"Would you mind looking in on Phee? At the new house."

"Sure. Is everything okay?" She didn't like the worry that had slipped into Quinn's voice. "She's working awfully late, isn't she?"

"As usual. And it's probably nothing, but she was feeling kind of puny when I took lunch by around one. I'm at the house here in town, but she's not home yet and she's not answering her phone. She's probably just working outside, but I'm out the door to a meeting at church and I'd feel better if somebody checked in on her. Maybe persuade her to go home if you can."

"Ha. You forget this is my stubborn big sister you're talking about."

"I remember. Believe me, I remember."

Britt laughed. "Let me get my groceries put away and I'll run over there. I have something to send home for you anyway."

"Oh?"

"It's a surprise, but you might want to save room for dessert when you get home from your meeting."

"My mouth is already watering. Thanks, Britt."

"No problem." Britt ended the call and

10

eased her Ford Escape up the lane. She frowned. Her oldest sister's pregnancy had been pretty routine, but Phylicia's morning sickness had dragged on for almost five months now — and not just in the mornings. Britt knew Phee was weary of it, especially when she had so many things she wanted to accomplish at the house she and Quinn were building on the property.

Britt peered up through the windshield and sighed to realize that the autumn colors were all but gone. The last smattering of leaves clung tenaciously to the poplars and dogwoods lining the lane. Before long, snow would blanket the countryside, leaching the landscape of the glorious golds and reds it had worn only a few weeks ago. Of course, winter had its own beauty here in southeast Missouri, but Britt wasn't ready for that yet. Especially not for how short the days had grown. She glanced at the dashboard. Not even six o'clock and it was already dark!

Still, her spirits lifted, as they always did, when the cottages came into sight. Lights gleamed from the cottage windows and even from a distance, Britt could see Joanna moving around inside, no doubt obsessing over the plans for her spring wedding.

Farther up the lane, she spotted Phee's car in front of the two-story home under

11

construction at the far end of the property. The house currently sported a roof and a pretty stone facade. If not for the field of mud where a front yard would be next spring, it almost looked like it might be occupied. Phylicia and Quinn were hoping to move in before the baby arrived in March. But since they were doing a lot of the work themselves, Britt had her doubts they'd make that deadline. Of course, she would never reveal those doubts to her oldest sister. Phee was nervous enough about being ready for the baby's arrival — a child she and Quinn jokingly declared had been conceived on their honeymoon in Hawaii. For now, they were living a few miles away in another house Quinn had built. Or at least that's where they slept. They spent nearly every waking hour at the construction site. Britt loved that they would soon all live here on the same property, but she sometimes worried that her sister overdid things. Half the time Phylicia forgot to eat lunch until Britt or Joanna reminded her. Or Quinn brought her a sandwich from town.

Remembering the cookies she'd baked this morning, Britt parked in front of her cabin and pulled her cell phone from her purse. She dialed Phee, but the phone went to voice mail. "This is Phee. You know what to do."

Britt waited impatiently for the tone. "Hey, you. I'm bringing over some cookies for you to take home. I made Quinn's favorite. Oatmeal scotchies."

The sisters all doted on Quinn Mitchell and for good reason. Britt wasn't sure how they would have managed getting their little Airbnb enterprise up and running without him. But things were going surprisingly well, despite some rather major hitches at the beginning. She and her sisters made a good team. In fact, only yesterday Phee declared that they'd built their renovation fund back up to the eleven thousand dollars they'd started with after purchasing the cottages free and clear. If Joanna's idea for opening a wedding venue here at the cottages took off, they could probably breathe easy where money was concerned.

She turned off the ignition and, as she did every time she arrived home, she stopped to admire the tiny stone cabin she'd claimed for her own. Dim lamplight outlined Melvin's silhouette on the windowsill, tail twitching, anticipating his nightly treat, no doubt. Her mother's tuxedo cat they'd inherited after Mom's death had decidedly become Britt's. Her sisters might argue with that claim, but Britt's cabin was where Melvin was fed, where he slept, and less happily, where his litter box resided. Mom would have loved knowing that Melvin had taken to country life so quickly. In some ways it felt surreal that the first anniversary of Mom's death was approaching, yet in other ways, it seemed an eternity since they'd had Mom in their lives.

Britt unloaded groceries from the back of the Escape and glanced toward Quinn and Phee's house. The lights were on inside, and she didn't see Phee outside. It wasn't like her to not return a call. She might be on the phone with someone else. Maybe Daddy had called from Florida. He'd been keeping in touch with Phee more often now that he was going to be a grandpa.

She heard the thud of Melvin jumping down from the windowsill and a second later he appeared in the kitchen. "Hey, buddy. Sorry, but you're going to have to wait a few minutes for your treat."

Britt gave him a quick head-to-tail stroke, then shrugged out of her jacket and put the groceries away before dialing Phee again. Straight to voice mail. Hmm. Well, no matter. She'd walk the cookies over and make sure everything was okay. The exercise would do her good after the three warm-from-the-oven cookies — and cookie dough worth three more — she'd snarfed while baking them this morning.

She slipped out of her boots, changed into tennis shoes, and donned her jacket again. The night air was cool and the ground soggy from recent rains, but she knew the lane by heart, rain or shine. Picking her way across the makeshift boardwalk Quinn had laid leading up to the house, she listened to the sounds of the Missouri night. A gentle breeze rustled the branches overhead, and a barn owl hooted above her somewhere in the canopy of the largest poplar.

Not that long ago, she would have been terrified to be alone in the night, but something about this beautiful spot of earth she and her sisters owned had cured her of that almost as soon as her name was on the title.

The porch light was on and Britt rang the bell. Muffled chimes sounded from inside. Good. Phee had been pestering Quinn to get the doorbell connected. Britt waited and rang again, knocking on the solid oak door for good measure. When that didn't rouse anyone, she tried the doorknob. Locked.

She knocked again. "Phee? Anybody home?"

Silence. She released a breath, set the paper plate of cookies on the edge of the half-finished porch, and stepped onto the boardwalk. Tiptoeing through the mud to the closest lit window, she was thankful she'd changed out of her favorite boots. She cupped her hands over her eyes and peered inside.

No sign of Phee, but a measuring tape and notepad lay atop a bolt of fabric on the kitchen counter. Britt remembered her sister saying she was going to try to sew all the curtains for this house. Not so much because she could save money that way, but because their mom had made the curtains for their childhood home, and Phee wanted to carry that tradition into the home her own children would grow up in.

Britt knocked on the window. "Phee?" she called again. It was too dark to see a clear path to the next lit window but she trudged blindly, the soft earth giving way beneath her feet. The landscape sloped downward on this side of the house, and by the time she reached the window, it was too high for her to look in.

She turned to retrace her steps but stopped, hearing an unfamiliar sound. Like the high-pitched mewing of a kitten. Holding perfectly still, she listened again. Only this time, she clearly heard her name.

It came again.

"Phee!" she shouted, heart in her throat. "Where are you?" Something wasn't right.

She slogged back through the damp sod and knocked again on the front door. Then pounded. She turned the handle and pushed with her shoulder, hoping maybe it was just stuck, but it didn't give.

She stopped to listen again, but only heard the night sounds — water sloshing the riverbanks below the cabins, the breeze, a distant hoot owl. Maybe she'd only imagined hearing her name. Joanna had accused her more than once of having an overactive imagination.

She dialed Quinn, thinking he might have a key hidden somewhere. But his phone went to voice mail and she hung up without listening to the familiar message.

Feeling more frantic by the minute, she retraced her steps along the side of the house and went around to the back door. To her relief, it was open. The cloying scents of sawdust and new paint mingled with the musty smell of rain.

Once inside the mudroom, she heard the sound again. Her name. And this time she was sure it was Phee, calling out to her, her voice weak and trembling. But unmistakably Phee.

Adrenaline surged through Britt's veins.

She ran down the hallway, following the sound. When she reached the kitchen, she stopped short.

Phee was slumped on the floor, her back against the kitchen island. Britt ran to her and knelt beside her.

Her sister's complexion had a gray cast, and she trembled like the last leaves on the poplars outside. "Britt? Thank God you're here. Something's wrong. Something . . . the baby . . ." Her words slurred and she clutched at her belly. "Oh, Britt . . . My baby . . ." She struggled to push herself up from the floor, revealing a puddle of blood underneath her.

"No! Stay there." Britt put a hand on her sister's shoulder. She worked to keep her own voice steady. But there was too much blood. Had Phee already lost the baby? "I'm calling an ambulance, Phee."

She felt like she was going to be sick. With trembling fingers, she dialed 911.

The dispatcher answered on the first ring. "Nine-one-one. What is your emergency, please?"

"We need an ambulance. My sister is —" She started to say "miscarrying a baby," but she didn't know that for sure and didn't want to scare Phee. But surely . . . surely you couldn't lose that much blood and still

18

carry the pregnancy to term. "My sister is pregnant but . . . she's bleeding. Pretty bad."

"Okay, I'm going to send an ambulance. I need you to clearly state your exact address for me."

Britt gave a little gasp. Quinn and Phee probably had a different address, even though their house was on the same property, but Britt didn't know what it was. "It's a new house . . . still being built. I'm not sure of the address, but tell them to come to 1585 Poplar Brook Road. There are four houses here. We're at the last house on the left at the end of the lane. You'll see a sign for The Cottages on Poplar Brook Road." The words tumbled out on top of each other.

The dispatcher repeated the address in a frustratingly slow singsong voice. "Is that correct? Could you repeat your phone number to me, please?"

Britt did so, growing more frustrated when the dispatcher repeated it back. "Yes. Yes, that's it. Please hurry!"

"I need you to stay calm and answer some questions for me. Tell me exactly what's happening. Is your sister conscious and breathing?" Frustrating calm permeated the woman's voice.

"Yes. She's breathing, but —" She turned

19

away, whispering into the phone. "There's a lot of blood. And she's so pale. And weak."

"But you're certain she's breathing and conscious."

"Yes, she's breathing. She's . . . sitting up."

"Okay. That's good. And how far along is her pregnancy?"

She scrambled to remember. "She's not due until March."

Phee gripped Britt's hand with a strength that surprised her. "March 28. Tell them I was having some contractions earlier. Not hard ones . . . I'm not even sure they were really contractions, but . . . Oh, Britt. It's too early! Way too early —" Her voice broke.

"Did you hear that?" Britt asked the dispatcher. "Her due date is March 28. And she had some contractions."

"Can you please state your name and your sister's name clearly?"

Britt did so, her panic escalating. "Please! She's really pale. Is someone coming? Did you send an ambulance yet? She's just . . . so pale."

"Yes. The ambulance has been dispatched. Your sister may be going into shock."

"Then what do I do?" Panic rose inside her. She thought shock could be life-threatening.

"I'm going to put an EMT — an emer-

20

gency medical technician — on the line. He will stay with you and talk you through everything until the ambulance gets there. Please stay on the line and I'll transfer you."

"No. Wait . . ." It felt as though her lifeline was being cut.

Almost immediately, a man's voice came on the line. "This is Rafe. I'm with the Langhorne Emergency Services. The dispatcher said you might be in labor? With some bleeding. Is that right?"

"No, not me. It's my sister. She's not due until March but she's bleeding and —"

"Your name is Britt? Is that right?"

"Yes."

"Okay, Britt. First, I need for you to stay calm. Your sister needs your help. I'm going to stay on the phone with you until the ambulance gets there. I'm going to talk you through what I need you to do while we wait. Do you understand?"

"Yes. Okay . . ."

"Britt, what is your sister's name?"

"Phylicia. Phylicia Mitchell. We call her Phee for short." She pronounced it again, then spelled it, feeling like every syllable she spoke wasted a moment that might mean the difference between life and death — if not for Phee, for her baby.

"Okay. That's good. An ambulance is on

its way for Phee right now, but I need you to answer a few more questions for me. Can you do that?"

The man's voice was calm and soothing and Britt nodded, determination rising in her. Nothing was going to happen to her sister or this precious baby. Not on her watch. She made her voice strong. "Yes, I'm here."

"Good." She thought she heard a smile in the man's voice, and it brought surprising encouragement. "Okay, is your sister having contractions?"

"Yes. She said she was earlier. She said they weren't too hard . . . But it's way too early."

"I understand. Now, I need to determine how much blood your sister has lost."

He asked a series of questions and Britt answered them as best she could, all the while keeping one eye on Phee, who'd relaxed and closed her eyes — a fact that didn't encourage Britt. She cradled her cell phone between her ear and her shoulder and spoke her sister's name softly.

No response. "Phee?" She shook her sister's shoulder.

"Is she losing consciousness?" The calming voice came again.

"I'm not sure. She's still breathing."

"That's good."

"But I can't get her to open her eyes."

"Try to rouse her. Have her stay awake." The EMT waited a few seconds. "Is she awake?"

"Phee! Come on, Phee. They want you to stay awake." Phee stirred and her eyes fluttered open, then closed again. "I'm awake."

"Then open your eyes. Please."

"I'm trying."

"She's talking to me, but she isn't opening her eyes. Is that okay?" She willed her voice to stay steady.

"The ambulance is almost there. I'll stay with you until I'm sure they've arrived. Be sure they can get inside."

The wail of a siren in the distance was the sweetest music Britt had ever heard. "Oh, I hear them now. Thank you!"

"Stay on the line, Britt. Until we're sure they've found the house." She didn't want him to ever hang up. His voice had been a lifeline, and she wasn't sure how she would have gotten through without his calming words to guide her.

"Yes, I'm here," she told him. She patted Phee's arm. "The ambulance is almost here. Stay awake, okay, sis?"

"I am." But Phylicia's words were frighteningly slurred, and the blood stains on her clothes seemed to tell the worst.

CHAPTER 2

Britt was terrified to leave her sister's side even for a few moments, but she knew the front door was locked. What she couldn't remember was whether she'd told the ambulance crew to come around back. "I'm going to go unlock the door for them, Phee. I'll be right back."

Phee seemed to have fallen asleep, the slight rise and fall of her chest the only indication she was still breathing.

Britt clutched the phone to her ear, the EMT on the other end her lifeline.

"Yes, go open the door." That smooth, low voice again. *Rafe,* he'd said his name was. Rhymed with *safe.* "But stay with me on the phone, Britt, okay?"

"Yes. I'm here." Britt raced through the house and unlocked the door. She looked out to see red and blue lights strobing through the trees down at the road. "I see them."

"Good." She flipped on the porch light and, leaving the door wide open, went back through the house flipping on light switches as she went. "Do they know which house to come to? It's the last one all the way down the lane."

"I'll let them know. You're doing great, Britt. When you get back to your sister, let me know how she's doing."

"I'm here. Her eyes are closed." She knelt beside Phee and patted her cheek.

Phee didn't so much as flinch.

Britt's grip tightened around her phone. "She's still breathing, but I can't wake her up."

"The team is there now. Just outside the house. Go show them where Phee is and let them do their job. You did great. You did everything you could."

Reluctantly, she left Phee's side and started back toward the front door. "Will they let me ride with her in the ambulance?"

"Probably not," he said. "It would be best if you follow them to the hospital in your own vehicle. Do you feel okay to drive?"

"I . . . I think so."

"Don't drive if you're feeling too shaky or upset. It'd be better to stay behind and be safe than —"

"No . . . I'll be okay. But I need to try to

get hold of Phee's husband. And Joanna."

"That's fine. Just let me know once the team is with your sister and then you can hang up and make those calls."

But she didn't want to hang up. She wished he could stay on the line with her until this nightmare was over and Phee was back home safe with the baby safe inside her. But was that even possible with as much blood as she'd lost? She opened her mouth to ask the EMT — Rafe — but closed it just as quickly. He couldn't possibly know how this would turn out, and it wasn't fair to make him answer her desperate questions.

Two EMTs — a middle-aged woman and a younger man — were hustling out of the emergency vehicle by the time she opened the door. They rushed up the steps, medical kits in hand, and Britt led them to the kitchen where Phee was still crumpled on the floor.

She should have thought to at least get a pillow under her sister's head to make her more comfortable. What else had she failed to do that might have made a difference for Phylicia and her baby?

She stood back watching as the man and woman worked over her sister, communicating almost silently, and when they did speak, their unfamiliar words resembled a foreign language to her. She couldn't sense from their tones how serious things were, but within a few minutes, they had Phee on a stretcher.

Something about seeing Phee carried from the house on a gurney sent a chill up Britt's spine. It was too familiar from the times they'd had to call the ambulance for Mom during those final days before cancer finally took her life. Those awful days . . . But Phee wasn't fighting cancer. She was fighting for the life of her baby. And maybe her own life too.

Desperate for someone to tell her that everything would be okay, Britt ran out behind the EMTs, hoping they'd offer to let her ride with Phee.

With the stretcher loaded into the back of the ambulance, the female EMT climbed in behind. She spoke in a clipped voice. "We're taking her to Southeast. You know where that is?"

"Yes. I . . . I'll follow you."

"Sorry, we can't wait for you. We need to get there as fast as we can. Just come on your own. Park in the ER lot when you get there and tell the front desk who you're there for. And drive safely!" Without another glance, the woman slammed the door, and the ambulance roared down the lane.

Fighting back tears, Britt ran back into the house, located her phone, and tried Quinn again. No answer. She dialed Joanna and almost cried when her sister answered.

"Jo! Where are you? An ambulance just took Phee to the ER. You need to get to Southeast Hospital right away."

"What? Why? What happened?"

Racing back to the house, Britt gave Jo the short version as she quickly closed up Phee and Quinn's house. The blood on the kitchen floor stopped her cold. So much blood. She prayed Quinn wouldn't find that before someone could come back and clean it up. But she couldn't take time now.

She ran back up the lane to get her Escape. "I'm on my way to the ER right now. And pray! Oh, Jo, she lost so much blood!"

"But did she lose . . ."

"I don't know. I don't think so, but it can't be good. Just hurry. They said we can park in the ER lot."

"I'm on my way. I'll probably beat you there."

"Okay. Don't wait for me. Go on in and tell them you're there for Phee. I still can't get hold of Quinn."

Fifteen minutes later Britt pulled in beside Jo's car in the small parking lot outside the

ER. Closing her car door, she realized there were smudges of blood on the door handle of her white car. She looked at her hands and realized where it had come from. Phee's blood. As she ran toward the building, she searched her purse for a tissue. But it did no good. The blood was already dried. *The life is in the blood.* "Oh, Lord," she whispered. "Please, please sustain that life for Phee and her baby."

She pushed through the doors and found Jo talking to a woman behind the window — a nurse, if her blue scrubs were any indication.

Britt pressed close to Jo and whispered, "Did she . . . lose the baby?"

Jo shrugged, her eyes dull with worry. "I don't know. I just got here."

"You're both her sisters?" the woman at the counter asked.

"Yes." They answered in unison.

"You can go on back. I'll buzz you in." She pointed to their left. "Through those doors, and take the first right. Your sister is in Three."

Thanking her, they hurried through doors that parted like the Red Sea before them.

Phee was sitting up in the bed, alert and talking to a nurse. They'd already changed her into a hospital gown and her hair was matted to her scalp. But already, her color was worlds better.

Relief washed over Britt, only to recede like a tide when she realized they didn't know yet about the baby.

Phee gave them a wan smile over the nurse's shoulder. "Sorry, guys."

"What on earth are you sorry for?" Jo went to the foot of the bed and tentatively touched Phee's toes beneath the blankets. "How are you doing?"

"Better. Now that I know the baby's okay."

Britt willed herself to swallow back the huge sigh that came. "Thank the Lord!"

"Oh yes," the nurse said. "Baby's still in there with a good, strong heartbeat. We're not completely out of the woods yet but baby is fine."

Phee frowned. "Is Quinn on his way?"

"We haven't been able to get hold of him," Britt said. "I talked to him about an hour ago. He said he had a meeting at church."

"Yes," Phee supplied. "He's at the church."

The nurse uncoiled some wires on a machine Britt didn't recognize. "One of you might want to go get him. There may be some decisions he'll want to be in on."

"I'll get him." Jo grabbed Britt's arm and tugged her toward the door they'd come in.

"I'll be right back."

"You may as well both go. We're taking this young lady back for some tests. It'll be" — she looked at her watch — "twenty minutes or so."

"Are you sure, Phee?"

Phee gave a weak laugh and held up an arm that already sported an IV line. "I'm not going anywhere."

"Well, hey there." Quinn smiled up at Britt from the table where he was seated with half a dozen other board members in the church basement.

His gaze went to Jo behind her, and he seemed surprised they'd interrupted his meeting, but quickly registered that something must be very wrong for them to do so. Quinn excused himself and met them at the doorway. "What's going on?"

"Everything's okay," Britt said quickly. She lowered her voice. "But Phee is in the emergency room."

"What?" He stepped into the hallway and pulled the door closed behind them. He glanced instinctively in the direction of the hospital, looking like he might run out the door to the ER. "What happened?"

Britt gave him the same quick update she'd given Jo earlier, leaving out the details about the blood. She was grateful she'd been able to clean her hands with some hand sanitizer in the car on the way here.

"The baby is fine," Jo reassured with a hand on Quinn's forearm.

"And Phee too," Britt hastened to add. She and Jo had decided not to tell him about the nurse's warning that they weren't out of the woods yet. "But they want you to be there while they're doing tests and trying to decide what's going on."

"Of course." Quinn fished in his pocket and produced his keys. "I'll meet you there. You said Southeast, right?" He didn't even go back to explain to the group in the meeting room.

"Yes, Southeast. Please drive carefully, Quinn." They were Jo's parting words to anyone getting in a vehicle ever since she'd been in a serious car accident last summer. She still walked with an almost imperceptible limp after getting the cast off her leg a couple of months ago.

Britt and Jo followed Quinn to the parking lot and climbed into Britt's Escape, but despite Jo's warning, they soon lost sight of Quinn's pickup as he sped for the hospital.

After a few minutes of silence, Jo spoke what they were both thinking. "Do you think she'll lose the baby?" Worry creased her brow.

Britt bit her bottom lip. "I don't know . . . Oh, Jo, I don't know how she could lose that much blood and still survive, let alone keep the baby." She took in a sharp breath, remembering. "We need to get things cleaned up before Quinn gets back home. It looks like a crime scene in their kitchen."

Jo pointed in the direction of home. "Let's go now then. That'll give them a little time alone together."

"Maybe you should text Quinn and let him know we're . . . running an errand and will be there soon. We don't want Phee to worry about us."

Jo spoke the message into her phone and pressed Send. But as they headed out to the cottages, Britt dreaded what they'd find at the new house and wished she'd taken the time to mop the floors — for *Jo's* sake.

CHAPTER 3

It was almost eight thirty by the time Britt and Jo got back to the hospital. Phylicia had been admitted, and they had to park in the visitor parking lot before going up to see her.

Quinn sat in an uncomfortable-looking vinyl chair scooted as close to the hospital bed as it would go. The TV overhead was on but with the sound turned down. Quinn's eyes flitted between a sleeping Phee and the monitors over her bed, as if he could will her vitals to remain at appropriate levels by keeping his eyes glued to the ever-changing numbers on the screen.

"How is she?" Britt mouthed when Quinn acknowledged them.

"She's stable. They got the bleeding under control and the baby is still doing great, but Phee has a condition — I forget what they called it — where she'll have to be on bed rest."

"For how long?"

He blew out a breath. "The rest of the pregnancy. Unless it resolves itself. Apparently that *can* happen, but it's not guaranteed. They just hope she can go a few more weeks."

"Oh wow." Jo shook her head.

"Tell me about it. How on earth are we supposed to keep this woman down?"

"She'll do it," Britt declared. "For the baby's sake. And yours, Quinn."

"I know." He shifted in his chair. "But she's not going to like it."

"She doesn't know yet?" Jo lowered her voice to a whisper.

"She was awake when the doctor told us . . . It has something to do with the placenta not being where it's supposed to be. Previous placenta? Something like that."

"Placenta previa?" Britt remembered a friend from her book club having the condition. She forgot exactly what it meant, but Mindy had been on bed rest for more than six weeks. They'd even held their book club meeting one month gathered around Mindy's bed. But Britt took great comfort in the fact that Mindy now had healthy twin girls. They had to be three or four years old by now. Of course, they'd been premature and in the hospital for several weeks before coming home. But you'd never know it now.

"Yeah, that sounds right. Placenta previa." Quinn rolled his tongue around the words, then shrugged. "I don't know anything about this stuff. I just know what Dr. Hinsen said about her being on bed rest for the duration."

Britt gave him a wry smile. "I don't envy you trying to keep Phee in bed."

"Oh, she'll do whatever she has to to keep the baby safe, but she's definitely going to be chomping at the bit." Quinn shook his head. "I just don't know how we're going to work out meals and laundry and all that. I mean, I can do most of that stuff but not if I have to keep up with work and the construc —"

"Don't even worry about that," Jo said.

"That's right," Britt echoed. "We'll take care of everything."

"Well, I'm aware that you both have lives too."

"No, we really don't." Britt laughed.

"Hey, speak for yourself." Jo affected a pout.

"Just kidding. But seriously, what are sisters for if not for times like this?"

Quinn swallowed hard and for a minute, Britt thought he might cry. But he straightened in the chair and turned to look between her and Jo. "Listen, you guys go on home. I'll text you later tonight and let you know how it's going."

"Are you sure?"

"Positive. Go home. I'll tell her you were here, and you can see her tomorrow — hopefully at home." Quinn shooed them away with a smile Britt knew was intended to prove to them that he was fine.

She wasn't so sure. But she and Jo navigated the hallways trying to find a shortcut to the parking lot.

When they passed a restroom, Jo held up a hand. "Wait for me. I'll be right back."

She disappeared into the restroom, and Britt looked for an out-of-the-way place to wait. A couple of employees were joking and laughing quietly behind the nurses station, and Britt's ears perked up when she recognized a familiar voice. It took her a minute to realize it sounded like *the* voice. The one that had calmed her so on the phone while she'd waited for the ambulance.

But she was certain it was his voice when the curly-haired girl he was bantering with called him by name: Rafe.

Feeling guilty for eavesdropping, she took a few steps back and leaned one shoulder against the wall, craning her neck for a glimpse of the owner of the silken voice.

Unfortunately, he was partially hidden by a pillar, and the part she could see had his back to her. But even with her limited view, she could tell he was tall and athletically built with a shock of blond hair. He wore street clothes — jeans and a sweatshirt.

Britt glanced toward the bathroom door, hoping Jo wouldn't emerge just yet. She was overwhelmed with curiosity about the man who'd been so calm and comforting on the phone.

"Would you have known what to do?" the curly haired girl asked.

"Oh, I could have talked them through it. I had the book open to the childbirth section, just in case."

She laughed. It sounded flirtatious to Britt's ears.

"I'm just glad it was only a phone consult. Let me deal with blood and guts any day. Just don't make me deliver a baby."

"Rafe, that's terrible! Besides, I hate to break it to you, but delivering a baby *is* blood and guts."

"Whatever." He shrugged the shoulder Britt could see from her vantage point.

"So did she have the baby?"

"Not on my watch." His voice turned serious and took on the well-modulated tone she remembered from the call earlier this evening. "But it would have been a miscarriage. She was only about eighteen weeks along. Do you know if they admitted her?"

The curls bounced as she shook her head. "Not that I know of, but I just got here. I haven't made rounds yet."

The girl glanced Britt's way and gave Rafe a pointed look, lowering her voice. He glanced over his shoulder, but Britt looked away before their eyes could meet, quickly pulling out her phone and trying to look oblivious to the conversation she'd been eavesdropping on.

She could hear the low murmuring of their continuing conversation, but she couldn't understand anything they were saying. She had half a notion to approach the desk and inform Rafe that her sister had, indeed, been admitted and that the baby was safe. But the girl — an aide, judging by her uniform — intimidated Britt for some reason. Probably because she was clearly flirting with Rafe — who seemed oblivious to that fact.

The door to the women's restroom swung open and Jo came through. "Ready?"

Making a split-second decision, Britt held up a hand to her sister. "Hang on. I need to go talk to someone."

"What? Who?"

"I see somebody I know. I'll meet you at the car in just a few minutes." She fished in her purse for the keys and handed them to Jo.

Jo hitched her purse up on her shoulder. "Okay, but please hurry. I have stuff to do tonight and if we have to clean Quinn and Phee's house first, then I —"

"I won't be long, I promise."

Jo hurried down the corridor and Britt considered following her out, her earlier resolve having dissipated. But she would regret it later if she didn't say something. She gathered her courage and approached the nurses station.

The two turned in unison to look at her. The girl — her name tag read Stefani — looked slightly annoyed at the interruption. But she said politely, "May I help you?"

Keeping her eyes on the girl, Britt pointed in Rafe's direction. "I wanted to talk to him."

"Me?" He pointed at himself, eyebrows lifted in surprise.

Britt met his gaze. "Yes. You're . . . Rafe?" Her breath caught. She knew this guy. She couldn't remember from where, but she'd definitely seen him before. Met him maybe.

"Yes, I'm Rafe." He took a step back. His furrowed eyebrows said he wondered how she knew his name.

And indeed, he wore no name tag.

"This might sound strange, but I recognized your voice. You were the EMT I talked to on the phone this evening, right?"

He gave her a strange look and for an awkward second, she worried she had the wrong guy. But it had to be him. That mellow voice was too distinctive. And Rafe wasn't exactly a common name.

"My voice?" He cocked his head and eyed her suspiciously.

She nodded. "I heard you talking out here and knew it had to be you." She quickly decided not to mention that she'd overheard the girl call him Rafe. And that she felt sure they'd met before.

"Wow." He shuffled his feet. "Yes. That was me. How is your sister doing?"

"They're keeping her overnight, but she's going to be okay."

"And . . ." He hesitated. "The baby?"

"Hanging in there."

"Oh. That's good." He shuffled again. "You said that you wanted to talk to me?"

"Oh . . . Sorry. I just wanted to thank you. You really helped me to stay calm during the whole ordeal. That's why I remembered your voice, I think."

"Well, I'm glad." He looked embarrassed

at her compliment. "Just doing my job."

"So, you work here at the hospital?"

The curly haired girl — Stefani — had taken a perch on a rolling stool at the counter a few feet away and was working at the computer, but Britt had the distinct impression she was eavesdropping on every word of their conversation. Not that *she* had any room to judge.

"No, I actually work for the Langhorne police department. As an EMT. Just . . . visiting here." He gave Stefani a sideways glance.

Ohhh . . . Britt looked between them, feeling like an idiot for not having figured that out by the way they were talking.

Rafe gestured. "Actually, if you'll excuse me, I need to be going."

"Of course." Britt gave an awkward wave. "I didn't mean to interrupt. I just wanted to say thank you."

"I appreciate it." He dismissed her with a nod, then took a step toward Stefani. "I'll see you tomorrow?"

"Sure." For being so flirtatious with him a moment ago, the girl had suddenly gone glacier.

Britt turned and hurried down the corridor toward the parking lot, feeling more than a little foolish. But she hadn't gone far when she heard the voice behind her.

"Excuse me . . . Wait up a minute, will you?"

She turned to see Rafe practically jogging to catch up. She stopped in the hallway and waited.

He eyed her with that suspicious gaze again. "Have we met?"

She gave a tentative smile. "I don't know, but . . . you look familiar to me too." She stuck out a hand. "I'm Britt Chandler. But I don't know where we would have met."

"Chandler? Do you have sisters?" Recognition dawned in his eyes. Pale blue eyes framed with lashes that matched his tawny hair. "Two sisters?"

"I do. Do you know them?" She and Joanna were often mistaken for twins. Maybe that was why she looked familiar to him, but that didn't explain where she knew him from.

"I don't know them by name, but I think I know where we met." A twinkle came to his eyes.

"You do? I'm drawing a complete blank."

"I don't want to embarrass you but . . ."

"Excuse me?"

"What if I told you I was a police officer with the Langhorne police department before I started working as an EMT there?

44

You, um . . ." His smile wasn't quite a smirk, but close. "You had a black-and-white cat, right?"

And suddenly, she knew *exactly* where she'd met Rafe Whatever-His-Name-Was. And she wished she could crawl under the gurney down the hall. "That was you?" She shaded her eyes and dropped her head, feeling her cheeks grow warm. "Of course, it was you. Oh boy . . ."

"Nothing to be embarrassed about."

"Oh, easy for you to say!"

"No, it just means you're human. As Mark Twain liked to say, 'Man is the only animal that blushes. Or needs to.'"

That made her blush twice as hard. She dared to sneak a look at him and couldn't help but laugh at the impish grin he wore.

A few weeks before they'd bought the cottages, she'd been staying alone in Dad's house with only Melvin to keep her company. The crazy cat had knocked over a vase in the middle of the night, scaring her half to death. She panicked and called 911. And Rafe was one of the policemen who showed up that night — along with two squad cars and another officer. The whole neighborhood had been awakened, and she'd been mortified for her false alarm. "So you know my brother-in-law?"

"Your brother-in-law?"

"Quinn Mitchell." Quinn had heard about the story — probably from Rafe himself — and further embarrassed Britt when he informed her that the story was all over town. By the time it made its way down the pike, the story involved a mischievous cat and "two hot chicks in pajamas" — no doubt the most exciting thing that had happened in the sleepy town of Langhorne in a while. She wondered if Rafe remembered the pajamas part and blushed at the thought.

Seeming not to notice, Rafe frowned. "Quinn? I know him. Sort of. He's a friend of a friend. But I'm not sure what that has to do with . . ." A light came on in his eyes, then quickly turned to worry. "Wait . . . Was it Quinn's wife you called the ambulance for? That's your sister?"

"Yes."

He rubbed his face. "Oh, man. I hadn't made all the connections yet. I'm so sorry."

"Oh no, it's okay. Everyone's going to be fine — Phee and the baby — thanks, in part, to you."

Again, he brushed off her praise. "I don't know about that. But . . . wow. I'm putting it all together now. So that was you and your sisters that night, huh? No wonder you looked familiar. That's funny."

She cleared her throat pointedly.

"Wait. Not funny ha-ha," he said quickly. "Funny strange — Oh . . . that didn't come out right either. What I meant was —"

She gave him a look. "Yeah, you just go ahead and dig that hole deeper."

He laughed again and suddenly seemed like an old friend.

"You wouldn't want to go get something to eat, would you?" Apparently he was feeling it too.

She hesitated. Was he asking her on a date? "Like, right now?"

He nodded, looking like an eager little boy.

"Thanks, but my sister's waiting in the car for me."

"Oh, sorry. I didn't mean to keep you."

"No problem." She moved toward the door. "Thanks again for your help on the phone tonight."

Following her, he gave a little salute. "Just doing my job."

"Well . . . Good night." She hurried ahead of him, not looking back.

She couldn't deny that their conversation excited her in a way she hadn't felt in a long time. She was only twenty-four, but she'd started to wonder how she was ever going to meet anyone given that her social life consisted of a book club with a bunch of women.

But she also couldn't deny that Rafe apparently had something going with the curly haired Stefani — including a date of some sort, if his "see you tomorrow" was any indication.

No thank you. She wasn't interested in breaking up a couple or being "the other woman." Besides, with Phee in the hospital and needing full-time help after she got home, they were all going to be busy making sure this precious baby came safely into the world a few months from now.

And somewhere in the midst of all that, Joanna and her fiancé, Luke, were going to be married up in the clearing, which needed a ton of work before it would be ready for another wedding.

The circumstances couldn't have been worse for her to finally meet someone. No matter how cute he was or how much his mellow voice stuck in her memory.

CHAPTER 4

Rafe watched the woman walk away, a longing he couldn't quite identify rising up inside of him. He looked back toward the nurses station. He should probably go say a proper goodbye to Stefani. She'd never been the jealous type — not that there was anything "official" between them — but he hadn't missed the frosty vibes coming from her direction while he and Britt Chandler talked.

Flirted. At least he'd been flirting. He thought she had too, but her brush-off — and the flimsy excuse — said otherwise.

He headed back down the corridor, rehearsing what he would say to Stefani, especially now that he knew it wasn't fair for him to lead her on. In the two months they'd been hanging out, she'd never stirred him the way Britt Chandler had in one brief encounter.

He thought about that night, almost a year

ago now, when he'd answered the 911 call she'd placed. He did not believe in love at first sight, but he couldn't deny he'd felt these same stirrings that night in Langhorne. Brian's friend, Quinn Mitchell, had razzed them about trying to get the scoop on the sisters. He didn't think Quinn and the older sister were married back then. Although he did remember the guy saying something about the sisters being spoken for.

He wasn't sure why he hadn't pursued the possibility of Britt Chandler back then. Maybe it felt inappropriate, given how he'd met her. Maybe he'd been too overwhelmed with the decisions he was facing. Switching departments — careers, really. And everything with his brother. Now that he thought about it, they'd probably been in the thick of things with moving to a different home about then. He raked a hand through his hair, as if he could brush away the unwelcome memories.

Stefani wasn't at the nurses station. Relief blew through him, followed by guilt. At least he could tell her he'd come back to talk to her and she was gone. And that was just one more reason he had no business leading the girl on. Too many games were played whenever the two of them were together.

He was as guilty as she was, but he'd had enough of game-playing to last a lifetime.

He'd break things off with her. Soon. And hope he didn't run into her every time he made a run to the hospital. He was tempted to find out what room Britt's sister was in and go by to check on her. But that might seem a little creepy to the sister. And to Britt. Unlike his first year as an EMT, he'd learned to compartmentalize, to not have to know the outcome of every call. He'd go crazy if he second-guessed his actions on every run he made. Or worse, if he took on guilt every time they lost someone.

Like they'd told them in the training, losing someone was part of the job. Sometimes — too often — they were gone before he even arrived on the scene. But when he could help someone, that's what this job was all about. And if he saved a life . . . Well, it didn't get any better than that.

He doubted Britt's sister had been in danger of dying tonight, but it must've been scary for both of them. He closed his eyes against the memories that tried to come . . . His mom lying crumpled on the bathroom floor, clutching her round belly, her face gray . . .

He'd turned ten the day before. If only he could go back in time —

But no matter how many times he went over everything that had happened that day, he couldn't change the outcome. Dad was still gone — living in Phoenix the last Ma heard from him. She seemed to grow more bitter and distant by the day. And Robby? Well, Robby was still Robby.

He fought against the oppressive thoughts, and thankfully, the memory of Britt Chandler's perky smile replaced them. What was it about the woman that moved him so? It wasn't just that she was drop-dead gorgeous — though she was that — but there was something he couldn't quite define . . . something more than skin-deep that made him want to hang on her every word.

Maybe he *would* ask her out. Not just the offhand test-the-waters invitation he'd issued tonight — one that had been soundly rejected. But maybe he'd have Brian get her number from her brother-in-law, Quinn. He'd wait a few days though. Quinn had other things on his mind with his wife in the hospital and a baby on the way.

Meanwhile, he'd just daydream about Britt Chandler and let the image of her smile keep his thoughts centered.

Jo's voice broke through the haze of sleep and Britt sat up in bed, wondering if she'd dreamed it. She peered at the clock. Two a.m.

"Britt? Are you awake?" A soft knock came at her bedroom door.

She slid out of bed and padded to the door, alarm rising with every step. Had something happened with Phee? She opened the door a crack. "What's wrong?"

"I'm sorry if I woke you up." She stopped short. "Well, of course, I woke you. It's two in the morning. But I couldn't sleep." Not waiting for an invitation, Jo slipped through the door. "I just keep thinking about Phee and . . . everything that could go wrong."

"I know. I had trouble getting to sleep too." Britt grabbed her robe off the end of the bed and went out into the hallway, motioning toward the kitchen.

"But you *did* get to sleep. Sorry." Jo gave her a sheepish look but followed her to the kitchen and placed her cell phone on the little bar counter. She opened a cupboard. "Do you have any decaf?"

"I'll put some water on for French press."

"Thanks. You can go back to bed if you want. I just didn't want to be alone with all those thoughts swirling around."

"It's okay. I'm awake now. Do you have to work tomorrow?"

"Yes, but I can go in a little late." Jo

turned her phone over absently.

"You haven't heard from Quinn?"

"Not since about eight."

Britt filled the kettle and ignited the gas under the front burner. The blue-tinged fire cast a comforting glow in the tiny kitchen. "Yeah. I got that text. We could call the hospital."

"I don't want to wake Quinn." Jo slid onto a high barstool.

"We could just ask at the nurses station."

"I doubt they'd tell us anything. Not without getting Phee's or Quinn's permission first. They'd just give us a cryptic answer that would make us think something horrible had happened."

Britt threw her sister a wry grin. "Good point. Besides, you know Quinn would call if anything changed."

"Is the cottage booked tomorrow?" She shrugged. "Sorry, I haven't checked the schedule since Sunday night."

"Both cabins are booked through the weekend. Same people all weekend. A sisters retreat."

"Aww, that's cool."

"Yeah . . ." She didn't dare meet Jo's gaze lest she burst into tears thinking how close they'd come to losing Phee. She turned back to the stove and needlessly adjusted the flame, then got two mugs down from the open shelving. "That means I'll be staying with you, don't forget."

"I know. And remember, we're booked every night over Thanksgiving week and weekend."

So far it had worked well for her and Jo to stay in whichever rental wasn't booked. And when they occasionally booked the cottage and both cabins, they all piled in at the house where Quinn and Phee were living now, just outside of Langhorne. Jo's cottage could sleep five and each of the cabins had a queen bed and a single, but the cottage rented for more, so the cabins usually booked first. She and Jo had a section of each other's closet and bathroom drawers stocked with clothes and toiletries so moving back and forth wasn't a huge deal, but sometimes Britt wished they weren't so dependent on the income from the Airbnb. "I wish we could afford to just block off a couple of weeks without worrying about guests."

"Well, you might get your wish."

Britt turned to study her. "What do you mean?"

"Britt, think about it. If Phee has to be on bed rest, one of us is going to need to be there all the time. We may have to adjust our calendar for the inn."

She hadn't thought that far ahead. Though she should have. "Could we hire someone to turn the rooms over?"

"And make breakfasts?"

"We could just serve bakery stuff for a while. We've done that before."

"Yes, and it cut our profits considerably. And somebody still has to go pick up the food. And plate it. And get the coffee ready. And then wash the dishes. And —"

"Yeah, yeah . . . I get the picture." She spooned ground coffee into the carafe.

"But am I wrong?"

"No. Not really. But we're kind of jumping the gun. We don't even know how . . . serious the whole bed rest thing is going to be. I've heard of some women who could get up for a few hours every day. It's not like they couldn't even take a step or go to the bathroom or anything."

"I don't want to take any chances with Phee though. If she lost the ba —"

Britt was glad Jo didn't finish. It was too hard to think about. They'd already lost so much.

They sat silent, mired in their separate thoughts until the kettle started its insistent whistle. Britt filled the French press and stirred, breathing in the rich aroma. She set the timer for four minutes.

Joanna lifted her empty mug to her lips, cupping both hands around it as if anticipating the coming beverage. But her sigh made Britt do a double take.

"What's wrong?"

"Oh, Britt. I don't want to sound like a selfish jerk, but how am I supposed to pull off a wedding if Phee's going to be laid up for the next four months?"

Joanna and Luke were planning a wedding in the clearing at the top of the ridge on the property. Phylicia and Quinn had gotten engaged there, and Jo had planned her sister's wedding in the breezy space beneath the canopy of poplars and silver maples. Ever since, Jo had dreamed of opening a wedding venue there and hoped her own wedding would be a grand opening of sorts. It really was the perfect match, given that Luke DJ'd when he wasn't working his advertising job at the radio station.

And though she and Luke hadn't set a firm date yet, Jo had been working toward April when the dogwoods and Eastern redbuds would be in glorious bloom. And when Phee wouldn't be waddling with pregnancy. Britt closed her eyes briefly, remembering how beautiful the property had been last spring with the flowering trees in bloom and

the woodland floor dotted with wild daffodils and grape hyacinths.

"We might still be able to work everything
out. Even for that spring wedding you
want."

Jo just shook her head and stared into the
empty mug.

Britt put an arm briefly around her sister's
shoulder. "Don't get all worked up about it
until we know what Phee's situation is."

"Yeah . . . Easy for you to say. It's not
your wedding that might get canceled."

Britt clenched her jaw, biting back the
response she *wanted* to give. "Postponed,
Jo. Nothing's getting canceled."

Her sisters didn't know how much she
envied the love they'd found. The lives they
were living. Lives of purpose and meaning.
Lives that had someone in them who would
worry if they didn't come home at night.
Who chose *them* to tell first if something
exciting or frustrating or life-changing happened. Or who would call just to say, "I was
thinking about you."

She blew out a little huff. She was lucky if
the book club gals remembered to tell her
when a meeting date got changed. If she
voiced her longing to her sisters, she knew
they would only tell her she was young. She
had plenty of time. But all the time in the

world meant nothing if all you wanted was someone to share it with. *Or if you never met that someone.*

CHAPTER 5

"Come on, Rob, time to get up. What are
you still doing in bed, lazybones?" Rafe
tugged at his brother's pajama sleeve.

Robby yanked the blankets over his head
and curled deeper into the fetal position.

"Come on! Chop-chop!" Rafe clapped his
hands, struggling to not take his frustration
with the nursing staff out on his younger
brother. It was after ten o'clock and they
still hadn't gotten Robby up and dressed
for the day. Rafe wondered if his brother
had even had breakfast yet.

Hope Village was short-staffed, but that
was no excuse to leave the kid in bed. He
playfully smacked his brother's backside
and tugged the blanket off the bed, revealing lanky, atrophied limbs. And reminding
him that Robby wasn't a kid at all any more.
At sixteen, he had the body of a young man
and probably would measure almost six feet
tall if they could ever get him to stand up

straight.

"I think it's pancakes for breakfast, bro. Come on . . . You're gonna miss out."

The promise of pancakes usually lured Robby just about anywhere they needed him to go, but this morning, he was having none of it. He grunted and grasped at invisible blankets with clenched fists.

Rafe finally wrestled him into sweatpants and a T-shirt that were a size too small and smelled faintly of urine. He made a mental note to bring his brother some new clothes. He quickly combed Robby's unruly mop of hair, so much like his own. Dishwater blond, Ma called it. He needed to talk to the nurse on duty about scheduling a haircut. He wouldn't complain about finding Robby still in bed at ten o'clock — and in need of a bath, judging by the odor that permeated the room. It wouldn't do any good anyway. The staff was overworked as it was.

They had fifteen people to get ready every morning — most of them in worse shape than Robby — and Rafe knew better than anyone that Robby wasn't the most co-operative resident early in the day. Not for the first time, he wondered if they had his brother on some medication that made him so sleepy all the time. No time to ask today, but he made a mental note.

"Come on, Rob. Up and at 'em, bro!" If he didn't get up, he'd miss out on physical therapy and whatever occupational therapy activities were on the schedule. Not that the therapy did any good. Robby had been here at the center for nine of his sixteen years and he still had the mind and mannerisms of a three-year-old, exactly like he had the day they'd moved him in.

At least he seemed happy here. And Rafe could rest assured that Robby was well fed and seen by a doctor on a regular basis. Rafe picked up the odd pairs of dirty socks strewn across the cold tile. Sometimes he still resented his mother for putting Robby in a home. But it wasn't realistic to think Ma could care for him and hold down the job she needed to make ends meet.

He helped out when she fell behind on the bills. His dad paid for Robby's care — a hefty sum and one that apparently absolved the man from ever having to come and visit his son. *Either* of his sons.

Not that Rafe was much better. Pulling extra shifts recently meant that he spent only a few hours a week with his brother, not making it to the center at all some days. It was a blessing that Robby had no concept of time.

"Come on, buddy. Let's get you down to the dining hall." He edged his shoulder under his brother's armpit and braced for the weight of his awkward high-stepping gait.

Robby knew the dance and gave his nasal, snorting laugh as they hobbled down the hall together. "Rafe came and got me up. Didn't you, bud?"

Rafe laughed. "I sure did, Rob."

"We're goin' to the dining hall, aren't we, bud?"

"Yep, bud, we sure are."

Robby wouldn't remember the promise of pancakes and would be blissfully satisfied with the peanut butter sandwich they'd probably give him in place of the breakfast he'd missed. But Rafe's conscience *wouldn't* be satisfied. Not until his next day off when he would bring Robby an order of to-go pancakes from Huddle House — with extra syrup.

Britt opened the door to Phee's hospital room a little wider, and she and Jo peered inside. "Hey, you're awake!"

Seeing Phee's smile, weak though it was, did her heart good. She closed the door behind them. No sign of Quinn. He must have gone home. Or maybe he was hunting

63

down some coffee in the cafeteria. "How are you doing, sis?"

Phee scooted up gingerly in the bed. "Hanging in there. I don't think I got much sleep, but at least they got the bleeding stopped, and the baby is still doing great. Don't you have to work, Jo?"

"I'm going in later."

Relief flooded Britt, hearing her sisters' matter-of-fact exchange. She was sure Quinn would have let them know if anything had changed during the night, but it was good to see for herself. Phee still looked a little wan but so much better than yesterday. "Have you seen the doctor this morning?"

"Not yet, but the nurse was pretty sure they wouldn't let me go home for another day or two. If that."

"Did they say why?" Jo asked.

"They want to monitor me for at least twenty-four hours from the time the bleeding stopped. That would be sometime tonight, and they probably will make me wait until I've seen the doctor tomorrow morning." She winced. "To be honest, I'm a little scared to go home anyway."

"I don't blame you. Have they said if you'll be on bed rest?"

"Oh, I'm afraid there's no question about that. They —" Phee looked past Britt and her face brightened.

Britt turned to see Quinn returning with a large to-go cup of coffee.

"Good morning, sunshine." He bent to kiss Phee, then lifted the cup in Britt's direction. "I would have brought you some, too, Britt, if I'd known you were coming by."

"It's okay. Jo and I drank coffee all night."

"All night? What happened?" Phee's voice held concern.

"What *happened*? Are you kidding?" Britt looked askance at her sister. "You scared us half to death."

"Oh . . . that." Phee gave a humorless laugh. "I thought something happened at the cottages."

"The cottages are fine. In fact, we were talking about that on the way here." Jo gave Britt a look that said, "Should we tell her?"

Britt nodded.

"If you *do* end up having to be on bed rest, Britt and I could take turns staying with you at your house" — Jo turned to Quinn — "if that's okay with you, of course."

"You guys . . ." He shook his head, but Britt could tell it was just to cover his emotions. Quinn was sweet that way. "Of course it's okay."

Phee frowned. "But you'll be at work, Jo. And who will keep the Airbnb going if Britt's not there?"

"Don't you worry about that. We've got it all figured out." Jo threw Britt a play-along glance.

She obeyed. "That's right. Your one and only job is to keep that baby cookin'."

Phee laughed but quickly looked over at the monitors — the baby's first, and then her own. She sobered. "That's the plan. But I've never felt so out of control in my life."

Quinn enveloped Phee's hand with his own. "Everything is going to be just fine. And you don't always have to be in control of everything, you know?"

"Hush," Phee scolded. But her smile acknowledged that she knew he was right.

Britt would have to agree. Phee did sometimes struggle with being in control. But Britt knew the feeling herself. At times it seemed as if her every move was being dictated by other people. Most of them in this room right now.

Being the youngest of the three sisters, it had been that way as long as she could remember, but it hadn't bothered her until recently, and she wasn't sure why. A counselor would likely say it had everything to do with losing her mother. Maybe so. That loss had been traumatic, life-changing for all of them. But she really didn't think losing Mom was the sole reason she'd felt so restless and adrift lately. In fact, she suspected it had more to do with losing her *sisters.*

Of course, she wasn't really "losing" Phylicia and Joanna. Just because one was married and expecting a baby and the other was getting married soon — and inheriting a twelve-year-old in the bargain — didn't mean Britt would lose them as sisters. But it did make her the odd man out. They both had someone — multiple someones — to care for now. And someone to care for them. They didn't *need* her, and she couldn't expect them to drop everything for her anymore.

"Right, Britt?" Jo's voice broke through her reverie.

She looked at them in turn, and the question in their expressions made her think Jo had said her name at least once already.

"I'm sorry . . . What? I missed that."

"Daydreaming there, little sister?" Quinn winked at her, as if he'd read her thoughts.

"Never mind." Jo took Britt's arm. "We'll see you guys later."

"What? We just got here."

"We're coming right back." Jo ushered her

toward the door. "I'll explain it on the way."

"On the way? Where are we going?"

That brought giggles, even from Phee. "Thanks, sisters. You're the best."

In the hallway, Jo turned to regard her. "You okay?"

Britt quickened her pace to avoid her sister's scrutiny. "I'm fine. Can't a girl have a moment to think to herself? Where are we going anyway?"

"You seriously didn't hear any of that?"

"Just tell me where we're going."

Jo shook her head as if Britt were a lost cause. "Phee's dying for some ice cream."

"At nine o'clock in the morning. Is that okay? I mean, is she allowed?"

"Sure. The hospital just doesn't happen to carry the Häagen-Dazs honey salted caramel almond she's craving."

"And they call themselves a *hospital*." Britt shook her head.

That drew laughter, and thankfully Jo forgot to cross-examine her about where her thoughts had roamed while they stood at Phee's bedside.

"Actually, I could go for some ice cream myself. Did Quinn want anything?"

"He said he'd share with Phee."

Britt lifted her eyebrows conspiratorially.

"You want to split a tub of chunky monkey?"

Jo threw her a look. "You want to jog six miles with me in the morning?"

Britt hung her head in mock disappointment. "Must be nice to be eating for two."

"Yeah, well, what's Quinn's excuse?"

Laughing, they climbed in the car.

Twenty minutes later, heading toward the checkout aisle with not one, but *three* tubs of ice cream and fifty dollars worth of supplies for the Airbnb, Britt left Jo to grab some things in the produce aisle and pushed their grocery cart around the corner — and almost collided head-on with a cart coming from the opposite direction.

"Whoa there. Where's the fire?"

Even without looking up, she *knew.* She would have recognized that velvety voice anywhere. Her gaze traveled from the embroidered EMT logo on his crisp uniform shirt to his slightly mussed blond hair, and she did her best to hide her embarrassment.

He backed his cart out of her path, grinning, recognition in his expression.

Britt clapped a hand over her mouth. "I am so sorry."

"No harm done. Worried your ice cream might melt there?" He nodded toward their cart.

"Yeah . . . That's it." Britt giggled.

Jo chose that moment to appear with an armful of bagged fruit. "Pomegranates are in season!" She stopped short, apparently unaware she'd interrupted.

Britt wished her sister had sent her on this errand alone. But she turned to Jo. "Jo, this is Rafe . . . ? Sorry, I never got your last name."

He extended a hand. "Rafe Stuart."

"This is my sister Jo. Sorry I didn't introduce you the other night. At the hospital."

"Nice to meet you, Jo."

"Oh, you're the one who talked to Britt on the phone?" Jo stole a glance at Britt as if trying to gauge how she felt about this encounter. "While she waited for the ambulance?"

"That's right."

"Thank you," Jo gushed. And Jo rarely gushed. "I'm not sure what we would have done without you."

Britt cut her a discreet look because, of course, she knew Jo really meant, *I'm not sure what* Britt *would have done without you.*

Rafe waved off the compliment. "Like I told your sister, I was just doing my job." His expression became serious and his gaze included Britt. "How *is* . . . Phee? Did I get her name right?"

"Yes, Phylicia. We call her Phee. And she's doing much better." Britt pointed to the cart. "That's who the ice cream's for, if that tells you anything."

"I'd say that's a good sign. Especially if she eats all three cartons." He winked.

More giggles, but then Rafe's smile faded. "It's funny we ran into each other. I was going to call you actually."

"Oh?"

Jo nudged her and whispered, "I'll go check out and meet you at the car."

"Thanks, sis. I won't be long." But oh, she wanted to linger here with him.

When Jo was out of earshot, he took a step toward her. "I really was going to call you."

"Because . . . ?" She didn't want to appear coy, but neither did she want to assume anything.

"I wanted to ask you out. On a date. Officially."

She frowned. "Did I miss something? Aren't you and that girl at the hospital . . . a thing?"

He hesitated a second too long, which told her what she needed to know. And deflated her mood considerably. As did the two college girls who walked by, not-so-discreetly checking him out. Not that she could blame them.

"You mean Stefani?" He scuffed at an invisible spot on the tile floor, not waiting for her to confirm. "We've . . . had a few dates, but we're not 'a thing.' " He chalked quote marks in the air.

"I appreciate the thought, Rafe, I really do, but I don't want to get in the middle of . . . something like that."

"I'm sorry . . . Something like what?"

"I'm just not interested in being a third wheel."

"Um . . . I think the expression is fifth wheel. A third wheel would be a tricycle." He didn't smile, but the twinkle in his eyes gave him away.

And she decided to play along. "Well, fifth wheel doesn't make sense. Unless you have *three* other girlfriends." She eyed him, feeling more than a little clever.

"I told you, I don't even have one girlfriend."

"Define girlfriend," she challenged, loving this exchange, but knowing it could lead nowhere with Jo waiting in the car with ice cream.

"Someone I'm dating exclusively."

"But you *do* have someone you're dating?"

"Occasionally," he admitted. "But there's nothing serious between us. I promise."

"Then maybe you shouldn't be dating her *occasionally*. That doesn't really seem fair. If you're not serious."

He shrugged one shoulder. "I'll take that under advisement."

Her cheeks heated and she glanced past the checkout counters toward the parking lot. "I really do need to be going. We have ice cream melting."

"Is that a no then?"

Why did he have to possess that persuasive, sexy voice? She sighed, wanting desperately to say yes, but somehow certain that was not the right answer. At least not now. "Tell you what . . . If you're ever unattached, I might reconsider. Sorry, but that's just a deal-breaker for me."

"Can I at least get your phone number?"

She gave a little laugh. "What? Are you planning to suddenly be unattached by tomorrow night or something?"

That earned her a nervous chuckle. Plus a sheepish look that said she'd read his mind. *Great.* And if she didn't get out of here right now, he just might wear her down. "Nice to see you again, Rafe. I really do need to run though. Häagen-Dazs is melting, you know."

She turned on her heel, and though it took every bit of effort — including any remaining resistance to the quart of dulce de leche

73

she'd sneaked into the cart — she did *not* look back.

CHAPTER 6

For the second time in as many days, Rafe found himself watching Britt Chandler walk away from him. And he didn't like the way it felt this time any better than he had the first.

He could have kicked himself for not dealing with the whole Stefani thing before now — so he could have honestly told Britt that there *weren't* any girlfriends to worry about. Period. But then, how could he have known he'd run into her today?

Even so, it seemed like a sign. Sure, this was a small town and the chances of running into her were pretty decent — especially in the grocery store. But their paths had crossed three times now — four if he counted the police incident that night almost a year ago — and his attraction to her hadn't dimmed from one encounter to the next. Quite the opposite.

There was just something special about

the woman — her shy smile that begged for someone to protect the woman behind it, her loyalty to her sisters, even her determination to keep him at arm's length. But who was he kidding? He came with a lot of baggage. Robby, Ma, the whole nine yards. That baggage was the reason he'd never gotten past a surface relationship with Stefani. Stefani didn't even know about Robby, except that he'd mentioned once he had a brother.

Of course, it said something that she had never asked any questions about anything that really mattered. They talked about work and movies and . . . that was about it. The few times he'd dipped his toe in the water and tried to bring up the subject of Robby or Ma or his childhood, Stefani changed the subject as if she'd seen a ghost. Or she acted like she hadn't heard a word he said and started talking about herself. Stefani liked talking about herself. A lot.

It was his own fault that he didn't push through and insist on having the conversations they needed to have to move their relationship forward. But he knew if he pushed, that would be the end of things with her. And the truth was, he didn't want to move forward with Stefani. Not now that Britt Chandler was in the picture.

Because he felt in his bones that Britt

Chandler was different.

And if somehow she turned out to be like all the rest, ditching and running when they found out about Robby, then he would give up. Just flat give up.

He grabbed the groceries he'd promised to pick up for his mom and got a few things he needed to get through the weekend. The cupboards were bare at his apartment, but he'd lost his enthusiasm for stocking up. His next shift didn't start until Sunday night but then he was on three straight.

His last weekend off for who knew how long, and he was going to waste it.

Phee and Quinn both seemed in good spirits when Britt and Jo returned bearing ice cream. The four of them sat around Phee's hospital bed trading bites from each other's Häagen-Dazs cartons and laughing at Quinn's corny jokes. But amidst the laughter, before Quinn left for work, they'd devised a plan for Phee's mandated bed rest that was workable, if a bit complicated.

Quinn offered to drop Jo off at her office, and as they readied to leave, Britt tried not to dwell on how much of "the plan" depended on *her.* But the more she and Jo discussed the details, the more it became clear that most of Phee's care would, indeed, fall on her shoulders. Just as it had with Mom when she was ill and then dying.

And not only would she be Phee's main caregiver, but she had a sneaking suspicion she might also get tasked with keeping an eye on Mateo, the preteen boy Jo's fiancé was guardian to. She loved the kid. Mateo had become like part of the family even before Jo and Luke announced their engagement. But she saw the handwriting on the wall: She would be the designated babysitter for Mateo. Just one more person on a long list she'd be responsible for. One more thing tying her to a life she had *not* signed up for. When would she —

A tap from the door halted her spiraling thoughts.

Phee's doctor stepped into the room. "How are we feeling this morning?"

"Well, I'm feeling hopeful that you'll let me go home today."

"Let's have a look."

Britt rose from her chair. "I'll be out in the —"

"You don't need to leave." Dr. Hinsen waved her off. "I'll only be a minute."

Still, Britt backed away and stood to the side, feeling a tad in the way.

After studying Phee's chart, Dr. Hinsen spoke softly. "I'd like you to stay tonight.

78

But I'll be around first thing in the morning and if nothing's changed, we'll dismiss you then." He turned and motioned Britt closer before giving Phee a stern look. "You understand you'll be on bed rest?"

Phee nodded.

"I'm only letting you go home on the condition that you have help when you get there." He'd spoken with Phee before about what bed rest would entail, but the way he said it now left no doubt that her condition was serious and ongoing.

"I understand." She nodded again, but her voice wavered.

Britt jumped in, aiming to reassure the doctor. "We worked out a schedule before Quinn left earlier. She'll have round-the-clock help."

"That's good." Dr. Hinsen turned back to Phee. "You can get up to use the bathroom and if you get a bath bench, you can take a quick shower each day, but except for a short drive to your checkup each week, that's it. Otherwise I want you in bed." He wrote orders for a physical therapist to show Phee some exercises she could do from her bed and with a look included Britt in the instructions for medications and the warning signs they should watch for.

"Is there any hope I can carry the baby

full-term?" The tremor in Phee's voice revealed more than her expression let on.

Dr. Hinsen shrugged. "Each case is different. I'll be pretty pleased if you can make it to thirty-six weeks." He flipped through her chart, then glanced at his watch. "That's twelve weeks in bed. We hope. You think you can handle that?"

Phee laughed nervously. "It doesn't sound like I have a choice."

"No, you don't."

Phee sighed. "There was a time I would have said a few weeks in bed sounded amazing, but after two days in this bed, I'm . . . a little more realistic about what that actually means."

"That's good. I want you to take this seriously."

"I do. I will. I'll do whatever I have to to keep my baby safe."

Dr. Hinsen shook his head. "Your baby, yes, but this is more about your own health." He went on to describe what could happen if Phee didn't take care of herself or if the bleeding started again.

Britt couldn't let herself think about it. If anything happened to Phee or the baby on her watch . . . She pasted on a smile and focused on the doctor's instructions.

But when Dr. Hinsen exited the room,

Phee grabbed Britt's hand. "I'm so sorry."

"Sorry? Why?" Her smile hadn't fooled her sister.

"That you're getting stuck babysitting." A smile quirked the corner of Phee's mouth. "No pun intended."

"Don't even talk like that, Phee. I'm just glad I can be there."

It wasn't exactly the truth. She wasn't glad about any of this. But she understood why she was the designated caregiver. It made sense. She was the one who didn't really have a job. Yes, she had plenty to do keeping the Airbnb going, but she could make her own hours and take shortcuts, like serving store-bought bakery treats for breakfast and even hiring someone to clean the rooms and make up the beds between guests, if it came to that. It would eat up their profits for a few months, but at least they could fulfill the bookings they already had and avoid a bunch of bad reviews that could ruin their reputation.

If she were a better person, she would just suck it up and graciously put her life aside to take care of her sister until the baby came. And she *would* do that. Of course, she would. But the "graciously" part wouldn't be easy. It was beyond frustrating to have circumstances always dictating her life. When would she ever get to make a choice about how her life looked?

She forced another smile, hoping this one looked more convincing. "Besides, between Thanksgiving, Christmas, and New Year's, time will fly."

"And Valentine's Day. Don't forget that."

"Okay, fine. Valentine's Day too. Be grateful if this had to happen, it happened in a season so full of holidays. But before you know it, it'll be spring and we'll be taking your baby in the stroller for walks between our houses."

The thought buoyed her as much as it seemed to cheer Phee. She only hoped her words were prophetic. And that these next weeks — taking them well into the new year — would fly by without incident.

CHAPTER 7

Rafe wiped his palms on his jeans. He hadn't expected to feel so nervous. After all, it was clear that Stefani had no strong feelings for him. Still, he felt mean wasting her supper break like this. And he wouldn't put it past her to make a scene. But it would have been far worse to ask her on a date and then break things off with her, and he sure wasn't going to break up via email or a note in her locker at the hospital.

The cafeteria was empty except for a janitor sweeping around a row of tables. Rafe chose a table in the corner farthest from the buffet line and pulled out a chair. A minute later, Stefani appeared around the corner. Coming toward him, she waved, but her smile dimmed as she got closer. He realized his expression must have cued her in that this wasn't just their usual supper date.

"What's wrong?" She hung back, eyeing him suspiciously.

"Don't you want to get something to eat before we talk?" He pulled out a chair and motioned for her to sit down.

"What's going on?"

He hesitated. "Why do you think something's going on?"

"I'm not an idiot, Rafe. And I'm not blind either. I see your face. What's this about?"

"Do you want to go outside?"

She glanced toward the windows. "Not unless the temperature has gone up by forty degrees since I came on shift."

"Oh, yeah . . . I kind of forgot about that. We could get some drive-through?"

"I'm not really hungry." She folded her arms across her waist.

He was. Hungry for something besides turkey and dressing anyway. Since last Thursday, he'd been living on Thanksgiving leftovers — and not the good homemade kind. Ma had ordered enough for a small army from the deli at Schnuck's and sent half of it home with him. In the end, Robby had balked at going to Ma's house, so Rafe had eaten a second institutional turkey dinner with Robby Thanksgiving night. The thought of another turkey-with-gravy sandwich made him queasy.

"How about you just tell me what you came to tell me and then you can go get whatever it is you want."

He frowned. "To eat, you mean?"

"Take it any way you want."

Okay, if she was going to play it like that, he may as well just get it over with. "I think we should stop seeing each other."

Her eyes went wide. "Well, that was subtle."

"You said to say what I came to say."

"So you think we've been seeing each other?"

He studied her for a long minute. She didn't flinch. "No. That's the problem. We don't see each other. We barely know anything about each other. We never go more than skin deep."

"Excuse me?"

"You don't even know I have a brother, Stefani. Or that my dad is a first-class jerk."

"No. No, I got that."

He smirked at her implication: It took one to know one. Or father one. He deserved that. He shook his head. He'd said it all so much better when he'd rehearsed it driving here. Instead he'd put the blame on her. *You've* been afraid. *You* don't even know . . .

"Listen. I'm as much at fault as anyone. I didn't ever press it. But I should have. I need you to know those things about me. How can we ever have a true friendship if

85

we don't talk about stuff like that?"

"You know I don't like talking about my family."

"Okay, but does that have to mean we don't talk about mine?"

She wrapped her arms tighter around her midsection. "You know what, Rafe? You've been wanting out of this for a long time. Just go. Far be it from me to hold you against your will."

"I didn't want it to turn into a fight, Stefani."

"Then your wish is my command. Go." She waved her hand with a flourish, then stood glaring at him.

"I'm sorry. I should have said something before. I take the blame. I mean that." And he did. He wasn't sure why he'd dragged things out with her as long as he had. Why had he been so afraid of letting her go? But he *did* know. Because letting her go meant he was alone again. It meant he'd screwed up yet another relationship. Three strikes, you're out.

And worse, the thing that was finally pushing him to end the charade with Stefani was the notion that he had something to offer any woman. He'd like to think he did. Had plenty to offer. But with that offering came responsibilities not many women were willing to take on. But that was a part of his life. Robby was part of his life. Taking care of his brother, his family. And that was a part that wasn't going to change.

He reached out to touch Stefani's arm briefly. He opened his mouth to say what he figured a woman in her position expected: *You'll find someone who's worthy of you.* And all that rot. But it wasn't *only* his fault. She had issues too. And he hoped she got them figured out before she got involved with someone else. So he simply touched her hand again. "I'm sorry. I truly am." Then he turned and walked away.

The lightness of being that came over him surprised him. And he was still smiling ten minutes later when he parked in front of Hope Village and psyched himself up for a visit with Robby.

Halfway home, he started — by sheer habit — to turn into the Aldi parking lot to pick up something for supper. And breakfast. But at the last minute he drove past the turn. Aldi was where he'd run into Britt Chandler and her sister. That had been a Wednesday, too, and he didn't want to chance that was their regular grocery shopping day and her taking him for a stalker.

He drove on to Schnuck's and parked in

the nearly empty lot. It might take him twice as long to find anything here since he rarely shopped at this store, but whatever.

He grabbed a small cart and pushed it through the automatic doors. Five minutes later, he had a frozen pizza, a carton of ice cream, and a two-liter bottle of root beer in his cart when he rounded the corner — and there she was.

Seriously? She hadn't spotted him yet, and he was tempted to turn his cart around and hide in the far corner of the store. But maybe it was a sign. And he *could* honestly tell her now that there were zero girlfriends waiting in the wings. She would not be a tricycle. The memory made him smile.

And when he looked up, she met his gaze, recognition dawning slowly. "Oh. Hi."

"Hi yourself." He shuffled his feet behind the grocery cart. "I'm really not stalking you."

She gave him a look that said she was doubtful.

"I promise. In fact, I started to turn into Aldi and then I remembered you shopped there and I came here instead. Promise. Scout's honor."

That earned him a smile. "It's a free country, Rafe. You can shop anywhere you like."

"I know. But I . . ." He waved a hand. "Never mind."

"I'm just picking up some groceries for my sister."

"Oh, how is she? Is everything okay now?"

Britt frowned. "She's doing okay. But she has to be on bed rest until the baby comes. She's going a little stir-crazy."

"I suppose that's not as wonderful as it sounds. Bed rest."

She laughed. "Definitely not. And I hope you won't judge me if I say that Phee is driving the rest of us a little crazy in the process."

"You'll get no judgment from me."

"Thanks. So . . ." She seemed to be grasping for something to change the subject. "Did you have a good Thanksgiving?"

He started to offer a glib yes, but given the conversation he'd just had with Stefani, he took a breath and dove in. "I've had better, to be honest."

She tilted her head, her blue eyes questioning. "I'm sorry. Is everything okay?"

"It's fine. Just some . . . family stuff."

Her eyes took on an impish spark. "Holidays. They'd be great if it wasn't for crazy family. I'm kidding," she added quickly. "We had turkey sandwiches around Phee's bed. It was kind of fun actually."

He laughed, and she looked relieved.

"I'm sorry yours wasn't the greatest. Anything you want to talk about?"

Her question genuinely surprised him. And he took a risk. "Don't you need to get groceries back to your sister?"

She looked into the half-full cart. "Oh, not until tomorrow."

"You wouldn't want to go for coffee would you? Or . . . maybe you were just being nice. Making conversation. And before you answer, let me say something, okay?"

She waited without speaking.

"Not that this would be anything more than just a shared cup of coffee, but I just want you to know that you wouldn't be a . . . third wheel. I'm not dating anyone. Not even occasionally."

"Oh? As of when?"

Trying to look sheepish, he glanced at his watch. "As of about thirty minutes ago."

She looked dubious. "Are you serious?"

"Is that a no?"

She considered for a few seconds. "No, I'd like that. Coffee . . ." She held up a hand. "As long as you aren't going to talk about stretch marks or Braxton Hicks contractions or daytime TV."

He laughed. "I can pretty much guarantee I have nothing to contribute on those topics whatsoever."

"Um . . . that ice cream might be a problem. And the pizza." She pointed at his cart.

"I'll put them back. They were an impulse purchase anyway." Could he look any more desperate?

"Don't do that on my account."

"No, I don't mind. Really."

"You could take them home and meet me somewhere."

He cocked his head and eyed her. "You're not just saying that and then you'll call me later and say never mind?"

She gave him a three-fingered salute. "Scout's honor."

His mood buoyed, he gave her his most winsome smile. "Okay then. Give me ten minutes. But . . . don't you need to do something with *your* groceries?"

"Nothing frozen. It's cold enough, they'll be fine in the car. Where do you want to meet?"

"How about Panera? I think they're still open."

"Sounds good."

"I'll see you there in ten minutes." He could hardly believe that mere minutes ago he'd been purposefully driving away from Aldi thinking to avoid her, and now they had a date for coffee. "My treat. And don't you dare back out on me." He tried for a teasing tone, but at the same time hoped she took him seriously.

"Don't worry, I'll be there."

CHAPTER 8

Britt's palms were damp when she placed them on the steering wheel to back out of her parking space at Schnuck's. The streetlights were coming on all along Kingshighway, and she flipped on her headlights as she eased into the line of cars headed south. She wasn't sure what had possessed her to say yes to Rafe's impromptu invitation to coffee. But she wasn't sorry.

Maybe she'd only agreed to his invitation because she was more than a little stir-crazy from all the time she'd spent in Phee's bedroom. She honestly didn't know how her sister was going to survive this bed-rest business. She wasn't so sure *she* would survive and she wasn't the one tied to that bed for the next three months — or longer if Phee made it to full-term.

But she'd entertained too many thoughts of Rafe Stuart in recent days to let this opportunity get away. Especially with his promise that she wouldn't be a third wheel. She smiled, remembering him teasing her about the tricycle. She was curious what had happened thirty minutes ago.

And yes, it *had* crossed her mind that Rafe might have set the whole thing up. If she ever found out that was the case, that would be the end of things. She wouldn't abide a liar. Or a charade. But she really thought he was telling her the truth about going to Schnuck's instead of Aldi for fear she'd be there and think he was stalking her. He couldn't just make that up on the spot, could he?

Maybe it was a sign. Not that she really believed in such things. Except that she had prayed that if it was okay with God, she could see Rafe again. And here he was. She could almost hear his low voice — Rafe's voice, not God's. Although if God had a voice, it very well might sound like Rafe Stuart's. She giggled at the thought.

She would have coffee with him, see where that went, and go from there. She wouldn't do anything stupid. Although she probably wouldn't tell her sisters about tonight. They were typical big sisters, always trying to boss her around and play protector — treating her as if she were fourteen instead of twenty-four and perfectly capable of taking care of herself.

That was one of the things that had been so hard about this whole thing with Phee. It had been a role reversal with Britt taking on the big-sister role. It felt strange. And worse, it reminded her too much of that awful year when she'd become her mom's caregiver after cancer took away Mom's ability to take care of herself.

Nurse was not a title she'd ever aspired to. So why did God keep forcing her into that role? Jo had quit law school when Mom got sick, and everyone saw that as such a huge sacrifice. And now Jo didn't even care to go back to law school. She wanted to run a wedding venue! Britt shook her head. Why couldn't anyone see that *she* had made sacrifices too? But hers seemed less to people — no, nonexistent — simply because she'd never had a chance to quit her great passion because she'd never had a chance to discover what it *was.*

She rubbed at her face, irritated that she'd let the heavy thoughts steal the excitement of seeing Rafe. She flipped on the radio and sang along with Luke Combs's "Even Though I'm Leaving." The song reminded her how crazy Phee's classical music drove her. But she didn't feel comfortable using her earbuds to listen to her own music, for fear Phee would need her and she wouldn't hear her sister call.

Cut it out, Chandler. Quit being so selfish. And don't ruin your one chance to do something fun. She immediately felt guilty. Not that Phee wasn't fun. She loved her oldest sister. Joanna too. Considered them her best friends. But over the last couple of weeks she'd had enough togetherness to last a lifetime. And the end wasn't even in sight. If Phee made it to thirty-six weeks as the doctors hoped, they still had ten weeks to go. Two down, ten to go. It sounded like an eternity. And already, Phee was getting a little testy. Not that Britt blamed her.

She had a feeling they were all a little on edge as the first anniversary of Mom's death approached. That had to hit Phee especially hard as she faced the possibility of losing her first baby so soon after losing Mom. *Oh, please, God. Don't let that happen. You* can't *let that happen.*

The light turned green and Panera came into view. Enough of these gloomy thoughts. She was just going to enjoy this evening. And hopefully get some answers to her questions. If it ended up being the last time she ever saw Rafe, so be it. At least she'd have him out of her system.

As she parked, she saw him waiting in the

entry alcove. She quickly slicked on some lip gloss, cut the engine, and locked the SUV.

Rafe opened the door for her, smiling. "You came."

"I told you I would."

"So you did." He led the way to the counter, and they ordered drinks. Hot tea for her, and hot chocolate for him. He paid, and they waited by the counter until their drinks were ready — served in real mugs, which Rafe specially requested. She liked that he'd done that. Maybe it wasn't his intention, but it made the evening feel like more than just an "accidental" coffee.

He led the way to a booth by the front windows. "This okay?"

"Sure."

He took the side facing the entrance, and Britt slid into the bench across from him. She put sugar in her tea and stirred it. Usually, she took her caffeine without sweetener, but stirring it gave her something to do. Mid-stir she remembered his comment about family stuff at Thanksgiving — perhaps the very reason they were here. "So your Thanksgiving wasn't the greatest? What happened?"

He looked surprised she'd remembered. "Oh, yeah . . . that. Just some stuff with my brother. And my mom. And my dad. And a girl that's ancient history."

"Oh, you mean ancient as in thirty minutes ago ancient?" Yikes. What had she gotten herself into? But at least he'd given her an opening to talk about the girl.

He checked his watch, then grinned across the table at her. "Almost an hour now."

"So tell me about that."

"Stefani?"

"The one at the hospital. Unless there are others?" She remembered the girl's name, but he didn't need to know that.

"There aren't any others. And yes, her name is Stefani. We were never serious. So I broke it off."

"Tonight."

"Yes."

"Like, an hour ago?"

He nodded.

She raised an eyebrow. "And that had nothing to do with us being here right now?"

"I swear it didn't. Well, wait . . . It had something to do with *you*. But I didn't know I was going to see you tonight. I promise. I . . . I was going to let a little time pass before I called you again."

So he *had* planned to call her. She raised an eyebrow in query.

"There was never anything serious be-

98

tween Stefani and me. We were more like friends . . . and not even that really. I honestly don't know why I didn't break things off a long time ago. She didn't know anything about me . . . and didn't want to."

"What didn't she know about you?" Britt felt bold given her resolute thoughts earlier. If tonight was about getting Rafe out of her system, that was fine with her. But still, hope was strong.

"That I have a brother for one thing."

"Why didn't she know that? You never told her?"

He chewed his bottom lip. "Well, she might've known I have one, but she didn't know anything about Robby. She never asked about him or wanted to meet him."

"Is he older or younger?"

"Younger. Ten years younger." There was deep affection in his voice. But an edge too.

"So he's . . . a teenager now?" She guessed Rafe to be about her age.

"He's sixteen." He fingered the handle of his mug. "But he acts about three."

She smiled. "Typical teen, huh?"

"No." His brow knit. "Not typical at all. Robby is . . . brain-damaged. From birth. He's developmentally about three years old. He's in a home."

"Oh wow. I'm sorry, Rafe. That must be

so hard." She *did* feel the sympathy she tried to convey, but at the same time, she was thinking of Joanna. She'd thought her sister was foolish to let twelve-year-old Mateo become an issue between Joanna and Luke early in their relationship. But suddenly, she empathized a little more. Rafe came with baggage. She gave a little gasp. Hadn't Joanna said those same words about Luke? And unlike Mateo, Rafe's brother would never grow up.

"Most of the time I don't even think about it." Rafe's mellow voice brought her back to the present. "Robby's a great kid. And the staff at the group home does all the really hard stuff. The hardest part — for me — is my parents. They're divorced. My dad pretty much checked out after they realized that Robby would never be . . . right. And my mom's bitter about all of it. She doesn't realize it, but she takes it out on Robby. And on me too, I guess."

"I'm so sorry, Rafe." And she was. But did she really want to get involved? Because as Mom had always said, *You don't just marry the man, you marry his family too.*

"It's not a big deal."

"It sounds like a pretty big deal to me."

"What I mean is, it's not *your* deal." He took a gulp of his hot chocolate. "Can I just be honest?"

"Please."

"Two things." He held up two fingers. "First, I didn't really mean to, but I think maybe I was testing you when you asked about my Thanksgiving. Back at Schnuck's."

"Testing me?"

"One of the things that didn't work between me and Stefani was that she never wanted to hear anything negative. She just tuned out if I ever started to talk about anything remotely negative. So when you asked about my holidays, I decided to just go for it and dump all that on you. That wasn't fair. At all. I'm sorry. I promise I'm not usually a whiner."

"And?"

"I'm sorry?" He looked confused.

"You said *two* things."

"Oh. I guess the other thing is that — because of Stefani — I decided I wasn't going to let that happen with you . . . I mean, with the next woman I dated. So again, I was testing. Totally not fair to you."

"It's okay. I might have been testing you too."

"Oh?" He looked intrigued.

"Well, not testing exactly. But I kind of needed to get you out of my system." She hadn't intended to spill her guts this way.

101

But as long as they were laying things out on the table . . .

"Get me out of your system, huh?" He gave her a crooked little half smile. "You *do* know that implies I was *in* your system in the first place?"

"I know, I know." She couldn't help but return his smile. "What can I say? You have a really nice voice."

"What?" He feigned a pout. "This handsome face, this studly bod, and you fall for my *voice*? What is wrong with you?"

She rolled her eyes. "Don't you know anything? Women don't care about handsome faces or studly bods."

"Hmm . . . It's all about the sexy voice, huh?"

"I never said your voice was *sexy.*"

"Oh." He had the grace to flush red. "I could have sworn . . ."

She laughed, elated that their conversation had covered so much territory in only a few minutes. "Okay, maybe it's a *little* sexy."

"Ha!" he crowed. "I knew it."

But she chose to turn serious. "I don't think you understand what it meant to have you stay with me — on the phone — that day when Phee almost lost the baby. Your voice was a lifeline."

"Well, I'm glad it all turned out okay."

"I've never been so scared in my life." That wasn't entirely true. She'd been equally terrified that first day Mom went into convulsions. Britt shuddered inwardly at the memory, remembering how terrified she'd been to see her mother that way. She couldn't have lived with it if Mom had died on *her* watch. And she would be forever grateful that instead, Mom had died surrounded by her family.

"You did everything right," Rafe said. "I wish all my calls went that well. And had such a happy ending."

"Well . . . again, thanks to you." Before he could deflect her gratitude like he'd done before, she held up a hand. "I know you say you were just doing your job, but that doesn't make you any less a hero in my eyes."

"I'm glad I could help." He bent his head briefly, but when he looked up again, there was a glint in his eyes. "So . . . Just so I'm clear, you think I have a sexy voice, and I'm a hero in your eyes. Is that right?"

"Oh, good grief." But she couldn't help laughing. "You just think whatever makes you feel good."

"That makes me feel good all right."

She shook her head. But she loved their

103

lighthearted banter. And that he could steer away from such a difficult topic without making her feel like he was dismissing her. "You said you wish all your calls had such a happy ending. Is it pretty common that . . . they don't?"

He grimaced. "Let's just say people don't call us when everything is peachy."

"No. I suppose not." She took the last sip of tepid tea. "So why'd you switch? From being a policeman?"

"Man! Our first date and you're asking all the hard questions."

"No, I'm saving the really hard ones for our first date. This" — she motioned between them — "is not a date."

"Oops. Right." But that impish glimmer came to his eyes again. "But if you're saving the hard questions, maybe we need to set up that *official* first date right away. So I can prepare." Oh, he was tricky. "We'll see. It depends on how you answer the easy questions."

He drained his mug and steepled his hands in front of him. "Okay. Shoot."

"We were talking about why you switched from police work to EMT."

"Right." The spark had left his eyes. "Technically, I still work for the Langhorne Police Department. I just have a different

104

position."

"Did you request the change?"

"I did." He seemed to be collecting his thoughts. "I guess the simple answer is that I felt like I could make more of a difference as an EMT."

"What's the not-so-simple answer?"

He moved his mug from one spot to another, then back again. A V formed between his pale eyebrows. "I think that might need to wait for the first date."

"Oh? I'm sorry. You don't have to tell me. I didn't realize . . ." She felt bad her question had put that furrow between his brows.

"No. It's not that I don't want to tell you. It's just . . . It's kind of a long story. It might take a while. Might even be second-date material."

"Wow. That serious, huh?" She wanted to reclaim the laughter they'd shared earlier.

"Let's get that first date scheduled and we'll see how it goes." His smile returned.

"I'd like that."

"How about tomorrow night?"

"I'm sorry. I can't. We have guests coming. At the Airbnb. With Phee out of commission and Jo working full-time, I really can't take the weekend off. Plus, we've promised guests the cottages will be decorated for Christmas, and I haven't put up so much as a strand of tinsel."

"Does that mean Saturday wouldn't work either?"

She shook her head. "Or Sunday either. I'm sorry."

"So what about Monday?"

She wrinkled her nose. "This week, that's my night to stay with Phee since Quinn has a board meeting at church."

"Tuesday?" He looked hopeful.

"I have book club Tuesday."

"You can't skip?"

"I'm hosting it. And it's our Christmas party."

"Book club, huh?" He cocked his head and eyed her suspiciously. "This isn't like the ol' I-have-to-wash-my-hair excuse, is it?"

"No. I do that on Wednesdays."

"Haha."

"Just kidding. And I promise it's not that kind of excuse. Did somebody really use that one on you?"

"No, but a girl did tell me once that she was busy the rest of her life."

Britt couldn't help laughing, and thankfully, he didn't seem offended.

But after a minute, he shook his head slowly, feigning — she thought — a disappointed look. "I didn't figure you for a book geek."

She wasn't sure how to take that, though she suspected he was stinging from her rejection — *five* rejections actually. She aimed for levity. "So you didn't think I could read or what?"

"No, but you know what they say: Books are for people who wish they were somewhere else."

She looked askance at him. "*Who* says that?"

"Mark Twain, actually."

"Are you sure about that? Seems like a funny thing for an author to say."

Rafe shrugged. "I guess it does, doesn't it?"

"Besides, what is that even supposed to mean?" Britt frowned, not liking the turn this conversation was taking.

CHAPTER 9

Rafe eyed Britt, trying to figure out if he'd offended her with his smart aleck quote. Mark Twain was going to get him in trouble if he kept slinging the man's quotes around. He'd written a paper on Samuel Langhorne Clemens in a college lit class. Figured it was a good topic since his hometown was named after the man. For some reason the quotes had stuck with him, and he'd memorized a few more in the years since.

So far, his little treasure trove of quotes hadn't served any purpose other than giving him something snappy to say when he was at a loss for words in a social situation. Now it seemed his so-called talent might have bitten him in the you-know-what. But seriously, if a woman wasn't willing to skip book club for him, he may as well abandon all hope.

Still, he had to try. "I didn't mean anything personal by that, you know — the book geek comment. Now that you mention it, Twain was probably saying something about how you could go anywhere without leaving your armchair, thanks to books."

She gave a little shrug. "Maybe. I'm not going to apologize for loving books."

"And I wasn't asking you to. I was asking you for a date . . . just to get this conversation back on track." He couldn't decide if she was genuinely busy the next four nights or if, after twenty minutes with him, she'd decided she wasn't interested. Either way, he probably owed her an apology. He tried to take full advantage of the voice she supposedly loved so much. "I really didn't mean to knock your book club or your love of books or . . . whatever." He shrugged. "I'm sorry if it came off that way."

He couldn't quite interpret the look she wore. "Well, regardless of what Mark Twain meant by that — if he even said it in the first place — there will be *one* person at our book club who wishes she were somewhere else."

"Oh?" He tipped his head, grinning, waiting for her to admit she wished she could have said yes to his invitation.

Instead she frowned. "My sister. We're meeting at Quinn and Phee's house, actually. It's my night to stay with Phee, so we're going to meet in her room."

He deflated but quickly recovered. "Why do you say she'll wish she was somewhere else? She doesn't like to read?"

"No, she does. Just not the kind of books we read. Our selection this month is John Grisham's latest. Phee is more of a Jane Austen type. But I figured this has to be better than watching *Sense and Sensibility* for the forty-eighth time."

"Forty-eight? Seriously? I could barely get through one time. And the book? Forget about it."

Britt giggled. She had a nice laugh.

"So, how much longer does she have to be down?"

"Oh, her entire pregnancy. They're just hoping she makes it to thirty-six weeks. That would be the end of February."

He blew out a slow breath. "That's a long time to be in bed."

"You're telling me. She's not even in our book club, but it was my turn to host and since I'm at her house most of the week anyway, we decided to host at her house. I can do my baking there . . . the hostess has to provide dessert," she explained.

"Well, now there's a reason to not wish you were somewhere else."

That got a laugh.

110

"Seriously, though, that's really sweet of you to include her that way. In book club, I mean."

"Yeah, well, we're trying to find ways to keep her from curling up and dying of boredom. And me too."

"You're bored?"

She winced. "Don't tell Phee I said so, but honestly, yes. I love my sister dearly, but sometimes it feels like *I'm* the one on bed rest."

"So what do you do while you're there?"

She shot him an exasperated look. "Well, I've already finished the next two book club selections. And I'm thinking about taking up cross-stitch."

"Wow. You *must* be bored. I don't think I've read two books this *year.*"

"Oh, I love to read. But I've cleaned about everything there is to clean in her house. And if I bake any more cookies or cakes I'll have to join Weight Watchers."

He laughed, but her expression said she was serious.

Britt frowned. "I have no reason to complain. You probably think I'm terrible."

"No, I don't." He placed a hand over hers on the table but pulled away quickly, realizing she might see it as too familiar. "Let's just say this is a safe place to whine

111

and complain."

Her shoulders relaxed slightly. "Thank you. But I don't want to get in the habit of whining. That's not pleasant for anybody."

"I don't mind."

"Oh, you would if I kept it up."

"I don't think so." He meant it, yet inexplicably, an image of his mother's pinched face and set jaw came to him. He pushed it away and focused on Britt Chandler's pretty face.

"Trust me, you would."

"Okay. I'll take your word for it." He pushed his empty mug to one side. "Now, can we get back to the subject at hand?"

"Which was?"

"You being busy Friday, Saturday, Sunday, Monday, and Tuesday. So the obvious question is what does Wednesday look like?"

She smiled. "You don't give up easily, do you?"

"Oh, you have no idea."

"You're not going to believe this, but Wednesday we have guests again — at the Airbnb. And that's my night with Phee because Quinn has another meeting at church. So after I welcome our guests and get them checked in, I head over to Phee's."

He affected a pout. "Well, that stinks. Because I have shifts from Thursday night

112

through the weekend, so it'd be the *next* Tuesday before I could do dinner."

She started to say something, but clamped her mouth shut.

"What?"

She wrinkled her nose. "Nothing. I'm just sorry to be so difficult. Maybe we can find a time the following week. If that's not getting too close to Christmas for you. I'd be happy to meet you somewhere."

His heart lifted. "You don't have to meet me. I can pick you up. Whenever it works out."

"If you don't mind, I'd rather meet you somewhere."

"Okaaay." He drew the word out, curious but sensing it would be best not to push.

She gave him an apologetic look. "The cottages — our Airbnb are a few miles out in the country. Down on the river — well, technically, a tributary of the Mississippi."

"I've seen the sign. I don't mind driving a few miles."

"Thanks, but I'd really rather meet you somewhere. I'll . . . explain later."

"Can I call you this weekend?"

"I guess that would be okay. But maybe you should text first. In case I'm with guests."

He couldn't tell if this was just another

excuse or if she was that conscientious. But she gave him her number.

He tapped the numbers into his phone. "Here . . . let me give you mine too. So you'll know it's not a telemarketer."

He rattled off his number and watched her copy it into her phone, hoping she wasn't going to block it once she got out of his sight.

The rest of the evening was spent in pleasant conversation. But if he had to guess, she wasn't falling nearly as head over heels with him as he was with her. In fact, he braced himself not to be surprised if she ignored his text.

And he would be lying if he pretended it didn't matter to him.

Putting the groceries away in the cabin, Britt replayed her conversation with Rafe. She wished she could take back all the complaining she'd done while they sipped their drinks. He'd insisted he didn't mind her griping. But she'd turned the conversation, too often, back on herself. It was a bad habit that had grown worse while Mom was sick. She wouldn't blame Rafe if he didn't call again, especially since she was the one who'd instigated their little coffee get-together. After all, the whole point of them getting together tonight was so Rafe could talk about his difficult Thanksgiving. Instead, she'd hijacked the conversation more than once.

Why did she always shoot herself in the foot that way? She liked this guy. A lot. But the more she thought about it, the more she wondered how she could add one more thing to her to-do list. She wadded up the empty grocery sacks and stuffed them into a tote bag in the closet.

She finished putting groceries away and texted Quinn to see how her sister was doing. Almost immediately, the little dots appeared on her phone indicating that Quinn was responding. But when the message came through, it was Phee:

It's me, sis. I'm fine. Just bored out of my ever lovin' mind. Quinn says hi. Will I see you tomorrow?

Britt texted a reply she hoped didn't sound terse. Of course, Phee would see her tomorrow. And almost every day after that for the foreseeable future.

Of all the times to meet the guy of her dreams! God must have some crazy sense of humor. She stilled as a thought came: Or maybe this was God's way of telling her that Rafe wasn't "the one." But how would she ever know if she couldn't find more than a couple of hours to spend with him?

Right now, the only truly important thing was to get Phee and Quinn through this trial. Get their baby safely into the world. Romance would have to simmer on the back burner.

Again.

CHAPTER 10

December

"Robby, you don't have a choice." Rafe worked to keep his voice even. It didn't take much to send his brother into a tantrum when he was like this. "You *have* to take a bath."

"Do not have to!"

"Yes, you do. You stink, buddy. Nobody wants to be around you when you stink."

"I don't stink. I don't stink. I don't!" Robby sniffed the air in front of him, as if to prove his point.

Rafe held his nose. "I'm here to tell you, bro, you *do* stink. Come on, Rob. It won't take long. And then you can watch cartoons."

"I wanna watch cartoons now."

If his brother were actually three years old, he would have put his foot down and marched him down the hall to the showers, knowing he'd be creating a monster if he let him throw a tantrum. But it didn't work that way with Robby. While he had the mental capabilities of a three-year-old, Robby didn't learn new things the way a toddler did. The kid was stuck in a time warp, forever three years old. And arguing with him when he didn't want to do something was an exercise in futility. Still, sometimes you had to force things and deal with the aftermath.

"Come on. You like bubbles, remember?" Persuading him with the promise of bubbles, Rafe clasped a hand roughly on his brother's shoulder and "guided" him in the direction of the hallway, grabbing a few items from the stack of clean clothes he'd brought as they went through the doorway. "And hey, I got you some new clothes." He held up navy blue sweatpants and a Spider-Man T-shirt.

The air in the hallway was only slightly fresher, but it reminded Rafe that his brother's room smelled like a high school locker room. He didn't have time today, but he would come back tomorrow and gather up his brother's dirty laundry and take it home to wash. At least the things that still fit him. He'd wash his sheets too. Until recently, Ma had done all of Robby's laundry, including his Spider-Man bed sheets.

But a few months ago, she'd turned it over to the staff at Hope Village. Apparently housekeeping hadn't gotten the memo.

Someone needed to call a meeting with the entire staff about Robby's care — or lack of it. It seemed the bigger he got physically, the less quality care he got. Rafe understood why. Most of the nurses and aides were female, and surely it had to be awkward to give a bath to a sixteen-year-old boy with the body of a man. Especially when that boy-man fought every effort at good hygiene. But it was a vicious cycle since the more unpleasant Robby smelled, the more unlikely he was to get the attention he needed.

"Okay, buddy. Let's get you cleaned up." Rafe tried to catch the eye of the CNA sitting at the desk as he went by, but she was suddenly intent on the papers in front of her — papers he suspected hid her cell phone. "I'm going to help him shower."

The woman looked up and nodded, unsmiling.

Half an hour later, Rafe was almost as wet as his brother, but at least they both smelled of shampoo and aftershave instead of week-old teenage sweat. Rafe requested fresh sheets for the bed and even helped the aide make it up. Robby would grumble plenty about giving up his Spider-Man sheets, but he'd be equally happy when Rafe brought them back fresh and clean tomorrow.

He told his brother good night and got an annoyed grunt in return. But he had the satisfaction of knowing that — for a day or two at least — his brother wouldn't repel every person who stepped into his room.

With Robby content in front of the TV and the annoying characters from *The Boss Baby* droning in the background, Rafe slipped out of the room without speaking to his brother again. He walked wordlessly past the nurses station, too tired to get into it with them tonight. Especially when he'd have to "get into it" with Ma. Why wasn't she the one taking care of Robby's laundry and making sure he got a bath more than once a week?

Am I my brother's keeper?

The question from last Sunday's sermon brought him up short. The story was from the book of Genesis, and when Cain had uttered those words in reply to God Himself, it had not gone well for him. The question was meant to be an excuse. But Rafe *was* his brother's keeper. As he deserved to be.

Britt had asked him why he'd switched to being an EMT, and he'd balked at telling

120

her the real reason. Maybe he never would, but if she remembered and asked again, he could tell her — quite honestly — that it was a good distraction from the troubles in his family. He'd come to dread his days off because it only meant spending time with his family, dealing with the fallout from everything that had happened, or sitting around in his apartment thinking about it, which was worst of all.

He drove to his mother's house, steeling himself for the confrontation that was sure to come. He parked on the street out in front, a subtle signal to her that he was in a hurry and couldn't stay long. The times he parked in the driveway had become fewer and fewer.

He rang the doorbell, then walked in without waiting for her to answer. "Hey, Ma. It's me. Where are you?"

"In the back." Her voice didn't carry its usual resignation.

He walked through the rooms, noting a kitchen that was cleaner than usual and window blinds that were raised all the way up, letting the winter sun inside.

In the family room, he stopped and his jaw went slack at the view. "What are you doing?"

"What does it look like? I'm putting the

tree up." She looked down at him from her perch on a low stepladder. Sparkly earrings dangled from her earlobes, and it looked like she was wearing lipstick.

Soft Christmas music wafted from the old CD player on top of the television, and a lone cardboard box of decorations spilled its contents onto the worn carpet.

"You need some help?"

"If you have time." Her demeanor seemed to brace for his rejection.

"I can stay a while." He was glad he hadn't brought Robby's laundry in with him as he'd been tempted to do. He shed his coat and went over to take the other end of the string of lights she wrestled with. He couldn't remember the last time the Christmas tree had been up in this room. Usually, if they did anything at all to celebrate, they went to the group home and sat with Robby for the residents' Christmas party.

"This is looking good, Ma. You want me to put the wreath up on the front door?" He was almost afraid to say anything lest he jinx this almost-cheerful version of his mother.

She eyed him as if trying to decide whether he was being facetious. Apparently he passed the test. "I'm not sure what I did with that wreath. But if you don't mind

122

checking the attic . . . it might be up there. To the left of the chimney in that big gunnysack, you know the one?"

He knew. The sack that had held the Stuart family Christmas decorations for the first ten years of his life had looked suspiciously like the sack carried by a Santa whose voice sounded suspiciously like his dad's. It was a good memory, but one tainted by everything that had happened in the years since.

He worked beside his mom for the next hour, wanting to ask her what had changed, what had brought about the lilt in her step and the soft smile that he'd almost forgotten. But he decided just to let it be. To enjoy the return of the woman he affectionately called "Ma" — for however long it lasted.

He'd do Robby's laundry himself and not say anything. It was a small thing, really. His resentment had never stemmed from the task itself but from feeling that it was a mother's place to take care of her children . . . as long as they were children. And maybe that was wrong of him. Maybe Ma needed a break. Needed some time to take care of herself. And heaven knew he was the only one who could give her that time. *Should* give her that time. It was the least he could do.

He helped her sweep up the plastic "needles" that had fallen from the artificial tree and stored away the empty box in the garage.

When he came back inside, she was admiring the tree with a look he hadn't seen on her face in a very long time. Almost a smile. It took ten years off of her face.

"It looks nice, Ma."

She looked up at him. "It does, doesn't it? Maybe I'll buy a couple of poinsettias to put on either side of the fireplace."

The fireplace was one of those boxes fitted with a fake flame. He hadn't seen it before and wondered where she'd come up with the money to buy it. He hoped she wasn't getting in trouble with her credit card again.

"Let me get the poinsettias for you. You want the red ones?"

"Of course. What else is there?"

"I saw some pink and yellow ones in Walmart the other day. At least I think that's what they were. They were pretty pricey though."

"You just don't worry about it. I'll get what I want. You keep your money."

He opened his mouth to ask if she planned to have Christmas at her house. But he swallowed the question unasked. No sense ruining her rare good mood. Especially when she'd just given him a brilliant idea.

Despite the forty-degree temperature, Britt wiped her brow and hauled another stack of boxes in from the car. When they'd ordered decorations for the cottage and cabins for this first Christmas for the Airbnb, they hadn't thought about where they'd store all the ornaments before — and after — the holidays. Quinn and Phee had come to the rescue and let them store everything in the basement of the new house.

They really should have had all the decorations up long before now. But with Phee out of commission, they were doing well just to honor their bookings. For the weeks leading up to Thanksgiving, they'd made do with a few pumpkins, cheap garlands of fall leaves, and some candles Joanna found for a quarter each at a garage sale. But recent weekend guests to the cottage had expressed disappointment that there were no Christmas decorations to be found. Britt had blatantly milked Phee's close call as an excuse, but despite the sympathy their guests expressed, they'd cited "a sad lack of holiday decor" as their reason for giving The Cottages on Poplar Brook Road only a three-star rating. Reviews were crucial, and they couldn't afford many more low ones like that.

Balancing the stack of boxes, Britt sighed and held the porch door open with one hip as she nudged open the front door. Joanna had left work to meet her at Quinn and Phee's to help load everything into her car. She was disappointed the three of them couldn't make an event of the decorating as they'd planned, and a little miffed that the task had ended up falling to her alone, even though she knew Jo was already behind at work thanks to the time she'd taken off to help with Phee. It couldn't be helped, and she was determined to make the best of it. At least it was a break from sitting with Phee.

She pulled up her favorite Christmas playlist on her phone, put the kettle on for tea, and went to retrieve the last boxes of ornaments.

Her phone pinged from her pocket, and she hurried to deposit the stack of boxes on the kitchen counter at the main cottage. She was expecting a text from the spokeswoman for a group of women who hoped to book the entire venue for two nights in January. They'd specifically requested to cook all their own meals, which would simplify things greatly. And the income from a complete booking for the whole weekend was always a boon to their dwindling bank account. They needed more bookings like that.

She sighed as she fished her phone from her pocket. They'd been doing so well until Phee had to go on bed rest. Not that they were in danger of not being able to pay their bills. But all three of them felt better when there was a little cash to spare in their savings account. They hadn't drained it yet, but they weren't adding to it either.

Her phone sounded again, and she clicked to view the message at the same instant she saw Rafe Stuart's name on the screen. He wasn't supposed to text her until next week. She read the text with wildly mixed emotions. Part of her would be relieved if he was texting to say "forget the whole thing." But a bigger part of her would be deeply disappointed. She'd never felt about any man the way she felt about Rafe after only spending a few hours with him.

Mom would have said it was dangerous to form such a hasty opinion about a person you might end up being married to someday. Not that Britt was going to rush into anything with this guy. But she'd waited so long for even an invitation, she was not going to let this one get away.

She read his text: "Would this be a good time to call you?"

Intrigued, she texted back a simple "yes."

Her phone rang almost immediately. She took in a breath and clicked Accept.

"Hey, I hope I'm not bothering you."

Oh, that voice . . . She could drown in it! She composed herself. "No. You're not. Sorry I'm out of breath. I've been lugging boxes in from the car."

"You're moving? See, I knew you'd try to get out of our date."

She laughed. "What date? I wasn't aware we'd been able to find a day in the next decade when we're both free."

"Funny you should mention that. It's exactly why I'm calling."

CHAPTER 11

"Oh?" Balancing her phone against one shoulder, Britt went to close the door to the enclosed porch and then the one between the porch and the house. "Now why . . . exactly . . . are you calling?"

"I think I've solved our problem." She could hear the smile in Rafe's voice.

"Oh you have? Have you added a new month to the calendar?"

"No, but that's not a half-bad idea. We could call it Brittober."

"Or Rafetember."

His laughter made her feel so clever. "Somehow I don't think that's going to go over very well with whoever's in charge of world calendars. But maybe we don't need an extra month. Maybe we just need to figure out how to use this one better."

"I'm all ears." She was intrigued. And relieved that it appeared he wasn't calling to cancel anything.

"You said the reason you couldn't go out with me this weekend is because you have to decorate for Christmas?"

"Yes . . ."

"Well then. Only hours ago, I finished helping my mom decorate her house for Christmas. It looked pretty good when we were finished, if I do say so myself, and I was struck by something my favorite author once said."

"Wait? Your favorite *author*?" She smiled to herself. This guy and his Mark Twain. But she happily played along. "I thought you didn't like to read."

"I don't. So it wasn't too hard to choose a favorite author from among the four I've read."

She smiled into the phone. "I bet I can guess who it is too."

"And I bet you'd be right."

"Mark Twain?"

"You got it. And he says you shouldn't wait, because the time will never be just right."

"Mark Twain *says* that, huh? Present tense? Funny, I thought he was dead."

Rafe didn't miss a beat. "A lot of people did. To which Twain replied, 'Reports of my death have been greatly exaggerated.' "

Britt remembered hearing that one. Being

a native Missourian and growing up in a town named after the man, they'd studied him in school in almost every grade. "So you and Mark are good buds then?"

"Just kidding. He's dead. For a while now. But an author lives on through his books."

"Or *her* books."

"Right. Anyway, if you'll let me finish . . ."

"Knock yourself out."

"So, I wondered if maybe you could use some help. Decorating. Would it help if I came and helped you this weekend? We could kill two birds with one stone."

"Two birds? Don't tell me . . . Mark Twain?"

"No, silly. That's an ancient idiom."

"Oooh, idiom? That's a big word for somebody who's only read four books in his entire life."

"Four *authors.* There's a difference."

"Point taken. So these two metaphorical birds would be helping me put up decorations and . . . ?"

"And spending time with me. I mean *together.* Spending time together. Contrary to popular belief, it's not *all* about me."

She laughed. "I like the way you think. The two birds part. I could use the help. But when were you thinking?"

"Whenever you were planning to decorate.

I have this whole weekend off, so just name a time. I'll even stop and get takeout. You're okay with cheeseburgers?"

"I love cheeseburgers." He could have suggested Liver-and-Onions-R-Us and she would have said she loved it.

"Alrighty then, burgers it is."

"I know beggars can't be choosers, but I have to have everything done before our guests check in tomorrow night."

"Oh. Well, then I guess we need to get hoppin'. When were you planning on decorating?"

"I don't suppose you're free right now?"

"Now? Like tonight?"

"Well, it doesn't have to be. I can get started and —"

"No. Tonight is great. You know what they say: Never put off till tomorrow what may be done day after tomorrow just as well."

"What? *Who* says? That doesn't even make sense."

He chuckled. "It doesn't, does it?"

"No. And I don't know who said it, but I have a feeling it was you-know-who."

"None other."

"Just so you know, if we were FaceTiming, you'd see me rolling my eyes."

"I don't blame you. So, what time should I come?"

132

"Beggars can't be choos —" She stopped short. "Please don't tell me I just quoted Mark Twain?"

That got a laugh. "Well, if it was, it didn't make my list."

"How long *is* that list, anyway?"

"You don't want to know." He cleared his throat. "Now, back to the question at hand. What time should I come?"

"Well, would now work?" She made a face, glad he couldn't see her. "The thing is, guests start checking in tomorrow around four, and I just brought the boxes of decorations over from my sister's house, and it kind of got me in the mood. To decorate. But I can get started and you can help me finish whenever you can . . . as long as it's done by tomorrow afternoon. There's plenty to do."

"Boxes, plural? Good grief. I did my mom's house in an hour. Are you outlining the river in lights or something?"

"Oooh. That's a great idea!" She laughed. But she *could* picture just how gorgeous that would look. "Our part of the river is only a tributary," she explained. "But no. We won't be lighting the riverbanks. But remember, there are three houses to decorate out here. We don't have to finish all three of them while you're here. If we just get the main

133

cottage done, I'll be thrilled."

"Oh no, I said I'd help, and I'll stay till the bitter end."

"You might want to bring your jammies then. Oh —" Her breath caught. "That did not come out right."

He laughed. "I know what you meant. How about this: I'll come and help for a few hours this evening. If we get along, work well together, maybe I can stay a little later. I don't have to be to work until eleven."

"Sounds like a plan. We'll see how we work together. Um, I might have to ask you to lay off the Mark Twain stuff though."

"What? Woman, you're taking away my best material!"

She might not have liked another man calling her "woman" that way, but coming from that voice . . . he could make just about anything sound perfectly divine and wholly appropriate.

By the time Rafe picked up burgers to go and approached the driveway to The Cottages on Poplar Brook Road, the temperature had dropped fifteen degrees and the wind had picked up. He drove up the lane in a swirl of yellow and red leaves. Sparkles of light from the river behind the cottages reflected against his windshield and added to the charm of the place. It was a nice property. Nicer than Britt had made it out to be. He could almost picture how it would look come spring. And though autumn had quickly turned to winter in Missouri, he could easily imagine what it must have looked like at the peak of fall.

He eased his car toward the largest of the three older houses. At the far end of the drive, he could see the roof and Tyvek-covered bones of the new house going up. He couldn't help imagining Britt there, on the phone in a panic that day her sister had almost lost the baby. He felt guilty that he was so grateful to not have been on that run — even though, God knew, it was almost as difficult being on the phone with her, fearing he wouldn't tell her the right things to save the baby. It had felt like he was reliving his worst nightmare that day. It was only his training that had kept his voice so steady while he talked to Britt, but he considered it a small miracle that she seemed to have no clue he'd been so un-done.

He shook away the memories. He'd come to spend time with the prettiest girl this side of the Mississippi, and he didn't need these dark thoughts clouding their time together. Especially given that it had practically taken an act of Congress to clear a space in their calendars.

He noticed lights on in both the small cabins, but Britt's Escape was parked in front of the larger cabin — she'd called it the cottage — so he parked beside her and locked the car, then felt a little foolish doing so, given the property's rather remote location on the outskirts of town.

He rang the bell. Within seconds, she opened the door and a cloud of aromas wafted out. Cinnamon, vanilla, almond, and pine — everything Christmas should smell like. It occurred to him that those scents were what had been missing from Ma's house. He made a note to buy her an early Christmas present of a scented candle or some of those bags of leaves and pine cones they sold to make houses smell good. The latter might be better, so she didn't burn down the house.

He held out the white bag. "Dinner is served."

"Wonderful. Come on in." She set the bag on the kitchen counter. "Thanks so much for picking up supper. And I made cookies for dessert. Chocolate chip."

"So I smell. *Everything* smells amazing." He inhaled through his nose to prove his appreciation.

136

She beamed. "I love the smells of Christmas. Do you want iced tea or hot?"

"Just water's fine."

As she took his coat and hung it on a hook near the front door, a black-and-white cat sauntered into the room. Rafe curbed a smile. He had this cat to thank for meeting Britt in the first place. She picked up the cat, who purred loud enough for Rafe to hear it from where he stood. She stroked the cat's large head. "This is Melvin."

"I remember Melvin."

She laughed. "Oh, that's right. You've met! How could I forget?"

Melvin stretched out a paw and gave a playful swat in Rafe's direction.

Britt pulled him back. "You're not allergic, are you?"

"Not that I know of. Never had a cat."

"Well, don't judge all cats by Melvin."

"That bad, huh?"

"No!" She drew the animal protectively to her. "That good. He is seriously the best cat you'll ever meet. Well, except when it comes to breaking vases in the middle of the night."

"He's a handsome fellow."

"He is, isn't he? He was my mom's — our mom's — but I kind of claimed him."

He put out a hand to pet the cat, then

withdrew it quickly. "He doesn't bite, does he?"

"Melvin?" Her voice went all baby talk. "Not this widdle pussy cat. You wouldn't bite a flea, would you, Melvin?"

He laughed and stroked the cat, happy for an excuse to be near the cat's owner. She smelled pretty amazing too.

Britt set Melvin on the floor and washed her hands before pouring water and distributing burgers and fries between two plates. She carried them to the round table in the dining nook, and he followed with their water glasses. She said a brief blessing over the food, and they made small talk while they ate.

When they were finished, she rose and offered him cookies from a fancy plate.

He took one and bit off half of it. "Mmm. These are good. You made them?"

"Just this morning. For our weekend guests. But those are in the freezer." She pushed the plate closer to him. "Help yourself. There are plenty."

"You don't know what you're saying. Cookies are my favorite dessert. Especially chocolate chip."

"I'm not worried. Unless I see you sneaking into the freezer."

"I wouldn't do that." He wriggled his

brows and sneaked another cookie from the plate. "So are you ready to get to work?"

"Ready when you are." She lifted a large lidded box from the floor and set it on the bar counter beside him. "We can munch on cookies while we work."

Stuffing the remainder of a second cookie in his mouth, he slid onto a high bar stool, one foot on a rung, the other firmly on the floor. He peeked inside the box she'd opened. "Just tell me what you need and I'll do my best."

CHAPTER 12

Britt covered the cookies loosely with plastic wrap and wiped off the counter. Rafe enjoyed watching her work. Not only because she was gorgeous, but because she had a certain grace and purpose to her movements.

She held up a long string of evergreen garland dusted with fake snow. "I thought we'd hang the garland first. Just on the fireplace inside, but there's tons more out in the shed, and I'd like to put it on the porch rails of all three houses. Almost everything is new, so we'll need to take the tags off first." She opened the box to reveal a mound of green garland with red berries.

"That I can do." Spotting scissors in a pencil holder on the counter, he took them and started cutting off the tags and labels.

When that was done, he carried the box to the hearth, and together they untangled the strands and laid them across the dining table. Britt showed him her plan for hanging the garland across the mantel. Swagging, she called it. And while they worked, they talked.

He told her about helping his mom decorate and how it was the first time she'd decorated for Christmas in years. "To be honest, I'm not sure what's gotten into her. She was wearing earrings. And lipstick. It just isn't like her —"

"No! Earrings and lipstick? That's awful," she teased.

"Go ahead and laugh, but you don't know how long it's been since I saw my mom dressed up."

"Maybe she met someone?"

He dropped his end of the garland and stared at her. "Met someone? You mean . . . like a man?"

"You seriously hadn't thought of that?"

"Not in a million years. My mom hasn't gone out on a date since my dad left. Ever." He rubbed his chin. "At least not that I know of."

"Speaking from experience, the kids are the last to know. My dad was practically married before my sisters and I even knew he had a girlfriend."

"Your parents are divorced too?"

"No." She swallowed. "My mom passed

away from cancer."

"I'm sorry." He rubbed at the bridge of his nose, not sure what to say. "So, your dad remarried?"

"No. They ended up breaking up. The woman was a lot younger than him. She'd been one of Mom's hospice nurses."

"Oh, ouch." He grimaced.

"Yeah. Tell me about it. It was . . . I guess, just Daddy's way of working through his grief. He's doing much better now. He moved to Florida and he seems to like it there. I miss him though."

"I bet. Do you ever visit?"

She shook her head. "We haven't yet. It's hard to leave the Airbnb. We book so far in advance usually, and we need the income. Plus, we'd all like to go together when we do. But Daddy came back for Phee's wedding last May, and I'm sure he'll come back for Jo and Luke's."

"When is that?"

"They haven't set a date yet. In the spring though. At least Jo hopes. But Phee's baby has kind of put us on hold with a lot of things." She sighed. "I'm sure God has it all figured out, but He hasn't let us in on things yet."

He gave a knowing nod. "Yeah, God's like that sometimes."

She untacked the strand of garland she'd been working on and studied him as if trying to decide if it was just a flippant comment.

He didn't want her to wonder, sensing it might be a deal-breaker for her. "I speak from experience. But I try to keep the faith anyway."

"Faith? So, you and God are tight?"

He crossed his middle finger over his pointer. "Like this."

She smiled. "Me too. I was hoping that was important to you."

"I'm glad it's important to you too."

"So tell me about that. Your faith."

He scratched his head. He couldn't remember anyone ever asking him that question. Not so point-blank anyway. "You mean *how* I became a Christian?"

She nodded, her expression making it clear that a lot was riding on his reply.

He thought how to answer and bit back a grin. "Sorry but, um . . . I can't answer that question without leaving out a pretty important part."

She tilted her head at him. "I don't understand."

"Because the story has to start with a quote from a certain person that I am not allowed to quote."

She laughed. "You're kidding, right?"

He shook his head, struggling not to smile. "I'm dead serious."

"Okay, then I lift the ban. Just for this one question. So, what's the quote?"

"Hang on." He held up a hand. "I have to set it up. So, I wrote this term paper in college. On you-know-who."

She smiled and set a package of tinsel aside, waiting.

"I liked Tom Sawyer and Huckleberry Finn in high school — mostly because I had a really good American lit teacher. That's where I first got interested in Twain, so I figured it would make an easy paper to write. But the research — such as it was — mostly led me to his quotes. So being the lazy bum that I am, I did my paper on that. His quotes. And kind of accidentally memorized a bunch of them in the process."

She shook her head slowly. "Only you could *accidentally* memorize four hundred quotes."

"Well, it's not quite that many. A couple dozen though." He loved the implication of her comment: that she knew him well enough to say *only you* . . . even though she clearly didn't. "But to answer your question, the one that really made me think goes like this . . ." He straightened and struck an

144

orator's pose. "The two most important days in your life are the day you are born and the day you find out why."

Her eyebrows rose. "Ooh, that's a good one. I thought you were going to say 'and the day you die.' "

"I know, and that's what got me thinking. What good is it if you die without ever knowing why you were born? So I started trying to answer that question for myself. Why *was* I born? I somehow knew, even as a kid, that God put me here on this earth for a reason. But back then, I couldn't have told you what that reason was if my life depended on it."

"No. I don't suppose I could have either." Her voice went low, and he sensed she was thinking about how she would answer the question. "So . . . what did you come up with?"

"I figured it had to be about helping other people."

She nodded her head. "Yes, having a servant's heart."

"Yeah, but I didn't know to put it that way. I wasn't brought up on the Bible. We were strictly C&E Christians — Christmas and Easter. And after Robby was born — and Dad left — we never went again."

"Oh. I'm so sorry."

"Thanks. But I must have learned something during those Christmas and Easter Sundays because I somehow knew that the answer to Twain's question — no, *my* question — had something to do with Jesus."

"Oh, Rafe. That's really neat. That tells you something about how important even those few times in church are for C&E people."

"True. Anyway, the rest is a long, boring story, but bottom line, by the time I was twenty, I figured out why I was born. And that it didn't just have something to do with Jesus . . . it had *everything* to do with Him. That — and some other stuff — led me first to police work, and more importantly, to becoming an EMT. I don't know if I'd exactly say it's a calling or ministry or whatever. It's just a job." He shrugged, wondering if it even made sense now. "But I feel like I'm doing some good. And helping others."

"You are! Believe me, I know that firsthand. And you're gifted at it, Rafe. Even the voice God gave you is part of your gift."

"Who knew a sexy voice could be a ministry."

"Would you stop?" She reached over and punched his bicep, giggling. "I never *said* sexy!"

"Oh yes you did. I heard it with my own two ears." He tugged at his earlobes. "You said — no, you *admitted* — my voice is a *little* sexy."

Her cheeks pinked. "Oops. I did say that, didn't I?"

"Admitted."

"Fine."

He gave her a smug look, but turned serious, wanting to hear how she would answer the question. "So, your turn. What's the reason you were born?"

She made a face. "That's a hard one. And I'm not sure I even know yet. I mean, I know the Westminster Confession and all that — the chief end of man is to glorify God and enjoy Him forever. Blah blah blah . . ." She frowned. "I guess I don't even do that all that well."

"Why would you say that?"

"I spend too much time thinking about Britt." She pointed to herself.

"Don't we all?" He shrugged, then curbed a grin.

"What's funny?"

"I was just thinking . . . Technically, I just admitted that I spent too much time thinking about *Britt.*" He pointed at her.

"Well, now, that probably wouldn't be a sin for you like it is for me."

"Good point. Seriously though, you really don't know? What you want to be when you grow up?"

"Not really. I dropped out of college after Mom got sick and just never went back. Never even considered it. Not that I could have afforded it after we pooled our money to buy this property."

"You didn't want to buy it?" He let go of a section of garland and Melvin pounced on it. "Hey!"

Britt laughed. "I can put him in the other room if I need to."

"No, he's okay." He toyed with Melvin for a minute, dragging the garland just out of his reach, and laughing at his antics. Like a kitten he'd seen in a pet store once. "So you were saying . . . You didn't want to buy the property?"

"Oh, I wanted to buy it. In fact, Phee was the holdout. Jo and I had to convince her. I just never considered any alternatives. Even though I like what I'm doing — mostly — it wasn't really my decision. I just kind of went along with what my sisters were doing."

"Nothing wrong with that. As long as you're happy."

"I guess not."

The way she said it made him wonder if she believed that. Or maybe she *wasn't*

148

happy. It struck him that he'd only known her in times of tension — when she'd called the police about what she thought was an intruder and when she'd called the ambulance for her sister. He hoped she wasn't one of those women who thrived on having turmoil in their lives. He got enough of that with his job, thank you very much.

CHAPTER 13

Britt studied Rafe as he climbed the ladder in front of the fireplace, a string of flashing twinkle lights coiled around one arm. She stood poised to look away lest he catch her staring. His confidence and strength reminded her of Quinn. She and Joanna had often jealously lamented Phee's catch, even though now they relished having their strong brother-in-law at their beck and call.

And now, of course, Jo had Luke. And — Britt sighed — she had no one. She knew herself well enough to realize she was in danger of falling for this man in front of her simply because he was . . . a man. Was she really that desperate?

And Rafe was all the more "dangerous" because he also happened to be a handsome and interesting man. With a swoon-worthy voice. And to make matters worse, Melvin had taken quite a liking to him. Of course, Melvin wasn't all that discerning.

The snarky thought made her stifle a grin and wish for an opportunity to try the line out on Rafe. It had been an evening full of laughter. Something she hadn't gotten enough of in recent months. But she and Rafe had joked and laughed together all evening, almost as if they'd been childhood friends.

She'd been relieved to hear him speak so unflinchingly about his faith. But while faith was an essential item on her checklist, just because a man shared her faith did not mean he was the one God intended for her. There was a lot more to it. She'd learned that from her sisters. There were a lot of pretenders out there . . . men who maybe even believed that they *were* Christians but didn't know the first thing about what it meant to have a relationship with God through Christ. Or what it meant to be a godly man.

It wasn't that Britt doubted Rafe's belief. Not that she'd needed convincing before, but if she had, he'd persuaded her as they talked. He wasn't just throwing spiritual words around. He spoke as if he knew the God he claimed to follow intimately. He was the real deal. But still, that didn't mean he was *the* one.

Guard your heart.

She wasn't sure if the words were that quiet voice of God's Spirit that she was just learning to recognize or if she was remembering something Mom or Daddy had told her. Either way, she took the gentle warning to heart. And promised herself she'd take things slow. Give herself time.

A promise Rafe breached five minutes later after he climbed down from the ladder and surveyed the room. "It's looking really pretty in here."

"I couldn't have done it without you."

"Sure you could have. It might have taken a week and a half, but you're the one who had all the good ideas. About where to put stuff. I never would have thought of half of this." He panned the room with his gaze.

"Pinterest."

"What?"

"You know what Pinterest is, don't you?"

"Sure. Oh . . . you mean that's where you got the ideas where to put stuff?"

"Mostly. My sisters and I talked about some of it. I can't wait till they see how it turned out."

"You did good." He playfully punched her arm like a big brother might.

She found it endearing anyway. "Thanks for helping. If you need to go, I can finish the two cabins tomorrow."

"I'm not in any hurry to get out of here. My shift doesn't start till eleven." He met her gaze. "Oh . . . unless that was your hint for me to leave."

"No. If you don't mind staying a while, let's keep going."

He eyed the table full of boxes. "Just tell me what to bring."

She reorganized some of the boxes and stacked three of them in his arms before gathering up the bags that held ribbon and pine cones. "Follow me."

She shivered as they walked over to the cabin, Melvin trotting just ahead of them. "It's starting to feel like Christmas."

"Yeah. Not crazy about that part."

"Me neither. Except I do like when it snows. As long as it doesn't cancel our bookings," she added quickly.

"Snow's okay, but it makes my job a beast."

"Oh, I never thought about that. I bet it does. Speaking of your job . . ." She turned away to slide the key in the front door of her cabin, feeling strange to be letting a man inside. "You promised to finish telling me about why you switched from police work."

"I never promised." His tone said he was being playful.

She copied it. "Basically, you did."

"No, I clearly remember telling you I'd save that for our first date."

"And this doesn't count as a first date?"

"I hardly think so."

She pouted.

Which made him laugh. "Tell you what. I'll start the story and we'll see how far we get. But first you need to tell me what we're doing in here." He touched the placard beside the doorbell. "Near Cottage? What does that mean?"

She rolled her eyes. "It means we didn't put very much thought into naming the houses. When we were working on the renovations, for convenience, this was Near Cottage because it was closest to the cottage where we were all living. Far Cottage" — she smirked — "well, you can probably figure that one out."

She opened the door, and Melvin slinked between them and scurried inside. Britt reached around the wall to turn up the lights, which had been set to dim, and motioned for him to go in.

He stepped inside and looked around. "Well, this is cool. I think I like this house even better than the bigger one." The cabin was simpler and had cleaner lines than the larger cottage. He liked the contrast of the rough wood floors and woodwork and white walls. The cottage was simply decorated, but he could see Britt's personality in the art on the walls and the muted colors in the pillows and blanket throws strewn about. "Smells good in here too." He took an appreciative sniff.

"Christmas candles. And this cabin is mine." She felt proud to say it.

"So each sister has a house? What'd you do, draw straws to decide who got the biggest one?"

She shrugged. "It just kind of evolved this way. We all lived in the cottage together when we first bought the place. Then by the time this cabin had been remodeled, Phee was getting married, so Jo took the cottage and I moved over here. We each have stuff at all three places — well, except Phee. She's pretty much moved everything to Quinn's house by now."

"But they're coming back to live here, right? In the new house?" He motioned in the direction of the construction site.

"Yes. And I can't wait."

"So you have an extra cabin now? Far Cottage?"

"Well, it's the one we rent first if we only have one guest. Unless they request the main cottage, since it will sleep four or five. But Far Cottage is going to be the bride's dressing room if Jo gets the wedding venue she wants going. When the weather is nicer, I'll have to show you the clearing where Phee got married. And Jo will too."

"It's here on the property?"

She pointed toward the clearing. "Up there."

"So is that where *you'll* get married?"

She ignored the grin that came with his question. "Wouldn't be surprised. If I *get* married."

"Of course, you'll get married."

"How would you know?"

"Nobody as pretty as you escapes marriage."

She looked askance at him, ignoring the compliment. "Escapes?"

"That probably wasn't the best word choice."

"Ya think?" She laughed, not offended, but wondering why *escape* was the word that came out of his mouth. She suspected it had something to do with his parents' divorce. And she had to admit it concerned her how that might have affected his view of marriage. "I wouldn't mind getting married, but I'm not putting my life on hold till that happens or anything. Just so you know."
Liar, liar, pants on fire.

"I never said you were."

"I never said you said I was. Just putting it out there." She lifted the top box off the pile he'd brought in. She took off the lid and set it on a narrow bench near the kitchen table. Melvin immediately jumped up and sniffed the box lid before curling up inside it.

"Well, make yourself at home, buddy." Rafe scratched Melvin under the chin.

Britt's heart warmed at the simple action. She was a little jealous of her cat. The thought made her blush and she busied herself with the other boxes, taking off each lid to reveal the contents. "I thought we could just do some of these strings of snowflakes in here. I already have quite a few candles around, and we can add some greenery around them . . . Maybe with some ribbon or —"

"You're not afraid of starting a fire?"

"You sound like my dad. Don't worry, I'm careful."

"I've just seen too many candle incidents in my line of work."

"Is that what they call them? Candle incidents?"

"That's what I call them. Sounds better than fatal conflagrations."

"Yikes. I'll be careful. I promise." She flashed a smile. "Now take one end of this garland and start talking."

"About?"

"You didn't really think I'd forget, did you?"

He looked sheepish. "I was hoping."

For the first time, it occurred to her that he might have a legitimate reason for not wanting to tell her about his job change. People had the right to choose what to tell about their lives. "If you don't want to tell me, you don't have to. I didn't mean to . . . pressure you."

"It's okay. It's not that big of a deal. Not even all that interesting even. I hope I didn't make it sound like it was going to be some great, edge-of-your-seat story."

She shook her head. "You didn't. And I'm not expecting the greatest story ever told."

He wiped his brow. "Whew. That's a relief because *that* story has already been told."

"Obviously, I would like to know your story, but it's really none of my business . . ."

"It's just . . . I thought I might want to be a doctor. When I was a kid, I mean. But ironically — since Robby was kind of the reason I went that direction — with all of his issues, med school was out of the question, so when a chance opened up for me to join the police force at Langhorne, I figured it was, you know, still a way to help people."

"I know you helped *me* that night . . . when Melvin made me call 911."

"Blaming Melvin, huh?"

"Of course."

"Figures." He shook his head as if she were hopeless, but then he frowned. "As much as I want to help people, I've just never been comfortable with people acting like it's some heroic thing. It's not. It's just my job. And — forgive me — but Mark Twain said that it's better to deserve honors and not have them than to have them and not deserve them."

He seemed so sincere that she let that one pass with only a smile.

He went back to his story. "Anyway, what I was saying . . . I don't know that there's such a big story about how I switched. I just . . ." He raked his fingers through his thick hair, leaving it pleasantly rumpled. "There were too many times when I couldn't do anything as a policeman . . . except wait for the ambulance. So when Langhorne instituted a policy that new law enforcement officers also had to be trained as EMTs, I asked the captain if I could take the training. One thing led to another, and it kind of made me remember that dream I had as a kid to do something in the field of medicine. Not that what I'm doing is anything close to being a doctor, but by the time I completed the training, I knew it was what I wanted to do. And I guess the rest is history. It wasn't a promotion. In fact, some might call it a demotion as far as the pecking order goes."

"But you're happier as an EMT?"

"I think so. It kind of fills the gaps I felt doing police work. For a while I thought I might consider med school again. But I'm honestly not sure I even want that anymore. Even if I could afford it. I get a lot of satisfaction from this job. And it lets me have some weekends to spend with Robby."

"So tell me about Robby." She said the words with a bit of fear and trembling, not sure she'd like what she might hear.

Rafe smiled, but Britt thought she sensed reserve and a deep sadness behind that smile. "Robby? That's a pretty long story. Are you sure you want to go into all that tonight?"

CHAPTER 14

"Robby, huh? Man, where do I start?" Rafe closed his eyes, scrambling for a way to change the subject. Why did he do that? He'd faulted Stefani for never asking him about his life, but realizing the way he "clutched" now when Britt asked about his brother, he wondered if he'd been more to blame than Stefani all along.

But even before he opened his mouth and forced himself to answer Britt's question, he knew why he was so reluctant. Because talking about Robby would mean reciting the story — no, the *lie* — he'd rehearsed too many times, told too many people. Or worse, it would mean admitting the truth of his own guilt in why Robby was the way he was. "Robby was born at home. He came early and fast and . . . he was deprived of oxygen during my mom's delivery. That's why he's like he is. Severe brain damage."

"Oh, how awful. I'm so sorry, Rafe."

Though she expressed shock at his revelation, Britt's pity wasn't cloying the way some well-meaning people's was.

He felt brave in the face of it. "I was ten when it happened.

And . . . I was there with Mom when he was born." It was the closest he'd ever come to telling the truth. The *whole* truth.

"Oh, Rafe . . ."

He watched her face closely. Behind the initial shock, it was clear that she was genuinely sorry and that her compassion was unfeigned.

"I know. It was pretty rough for a kid that age."

"I can't even imagine. So who delivered the baby?" A light came to her eyes. "Is that what inspired you to become an EMT?"

He shook his head. "Maybe. In a roundabout way. And . . . nobody delivered him. Mom was there alone. Well . . . with me. She just . . . had him. Finally."

"You must have been terrified!"

"Beyond." The memories threatened to drown him. "To be honest . . . it's kind of hard to talk about."

She gave a little gasp. "I'm sorry. I didn't mean to —"

"No. It's okay." He held up a hand. "It just . . . Every time I tell the story — or

162

think of the story — it makes me wish I could rewrite it." That much was true. *Rewrite it. Get a do-over.*

"I'm sure. Oh, if only we *could* rewrite history."

"You asked if that was what inspired me to become an EMT? If anything, I'd say that's what made me consider becoming a doctor. Because then . . . I could have saved Robby." He swallowed hard, struggling with his emotions.

Her mouth tipped in a soft smile. "Except you would have had to start med school when you were two."

"Well, there is that, yes." He gave a humorless laugh. "I guess I never thought of it that way."

"It's only natural that you'd look back and wish things could have been different, but Rafe, if you were ten . . . I mean, what ten-year-old even understands what childbirth looks like, let alone would know how to deliver a baby in distress."

"Well, believe me, I knew what childbirth looked like after that day." He winced at the image that came. His mother's agony.

"Oh, Rafe." She laid down the string of snowflakes she'd been untangling and came toward him, arms out as if she might hug him.

163

He would have welcomed it, actually, and yet he didn't want his first embrace with this woman to be one of pity. For the sake of her feelings he resisted taking a step back, but he was grateful when she simply gripped his forearm briefly, then took his strand of snowflakes from him.

Silence fell between them — the first since he'd stepped through the doors of the cottage next door a few hours earlier. Yet it wasn't an awkward silence. At least not for him. He picked up another snowflake garland out of the box and untied a knot between two of the glittery flakes.

"I'm so sorry," she said quietly. "I didn't mean to put a damper on the night."

"You didn't." And he found it was true. Her response to his story was one of surprise and dismay, but there was no judgment in either emotion. And it tempted him to tell her all of it. He sensed she wouldn't judge him too harshly for everything that had happened. She'd already intimated as much.

But was he willing to risk that he hadn't misunderstood? Certainly, he wanted more transparency than Stefani had been willing to give him, but complete transparency wasn't worth losing Britt Chandler over. Maybe no romance ever had that kind of openness. Or maybe no relationship survived it.

"Here."

He started, realizing she'd been speaking to him.

"Trade me." Britt handed him a strand of detangled snowflakes and took the one he'd only pretended to work on.

"Sorry. Got a little . . . sidetracked there."

"I understand if you don't want to talk about it, Rafe, but . . . I'd like to know the whole story. About the day Robby was born."

No. He liked this girl too much. "There's not that much to tell. It was a breach delivery, and by the time he made it through the birth canal, Ma was exhausted and hysterical, and Robby had been without oxygen for too long."

"Oh, Rafe, that must have been awful. Did you ride in the ambulance with them?"

He shook his head, remembering — against his will — things he hadn't thought of in years. Things he'd purposefully pushed to the far corners of his mind. "Mrs. Schofield, our next door neighbor, came over and stayed with me. I assume the ambulance attendants — Langhorne didn't really have trained EMTs yet back then — went and got her. Or maybe she heard Ma screaming."

Britt looked like she might cry.

He should have shut up then, but something in her expression compelled him to continue. "I thought the baby was dead. He never cried. He just lay there, still and blue. Ma wasn't in much better shape, but I could tell she was alive at least. They wrapped the baby — *Robby* — up in blankets. The blankets were blue. Pale blue. I remember, because the blood . . ." He shuddered involuntarily. "This is getting too gory. Sorry. And you pretty much know the rest."

Except she didn't. Nobody did.

Britt desperately wanted to know more. She had so many questions. How did a ten-year-old boy process something like that? Watching his mother give birth would have been traumatic enough if everything had gone well and there was a healthy baby at the end. But to see his mom suffer that way, to believe that his baby brother had died. She couldn't even imagine the horror of it. And she didn't blame him for not wanting to talk about it.

It would be cruel to try to drag it out of him. Wanting to give him a moment to compose himself, she went to move the ladder in front of the fireplace. "I'm so sorry you had to go through that, Rafe. And I'm sorry about Robby too. I . . . I hope I get to meet him someday."

It seemed like the right thing to say, even though she had qualms about meeting Rafe's brother.

But Rafe's countenance brightened. "I'd like that. Robby will love you too —" He stopped, and his face flushed as if he'd just realized the implications.

Britt felt her own cheeks heat. But it was with pleasant warmth, not embarrassment. "I just wish circumstances were different."

"What do you mean?"

"Just that . . . I don't know when we'll ever find time to see each other, let alone meet each other's families." She knew she was speaking as if their friendship would certainly go beyond this night. She'd never been that bold with a man before. Maybe that was why she'd seldom had more than two or three dates before the guy lost interest. Not that she'd ever met anyone she wanted to go on seeing. Until Rafe.

He helped her set up the ladder, then surprised her by taking both of her hands in his. "I don't know when we'll find the time either, but please tell me you'll try. I like you, Britt Chandler. A lot."

She smiled up at him. "I like you too, Rafe

167

Stuart. But between your work hours and my commitment to my sister, I can't see how we'll ever —"

He shushed her with a gentle finger to her lips. "We'll just have to get creative, that's all."

"Creative?"

"Like . . . Do you think your sister would mind if I came with you next time you're on duty?" He shrugged. "I don't know. Maybe that would feel awkward . . . for her. I mean, do you have to be in her bedroom with her the whole time you're there?"

"I don't know that I *have* to, but it's not just about making sure someone is there if she should go into labor or start bleeding again. It's also about keeping her company — so she doesn't go stark-raving mad."

He laughed, then sobered when he saw that she wasn't exactly kidding. "I don't want to make you feel uncomfortable or like you're shirking your duties or anything, but we could play board games or cards or something with her — if she's up to it."

Britt wasn't sure why she hadn't thought of that. Except that it would feel a little awkward trying to get to know Rafe under the watchful eye of her sister, who most definitely would be watching their every move, their every expression. And who would have a strong opinion about whether or not Rafe was good enough for her baby sister. "Maybe we could do that. Especially if we found a night when Joanna and Luke could come too."

His shoulders fell. "You're going to make me meet the whole family?"

"Oh, don't worry. My dad won't be there. Or Quinn either because whenever he's there, Jo and I don't need to be."

"I already know Quinn."

"Oh, that's right. I forgot."

"Not that well. But we've met." He blew out an exaggerated sigh. "I guess he didn't seem like the kind of guy who would bite my head off or anything."

"As long as you treat his sister-in-law well."

"Hey, I came and rescued you from that big, bad imaginary burglar, didn't I? That ought to get me a few brownie points with the family."

"Very funny." She threw him a sardonic smile, but excitement rose inside her along with the trepidation about falling in love with Rafe while her sisters looked on.

CHAPTER 15

Britt fluffed the pillows on Phee's sofa for the tenth time in as many minutes. Rafe would be here soon, and she seriously doubted he would even look at the sofa. Still, she wanted everything to be just so. Quinn and Phee's house epitomized "a sad lack of holiday decor" with not a Christmas decoration in sight. It was especially notable now that the cottage and cabins on the property were decked out for the holidays, but Phee hadn't wanted Quinn to have to mess with taking decorations down before they listed the house, plus they were trying to get things packed for the move.

Britt had rather enjoyed helping pack boxes, and it made the time go a bit faster while she was on "Phee-watch."

"Britt?" Phee called from her bedroom. "Could you bring me a new box of tissues from the hall closet?"

"Hang on a sec."

"I'll get them," Jo said.

"Thanks, Jo. No rush. Britt, what time did you say your guy is coming?"

Britt went to the bedroom doorway, a sofa pillow still inhand. "His name is Rafe, Phee. And he's not *my* guy. Please don't say anything like that while he's here. Please."

"I'm not going to say a word. I shall just sit upon my tuffet, eat my curds and whey, and keep my mouth shut."

Jo laughed. "You're going to have a hard time eating curds and whey with your mouth shut."

"No, you can't keep your mouth shut." Britt worried the fringe on the edge of the throw pillow. Her sisters never listened to her. "We're playing games, remember? I told you that already."

"Don't forget Luke is picking me up around seven, so I'll have to bow out then. We're taking Mateo to that live nativity at La Croix church."

"Jo! You promised to be here for at least the first hour."

"I can play for a little while."

"What, forty minutes?" She glanced pointedly at the clock.

"Well, excuse me if I'd like to have *one* date with my fiancé this week. If you can even call it a date since Mateo will be with

171

us. But you're not the only one juggling things trying to get time with your guy, Britt." Jo seemed to realize they were treading on thin ice, indirectly blaming things on Phee, and she quickly changed the subject. "So, what game are we playing anyway?"

"I haven't decided yet. Maybe just Uno or gin rummy. Something simple."

"I know!" Phee clapped her hands, seeming oblivious to the implications of Jo's earlier comment. "How about spin the bottle?"

Britt swung the pillow at her sister's pink-stockinged feet. "Cut it out! You two are making me a nervous wreck!"

"You're making *yourself* a nervous wreck. And you're going to destroy this poor pillow." Jo grabbed it out of Britt's hand.

Britt snapped. "You two just don't understand how important this is to me! And you never listen either. He's not 'my guy.' At least not yet. And he might never be if you two don't stop with the teasing."

Jo and Phee exchanged a look, then Phee's eyes misted.

"Oh, sis! I'm sorry. You're right, we shouldn't tease you. And I promise I'll be on my best behavior. *We* will, right, Jo?" She shot Jo her infamous big-sister glare.

Which made Britt feel even worse. She

slumped. "It's not that. I just . . . I don't want to blow this. I really like this guy."

Phee stretched from the bed and took Britt's hand. "And how would you blow it? Just be your sweet self, and if it's meant to be, the rest will fall into place."

"How can I be my sweet self when I don't even know *who* my sweet self is, Phee?"

Jo gave her a look that wasn't nearly as compassionate as their oldest sister's. "Why are you having an identity crisis all of a sudden? It seems like maybe this guy is wanting you to be someone other than who you are."

"No, he's not. You don't even know him, Jo. Why would you even say that?"

"Because I see my sister freaking out over a guy coming over to play a few games."

"I seem to recall you having a few freakout moments when you and Luke first started dating."

"That was different."

"How was it different? It's exactly the same."

"For starters, I never —"

"Stop it, you two." Phee's strident tone made them both turn.

Britt studied her to be sure she wasn't getting overstressed.

Jo rushed to her bedside. "Are you okay, sis?"

"I'm fine. I'm just sorry I'm making everything so hard for you two. For everybody."

"Phee . . ." Britt felt awful. Couldn't she keep her big mouth shut for five minutes? "It isn't your fault. And even if it had something to do with you, it wouldn't be *your* fault. You couldn't help what happened."

"Still, I know it's not easy for you guys to always have to babysit me. And poor Quinn is working overtime trying to get the house ready before the baby comes and —"

"Stop it, Phee." Jo shot Britt a look that said *she* was the one who needed to stop. "You know we'd do this a thousand times over to get this precious baby here safely."

Hearing the silent-but-oh-so-loud accusation, Britt gritted her teeth. She'd deal with Joanna later. Right now, she just wanted to smooth things over with Phee so there wouldn't be tension when Rafe got here. Fighting tears, she straightened the blankets piled on her sister's feet. "It'll soon be over and you'll be in that gorgeous house chasing after a darling little boy."

Phee gave a little laugh. "Stop. You don't know it's a boy."

174

"Pretty sure it's a boy." Britt smiled, happy the subject had moved to a happier topic.

Jo scoffed. "I don't know why you'd say that when Mom and Dad produced *three* girls. No doubt about it, this is a girl."

"We'll see about that." Phee and Quinn had decided not to find out their baby's gender, but the whole family was hedging bets on whether it would be a niece or nephew in their future. Phee patted Britt's hand. "But thank you for reminding me *why* I'm in this infernal bed. I sometimes forget."

"I don't see how you could possibly forget with that belly," Britt teased.

"Very funny." But Phee smiled and patted the mound under the covers.

"It'll all be worth it," Britt said, turning serious again.

"Yes, it will." Jo gave the blankets a pat too and shot Britt a look that said *Let's call a truce for now.*

Britt ignored her. Let her stew for a while. Jo had no call to say that about her freaking out. Things hadn't been smooth as butter when she and Luke first started dating either, and Britt had spent more than a few hours listening to Jo whine. Why couldn't her sister remember that now and give her a break? Have a little compassion?

"So back to the question: what time is Rafe supposed to get —"

The doorbell answered the question for them.

Britt's heart stammered. "Right about now." She grabbed the pillow back from Jo and tossed it on the sofa as she went through the living room to answer the door.

"Just be yourself!" Phee called from her bed.

"Your *nice* self!" Jo chimed.

Rafe took a deep breath and waited for someone to answer the door. In his job, he'd lifted injured children out of crumpled cars, been shot at, even literally walked through fire, but he wasn't sure any of those took as much courage as he'd had to muster to come and meet Britt's sisters tonight.

It wasn't that he was scared of three sweet women. But he knew he was being judged by a jury that mattered tonight, and he didn't want to blow it. For a man who wore a uniform to work and rarely gave a thought to the clothes he put on, he'd changed shirts and shoes an inordinate number of times before he finally settled on jeans, plaid flannel, and boots, then climbed into his car to head to the Mitchell home just outside of Langhorne.

176

Quinn and Phee Mitchell's house was nice. It looked fairly new, which made him wonder why they were building another new house. He assumed it was because they wanted to be near the Airbnb properties. He wondered if they would put this house on the market once they moved into the new one out on Poplar Brook Road.

He'd never thought about owning property before but wondered if that was something Britt would expect of the man she married. Would she expect her husband to live on their property? It was beautiful with the wooded acreage and a slender finger of the river running behind the cabins. But they were small cabins, and it sounded like the sisters played fruit basket upset every time they had guests.

He thought Britt had said that Luke and Joanna would live there in the larger cottage so they'd be close enough to run the wedding venue she was hoping to start. But frankly, it seemed a little . . . *cultish* to him that all three sisters would marry and live on the same property. If they offered him Kool-Aid, no way was he drinking it. But then, it happened all the time on family farms and ranches. He supposed it wasn't that different when the family business was renting out Airbnbs. He was getting ahead of himself, but if things did work out between him and Britt, he hoped she wouldn't expect him to quit his EMT job and clean toilets or make beds —

Cut it out, man. You don't even know if —

The door flew open and Britt stood there smiling, looking a little nervous herself. "You found it. Come on in."

"I did." He stepped inside to a small foyer that opened into a large living room and kitchen all in one — open concept, he thought the style was called. "Nice place."

"Well, except for the moving boxes." She pointed to a stack of labeled boxes against a far wall. "Hopefully by the time this baby comes, Phee and Quinn will be in the new house. That's why there aren't any Christmas decorations up. They were in the process of getting this one ready to list when everything happened with Phee."

"So they're selling this one?"

"That was the plan, but I don't know when they'll do that now. Obviously, they can't show it while Phee is on bed rest." She turned and looked at him, a spark of curiosity in her blue eyes. "You don't know anyone who's looking for a nice house, do you?"

At least she hadn't asked if he was interested. "No, not really. But I can ask around

at the station if you're trying to find someone."

"It's no big deal. I just thought . . . the
way you said it . . . about if they were selling, that maybe you knew someone."

"Oh. No. Just curious."

"Here, let me take your coat."

He shrugged out of his parka and she
hung it on a hall tree by the door, then
started across the living room toward a
hallway that led to the back of the house.
"Come on back . . . My sisters are in Phee's
room."

He caught up with her and pulled at the
sleeve of her sweater. "Promise me your
sisters won't bite."

She laughed, her eyes twinkling. "Are you
nervous?"

"More like terrified."

"Silly. You've already met both of them.
They didn't bite then, did they?"

"No, but this is different. This is official.
There weren't any stakes before."

"Oh, and now there are?" Her eyes spar-
kled more, but then her expression sobered.
"But to tell you the truth, I'm a little
nervous too."

"Then let's get out of here. Just ditch this
and go get coffee or something?"

She opened her mouth to protest, but he

quickly interrupted. "I'm only kidding. I know you can't leave. I'll survive. I just hope they —"

"They're going to love you. Just be yourself." She cringed. "I sound like my sisters. That's what they just told me."

"Be yourself?" He studied her. "So you're nervous too, huh?"

"A little."

"Why would *you* be nervous? They're *your* sisters."

"I don't know. I just want them to like you and —"

"Oh, and you don't think they will?" He threw her a smirk.

"It's not that. They're just . . . I'm the baby sister and sometimes they take their big-sister roles way too seriously. Especially since Mom died."

"Well, you can't blame them." He wondered if Robby thought he took his big-brother role too seriously — or would, if he could think at that level.

"Oh, just watch me blame them."

He laughed, but he wasn't sure she was teasing. "I could tell that night we answered your 911 call, when Melvin broke the vase, how close you and your sisters are."

"Really, you noticed? All I ever heard was how hot you thought we all were."

"Well, that too." He grinned, but had the decency to look sheepish.

She gave him a sidelong glance. "My sisters are both spoken for, just so we're clear."

"Oh, I only ever had my eye on one of the sisters." He lowered his voice to a whisper as Britt stopped at a door and reached for the handle.

She raised her eyebrows at his comment, then turned the knob and motioned for him to precede her.

CHAPTER 16

Rafe gave a small wave, feeling awkward being in this bedroom where two women sat on the bed. Britt's oldest sister lay atop the patchwork quilt and she appeared to be wearing clothes — not the pajamas he'd expected. But it was hard to tell, swathed as she was in white blankets, her pregnant belly underneath creating a small mound that looked like a beginners' ski slope. She wore her hair in a bun on top of her head, and fuzzy pink socks peeked out from under the covers at the end of the bed.

Sitting beside her sister on the bed, Joanna looked like she was dressed to go out — except for her stockinged feet. She wore pink lipstick and her hair was curled in loose waves the way Britt sometimes wore hers. The sisters both waved back.

Britt tucked her hand in the crook of his elbow. "Guys, you remember Rafe."

"Hi, Rafe!" they said in unison, maybe a

tad overeager.

Phylicia reached from her bed to pull over a nearby chair, and Joanna and Britt both rushed to relieve her of it.

"Would you stop that, Phee!" Joanna chided. "You know you're not supposed to stretch like that."

"I *need* to stretch."

"Fine, but not like that, and you're definitely not supposed to lift anything as heavy as that chair."

Phee looked at Rafe and rolled her eyes. "These two don't let me get away with anything."

He laughed nervously. "I see that."

After an awkward pause, Phee asked, "So, Rafe, how do you feel about Uno? The card game?"

He shrugged. "I haven't played in a long time, but I think I'll catch on pretty quick."

Joanna scooted off the bed and opened a cabinet on the opposite wall that revealed an arsenal of board games and playing cards. "You need to know," she called over her shoulder, "that the three of us have been practicing ever since Phee had to go on bed rest. It can get pretty cutthroat."

He drew himself to his full six feet. "I'll have one of you on my team, won't I?"

That garnered laughter.

Joanna went into the hallway, and the sound of dog toenails on the wood floors preceded her reentry into the room. A brindle-coated dog bounded in and made a beeline for Rafe.

"Mabel, get down!" Phee yelled. "Jo, why'd you let that dog in? Sorry, Rafe."

He held up a hand. "It's okay. Hey, girl." He bent to scratch behind the dog's ears, which were attached to a massive head. He looked up at Britt. "Is it safe to assume Mabel is a girl?"

"She is."

"How do she and Melvin get along?" Mabel pressed her nose into Rafe's open hand, nuzzling.

"They've only met once," Phee said.

"And once was enough. Melvin has mostly lived with me since Mom died," Britt explained. "And Mabel was Quinn's dog."

"That dog played a very important role when Quinn and I were dating."

The sisters giggled at some shared secret.

"Hmmm. Maybe I need to get a dog." Rafe winked at Britt. "Or Melvin could do the job."

The sisters laughed harder, as if that was the funniest thing ever. Rafe looked from one to the other.

"Sorry," Phee said, between giggles. "You

184

obviously haven't gotten to know Melvin very well yet."

"Or any cat," Jo deadpanned.

"Cats chaperone *if* and when they feel like chaperoning," Britt said.

Phee nodded. "And Melvin clearly never feels like chaperoning."

That sent the sisters into another fit of giggles.

He didn't tell them he'd never owned a cat in his life. Or any pet for that matter. And he wasn't exactly getting the joke. But it was fun to hear them laugh. Even while their laughter made him realize what he'd missed not having a brother — a normal brother — to share inside jokes with.

No, that wasn't fair. He and Robby had exchanged their share of jokes. Even if Robby usually laughed before the punch-line.

"Okay, guys, settle down or Rafe is going to think we're crazy." Britt giggled again and scooted another chair close to Phee's bed.

Rafe took the chair closest to the foot of the bed, Britt beside him, and Jo climbed onto the bed.

The sisters worked together clearing Phee's things off the rolling bedside table, which made a surprisingly good card table.

They quickly got a game of Uno underway, and Rafe's nerves vanished as the four of them laughed together.

They were in the middle of the third round — a rubber match that he cared a great deal about winning — when the doorbell rang. Jo jumped up and slipped on her shoes. "That'll be Luke."

"Come back though," Britt yelled. "You have to finish this round."

"I will."

A few seconds later, Rafe was introduced to Joanna's fiancé, Lukas Blaine, and twelve-year-old Mateo, the boy Luke was guardian to. Mateo went to play with the dog, and Luke stood behind the chair where Jo had settled, making faces as she played her cards while they finished out the round. But Rafe could tell Joanna had lost the spirit of the game and just wanted to get going wherever she and Luke and Mateo were headed.

He and Britt won the round handily, but the conquest felt unearned. Luke and Jo slipped out a few minutes after the game ended, and Phee's husband came home shortly after that.

Britt dished up brownies and ice cream for the four of them. Rafe had met Quinn through a mutual friend. He didn't know him well, except that Quinn was the one who ratted him out for calling the Chandler sisters "hot chicks." He liked the guy though. Quinn seemed to go out of his way to make him feel welcome.

Over a bite of brownie, Quinn said, "You don't happen to know anyone looking for some hourly work, do you? We can't offer full-time hours or benefits or anything, but we're looking for some help with the finish work on the house. Mostly painting and sanding, but maybe some landscaping too, once the weather gets nicer."

"I don't know of anyone right now, but I'll let the guys on the force know. Since it's shift work, they sometimes try to pick up extra hours. Especially around Christmas. You'd have work right away?"

"Tonight, if they're interested."

Phee swatted at her husband and threw Rafe an apologetic look. "He doesn't really mean tonight."

"No, but tomorrow would be great. My builder is shorthanded, and I want this house ready before the baby comes." Quinn fished his wallet from his back pocket and handed Rafe a business card that read Langhorne Construction and listed Quinn as contracting supervisor.

Langhorne Construction was Britt's dad's company. Rafe swallowed. This family gave

187

new meaning to the word *tight-knit.* He wasn't sure how he felt about that, but he put the card in his shirt pocket. "My next shift isn't until tomorrow night, but I'll let the guys know."

"I appreciate it," Quinn said.

When they'd finished their brownies, Britt gathered up the empty bowls and carried them into the kitchen. When she returned, Phee made a shooing motion with her hands. "You two don't have to stay. I'm sure you have better things to do. Besides, I haven't seen my husband all day."

As much as he'd enjoyed the evening, Rafe appreciated an excuse to have Britt all to himself. Unless that was *his* cue to go home.

In the hallway with Britt, he whispered, "Was that a hint for me to leave?"

"No, silly. Phee is just trying to give us some time alone."

"I like your sisters."

"Yeah, they're okay, I guess." Her grin told him she was joking.

She led the way to the living room and curled up in the corner of the sectional sofa. He plopped down across from her on the comfy ottoman.

"So? That wasn't so bad, was it?" she asked, hugging an overstuffed throw pillow.

"Not bad at all. I actually really enjoyed it."

"And we won at Uno too."

He shook his head. "Technically."

"What do you mean?"

"Jo wasn't even trying that last round. I want a rematch."

She smiled. "That could probably be arranged."

"I'd like that. But . . . what I'd really like is a *real* date with you. Any chance of that happening before next year?"

She laughed as if he were exaggerating.

But he frowned. "I'm serious, Britt. When we looked at our calendars last time, tonight was about it for this year."

"Technically, next year isn't *all* that far away."

"More than two weeks. That's an eternity."

She offered him a coy smile. "I'll take that as a compliment."

"As I intended. But you'll probably forget all about me by next year."

She leveled her gaze at him. "Not likely."

"So can you please prove it and carve out a day on your calendar for me?"

"Do you have to work the nineteenth?"

"What day of the week is that?"

"Tuesday. A week from yesterday. It's kind of late, but it's the only day I have to do some Christmas shopping. We have guests coming in that night — and every day until the holidays — but I can make sure I have everything ready for them to check in that night."

"That's still a long ways away." He feigned a pout. "But I'll take what I can get. What time should I pick you up?"

"I . . . I'd rather meet you downtown if that's okay."

"Oh, sorry. I forgot. You told me that before. May I ask why?" He didn't want to push her, but she had said she'd explain it to him later.

"It's something I learned from my sisters. Jo had a bad experience with a guy . . . before Luke. Long story, but she could have been saved a lot of grief if she hadn't been at this guy's mercy and could have taken her car home."

"I'm sorry. Guys can be such beasts."

"Well, this one really was. His name was Ben. Jo ended up in a bad car accident with him last summer. On Highway 60 out by Dexter."

"Wow. I'm so sorry. By Dexter, you say? I wouldn't have worked that one. Was he drinking?"

Britt shook her head, her expression sober with remembrance. "No. He was just stupid.

And liked to take risks with other people's lives. Jo was in the hospital for almost a week. And in a cast — her leg — for the rest of the summer."

"I'm sorry," he said again. "I didn't know. So, do you feel like you'd be . . . at my mercy?"

"No. Not now. But I still don't know you, Rafe. Not that well. I'm just —"

He held up a hand. "I understand. You're being cautious. And I shouldn't give you a hard time about it. That's smart. And you're right: You don't know me. Yet."

"But I want to."

He cocked his head and gave her a wry smile. "Are you *sure*?"

"I'm very sure."

He would have kissed her right then if they'd had at least one real date under their belts. Maybe it was a good thing they didn't.

CHAPTER 17

Langhorne, small as it was, knew how to dress up for Christmas. Every street light along Main Street bore a wreath and festive lantern, accents to the garlands of tinsel zigzagging across the street between the light posts. As much as Britt hated switching from daylight saving time, tonight she was glad that it was almost dark at four forty-five in the afternoon. The lights made everything look magical. Just like she had a feeling this evening was going to be.

She was glad Rafe suggested they get an early start on their first "official" date. Since she'd insisted on meeting him in town, once they'd finished their last-minute Christmas shopping, they would part ways for the evening.

She spotted his car in front of Coffee's On where they'd agreed to meet. She pulled in beside him and, even through the tinted window, could see his smile. They both climbed out and met on the sidewalk in front of the little bakery and coffee shop. He gave her a hug that she readily returned.

"Everything sure looks Christmasy." His breath hung in a mist in front of him.

"It's gorgeous," she squealed, clapping her mittened hands and beaming up at him. Thanks to his help decorating the cottages last week, she was fully in the Christmas spirit, but if she hadn't been, this would have surely done the trick.

He reached over and tugged on the ball of her fluffy stocking cap. "Do you want to get some hot chocolate before we get down to business?"

"That'd be nice. We might not be able to take it into all the stores, but it'll keep our hands warm while we window shop."

"Let's go then." He held the door to the shop open for her. Country music spilled out into the street, and Britt did a little dance with her head and shoulders. Rafe laughed. Their love of country was another thing they'd discovered they had in common. She inhaled the scents of coffee and cinnamon and something else delicious as Shayla Whitman, co-owner of the shop, greeted them by name and took their orders.

"To go, please," Rafe told her. "This is fuel for a night of Christmas shopping."

Shayla laughed. "Are you sure one will be enough? I could make it a double shot."

Rafe put up a hand. "Better not. We'll come back later if we run low."

"We're open till eight. Every night until Christmas Eve."

"That's great that you're doing that. I'm sure shoppers appreciate it," Britt told her.

"They seem to. How is Phee doing? I heard she had to go on bed rest."

"She's going a little stir-crazy, but the baby is fine, and the holidays will help time fly."

"I'll pray it does. And hey," — Shayla held up her finger — "let me send a loaf of bread home with you. Maybe it'll help to have something for sandwiches on hand." She reached behind her and pulled a large, sliced loaf from a baker's rack.

Britt took it with a smile. "That's so sweet of you. Thank you, Shayla. And tell your family hello." This was what Britt loved most about small towns. Everybody knew everybody. And their business too. The latter could be annoying at times, but when news spread about what had happened to Phee, so many people had brought food, sent gift cards, and offered help, that she and Jo hadn't had to do much cooking at all.

Armed with their drinks, Britt and Rafe headed down the street. For a while, they just sipped their drinks and walked, commenting on the window displays in the shops and sharing remembrances from childhood Christmases.

She noticed that the memories Rafe shared all seemed to have happened before he turned ten. It didn't take a genius to figure out that Robby's entry into the family had been a stressful turning point.

"Six days till Christmas. You seem like the kind of girl who would've had all her shopping done a long time ago."

"I usually do. Everything with Phee has really thrown me off kilter. But I went through my list before I left home, and it's not as bad as I thought. I was able to get a couple of things online and the rest I at least know what I want to get. That's usually the hardest part — just coming up with ideas. So, are you done with your shopping?"

"That depends." He stopped walking and turned to her. "Are *we* exchanging gifts?"

"No! Oh, I didn't mean that. No. In fact, Jo and I were just talking about how awkward it is to start dating someone right before Christmas — or Valentine's or whatever holiday. But those are the worst. Seriously, let's decide right now not to get each other gifts. At least not this year."

"You're sure? You won't be disappointed?"

"No. And I'll be mad if you do get me something because I'm not getting you anything. Okay? Deal?"

He stuck out his hand and she shook it, relieved, then peered up at him. "There is one thing I'd like for Christmas though."

"Now wait a minute . . ." He pulled her to his side in a playful hug. "You just got through saying we were *not* exchanging gifts."

"This isn't a gift. But I guess you could call it an exchange."

"Okay . . . I'm listening."

She peered up at him coyly, loving the feel of his arm around her waist. "You got to meet my family. I'm just wondering when I get to meet yours? Your mom. And Robby . . ." She tried to smooth out the trepidation she heard in her own voice. "And any other relatives you might have hiding in your closet."

"Oh, you don't even want to know about those. The ones I *have* to claim are bad enough."

"What about your dad? Will you see him for Christmas?"

His jaw tensed. "If I do, it'll be the first time I've seen him since I was eighteen."

He paused and the stunned look on his face said he hadn't done the math in a while. "Eight years."

"Oh. I'm sorry. You said your parents were divorced, but I didn't know you never see your dad. Is that . . . your choice or his?" She didn't want to press. And for sure, she didn't want to ruin the night. But this was important.

A group of rowdy high school students approached them on the sidewalk, and Rafe steered Britt under the covered entrance to the flower shop until the kids had passed. Then they walked slowly, admiring the window displays and talking quietly. He was grateful for the respite from her probing questions. But he didn't want to retreat from her either. He'd done that too many times.

"You asked earlier if it was my choice or my dad's?" He opened his mouth to continue, but his phone chirped with a text message. Ma. "Sorry, I really need to check this."

"Convenient," she whispered under her breath. But her expression said she was joking.

"Would it make a difference if I said it was my mom?"

Her grin widened. "It might if it really *was* your mom."

"I promise."

She gave a thumbs up, and he opened the message: "Give me a call when you get a chance. No rush, but I need to talk to you ASAP."

Despite the alarm her message raised, he chuckled. "Leave it to my mom to use 'no rush' and 'ASAP' in the same sentence."

Britt laughed. "Is everything okay?"

"I think she would have said if it was truly urgent. She would have just called if it was *that* important. But my thoughts always go straight to Robby whenever I see her name on my notifications."

"Does your brother have medical issues that . . . worry you?"

"Not really. Robby has some physical issues — muscle atrophy and things like that — which means he doesn't get as much exercise as he probably should. But hey, a lot of healthy people have that problem."

She winced. "Tell me about it."

He appreciated her laid-back attitude about it. He hadn't missed the reluctance in her voice when she mentioned meeting Robby earlier this evening. He didn't blame her. There'd been a time he would have been most nervous about Britt — or any girl he was interested in — meeting Robby. But right now, it was Ma who worried him. He didn't have a clue what this latest message was about, but *something* was up. And whatever it was, she wasn't telling. When he'd stopped by her house after his shift on Sunday, he noticed immediately that she'd bought some new furniture. When he mentioned it, she brushed his comment off as if she bought new furniture every day.

She'd had on a new outfit too — at least one he'd never seen her wear before. And strappy sandals with heels. The last time he could even remember Ma wearing heels was at his grandpa's funeral some . . . what? twenty years ago? He didn't know the first thing about fashion, but the shoes she'd worn didn't look like something from Walmart.

No, something was definitely up with her. And until he knew exactly what was going on, he wasn't keen on introducing Britt to her.

"Anyway, to answer your question, I'm anxious for you to meet Ma and Robby."

"Anxious? Or eager?"

"There's a difference?"

"We actually just discussed this at book club the other night."

"What are you, a bunch of dictionary nerds?"

She laughed, and he was grateful to return to the playful tone of earlier. "There are a couple of those, actually, but it was just a word choice of the author, and someone brought up the difference."

"Which is?"

"Eager is positive. Excited and looking forward to. Anxious comes from *anxiety*. It really means you're worried and concerned. So are you anxious for me to meet your family? Or eager?"

Her tone was teasing, but he was pretty sure *she* wasn't.

He slowed his pace for a minute, pondering her question. "A little of both, I guess."

"That's something probably any guy could say. But I want you to know . . . I'm not scared."

"You're not?"

"Well, maybe a little *anxious*." She quirked a little smile. "But I seem to recall you were terrified to meet my family."

"Oh, yeah. There was that. But you were nervous for your family to meet me. I don't have that problem at all. Ma and Robby will love you. Guaranteed."

She gave him a smug grin. "And I'll love them because you love them."

With those words, Britt Chandler went up about seventy notches in his estimation.

But the look in her eyes said she wasn't going to let him off the hook so easily. "So, what about your dad?" She motioned to the cell phone still in his hand. "You were about to tell me that story when your mom texted."

He pulled his jacket tighter around his midsection. "Didn't you have some shopping you wanted to do?"

Her brow furrowed. "I'm not going to drag things out of you, Rafe. If you don't want to tell me, just say so. I won't push you. But I would like to know. When you're ready."

He blew out a sigh. "Guess there's no time like the present."

"That's not Mark Twain is it? No time like the present?"

He smirked. "Nope, that's Rafe Stuart."

"Okay, Rafe Stuart. I'm here to listen when you're ready."

CHAPTER 18

Britt had mixed emotions about Rafe's sudden willingness to talk about his father. She hated the red flags that were waving. Because she was falling hard for this man.

"I'll tell you what . . ." Rafe turned to her and reached up to tuck an errant strand of hair into the stocking cap perched on her head. "You look cute in that cap, by the way."

"*That's* what you wanted to tell me?"

"No. That was just a comment that needed to be made."

"Well, thank you. That's sweet." She reveled in the compliment, but she wasn't going to let him change the subject again.

"No, what I was going to say is why don't we pick up the things you were shopping for. I know your time is limited, and I don't want you to feel like the night was wasted —"

"Oh, I don't," she protested. "Not at all.

But I do need to get those gifts."

"Let's do that then, and then we can go somewhere and talk."

She pointed to a store down the street. "I can get two of my items there."

"Lead the way." He waved his arm as if brandishing a matador's cape.

Laughing, Britt took the lead, and half an hour later, she'd completely finished her shopping. Rafe found gifts for Ma and Robby to add to what he'd already ordered online for them. "You're either making me a hero or breaking the bank."

"Probably a little of both. But you didn't spend that much. And your mom will love that scarf."

"She'll know I didn't pick it out myself."

"Is that so bad?" She gave an exaggerated wink. "Maybe you can use that as an entry point to introduce us."

"Okay, since you brought it up, let's go find someplace we can sit and talk. I'll tell you everything you want to know. And then you can decide if you still want to hang out with me."

His grin said he was teasing, but she thought there was an undercurrent of worry in his eyes. She couldn't imagine anything he could tell her that would make her feel differently about him. But Jo's experience with Ben had taught her that men weren't always what they seemed to be. Or pretended to be.

"We could just go back to the bakery," Britt said.

"You don't mind?"

"Not at all. They have that cozy place in the back to sit." They crossed the street and walked back to Coffee's On, admiring the Christmas lights as they went.

When they opened the door, Shayla gave a little cheer. "See, I told you you needed that double shot."

Britt held up a hand. "Not for me. Maybe a hot chocolate this time. Small, please."

Rafe gave a nod. "Sounds good. I'll have the same."

"For here or to go?"

"Here," they said in unison.

"Coming right up. You two can sit wherever you like. I'll bring your drinks out when they're ready."

"Thanks, Shayla. And thanks again for Phee's bread."

"Happy to help."

The jukebox still spilled country music into the space, and Britt was glad to see there were only half a dozen other people in the shop. She pointed Rafe to the open corner of the café decorated with clever curtains made from coffee sacks, cozy benches piled high with burlap pillows, and coffee-themed art on the walls. "Let's sit back here. That okay?"

"Sure." He chose a seat in the far corner with his back to the wall, something she'd noticed when they were at Panera.

"Is that a cop thing?"

"Excuse me?"

"Sitting with your back to the wall like that?"

He grinned as if she'd exposed a secret. "I think it's a man thing. But yes, a cop thing too. Have to be able to case the joint, you know. Never turn your back on danger and all that."

"I like it. It makes me feel safe."

"Ah, then we're making progress."

"We are?"

"Sure. We went from 'at my mercy' to you feeling safe."

She laughed. "You remember that, huh?"

He looked offended. "Believe me, a man remembers when the woman he . . . really likes feels like she's at his mercy."

"I'm sorry. I hope you know it really was more about what happened to Jo than any way you've ever made me feel."

"You sure?"

"Positive. Shoot, I might even let you pick

me up next time."

"Ah, so there's going to be a next time?"

"That's up to you."

That furrow appeared between his eyebrows again. "Well, then let's get this conversation out of the way."

Shayla brought their drinks and set them down without comment, as if she knew they were having a serious discussion.

When she was out of earshot, Britt said, "You're sure you want to talk about it?"

"I don't, but I know we need to."

"I don't want to make you feel . . . *forced* to talk about something you'd rather not."

"No. It's okay. It's my story. You should know it." A small smile appeared. "Of course, turnabout is fair play, right?"

"I don't have much of a story."

"Be glad. That's a blessing."

"Maybe. Sometimes I think life would be a lot more exciting if I *had* a story. I don't even have a good Jesus story."

"What? Every Jesus story is a good story."

She laughed. "I know. That didn't sound good, did it? I just mean that we went to church every Sunday, I gave my life to Jesus when I was five, and I've been following Him ever since." She held up a hand. "Not that I'm a saint or anything, but . . . boring."

"*Not* boring. Do you know how many people would envy your story? Shoot, I'd trade you in a heartbeat."

"I know. I shouldn't have said that. I was mostly kidding. So, tell me about your dad."

He chewed the corner of his lip, as if trying to decide where to start. "You know, I don't think the whole thing would bother me as much if my dad had been a jerk his whole life. But he wasn't. The first ten years of my life were the happiest any kid could have asked for. Our house was full of laughter and jokes. Ma would have cookies waiting, fresh out of the oven, almost every day when I came home from school, and then she'd scold Dad for eating the rest of them after I went to bed. He was the kind of dad who played catch with me and took me fishing . . ." He stared off into the past.

"So what happened. What changed? Was it Robby?" He'd hinted at that the night they went to Panera.

Rafe nodded. "I don't know what the breaking point was, but when it became clear that Robby wasn't going to be normal . . ." He chalked quotation marks in the air. "When he didn't walk until he was almost three, and then he walked with this awkward gait — still does — Dad couldn't take it. Ma says he couldn't accept that his son would never be normal. But . . . come on. Aren't you supposed to love your kids unconditionally? I don't want to sound vain, but I think *I* would. I truly do. In fact, I'd consider myself more of a father to Robby than his real father is."

"I'm glad you're there for him." And she was. But she couldn't help but wonder how much *she* would have to be there for Robby if she and Rafe were to marry someday. It wasn't exactly a comforting thought.

Rafe sighed. "I just don't understand why God would give me those ten great years and then pull them out from under me like some kind of cosmic rug. If you want to know the truth, it seems kind of cruel."

"I can see why it would. But Rafe —" She took a sip of hot chocolate, trying to think of how on earth to reply when it *did* seem cruel. And the words came to her in a flash. "Just think of all the things you learned during those ten years . . . how to be a good dad, what a happy family looks like. I think that's the thing that makes me the saddest about broken homes. Too often, those kids grow up to repeat what they saw with their parents. The fighting and anger and resentment. Some of those kids don't even have a clue what they're missing because they've never seen a happy marriage. I hope it doesn't sound . . . trite for me to say that you should be thankful you had those ten years."

"I guess." He shrugged. "I hadn't ever really thought about it that way. But if Dad could go off the rails like that . . . It's hard to believe he was ever really that man I remember . . . laughing and loving and kind."

Britt shook her head, her heart breaking for Rafe's loss, and she whispered a prayer of gratitude for her own loving father. "I don't know the answer to that. I wish I did. But Rafe . . . I don't know, maybe your mom's influence overcame your dad's? But whatever happened, look how you turned out! That's a victory in itself."

He bent his head and studied the lid of his hot chocolate cup for a long minute. "You said something about Ma's influence?"

She nodded, curious.

"That's the worst of it. I mean, not that Ma's a bad person or anything, but after Robby came along, and then Dad left, Ma . . . changed. I understand it had to have been a huge burden for her to take care of Robby's needs — and mine, too — while resenting Dad for leaving her to do that all on her own. But it was more than that. She just became a different person. Still is. She rarely laughs, she always sees the negative in people. To be honest, she's kind of hard to be around. Except . . ." A faint smile touched his lips.

"What?"

"I think I told you that when I went to help her put up her Christmas tree, she was . . . just happier, more like the mom I remember from my childhood than I've seen in years."

She grinned. "Right. She started wearing lipstick."

"Cut it out." But his smile said he was glad she remembered.

"So, was I right?"

"Right?"

"That your mom is seeing someone?"

"Oh. No, I don't think so."

"You didn't ask her?"

"No. I'm not sure she'd tell me if she was. I don't know . . . maybe she would."

Britt swirled the last inch of hot chocolate around her mug. "Or would you rather just not know if she is . . . seeing someone. Believe me, I understand that."

"Maybe. But maybe more than that, I'm just glad to have the old Ma back."

"I'm glad. I hope she's here to stay." *Ma.* She found it endearing that he called his

mother "Ma." It seemed old-fashioned —
and maybe a tiny bit hillbilly. Except that
Rafe always spoke her name with such
respect. "What about your dad? When was
the last time you saw him?"

"He came to my high school graduation. I
didn't talk to him, but I saw him standing
in the back of the gym."

"But why didn't you talk to him?"

He combed his fingers through his thick
hair. "I didn't think he deserved it. He
hadn't bothered to come and see me since I
was fifteen. He *never* went to see Robby. At
least not that Ma and I knew of. He paid
the bills for the group home, and I guess he
thought that got him off from being a dad."

Britt touched his hand briefly across the
table. "That had to hurt."

"Yeah. It hurt. And not to sound all heroic
or anything, but it hurt most for Ma and
Robby. Ma hung in there as long as she
could, but when Robby was nine and almost
as tall as Ma . . ." He smiled softly. "She
said he outweighed her by ten pounds then.
Anyway, she couldn't handle him physically
anymore. She had no choice but to put him
in a group home."

"I'm so sorry, Rafe. I can't even imagine
how hard that must have been."

"Yeah, well, for a while, it seemed like

things might be better. For the first time since Robby was born, I'd come home from college and the house was tidy and there were hot meals on the table. But Robby, even though he has the mind of a three-year-old, seemed to resent being sent away. And he took it out on Ma. She stopped going to see him every day. She'd go on the weekends and holidays, stuff like that . . . But after a while, she just quit going. She'll take food to the home for him — he *loves* pancakes — and sometimes she does his laundry. But most of the time, it's just easier to stay away.

"And honestly, I didn't blame her. He's hard to be with sometimes. He's a little better now, but he throws tantrums if things don't go his way, like if he doesn't get his pancakes. Or if someone, God forbid, puts blueberries in his pancakes. And when he gets like that, there's not much you can do but wait it out."

"That has to be devastating. For your whole family." She pushed her empty mug to one side of the table and scooted her chair closer, leaning across the table. "You know, I've always heard that a huge percentage of marriages end after the death of a child. It seems like Robby's . . . issues were kind of like a death for your parents. And probably for you too. I'm truly sorry, Rafe."

He was silent for a minute and when he looked up, she couldn't quite read the expression in his eyes. "Thanks. Yeah, it was kind of like a death."

She swallowed her fears, deciding to trust him. "I haven't told anyone else this, but in those early days when we were afraid Phee might lose the baby I was terrified it might destroy their marriage too. Phee and Quinn are so deeply in love that I couldn't imagine them ever splitting up over something like that. I mean, shouldn't that be when the strength of a marriage is forged? When something awful happens? That's when you should have each other to cling to."

He nodded. "Exactly. I don't know why my parents couldn't see that. But then, I couldn't know what it was like to lose a child — or, I guess . . . a dream. Because they *didn't* lose Robby. He's still there, still needing their love. And instead, one of them throws money at him, and the other one assuages her guilt by taking pancakes and doing laundry. As if he could possibly even understand how that equates to love in their eyes."

"But it sounds like you're there for him."

"I kind of don't have a choice. Who else does he have?"

"Yes, but I can tell by the way you talk about him and the way your eyes soften when his name comes up that you're not doing it because you don't have a choice."

"Wow." He shook his head. "You make me nervous!"

"Nervous? Why?"

"That you see that . . . in my eyes. I'm not sure I like that you seem to be able to know what I'm thinking. But you're right. I do love my brother. Still, I feel an obligation to him too. And it gets heavy sometimes. Really heavy."

"I can barely imagine, Rafe." She tried not to let her own fears — about how Robby might impact her relationship with Rafe — prevent her from being a listening ear. It wasn't easy.

CHAPTER 19

Britt glanced at her phone. "I really, really ought to get home." It was the second time she'd said those exact words in twenty minutes. She heard the apology in her own voice and tried to temper it. But it was after nine o'clock and the bakery had closed an hour ago. Shayla urged them to stay as long as they wanted while she cleaned and closed up. Britt suspected the sweet girl had purposely taken her time closing the bakery down for the night, sensing what was happening between her and Rafe.

And what was happening was that she was falling head over heels — and she suspected he felt the same. She didn't want to leave, but she *needed* to, if for no other reason than she desperately needed some space apart from this man to sort out her feelings. Because if Rafe asked her to marry him right this minute, she just might say yes. And that meant she was thinking with her

215

emotions, not the rational mind God gave her.

"I'm not kidding, Rafe." She smiled up at him. "I really do need to go."

"Yeah, me too." But he made no move to budge from the cozy corner of the bakery where they'd settled in for the evening. Their hot chocolate was long gone, and Shayla had cleared the table of their mugs. But Britt still felt the warmth of it.

Brad Paisley's "Today" started playing on the jukebox and Britt sighed inwardly. One of her favorite songs. And tonight, the lyrics were so poignant and fitting.

Rafe nodded toward the speaker in the ceiling above their heads. "I like this song."

"Me too."

He grinned. "I could tell by the way you were dancing."

"I was not dancing."

He mimicked her, swaying his head and shoulders in time to the music. She waved him off, and they sat in silence for a while just listening to the words. She might have felt awkward at the implications of the romantic lyrics. But instead she just smiled across the table at him.

"That's true, you know?"

"What's true?"

He pointed to the ceiling again. "Right

now, the whole world feels right."

"It does. But . . ." She grinned and echoed the lyrics. "We're going to have to get by on the memories because I *really* do need to get home." She gathered their crumpled napkins and scooted back her chair.

Looking as reluctant as she felt, Rafe rose. "The day's not over yet and already I miss you."

She laughed. "That's not exactly how the lyrics go, but I kind of like your version."

He helped her with her coat and scarf, taking far more time than he needed. Passing by the counter, they shouted a thank-you to Shayla, who stuck her head out of the kitchen to wish them a good evening.

Rafe held the door open for her and gave her a wink as she stepped out into the cold. But it was the wonderfully possessive hand he placed at the small of her back as they walked to her SUV that made her melt, despite the biting cold. Waiting as she unlocked the door of her SUV, he stepped closer. He held the door open for her, but before she could climb behind the wheel, he captured her hands between his. "Hey. Thank you."

"I didn't do anything. Thank *you.* For the hot chocolate and for coming with me to shop."

"I had a great time tonight." His eyes hinted at what was about to happen.

"I did too. Thank you again."

He leaned closer, but he waited, still enveloping her hands with his. "I'd really, really like to kiss you right now." He reached up a hand and brushed back the same wayward strand of hair he'd tucked under her cap earlier in the evening.

She freed one of her hands and placed it on his cheek.

He took the gesture as permission and cradled her face between his hands, bending to match his lips to hers. But only briefly. Too briefly.

Yet as much as she wished the kiss would deepen, she was grateful that he'd shown mercy. And that they were standing on a public street in the middle of Langhorne.

"It was a really good day." She touched his cheek again. "Sweet dreams."

"Oh, they will be." He ran a gentle finger down the bridge of her nose, smiling. "I'll call you, okay? We'll figure out a next time."

"We'll have to get creative," she said, echoing his comment from the other night.

He took a step away from her door. "I'll call you."

"You'd better, buddy."

"Don't you worry." And with that, he

turned and walked to his own car without a backward glance.

All the way home, Britt kept touching her lips where his had rested so briefly and thanking God for putting this man in her life. Surely they could figure out a way to get over the hurdles that seemed determined to keep them apart. After all, most of them were temporary. Phee's bed rest, Joanna's wedding, Rafe's overtime . . . at least those would end in the spring.

But tonight, with his tender kiss still warming her lips, spring seemed like a lifetime away.

Rafe waited until Britt's Escape disappeared from sight, but when he looked up at his rearview mirror to back out of the parking lot, his own mug was smiling back at him like a lovesick fool. And that's exactly what he was.

How could he ever have been content with a girl like Stefani, when someone like Britt Chandler — kind, selfless, funny, talented, and gorgeous, to boot — had been in this world, in this very town, all along. He'd even known her — and been attracted to her. But back then, he hadn't really been looking for the woman of his dreams. He hadn't yet been twenty-five, and he'd been heady with his new job.

But he'd noticed her. He should have made a note to himself to look her up in a year or two, but he hadn't been thinking of anything back then but having fun in the newfound freedom of adulthood. "Thank You, God, for bringing her back into my life." Whispering those words into the quiet of his car made him smile even bigger. He flipped the mirror up to night mode so he wouldn't have to look at that goofy grin.

He checked his cell phone and saw Ma's text message still waiting on his phone. As much as he just wanted to go home and let this evening settle over him, he couldn't really ignore her call.

He'd drive by her house and if the lights were on, he'd take that as a sign that he needed to stop and see what she wanted. He prayed all was dark on her street.

But no, the Christmas tree blazed in the front window and there were still lights on in the kitchen and the sitting room behind it where she watched TV in the evenings. He pulled slowly into the driveway and parked. Walking to the front door, he texted her so the doorbell wouldn't scare her.

A few seconds later, the porch light came on and Ma opened the door. "Rafe? What are you doing here?"

He gave her a quick hug and ducked into the darkened foyer. "You said you had something you wanted to talk about."

"Well, you didn't have to come *over*. You could have just called. Or texted."

"It's okay. I was going by here anyway."

"You're not on duty, are you? I don't want to get you in trouble," she scolded.

He tugged at his civilian clothes. "Do I look like I'm on duty?"

"Don't get smart with me, young man." She swatted at him playfully, but her smile faded a little too quickly.

He drew her into another hug. "You know I'm just giving you a hard time. So tell me what's going on."

They walked through the living room where the new furniture sat looking out of place and too stiff and formal for Ma. He didn't comment.

But the minute she stepped under the kitchen lights, he could tell something was wrong. The lipstick and earrings were gone. Of course, it was almost bedtime, but it was more than that. The haggard expression that creased her brow and rounded her shoulders was back.

"You don't look so good, Ma. Is everything okay?"

She pulled out of his embrace and looked

up at him. "Two insults and you've barely been here five minutes?" Her voice held teasing, but her eyes said his comment hurt.

"I didn't mean it that way, Ma. Come on. I just meant you look tired. You've been so happy the last few times we've gotten together. So tell me, what's changed?" What he really wanted to ask was what had *caused* that happiness in the first place. Except, he wasn't really sure he wanted to know the answer.

She slid into a chair at the kitchen table and rested her head in her hands.

"What's wrong, Ma? Are you having to work extra shifts?" He knew they took advantage of her at the daycare where she cooked.

She looked up, but fingered the stained tablecloth, not meeting his eyes.

"Is everything okay with Robby?" His brother had been fine when Rafe stopped by two days ago.

"Robby's fine. This has nothing to do with Robby."

"What then?"

She glanced up at him, and her eyes brimmed with tears. He pulled out a chair at the table and sat beside her, put his hand over hers. It felt so frail, the skin on her knuckles papery thin.

"I've gotten myself in a pickle, Rafe."

"What kind of a pickle?"

"I need some money. To pay off . . . a loan."

"What do you still have a loan on besides the house? I thought we got your car paid off a year ago."

"It's not the car."

"What then?"

"I . . . I borrowed some money from a friend, and I'm having trouble paying it back. I was making payments every week, but now they want it all paid back by January 1."

He eyed her. "What friend?" He couldn't think of one friend of his mother's who would be in a position to loan her money. "And what did you borrow it for?"

She winced. "I know you're going to say this was foolish, but I went to the casino one night and things —"

"To gamble? Ma, what were you thinking?" He worked to keep his voice level, but it was a struggle. "You *know* nobody ever wins anything worth a hoot out there."

"Now that's not true, Rafe. *I* won. I won big. And my friend did too. It must have just been my lucky night because I went with a few hundred dollars —"

"A couple hundred!" He lost the battle

with his voice.

"Just wait. Let me finish my story." A spark of defiance lit her eyes. "I went with three hundred dollars and I came back with six thousand! I could hardly believe it!"

"You won six *thousand* dollars gambling?" He remembered the new furniture and the clothes. The jewelry she'd worn that was so out of character for her. It all made sense now. Even while it made no sense whatsoever.

"I know," Ma said. "I couldn't believe it myself."

"Then where's the money now? Why do you have a loan? I don't understand."

"I know . . . I know it sounds stupid. I *should* have known it was too good to be true. But after that first time when I couldn't hardly lose if I tried, there was just . . . so much hope. So much hope, Rafe. I thought I could finally get out from under the house payments and —"

"So you went back?" His shoulders slumped, and he knew the rest of the story merely by looking at her careworn face.

"Yes. And every time I walked onto that floor, honey, this whole world of possibilities opened up." The lines in her face softened. "I mean, if it happened once, it could happen again, you know? So we

224

started going —"

"Wait. *We*? Who did you go with?"

"A friend. You don't know them," she added quickly. "It's somebody I met that first night I was there."

"Ma . . ."

She waved a hand. "I know. Believe me if you live as long as I have, you'll understand. And I know you don't care that much about money, but oh honey, so many of this world's ills can be solved with money."

He shook his head. "And so many of this world's ills are *caused* by people wishing they had money they didn't do a thing to earn!"

She hung her head like a shamed child.

Rafe immediately felt chastened. He leaned over and put an arm around her. "I'm sorry, Ma. I shouldn't have said that. So who do you owe money to? The casino?"

"No! I would never do that. I'm not an idiot. My friend said . . . they'd loan me some money. Since I was having such a lucky streak. But . . . I guess my luck ran out. And now they want the money paid back."

He blew out a hard breath. She was being awfully careful with her pronouns. For the first time, he wondered if Britt was right and Mom was seeing someone. "We'll figure something out, Ma."

"I can sell the furniture. This lady at work does it all the time . . . on one of those Facebook groups. Or maybe it's Craigslist. I forget."

He took a step away from her. "You wouldn't get anywhere near what you paid for it, Ma. And then you'd be left with an empty house. And you'd still have that payment."

"Well, what do you want me to do then?"

He cupped his hands and rubbed his face hard. "I don't know. Let me think about it for a while. And I'm sorry . . . I shouldn't have said what I did a few minutes ago."

She shook her head, looking utterly defeated. "I'm sorry I've made such a mess of things."

"We'll get it worked out. Just . . . don't gamble any more. Do you . . . do you need to get some help?"

She looked at him like he had three heads. "What are you saying? You think I'm addicted or something? I'm not an idiot, Rafe. I know how I got into this pickle, and I'm not about to make it worse."

"Okay. I just wanted to be sure. And I'm going to ask you again: Who is this friend anyway? Maybe you need to stay away from . . . *them*. If it's going to cause this

226

much trouble."

"Don't worry. I won't fall for a stupid scam like this again."

"*Was* it a scam? I thought you said you *borrowed* the money from a friend."

"He claimed to be —" She clamped a hand over her mouth. "Okay, so yes. It was a man. And I don't think he was really trying to scam me. He just *used* me is all. And I fell for it like the —" She stopped short, then bent her head. "Like the fool that I am."

Again, he put an arm around her. "Stop it, Ma. Of course you're not. We'll figure this out. There has to be a way to get this taken care of."

But right now, he didn't have a clue what that would be.

CHAPTER 20

Britt fluffed the bed pillows in the master bedroom one more time and then carried a bucket of cleaning supplies back to the kitchen and tucked them in the broom closet. The cottage smelled of lemon oil and pumpkin bread, and it looked charming in its Christmas finery. She suspected she was slightly prejudiced since every time she looked at the decorations, she remembered the night Rafe came over to help her put them up. She loved that he had been creative enough to figure out a way they could have a "date" even if it wasn't dinner and a movie.

She walked through the rooms of the cottage one last time, making sure it was guest-ready, then locked the door and hid the key in its designated place — on the porch in the bird's nest under the old church pew Joanna had found at an estate sale. As much as she enjoyed guests' reactions when they first saw the cottage or cabins, sometimes it felt like a waste to have everything sparkling clean and then not even be able to enjoy it themselves. She was afraid the newness of owning an Airbnb was quickly wearing off. But even if it did, she could think of worse jobs to hold. And now that she'd met Rafe, she didn't feel nearly as lonely out here on the property, pining and worrying that she'd never meet someone.

She touched her lips, remembering the warmth of his kiss. She'd been walking around with her head in the clouds ever since that night outside of the bakery two days ago. A lifetime. She hadn't seen him since then, but he'd texted her several times with silly, fun questions and had left a voice mail on her phone, apparently while she was out sweeping the cottage's porch.

At first, she'd been disappointed to miss his call, but now she was glad she had the recording of his voice — that incredible voice — to listen to whenever she wanted to — which was, oh, about every five minutes. She smiled to herself at the thought. She was definitely falling and falling hard.

Back at her cabin, she tidied up, changed into jeans and a sweater, wrapped the extra loaf of pumpkin bread from the batch she'd baked for their guests, and headed for

Quinn and Phee's house. She'd be glad when they got moved to the property.

Joanna had offered to bring lasagna for dinner and said she and Luke wanted to talk to all of them about something. Britt suspected they had set a date and wanted to announce it and make sure everyone made room on their calendars. They'd probably be asking her to look after Mateo while they were on their honeymoon since Phee and Quinn would have a tiny baby by that time.

At least Britt hoped Joanna had the sense to wait until Phee's baby was safely here before they got married. Joanna was set on having her wedding up in the clearing on the property, and it wouldn't even be nice enough weather-wise until late April or early May. That should be enough time . . . if everything went well with Phee's delivery.

When Britt pulled into the driveway a few minutes later, the lights were on in every window, and Luke's truck was parked in the driveway. She grabbed the pumpkin bread and hurried up the sidewalk.

"Anybody home?" She knocked on the front door, but could hear the laughter even before she stepped inside. For a brief moment, she paused and listened to the sounds of her family living life, messy and wonder-

230

ful as it was. The sisters she'd grown up with, the men they'd chosen to spend their lives with, and the others God had placed in their care — Mateo and Phee's baby — were beyond dear to her. She wished her mother could see them now, although Mom would have been sad to know that Daddy was no longer a part of their everyday lives. That seemed so strange, given how close they'd been only a year ago before losing Mom. Thankfully, they still spoke to Daddy weekly on the phone and longed for his too-infrequent visits.

It seemed even stranger that in a little more than a year since Mom's death, this family had grown by four people — counting Phee's baby — that Mom had never known as part of the family circle. Yes, she'd known Quinn as Daddy's coworker — and adored him — but she hadn't lived long enough to see him and Phee fall in love.

Britt loved this family and she could so easily imagine Rafe in their midst, completing the family she'd always dreamed of. If only she could see into the future and know whether that was the plan God had for her life. She had a hard time seeing how it could be if she and Rafe couldn't even find time for a real date.

"Oh! There you are." The door swung

wide and Joanna pulled Britt inside. "Dinner's just about ready. Everything's ready to serve in Phee's room."

"I'm not late, am I?"

"No, we're just hungry." She looked down at the loaf of bread in Britt's hands. "Does that need slicing?"

"No, it's ready to go."

"Great. Take off your coat and come on."

In Phee's room, everyone greeted her, and Mateo patted the chair beside him, motioning her to sit with him. "Hey, buddy. How's basketball going?"

"Pretty good. Except we lost by one point last weekend."

"Bummer. Well, there's always next time."

"That's not what Coach said."

Not sure how to respond, Britt looked to Luke to bail her out.

"Coach gets a little worked up sometimes, but they played a good game even if they did lose." He squeezed Mateo's shoulder affectionately. "And *this* guy had six points in the first half."

"Yeah, and zero points in the second half." Mateo rolled his eyes.

"Hey, six points is six points, buddy." Luke patted his back.

Britt was always amazed how much Mateo and Luke resembled each other with

232

their dark eyes and almost-black hair. They shared not a drop of blood, but no one would have doubted the truth of it if Luke had claimed to be his birth father. And since Joanna had finally accepted that Mateo was part of a package deal with Luke, the kid had blossomed.

"Hey, Britt's here!" Quinn came in from the hallway with a pitcher of water. "Let's eat! I'm starved." He turned to Luke. "Would you bless the food, Luke?"

"Sure." Luke motioned silently for Mateo to take off his ball cap, then slipped a possessive arm around Jo and bowed his head. "Lord, thank You for this food and this family. Please bless both, and we continue to put Phee and the baby in Your hands. Thank You for bringing them this far and we trust You, Father, to bring this little one safely into the world in Your perfect time."

The minute Luke uttered the "amen," the decibel level went up with everyone talking at once and jockeying for position around the card table where the food was laid out. Phee was propped up in the middle of the bed, and as he'd done for their little Thanksgiving Day dinner, Quinn had ingeniously placed the leaves from the dining room table — with tablecloths spread underneath to protect Phee's pretty quilt — on each side

of the bed, making table space for everyone
to sit around the bed.

"I feel like a queen or something," Phee
joked as everyone doted and waited on her
as she reclined at the head of the "table."

"Don't let that go to your head," Quinn
teased. "This is a limited reign, Your High-
ness."

"Don't you worry. I can't wait to get
demoted to kitchen serf."

"And nursemaid," Britt chimed.

They ate amidst the comfy chatter of family until Quinn cleared his throat and got
their attention. When the room was quiet,
he looked to Luke. "I believe Luke and Jo
have something they wanted to share with
us."

The couple looked at each other with
knowing smiles, and Joanna nudged Luke
to do the talking.

"We do," Luke said. "Jo and I have finally
set a date and we wanted to make sure it
works for everyone before we send out our
announcements." He turned to Jo. "Why
don't you do the honors?"

Beaming, she told them, "The wedding —
up in the clearing, of course — will be May
12. That's the Saturday before Mother's
Day, and we thought" — Jo's eyes filled with
unshed tears — "we thought it would be a

nice way to honor Mom and celebrate Phee and Quinn's new little one."

Phee clapped from her tower of pillows. "That's perfect, Jo. The baby should be old enough by then."

"We're hoping the weather will be warm enough by then too," Luke added.

"And the trees should be leafed out and a few things blooming." Jo smiled. "We already talked to Dad and he can come then. Will that work for everyone else?"

Murmurs of affirmation fluttered around their little circle.

"It'll be beautiful up there in May, you guys. Just perfect!" Britt felt close to tears herself — but the happy kind. After a hard season of loss and change, Jo and Luke's announcement held such hope for this family.

"Wait though. We're not finished." Luke held up a hand and waited for it to quiet again. "We have something else to share."

They all exchanged curious glances as Luke took Joanna's hand on one side and put his arm around Mateo on the other. "Do you want to tell this one, buddy?"

Mateo ducked his head. "No, you." But he couldn't seem to keep the grin off his face.

"Jo and I . . ." Luke swallowed hard,

composing himself. "As of January 19, Joanna and I will be legal guardians of Mateo. He's going to keep his mama's last name, of course, but he's asked to legally use my name — what will soon be Jo's name too — as his middle name."

"Mateo Blaine Castillo." Phee tested it out, smiling. "That is a great name, buddy!"

"I know."

Everyone laughed and Mateo's golden brown skin took on a pink glow.

"This way," Quinn said, with an ornery glint in his eyes, "if you get to be famous someday, you won't have to change your name. You'll already have an über cool name."

Phee nudged him. "Babe, I don't think anyone says *über* anymore."

"Sure they do. Like, if Mateo becomes an Uber driver, he'd have the coolest name on the whole app."

They all groaned but laughed just the same.

"Nah, that won't work, Quinn," said Mateo, warming to the spotlight. " 'Cause I'm gonna get a Mini Cooper when I'm old enough to drive. Won't be able to Uber because I couldn't fit anybody in there. Except maybe a petite girl."

Luke rubbed his knuckles on the boy's

dark head. "A girl! Since when are you interested in girls?"

Mateo flushed bright red, and Luke quickly changed the subject. "I'm just wondering how you're going to afford this Mini Cooper. You might want to start filling out job applications as soon as we get home tonight."

"I was hoping maybe you'd just give me one for my birthday. That'd be a lot cheaper." His grin said he knew it wasn't going to happen, but no one could blame him for trying.

When the laughter and congratulations finally quieted, Phee's stifled yawn caused Quinn to pat her belly beneath the covers. "This baby needs a nap." He planted a kiss on Phee's forehead. "This one too. Everybody out."

Quinn jokingly shooed everyone from the bedroom.

"But don't forget there's dessert," Jo said, gathering the dishes from the table leaves. "Come on out to the kitchen and I'll dish it up."

Before leaving the room, Britt straightened the covers over her sister's feet. "Don't worry, Phee. We'll save some for you and the baby."

She brought up the rear of the happy

parade marching down the hallway to the kitchen for apple crisp and ice cream. The only thing that would have made this day more perfect was if Mom and Daddy could have been here.

And Rafe.

For the third time, Rafe hit End and stuffed his phone back in his pocket. When Quinn had asked him if he knew anyone who was looking for part-time work, it had never crossed his mind that *he* would be a candidate. But Ma's revelation threw him for a loop. And presented him with a huge problem.

He'd offered to help her pay off her gambling debt — and he would. But it wasn't like he had thousands of dollars lying around with no place to go. He made decent money as an EMT, and he would draw an adequate pension when it was time to retire. But right now, what money he had saved was tied up in a long-term CD. If he pulled it out now, he'd forfeit what little interest the money had earned and pay a penalty besides.

He supposed most people saw his switch from cop to EMT as a demotion. It probably was, in the sense that he'd taken a small cut in salary — ostensibly because he wasn't directly putting his life on the line every day as an EMT the way he had as a cop.

Not that he'd faced a whole lot of risk as a cop in tiny Langhorne, Missouri. In fact, sometimes he thought he faced more risk now, as an EMT — certainly when he worked the scene of an accident or a fire or when he got called in on a domestic violence incident like the one last June where a gun-wielding woman threatened to kill her husband while their two toddlers cowered under the kitchen table. He cringed at the memory. Not for what he'd witnessed, but for those poor kids. And as he did so often whenever he thought of that night, he shot up a prayer that God might wipe the memory of that night from those little boys' minds.

He would help Ma however he could, but that bill wouldn't get paid overnight. He sighed. He'd heard several of the older guys at work talk about the burden they had caring for parents who hadn't been wise with their money. Most of them at least had siblings who were helping out with the bills. But not only could his brother not help, but Robby came with his own expenses. Yes, their father paid the bills at the group home, but there were always incidentals that came out of pocket. And since he'd started with the Langhorne force, he paid those bills so Ma wouldn't have to.

He pulled his cell phone out of his pocket again, clicked on Contacts, and stared at Quinn's name and number on the screen.

He and Britt already had a major challenge trying to find time together. If he took on additional work, that might be the end of them until the Mitchells' house was finished and their baby safely born. And that was a ways off.

Worse, if he took that job, he'd be working out at the sisters' property. Britt — and her sisters too . . . even Quinn — would have every right to think it looked suspiciously as if he was stalking Britt. But it might also give him a chance, however brief, to see her and keep alive the friendship that had deepened between them. It was hard to believe that he'd only really known her for three weeks now.

Was it foolish to even think of applying for that job? Or was it God's answer to his prayers?

CHAPTER 21

"Good night everyone. Merry Christmas." Britt closed the door of Quinn and Phee's house and headed for her SUV. She heard Jo and Luke laughing with Mateo behind her and though it made her feel even lonelier, she just wanted to get back to her cabin to be alone with her thoughts.

It had been a strange Christmas, spent in Phee's room, like at Thanksgiving, except today's gathering had ended early since Phee wasn't feeling well.

Britt stared into the white beam of her headlights on the dark highway, the striped middle line ticking, ticking, ticking past. The holidays hadn't been the same since Mom died. It didn't help that Daddy had bowed out of Christmas at the last minute, citing his desire to come when Phee's baby was born instead. March felt a long way off, and she knew Dad could afford to make the trip twice. Maybe he just couldn't take off work both times, but he hadn't said that, and she worried there was more to it than he let on.

She angled her neck from side to side, feeling a headache coming on and doing her best to push off the blanket of melancholy that settled over her.

But it wasn't only Chandler family matters that had put a pall over the holidays. Apparently, it was Rafe's family too. He seemed distant lately and even though they'd spoken on the phone several times, he told her last night — via text, no less — that he was dealing with some family issues and that it might be a while before he could get away.

For once, they didn't have guests at the Airbnb, so she could just go home and relax. Maybe get started on the next book club selection. She blew out a little huff. Who was she kidding? She would go home and mope.

At the cabin, she unloaded the empty dishes and leftover food she'd taken to Quinn and Phee's. As she was coming out for the last load, Jo's car came up the lane, but instead of parking in front of the cottage, Jo pulled up beside Britt. Great. She didn't really feel like talking.

Jo got out and came around to the passenger side. "Need help?"

"Nope, this is the last of it. Do you need help unloading?" As soon as she'd offered she wished she could take it back. She just wanted to be alone.

"No, I just have a couple of things to take in to the fridge. I sent most of my leftovers home with Luke."

"That was sweet. But don't think you can come over and eat mine."

"Haha. No, I'll probably have to go over tomorrow and show him how to heat up leftovers. So I'll get my share after all." She tilted her head and studied Britt. "Is everything okay, sis?"

"Everything's fine. Why?"

"You were awfully quiet tonight. And . . . I kind of thought Rafe might join us."

"No. Like I told you before, he had family stuff going on."

"Are you guys still . . . getting along? I know you really like him." Jo took a heavy casserole dish from the top of the stack in Britt's arms and they started toward the house.

She sighed. May as well spill, as long as Jo was willing to listen.

"I do really like him. But as of today it's been almost a week since I've laid eyes on the man. A week, Jo, with no future date in sight!"

"Why is that?"

She shrugged. "You've got me. I mean, it is Christmas, after all. He told me he's dealing with some family stuff, but he didn't go into detail. I don't know, Jo. Maybe he really does have family stuff going on, but I just can't shake the feeling that something's off."

"Do you think it's his brother? I know Luke sometimes seemed a little . . . *distant* when we were first dating, especially where Mateo was concerned. But then he knew I was really hesitant about Mateo."

Britt smiled. "Kind of hard to believe you ever had a problem with that sweet kid, isn't it?"

"I know. I was a total jerk. It's a miracle Luke put up with me as long as he did."

"I'm guessing he thought you were worth it."

Jo returned her smile. "Thanks. I'm trying to make up for lost time."

"I don't think you have anything to worry about. It's obvious Mateo adores you."

"Almost as much as he adores you."

Britt eyed her. "You're not jealous are you?"

"No! I'm thrilled Mateo likes my sisters as much as he likes me. I mean, he's stuck with us. All of us."

Britt chuckled. "Poor kid."

They went inside and worked together putting leftovers in the fridge and washing up the empty bowls and pans.

"I never let you answer about Rafe." Joanna hung the dish towel to dry before turning to her. "Do you think the issues he's dealing with are about his brother?"

Shaking her head, Britt gave the counter one last swipe with the sponge. "No. Rafe said it has something to do with his mom. But he didn't offer any details. Not that he owes me that. I mean, we're still just getting to know each other. I don't expect to be in on family decisions or anything like that. But . . . it feels like there's too much he's *not* telling me."

"You think he's hiding something from you?"

"I don't know. Maybe I'm just not asking the right questions. But I don't want to be that woman who chases a guy off by being overly pushy or possessive or . . . I don't know. It seems like he's withdrawing. And just when I felt like we really had something between us. I don't want this to fizzle out for reasons I can't control. Or even understand. I keep replaying our conversations in my mind, wondering if I said something that ticked him off."

"Like what? Unlike me, you're not the type to rub people the wrong way, Britt."

"Well, for one thing, when we were Christmas shopping last week I had to open my big mouth and tell him I didn't want to exchange gifts."

"Why'd you tell him that?"

She waved her sister off. "It's not like I made a big announcement or anything. You had to be there to hear it in context. But . . . I don't know, maybe he took it the wrong way, because he sure took it to the next level. No gifts, no date, no nuthin'. And as adamant as he was at first about being creative and making time to see each other, he hasn't mentioned getting together at all, let alone during the holidays."

Jo clucked sympathetically. "Maybe he just doesn't know how important it is to you."

"Yeah. Or maybe he's having second thoughts about me."

"So . . . You haven't talked to him in a week? How did you leave things last time you were together?"

"Oh no, we've talked. On the phone. And texted. But something has definitely changed. And when I think about how he broke up with his last girlfriend, it worries me that he has commitment issues or some-

246

thing." She briefed Jo on how Rafe had broken things off with that girl at the hospital the same day she and Rafe went to Panera. "It all seemed perfectly logical when he was telling me about breaking up with her, but now I'm second-guessing myself."

"Talk to him, Britt. If there's one thing I've learned from my relationship with Luke, it's that you can't expect a guy to read your mind or know what you want unless you tell him. If Rafe takes that as you being pushy and forward, then maybe he's not the guy for you. I know you might not want to hear —"

"Oh, but I *want* him to be the guy for me, Jo. So bad! I've never felt this way about any other man. You might think I'm crazy for saying this when I've only known him for a few weeks, but . . . I think I *love* him!" She hadn't meant to say the words out loud, but they were out now.

"Then, Britt . . . *talk* to him!" Jo held up a warning hand. "I'm not saying tell him you love him. It might be a little soon for that. But tell him you're worried about how he's withdrawn. Give him a chance to say yay or nay to whether it's true. You have nothing to lose and everything to gain."

"You really think I should? Tonight?"

Jo shrugged. "No time like the present.

It's still early. Unless you know he's celebrating with family tonight."

"That's just it. I don't know where he is or what he's doing. On Christmas night. That's not a very good sign for our relationship."

"Don't jump to conclusions until you know for sure. You'll just have to pray about the timing and then decide. And you know I'll be praying too. But talk to him. If you care about him, don't let things just fizzle out without at least talking it through. Otherwise you'll always wonder."

She gave her sister a grateful smile. "I wasn't really in the mood to talk, but I'm so glad you came by."

"Merry Christmas, sis."

"You too." Britt leaned in for a hug.

"Now, I'm headed to Luke's for a movie with my guys. Do you want to come?"

"No. Thanks. You're sweet to offer, but I need time to think and pray and decide what to do."

"Attagirl."

Rafe tossed his phone on the bed, the calculator app still showing the ugly numbers. As devastating as it would be to his own financial future, tomorrow he would cash in his CD and pay off as much of his mother's gambling debts as he could.

He ran a hand through his hair and yanked on the ends, as if he could fix the problem by sheer will. How Ma had gotten in this deep, he couldn't even imagine. But the several thousand dollars she'd told him about that night had somehow suddenly become *eleven* thousand.

According to Ma, the supposed friend who'd lent her the original money had fronted her the cash to play the slots, insisting she could make enough to pay him back for the original loan. But it had all backfired. Ma's winning streak was over, and now she was in twice as deep and the man was making demands — Rafe considered them threats — to be paid back in full before year's end.

He pulled up his bank account on the laptop again, even though he knew that opening the accounts one more time was not going to change the numbers. Ma's predicament had consumed his thoughts and energy every waking moment. It didn't help matters that he'd worked a traffic fatality last night. The darkness of that always hung on for a day or two. Especially when it was a seventeen-year-old kid with his whole life ahead of him. Now a family would spend their first horrific holidays without their beloved son, brother, grandson, nephew.

He'd spent what was supposed to be the hap-hap-happiest day of the year between Ma's house and the group home with Robby. And they'd both been testy and restless and completely lacking in holiday spirit. Worse, he'd all but ignored Britt. The few texts he had sent her were terse and almost dismissive. His intent wasn't to take out his frustrations on her, but he knew that's how she would see it. And of course, she had no idea of what was happening with his mother. Or with work.

He owed her an explanation, but again and again, he'd put it off because he wouldn't blame her if she dumped him when she found out what he was up against. And realistically, he had no business trying to date anyone, let alone Britt Chandler. Until Mom's loans were paid off, he wouldn't have a minute to spare. And once the loans were paid, he would have little money and even more to hide. He had nothing to offer a woman who deserved everything.

There was only one last wild card he was willing to play. He'd wavered back and forth about calling Quinn Mitchell. He didn't want to risk Britt — or the rest of her family — thinking he was stalking her. But now he had no choice. And Quinn's job would be a lifeline, given the flexibility of the hours. He fished his cell phone from his back pocket and dialed the number.

CHAPTER 22

"That's the last of it." Britt placed the lid on the shoebox of decorations left over from the cottage and cabins. Jo had insisted they put up a few lights and a garland of greenery in Phee's room before their sad little Christmas dinner around her bed. With Christmas plates and napkins it had looked festive enough, even if their spirits were all low.

She hated to admit what a relief it was to have this holiday over. One that used to be her favorite. Now, if she could just get through New Year's Eve, she thought she might breathe easy again.

Phee's doctor wanted her to make it until at least the end of February before she went into labor. She would be thirty-six weeks then. Once the calendar turned to the new year, that would seem possible. Less than eight and a half weeks. Single digits. Surely they could all make it through till then. And if by some miracle Phee made it past that, every day in March closer to her due date would be a victory.

Britt carried the box to her SUV and then went back in to say goodbye. Quinn was home all week, so she and Jo had planned to get caught up on cleaning and upkeep at the Airbnb. But now, both cabins were booked through the first week of January, so Britt would be staying with Jo at the cottage. Still, it would be a break from the boredom of sitting with Phee.

Jo had suggested setting up a baby monitor in Phee's room, but she balked at having a camera trained on her every move. Instead, Quinn installed an intercom system so Phee could call from her room to the kitchen or living room. It gave whoever was on Phee-watch a little more freedom. Still, though they'd supplied Phee's bedside table with everything she could possibly need, there was so much she simply couldn't do for herself without getting out of bed. Thankfully, over these weeks Britt's earlier annoyance had turned to compassion. Ironic though it seemed, bed rest was not for the faint of heart.

When she entered Phee's room, Quinn was on the phone at the desk they'd moved into the bedroom so he could work but also keep Phee company. Britt gave him a little wave and went to speak quietly to her sister. "Anything else you need me to do before I head home?"

"Nope. We're good. You go home and enjoy some time off. And thanks for everything, sis." She scooted up in the bed, groaning with the growing weight of the baby.

"You're still feeling okay?"

"I'm fine. Just bored silly."

"Well, if Quinn needs to go out, don't hesitate to call. I'll be home most of the week."

Phee waved her off. "We'll be fine. But thanks."

"Tell Quinn goodbye. And happy new year in advance."

He apparently heard her and turned to wave at her, smiling. She started to leave, but he motioned to her and mouthed, "Wait."

She looked to Phee, thinking she might know what Quinn wanted, but her sister only shrugged.

Britt sat on the edge of the bed to wait. She couldn't help overhearing Quinn's end of the phone conversation.

"I'm okay with that," he was saying. "Hey, I'll take whatever hours you can give me. So when could you start?" A pause as Quinn

254

listened, then, "Great! You bet . . . glad it will work out. See you on Tuesday."

He must have found someone interested in the hourly work she'd heard him talking to Rafe about. Rafe must have steered a friend his way. The thought made her realize how desperate she was for a connection, however frail, that would keep her tethered to Rafe.

Quinn continued, eyeing her as he spoke. "No, you can just come out to the construction site. You've been here, right? The Airbnb on Poplar Brook Road? Good deal. See you then." He clicked End and laid his phone on the desk. "That was your friend Rafe. Did you know he was going to call?"

She shook her head. "About what?" Had Rafe known she was here?

"He's going to help me with the finish work on the house. I talked to him about it a couple weeks ago and —"

"Yes, I heard that. I guess I didn't realize you meant him."

"Actually, I didn't. I just thought he might know someone at work who'd be interested. But it turns out he's interested himself. You should have said something!"

She shrugged. "He never said anything to me about it." She felt a little silly and embarrassed that she hadn't even known he was looking for other work. Her spirits deflated further. What else didn't she know about this man? Not to mention, already she and Rafe could scarcely find an hour or two they were both free. This would pretty much seal their doom. And she couldn't help but wonder if that was exactly Rafe's intent.

He'd texted her a fancy snow globe meme with a Merry Christmas wish late Christmas night, which she'd pretended not to see until the next morning when she responded with what she hoped was an appropriately frosty, "Yeah, you too." That was the last she'd heard from him. And now Quinn was telling her that Rafe was taking a second job? On her property? *What on earth . . . ?*

"Are you comfortable with that, Britt? He'll be on the property . . . working. I hope that won't be a problem." Quinn had a way of cutting to the chase.

She shrugged. "It's whatever you want. I'll probably be here with Phee anyway. I have no problem with it." That wasn't exactly true. But her problem wasn't with Quinn.

And right then, she decided to get to the bottom of things. She'd moped around far too long, wondering and worrying and not knowing where she stood with him. *Far* too long. "I need to get going, you guys. See you next week."

"Bye, sis. Love you."

"You too. Jo will be here on Tuesday. I'm taking Wednesday and Thursday. We'll figure out the rest of the week later."

"See you later, Britt. Thanks again." Quinn waved a hand. "And hey, I'll be at the house to get Rafe started Tuesday morning. I'll try to get there before he does. But . . . I'll need to wait for Joanna to get here."

Britt and Phee exchanged glances and gave identical wry laughs.

"Well, we all know what *that* means," Britt said.

Joanna was notoriously late. Luke teased that she'd probably be late for their wedding — which Britt doubted. But it did likely mean that Rafe would get to the property before Quinn Tuesday.

"Don't worry about it. It's no biggie." She gathered her things and hurried to the Escape before Phee could question her.

Not until she was going up the lane to the cabins did she find the courage to make the call. And even then, she texted him first. "Is this a good time to call?"

A few long seconds went by before her message showed as Read.

Even so, she jumped when her phone started ringing. She inhaled deeply and blew out her breath slowly before answering. "Hi. Thanks for calling."

"Sure . . . What's up?"

"That's what I'd like to know." She pulled her Escape over to the edge of the lane and put it in Park.

"Sorry?"

"I don't mean to be pushy, Rafe, but what is going on with us?"

He sighed into the phone. "First, just so you know, I'm on call right now, so don't be offended if I get called away, okay?"

"Okay, so . . . this isn't a great time."

He gave a humorless chuckle. "There wouldn't exactly *be* a good time."

"What's that supposed to mean?" Already she could feel her hopes, her *heart,* sinking.

"It's not you, Britt. I promise you that. But I'm in a mess that's going to take some time to get out of. And . . . I have no clue how long it might be."

"What kind of mess?" His voice said it was serious.

"It's family stuff. With my mom."

"So talk to me about it. What's going on? You're scaring me."

"There's nothing for you to be scared about. It has nothing to do with you. And I don't want to drag you into it."

"Is that why you've been so . . . distant lately?"

"Yes. And I'm sorry. I should have told you and just let you off the hook. I'm sorry."

"What do you mean 'let me off the hook'?"

"Britt . . ." He gave a low growl of frustration. "My mom is in deep financial trouble, with no way out . . . except me. Long story, but she got caught up in . . . gambling."

"Oh, Rafe. Wow. I'm sorry."

"Yeah. It's a mess. And you were kind of right. There was a man involved all right, but it wasn't Ma he was interested in. He used her."

"I'm so sorry." And she was. That had to be humiliating. But it was hard, knowing that Rafe's reasons for putting her off were caused by such a stupid mistake.

"I don't know if your brother-in-law told you, but I'm picking up some extra hours working for him. It's the only thing I know to do to help Ma. And between that and my job . . . and Robby . . . it means I'm not going to have one extra minute, let alone a free evening. It's not fair to ask you to wait for me. For all I know, I might still be in this mess a year from now."

"Hang on . . ." She forced a calm she didn't feel. "Are you trying to break up with

me or are you just telling me you'll understand if I break up with *you*?"

"The latter, I guess. I don't want to break
up with you, Britt. But right now, I've got
nothing to offer you. *Nothing.* Not time, not
money, not a future . . ."

"Rafe . . . There's always a future. What if
I told you —" She stopped, throwing up a
wordless prayer, not wanting to speak the
words until she was absolutely sure in her
heart of hearts that they were true. The
peace that came over her was her answer.
"I'm willing to wait, Rafe. I'm willing to be
here as long as it takes. You're worth that to
me."

"You don't know what you're saying."

"Let me be the judge of that, okay?"

Another sigh. "I don't know . . ."

A scene from a book they'd read in book
club a couple of months ago came to life in
her mind. "Rafe, people have waited — for
things that really matter — since the beginning of time. In war, in sickness . . . Shoot,
in the Bible, Jacob waited for Rachel for
seven years."

"Um . . . I hear that didn't turn out so
well for Jacob, even after seven years."

She ignored his joke. "My point is, if
something is worth having, it's worth waiting for. If what you and I have going be-

tween us matters at all, then why shouldn't we be willing to wait?"

"I don't know," he said again. "Could you be content with hardly ever actually seeing each other? With only texts and once-in-a-while phone calls?"

"As long as they aren't cryptic and weird like the ones you've been sending these last couple of weeks."

"Yeah . . . I'm sorry about that."

"And as long as we can talk things out — or at least say, 'I'm not quite ready to talk about that yet.' "

"I think . . . I think I could do that. But . . . are you sure, Britt?" She heard the smile in his voice and her spirit soared.

"I'm sure. I know it won't be easy, Rafe, but what do we have to lose . . . except each other?"

"That's the one thing I *don't* want to lose." The tenderness in his voice made her want to weep.

"Me neither."

"If it helps, I'm pretty sure you won't have to wait seven years."

She laughed. "Thank You, Lord."

"I think I can probably get my issues wrapped up in three or four."

She groaned, hoping he wasn't serious.

"Just kidding. Well . . . Okay then. Let's

give it a go, and if we —" His voice cut out for a split second, and he growled under his breath. "Hey, I've got a call. Work. I'm sorry. But . . . this is how it's going to be, Britt. Just so you know. I'll text you later."

"Promise?"

"I promise." The line went dead.

She sat in the dark car for several minutes, replaying their conversation. *Could* she live this way? With every meaningful conversation interrupted and rarely getting to actually see him? To feel her hand in his? His kiss on her lips? Maybe for a long time?

As she parked in front of Near Cottage, the questions answered themselves with a sure knowledge: It seemed like her whole life had been spent waiting. But now, she had something worth waiting for. And she would take Rafe Stuart however she could get him, because now that she knew the man, she did not want to live without him.

Chapter 23

January

Even though he had no intention of seeing her, doubted she was even on the property this morning, Rafe checked his reflection in the rearview mirror as he pulled off of Poplar Brook Road and headed up the lane to the construction site. He forced himself not to look toward Near Cottage, even though he smiled, remembering their conversation that night he helped her decorate the cottages for Christmas about how Britt's little cabin got its name.

He spotted Quinn at the side of the house talking to a crew of men in painters overalls. He wasn't sure what kind of work he would be doing, but Quinn had promised it wouldn't be rocket science, and that he would talk him through it before he left the site for the day.

He'd packed a lunch and planned to stay till three, because he knew he'd need a few hours of sleep before he started his shift at the station tonight. His supervisor hadn't been too keen on the idea of him taking another job, but when Rafe explained that it was part-time and temporary, he agreed. Rafe was just glad he hadn't had to explain the reason he needed this job in the first place. He hadn't told anyone but Britt that information. And he hadn't told her the whole story, though he would — if they ever got more than five minutes to talk.

Quinn met him at the door. "Hey, Rafe. Good to see you. I appreciate you taking this on."

He offered a hand. "Hey, it's you who's doing me a favor."

"Well, let's get started. Follow me and I'll show you today's project. This one isn't going to be a whole lot of fun, but it should go pretty quickly." He led Rafe to the basement of the house where half a dozen sawhorses were set up on painters drop cloths. Wide trim boards were stacked on a makeshift table to one side.

"Phee decided she wanted old-fashioned stained trim board and crown molding, so that's what I'm going to put you on today. Believe me, I've done the hard part, trying to get the exact color of stain that woman had in mind."

Rafe laughed. "Well, I hope you got it right."

Quinn pulled a wedge of wood from his pocket and held it out. "This has received the stamp of approval. So as long as you only use what's in these cans, you should be safe. You ever done finish work before?"

"Sorry, no, I haven't."

"No worries. I'll get you started."

For the next ten minutes he worked beside Quinn, matching his strokes as he rubbed the stain onto the trim boards with a soft cloth.

"Personally, I prefer a brush, but my wife thinks the texture is better with a cloth, so cloth it is. You know what they say . . . If Mama ain't happy, ain't nobody happy." He winked good-naturedly and went on to show Rafe the other steps in the process Phylicia had approved. But he could tell after fifteen minutes with Quinn Mitchell that he was as much a perfectionist as Phee apparently was.

This house was going to be quite the place.

After a while, Quinn looked at his watch and blew out a breath. "I need to get going. But call me if you have any questions the paint crew upstairs can't answer for you. I'll take as many hours as you can give me, but you leave whenever you need to. Just keep track of your hours."

"I'm good till about three today."

"Good. You'll probably finish this up in a couple of good days, maybe three. But I have another project I want to talk to you about when this is done. Assuming you're still willing." Quinn checked his watch again. "Man, I've really got to run."

Once he got into a rhythm, Rafe found the work satisfying, relaxing even. Nothing like his day job. He finished the first coat of stain shortly after noon, cleaned up, and ate a sandwich sitting on the basement stairs. While he ate, he tapped out a text to Britt:

"It is killing me to know you're two minutes away. Hope you're having a good day."

But he deleted it before he hit Send. She'd either think he was hinting for her to come see him, or she'd have her hopes up that he'd come and see her. And there wasn't time for either without cheating Quinn out of minutes he'd promised.

He'd been back to work for a couple of hours rubbing down the boards he'd stained earlier with fine steel wool when laughter came from the crew upstairs. He'd been hearing the muffled voices of the paint crew — five or six guys — throughout the day, but now they were cheering. He checked his phone. Maybe two o'clock was quitting time for them.

But a minute later, footsteps sounded on the stairway and he looked up to see Britt round the corner, smiling, a foil-wrapped plate in hand.

"Hey, you!" He'd never seen a cheerier sight. "Are you the one who got the paint crew all rowdy up there?" He angled his chin toward the trusses above his head, not missing a beat with the steel wool in his right hand.

She smiled. "I'm guessing it wasn't so much me as the cookies I brought."

"Don't be so sure." He eyed the pan in her hands. "I don't suppose they left any for the poor guy working in the dungeon?"

"I made sure."

"You're the best. Let me wipe my hands." He laid down the wad of steel wool he'd been sanding with. "I already took my lunch break, and I'm leaving at three, so . . . I can't take long."

"I know. But it struck me that . . . you might be able to talk while you work." She suddenly looked shy and vulnerable. "You said we'd just have to get creative. Before."

"I said that, didn't I?"

She nodded, looking like she might cry.

"Tell you what . . ." He picked the steel wool back up and rubbed on the stain in long, smooth strokes. "You feed me cookies while I work and we can talk all you want."

She laughed. "You might have a little trouble talking with your mouth stuffed full of cookies."

"So *you* do all the talking." He opened his mouth, waiting for her to offer up a cookie.

That elicited more laughter, but she pulled a cookie from beneath the foil and held it to his mouth. He bit off half of it and chewed. Oatmeal. Did she know that was his favorite? "Mmm. These are good," he mumbled over a mouthful of cookie. He swallowed and opened wide again.

She pushed the last of the cookie into his mouth, shaking her head and rolling her eyes. "The things a woman has to do to have a conversation with a man."

"I'm thinking this works out pretty well."

She offered another cookie, shoving the whole thing into his mouth and reaching for another.

Laughing and chewing, he shook his head. "Umhph-huh. Enumph."

"What's that? I can't understand you." But she put the cookie back and set the plate on the steps. "Anything I can help you with?"

"I thought you had to stay with your sister today."

"That's tomorrow. Today is Jo's day. But we kind of had a sisters' day at Quinn and Phee's house, and I made these cookies there. I was planning to bring them by later, but Quinn came home for lunch and practically pushed me out the door. If I didn't know better, I'd think they were conspiring."

He swallowed the last of the cookie. "What do you mean?"

"It's just a theory, but I think Quinn was checking you out, making sure you were a decent guy. He apparently decided you were, and . . . Did he know you have to leave at three?"

Rafe nodded.

"Yep." She gave a decisive nod. "He made sure I would bring them while you were still here. He's playing matchmaker."

Rafe grinned at her, happier than he'd felt in a long while. "I knew there was a reason I like that guy."

"My sister is probably in on it too."

He cocked his head, studying her. "So, do you always bring cookies for the work crews?"

She blushed. "Let's just say, I've done it once or twice before. Not recently."

He laughed. "So you fed half a dozen burly painters just so you could bring me my favorite cookies?"

"Really? Oatmeal is your favorite?"

"You know, this just might work."

"What might work?"

"This waiting thing." He felt the slow grin take over his face.

She flashed a triumphant smile in return.

"Come here." He put down his tools and beckoned her with one finger.

She stepped closer, cursing the stupid sawhorse between them.

He tapped his cheek just under his eye.

Her eyes never leaving his, she stood on tiptoe, leaned across the sawhorse, and kissed the spot he'd marked.

"Okay. Now you'd better get out of here so I can get some work done."

She gave a knowing nod, turned, and headed for the stairs, scooping up the plate of cookies as she went. She never looked back, but he watched her until she disappeared at the top of the stairs.

Britt smiled all the way home. She'd been so afraid her "cookie ploy" would backfire and either Rafe wouldn't be there, or he'd be too busy to talk, or a thousand other things she'd thought of that could go wrong. But the afternoon had gone even better than she could have hoped, and she floated on a cloud all the way back to Phee's.

Quinn would be home in a couple of hours, and she had guests checking in to the cabins after dark, which meant she would be staying with Jo in the cottage tonight.

In Phee's room, she feigned interest in the newest book club novel — she was already reading February's selection — hoping her sister wouldn't be too talkative because all she wanted to do was replay the afternoon in her mind. She daydreamed through half a dozen pages not remembering a word she'd read. But now, without Rafe's touch to distract her, she saw things a little more realistically. The truth was that every time she saw him, it would only be harder to bear the waiting time.

Still, their interaction today had given her hope that their relationship could stay alive, even deepen as long as he was working right here on the property. She didn't know how long Quinn had hired Rafe for, but she'd take what she could get.

"What are you smiling about over there? That book cover doesn't look like a comedy to me." Phee's tone said she knew very well what Britt was smiling about.

"It's not. I was just . . . thinking." She turned a page and pretended to read.

"Quinn said you took cookies to the guys today. I guess they really appreciated it. I hope you don't spoil them."

She closed the book and tilted her head at her sister. "Why don't you just come out and say it, Phee."

"Say what?"

"You know very well what. You're wondering if I saw Rafe."

"Well, I happen to know you did see him."

She stopped and stared at her sister. "How do you know?"

Phee grinned. "Apparently, Rafe told my husband that you came over with cookies."

"Really? Oh, Phee. Today was so . . ." She struggled to find the right words. "It was wonderful and fun and exciting. But it's going to be so hard."

"Waiting?"

"Yes." She gave Phee a shortened version of the issues with Rafe's mom, not mentioning that the money she owed was a gambling debt. And even then, she felt like she was betraying a confidence. "He hasn't said how much money she owes, but it must be pretty bad."

"Why is *he* paying it back? Doesn't she work?"

"She does, but . . . I don't know the details for sure. You know he has a brother in a group home. Maybe that has something to do with it."

Phee frowned. "I hope he'll explain it to you. Have you asked him about it? The details, I mean?"

"Not really. I don't want to be nosy."

"It's hard, isn't it? Trying to figure out when you've crossed that threshold where you share the deeper, more secret things. I remember with Quinn." She sighed. "Oh, Britt, I'm so glad we're past the dating stage. Seeing you all moony-eyed over Rafe makes me remember how it was, falling in love with Quinn. But I love where we are so much better. Well, except for this stupid bed."

Britt laughed, glad after all that her sister had decided to be talkative. "I love where you are too. And I'll love it even more when you give me that nephew or niece."

"You and me both." Her expression turned somber. "Think about what I said, sis. You don't want any secrets between you. And maybe Rafe needs to talk about it with somebody. That's one way you'll know if you're right for each other — if you can talk about even the hard things. And this sounds like a pretty hard one."

Britt nodded, knowing her sister was right, but wishing she could just go back to daydreaming about the good stuff — the kisses and the smiles they'd exchanged.

Phee scooted up in the bed, wincing as she did.

"You okay?" A frisson of alarm went through Britt.

Her sister nodded, but lines still creased her forehead.

"You sure?"

"I don't think the baby has anything to do with all my aches and pains. It's all the time I've spent in this infernal bed that's giving me fits."

Britt watched her sister's face closely for the next few minutes. Once, Phee gave a little gasp and clutched her belly. But her concern turned to a smile. "This baby is having a party in there tonight."

Britt put a hand on her sister's belly, amazed when she felt the baby roll and stretch inside Phee. "What a miracle."

"I know. Isn't it? I still can hardly believe I'll be holding this baby in my arms in a few short weeks."

"It'll go faster than you can imagine."

Phee sighed heavily. "I hope so. I'm about

to go mad. And speaking of about to go . . . I need to get up and go to the bathroom."

Britt helped her out of bed and walked beside her down the hall. There was a bathroom in the master bedroom, but Phee insisted on using the one down the hall. "It's the only time I get to see the outside world . . . and by outside world, I mean the rest of this house."

"Just a few more weeks and it'll all be over, and you'll be so happy you won't even remember the waiting."

Phee stopped in the hallway and cast her a sideways glance. "Just who are we talking about?"

Britt laughed. "Both of us, I hope."

CHAPTER 24

"It's looking good in here. These are going to make my wife very happy." Quinn aimed his phone's camera at the crown molding that he and Rafe had just finished installing in the dining room and snapped several more photos from every possible angle. "I've had to learn to think like her since she can't come out here to check on things. And believe me" — he shot Rafe a sardonic glance — "I'm only shooting half as many pictures as she would have."

Rafe laughed and agreed. "It does look good. It's going to be a beautiful house." He'd never really considered buying a home, but if he ever did, it would be something like this one. Maybe not quite as old-fashioned in decor, but the size of it and the way it sat in relation to the river . . . it felt solid and substantial. Like a man could raise his kids here and then die in the knowledge that his great-grandkids would grow up in the same house.

Quinn went to talk to the electrician who was wiring a fancy light fixture in the breakfast room, but he returned to the dining room and sought out Rafe. "If you have time, I wanted to talk to you about that other project before you leave."

"Sure."

Quinn looked around the room and out into the foyer, as if worried someone might overhear him. "Luke and I are working on a little project — it's a secret from Joanna . . . and all the sisters right now. We'll let Phee and Britt in on it soon, but for now, don't say anything."

He nodded. "My lips are sealed until you give the word."

"I don't know if you knew that Jo's been wanting to set up a wedding venue on the property?"

"Britt said something about it."

"Well, Luke and I are going to do some building toward that end, but they've set their wedding date for May 12 and we're going to need some help to make that date since what we're building will be used for Luke and Jo's wedding first. We plan to put in a large deck that can serve as a permanent dance floor, a tent frame that we hope to eventually cover, and then permanent seating for one hundred."

"Sounds like a pretty big project."

Quinn acknowledged that with a low whistle. "I'm more worried about the surprise part. But thankfully, Luke has Joanna's sketches and notes to go from, so we're not making this up as we go."

"How are you going to keep her from finding out what you're doing?"

"For starters, we'll work while she's at work. I know your real job may not let you do that, but if you do have any hours free, we could sure use you."

"I usually know my shifts a month or so ahead of time. I'll give you what hours I can."

"And we're going to do as much of the building as we can at our shop in town. It'll take a few days to assemble everything on site, and we may not be able to keep her from figuring out what we're up to at that point. But she'll have to see it before they start decorating for the wedding anyway. I'm sure Luke will figure out a way to make a splash with his gift."

"I'm glad to be part of this. Sounds like a pretty good surprise from what I know of Jo."

"The best." Quinn clapped Rafe briefly on the shoulder. "I didn't mean to keep you but wanted to give you the hours if you're interested. Of course this house will be the priority. I want to be in it before that baby gets here."

"Understood. But I'm definitely interested."

Quinn started to turn away, but Rafe stopped him. "Hey, I wanted to talk to you about something too."

"Oh?" Something about Quinn's expression told him the man had an inkling of what he was about to say.

"I think you know that Britt and I are . . . becoming good friends."

"It's a lot more than that from what I hear. But go on . . ." The good-natured smirk he wore gave Rafe courage.

"Okay, then. I just wanted to make sure you were okay if she comes to the house to talk once in a while . . . while I'm working. I wouldn't let it interfere with the job. It's just that . . . we're both so crazy busy that we can hardly find a night to have a real date. But we'd like to . . . keep getting to know each other."

"You have my blessing." Quinn clapped his shoulder again. "You can put that girl to work while she's here too, you know. The sooner this house is finished the more my wife can chill, and the more my wife can chill, the less grumpy I'll be."

Rafe laughed. "We'll see what we can do." He doubted Quinn Mitchell had been grumpy a day in his life, but he refrained from saying so.

He felt considerably less grumpy himself now that he had not only Quinn's permission, but the man's *blessing* to see Britt as long as he was working here at the house. A thought struck him and he caught Quinn before he left the room. "If we know when it's Joanna's turn to stay with Phee, we could enlist Britt's help on the wedding stuff. That would see to it that Joanna didn't find out what you're up to. For a while at least."

Quinn wore that smirk again. "I see where you're going with this. It would also buy a certain couple some time together, even while one of them was working."

Rafe feigned a hangdog look. "You're on to me. But . . . okay, that might have something to do with my brilliant idea."

"I just might have to give you a raise, young man." Looking serious, Quinn shook his hand and strode to the front door, but Rafe could swear the man's shoulders were heaving in silent laughter.

"There you are. We were starting to wonder." Quinn closed the door to the shop behind Britt. The massive shop behind Langhorne Construction was the site of Project Surprise Joanna tonight, and the operation was in full swing.

Britt sighed. "Stupid guests were almost an hour later checking in than they said. But they're booked for almost a week, so the place should run itself for a few days." Looking past Quinn, she searched the massive shed for Rafe.

"He's not here yet, but he's on his way."

She gave her brother-in-law a sheepish grin. "Am I that transparent?"

"Even more than that."

She gave him a sisterly punch in the bicep and swept past him to where Luke and Mateo were nailing sheets of plywood to multiple wooden frames. "What can I do?"

"Hey, Britt!" Mateo beamed when he saw her. "Don't say anything to Jo! It's a surprise!"

"I know, buddy. It's a good one too. What have you got going here?" Britt pulled off her stocking cap and mittens and warmed her hands over the space heater that was running beside the sections of decking they were building.

"This is gonna be the dance floor." He hopped on top of one of the finished frames

281

and danced a little jig.

Britt laughed. "Are you practicing your number for the wedding?"

"I am." He tossed his head, sending his thick bangs bouncing. "Not a solo, but I'm gonna dance with Jo. At the reception. But not till after Luke dances with her."

"Good idea. Better let the groom go first."

"I think I hurt Jo's feelings when I didn't dance with her at Phee and Quinn's wedding. I didn't like to dance back then."

Luke struggled to his feet and stood behind Mateo, resting his hands on the boy's shoulders. "That was a long time ago, though, right? What . . . seven months now?"

"Yeah, I was only twelve then."

"You're only twelve *now,* bud." Laughing, Luke rubbed Mateo's mop of hair with his knuckles.

The boy's olive complexion pinked. "Yeah, but I'll be thirteen in a few weeks."

"That, you will."

"So, these are getting painted?" Britt tapped one of the wooden frames with the toe of her boot.

Nodding, Luke pulled a sheet of paper from his back pocket. "Grey and white checkerboard, according to your sister. Not sure how we're going to pull that off."

"Checkerboard? No problem. We painted

two bathroom floors like that in the cabins. It takes some measuring and taping, but not much to it after that's done. You want me to head that project up?"

"That'd be great. We won't put the sections together until we get them up to the clearing though. Won't they have to match up just right?"

"We can number them. Or . . ." She tried to picture the configuration in her mind. "If we divide the squares right, we should be able to make it so any slab matches up with any of the others."

"I'll leave that to you." His lips curved into a knowing grin. "And I hear Quinn hired another guy to help. Some rookie. Okay if I put him on your team?"

"You'd better!" She beamed, not caring if they teased her about Rafe.

"Speaking of that guy, where is he?"

"I'm not sure. Quinn said he was on the way."

"Okay. Let us finish nailing these last two sections and then they're all yours. I've got the paint in the back. I'm sure Jo had exact color names and paint companies in mind, but she'll have to be satisfied with what we got on sale cheap."

"I don't think you can mess up gray and white too bad."

Over Luke's shoulder, she saw the shop door open and Rafe strolled in. He spotted her and nodded, but went to talk to Quinn first.

A few minutes later, he came to the work table where she was plotting out the checkerboard pattern on paper. "So, I hear you're my boss on this project."

She scoffed. "Who said that?"

"The real boss."

"Well, okay. It's official then." She smiled at him over her shoulder. "You can start by helping me figure this out." She explained the checkerboard plan, and he pulled up a stool and straddled it.

He bent his head close to hers and whispered, close enough that his breath tickled her cheek. "I might like having you for a boss."

"Don't get too comfortable there, buddy," she teased. "You know how to paint?"

"I've painted a room or two in my day. But I'm not sure about the measuring and taping stuff."

"How about I'll do that, and you do the painting."

"A match made in heaven."

"But first you have to help me figure out if this pattern will make all six of the decks

284

fit together no matter which way they lay them."

Heads together, they worked, laughing and joking. For a while, Mateo hung out with them, making Rafe laugh and annoying Britt just a little because she wanted Rafe to herself. But after a while, Luke and Mateo moved to a far corner of the shop, and Britt suspected Quinn had given some sort of assignment that involved leaving her and Rafe alone. She'd have to remember to thank him later.

Half an hour later, Rafe looked up, seeming to realize for the first time that Mateo had disappeared. Spotting him with Luke, Rafe nodded in his direction. "He's a great kid."

"He is, but I kind of like having you to myself, if you want to know the truth." She was flirting blatantly, as long as she had Quinn's blessing.

Rafe ignored her comment. "It seems like he fits right into your family. He had a lot to overcome from what you've said."

"He really did. And he really has become like part of the family. He'll be one of us officially next Friday. Did I tell you? Luke and Jo are becoming his official guardians."

"That's really cool. But . . ." He shook his head.

"What?"

"That makes me kind of . . . sad, I guess."

"Sad? Why?"

"Not for them, of course. It's just that . . . I can't help wondering what Robby would have been like if he'd been born . . . normal."

"Oh, Rafe. I never thought about that. I'm sure he would have been awesome. I mean, I'm sure he *is* awesome."

He gave a nervous laugh. "I didn't mean to change the subject. And Robby is awesome in his own way, but he can be a little hard to take sometimes too."

"I know time is an issue for both of us, but . . ." She spoke quickly before she could change her mind. "I really would like to meet him."

"I want you to. It's something I've been thinking about. I . . . I want you to know what you're getting into."

"Getting into?"

"Being with me. Maybe someday being . . . *really* with me."

She liked the way he was thinking. Except the way he talked made her wonder if Robby was more than she'd bargained for. If maybe Rafe had painted a softer picture than reality when it came to his brother. She felt guilty for being a little bit glad that their schedules meant the meeting would be put off a little longer.

"I work all this week, but what about Sunday? Do you have to deal with guests or . . . could you maybe come with me to see Robby Sunday afternoon?"

She swallowed. So much for putting it off. "We have guests checking out Sunday, but . . . I don't have to be there."

"Okay. Will you go with me?"

"Sure."

"Can I pick you up? Say two o'clock?" He smiled, obviously remembering her rule about meeting him in town.

"I think that would be okay. After all, you've passed Quinn's approval."

"Yes. Yes, I have." He looked around the shop before stealing a quick kiss. "I'll see you Sunday."

Oh, Sunday was such a long way off.

CHAPTER 25

Rafe pulled up in front of Near Cottage and smiled, seeing Melvin perched behind the curtain in the front window. Surveying his kingdom, no doubt. Rafe got out of the car and started toward the front door, but Britt came out before he was halfway up the short walk. He'd had to fill in extra shifts at work all week so he hadn't seen her since Monday. It felt like a lifetime.

She looked good, with her hair in those bouncy waves he liked and shiny earrings bobbing as she walked. He wondered if she was still dressed up from church this morning or if she'd dressed up for him — or Robby.

He opened the passenger door for her, then went around and slid behind the wheel. Before putting the car in gear, he gave her an appreciative once-over. "You clean up nice."

That earned him a smile. "Thank you.

That was sweet. You know, they say you can live for two months on a good compliment."

He cocked his head. "They?"

She shrugged. "Whoever said it."

"You really don't know who actually said that?"

She narrowed her eyes at him. "Don't tell me . . . Mark Twain?"

He broke into a grin. "None other."

"Oh, for heaven's sake! This is getting downright eerie."

"For a minute there, I thought maybe you'd been studying up."

"No, thank you. And by the way, you don't look half bad yourself."

He instinctively stretched to peer into the rearview mirror, wondering what she saw that spurred the comment. He finger combed his hair and readjusted the mirror. "I try."

"Although I do miss seeing you in uniform."

"Please . . ." He groaned. "I've spent so many hours in uniform this week, I don't even want to think about it. Which reminds me, I need to do laundry when I get home tonight."

"Aww, I'm sorry you're having to work such long hours."

He shrugged. "I'm grateful for the overtime. How was your week?"

"Long too. But good. Luke and Jo had their court date with Mateo Friday, so we celebrated with tacos Friday night. In Phee's room, of course."

"That's cool. So everybody was there?" There was no reason he should have been invited to the family event, and he couldn't have come anyway because he was on shift. But he felt mildly jealous to have missed out.

"Everybody was there for tacos, but not the court hearing. That was just the three of them. But Jo said they had a little ceremony and everything. Mateo was so excited. It was really cute to see him strutting around and practicing his new name."

"They changed his name?"

"Well, don't tell Mateo, but apparently that part won't be official for a while. Jo and Luke have to be legal guardians before they could file for a name change on Mateo's behalf. And since they're just adding Luke's last name as a middle name, not changing Mateo's surname, the judge said he can go ahead and start using his new name unofficially now."

"Joanna's legal background must be coming in handy, huh?"

"It is. It was pretty impressive to see her

handle all the details."

"That's really cool. Tell them congratulations. Your whole family."

They rode in silence until he pulled into the driveway of the group home and parked near the main entrance. He cut the engine and wiped his palms on the knees of his jeans. "Well, here we are."

He watched Britt closely, wondering if she felt as nervous as he did. He'd called the office at Hope Village when he got off work yesterday and asked them to be sure Robby got a shower and a clean change of clothes, but he was never sure whether that would actually happen or not. Weekends, they were usually short-staffed.

He went around and opened Britt's door, and they walked into the building side by side. Rafe stopped at the front desk. "Hi, Angie. Is Robby in his room?"

She gave Britt a curious glance before motioning down the hall. "Last I saw him he was in the day room watching the game."

"Okay. Thanks."

Almost without thinking about it, he took Britt's hand as they neared the door to the day room. He wasn't sure if it was to calm the fears he saw in her demeanor — or his own. But she didn't seem to mind and gave his hand a squeeze.

Robby was flopped on a vinyl sofa, his eyes half-mast as if he was either about to go to sleep or had just awakened from a nap. Three other men sprawled in the recliners lined up in front of the big-screen TV. Two of them were engaged in an argument about which channel to watch. They sounded like first graders, and Rafe could imagine Robby jumping into the fray at any moment. If he didn't fall asleep first.

Paul — who had Down syndrome and was probably in his thirties but looked closer to Robby's age — spotted Rafe and his eyes lit up. "It's Robby's brother! Hey, Robby, it's your brother!"

Robby looked up, then sprang from the sofa, tripping on an errant sofa cushion before starting across the room in his staggering gait. "It's Robby's brother!"

Rafe laughed, his throat tight with nerves. "Hey, bud." He hurried toward him, walking faster than necessary. He greeted his brother with their usual long hug, then stood with one arm around Robby's shoulder, supporting and steadying him, not wanting Britt to get the full impact of Robby's disability before she'd had a chance to say hello.

"Rob, this is my friend Britt."

"I had only one pancake. Only one, Rafe.

They said no more."

Britt took half a step forward. She put out her hand for a handshake, but when Robby didn't respond, she touched his wrist briefly. "Hi, Robby. I heard how much you like pancakes."

He drew back and gave her a look that said, rather rudely, "How would *you* know?"

Rafe laughed, but wished he could let go of his brother and hold up Britt, who looked like she needed it more. "Yeah, Rob, I told Britt about you and your pancakes."

"*She* didn't bring me pancakes." Robby glared at Britt. "I don't see pancakes. No pancakes." His voice escalated the way it did before a full-on tantrum.

"I'm sorry." Britt spoke to Robby, then threw Rafe a look of desperation. "Maybe . . . we can bring some next time we come."

"No! Next time is not good. Pancakes *right* now."

"I'm sorry."

"Not next time. Now."

"Shut up about the pancakes," Paul shouted from across the room.

"Yeah, shut up about the pancakes," Gregory, the newest resident, chimed from his spot in front of the television.

"You shut up!" Robby yelled back.

"Hey, hey . . . Come on, Rob." Rafe ducked to wedge his shoulder under his brother's armpit and deftly turned him toward the hallway. "Let's go show Britt that puzzle you were working on in your room."

"It broke. That nurse broke it. It's back in the box."

"That's okay, we can start all over and do it again. Or maybe pick out a new one?"

"I don't wanna new one. I want pancakes."

"Shut up about the pancakes," Paul and Gregory yelled in unison.

Rafe couldn't help but laugh. But the look of impending panic on Britt's face sobered him quickly.

"Hey, Rob. Let's go back and show Britt your room. She hasn't seen those new Spider-Man sheets, remember?"

"They're not new. No. Not new."

"Well, they're *pretty* new."

"They're not pretty. They're Spider-Man."

That got a smile from Britt, and Rafe's pulse settled back nearer to normal. He started walking, guiding Robby, and motioning with his chin for Britt to follow.

In Robby's room — which, thankfully, smelled decent — he and his brother sat side-by-side on the Spider-Man sheets, and Britt sat across from them at Robby's desk.

"I like the sheets, Robby. Spider-Man is

294

cool." She glanced at the clock, calculating, Rafe guessed, how long before they could get the heck out of Dodge.

He threw her a smile meant to encourage, but she looked near tears. Best get her out of here sooner rather than later. He always forgot that he'd become a bit immune to the awkwardness of this place and the people who lived here. Britt lived in a world where too many Robbys were hidden away in places like this. Indeed, he sometimes felt guilty that his brother was here. Until he remembered that caring for Robby was a 24-7 job. And he already had a job. An important one. And these days, *two* jobs.

For the next half hour, he grasped for things to talk about that would magically connect Robby and Britt. She held her own, but as hard as she tried to work with him, Robby was having none of it.

Rafe sighed. He should have anticipated that his brother wouldn't like someone else in the room — in the *world* — vying for his attention.

Britt cast about the room, her eyes landing on a poster on the wall. "I like your lion poster, Robby."

He looked from Britt to the poster and back. Then squinted, staring very obviously at her chest. "You got fur. Lions got fur."

Britt's brow knit, and she followed his gaze to the front of her blouse. Laughing, she pulled the fabric out and picked off a clump of fuzz. "Wow. You have good eyes." She held the tiny clump out to Robby, catching Rafe's eyes before turning back to his brother. "This is from my cat, Melvin. He's black-and-white, and he sheds all over the place."

"I want a cat. Rafe, I want a cat."

Rafe didn't miss Britt's almost imperceptible cringe, probably afraid she'd started another tantrum. "That would be cool, buddy, but I don't think they'll let you have a cat here."

"But I want a cat. I want a black-and-white cat. Right here." Robby patted the space between them on his mattress.

"We'll see. But right now, I need to get Britt home. She turns into a pumpkin if she doesn't get home in time."

"Like Cinderella."

"Yep, like Cinderella." He breathed easier. Tantrum averted. "Do you want to go back down and watch the game?"

"They're fighting. Those guys."

Rafe cupped a hand to his ear. "I don't hear anything. I think they're done fighting now. Let's go on down."

He rose and pulled his brother up beside

him. Robby did an awkward hop trying to get his balance. Rafe turned to Britt. "Do you want to just meet me in the car?"

"*I* want to meet you in the car."

It took Rafe by surprise. Robby usually fought leaving the grounds. On days when Rafe had to accompany him to an appointment, Robby was surly and uneasy until he was safely back at the home. Apparently jealousy was a stronger emotion than fear.

Rafe gripped his brother's shoulder. "You can meet me in the car another time, okay, buddy? You don't want to miss the rest of the game, do you?"

"The rest of the game, the rest of the game," Robby singsonged.

Britt gave an awkward wave. "It was nice to meet you, Robby."

Robby grunted and took a giant, gangling step toward the door. Rafe looked over his shoulder and mouthed, "See you in the car?"

She nodded, her expression inscrutable.

It wasn't inscrutable ten minutes later when he opened the car door. Britt's cheeks were wet with tears, which she tried unsuccessfully to brush away before he could see.

"I'm sorry." He climbed behind the wheel. "I'm so sorry, Britt. I know that wasn't easy for you. Maybe it was . . . too soon. Please don't take it personally that my brother was rude. You were amazing with him. You couldn't have been better. It's just the way he is and —"

"No. No, Rafe. That's not why I'm crying. Not at all. I'm just . . ." She took a jagged breath. "I'm just so sad for you. It breaks my heart."

"Hey . . ." Her emotion — and her words — caught him by surprise. He reached for her hand and twined his fingers with hers. "It's okay. I've had a few years to get used to it."

"But . . . do you just accept what happened, Rafe? Or . . . doesn't it sometimes make you mad? Like, it's not fair that God would let that happen to your brother? I'm sorry, but it makes me a little mad. That God would allow that."

"Oh, it makes me mad sometimes. But it's not God I'm mad at."

"Then who?"

"Me. Myself. I." This was not the conversation he'd expected to have with her today.

"What? Why would you say that?"

He raked a hand through his hair. "You don't know the whole story, Britt. Robby's whole story . . . *My* story."

"Then . . . tell me. What am I missing?"

CHAPTER 26

"What is it, Rafe?" His complexion had a gray pallor to it that frightened Britt. "Can you tell me? Please, you're scaring me."

He gave a humorless laugh. "You won't like me quoting him, but a certain you-know-who said that a half-truth is the most cowardly of lies."

"What half-truth are we talking about?"

He closed his eyes briefly before looking back down at her. "I don't want you to think I've ever out-and-out lied to you, Britt. But I guess there's something to that truth, whole truth, and nothing but the truth thing they make people swear in court."

"So . . . what don't I know?" She held her breath. And prayed. *Please, God. I already love him. Don't let this be bad . . .*

"First of all, you need to quit thinking of me as a hero . . . that night you called when Phee was in trouble. You've thanked me a dozen times and your sisters almost that many. I am no hero, Britt."

She shook her head. "I don't understand. Of course you are."

"I was more scared that night than I've maybe *ever* been on a call."

"What? Why? You didn't sound scared. You sounded calm and completely in control. You — your voice — was the only thing that kept me from totally freaking out."

"Sorry to disappoint you, but it was all a charade."

"How could that be a charade? You told me what I needed to do and it was exactly right. I'm . . . confused."

"It was a charade because I was terrified."

"There's nothing . . . unheroic about being terrified. It wouldn't be called courage if you were doing something that didn't scare you at least a little."

"Oh, I've handled a lot of hard calls. I've removed dead bodies from mangled vehicles and walked through fire. And yeah, I was scared. But not terrified. I live in fear of getting the call I got that night . . . when they transferred you to me. The only thing worse would be if it wasn't . . . on the phone."

"But why? That makes no sense."

He closed his eyes again. "It makes sense when you know . . . the whole truth."

"So tell me the whole truth, because I'm confused right now."

"Britt, Robby is the way he is — brain damaged — because he was deprived of oxygen when he was born."

She nodded slowly. "You've told me that."

"Yes, but I didn't tell you that it was my fault."

"What do you mean?"

"I was there when my mom went into labor. I was there when she was screaming in pain, calling out for help."

Rafe had told her all of this before. "Go on . . ."

"Ma told me years later that she crawled to the phone — most phones had cords back then, remember" — he shot her a smile he wasn't feeling. "She managed to call 911 before she passed out."

Britt shook her head, overwhelmed with what he must have been through. "How awful, Rafe. I . . . can't even imagine."

"I did nothing, Britt. *Nothing.* I cowered in a corner shaking like a bowl of Jell-O. I — Knowing what I know now, I realize I was probably in shock. But that's no excuse. I did *nothing.* Do you understand? My mom could have died. My brother could have been stillborn." He scrubbed his face with his hands. "Sometimes I think it might have been better if he had. But the point is . . . the awful *whole truth* is that it's my fault. If I'd just done something . . . anything . . ."

"Rafe. You were ten." Did he really think he was responsible? "You couldn't have known."

"Why didn't I call 911 for Ma? I knew about *that* at ten. I just — It was like I was paralyzed. I couldn't move."

"Anyone would have felt the same. *I* felt that way when I found Phee bleeding all over the kitchen floor."

"Yes, but you *did* something. You called. You got the help she needed."

She made her voice stern. "I was twenty-four, Rafe. Not ten. I knew where babies came from. It was my sister, not my mom. It's totally different. Can't you see that?"

"I just —" He swore under his breath. "I play that scene over and over, and it kills me that I can't go back and change it. Fix it. If only I could go back, knowing what I know now. *Everything* would be different. I could have gotten him out — Robby — before he'd been without oxygen for so long. Thirty seconds, just thirty seconds, might have changed the entire course of my family's history."

Everything started to become clear to her.

"Do you blame yourself for your dad leaving?"

"I don't know . . . Maybe not directly." He rubbed his face again. "But he left because of Robby. And that was my fault. Mom grew bitter . . . because of Robby. So in a way, yes! It *is* my fault! All of it. And . . . rationally, I know that I was just a kid. I think, in my heart of hearts — except for Robby — I know these things weren't *entirely* my fault. But, *no one* — not Ma, not Dad, not *one* soul — has ever said that. Has ever absolved me of that guilt. And if *they* can't . . ." He shook his head, looking hopeless. "You know, the Bible says the heart is deceitful above all things. So maybe my heart of hearts is wrong. And maybe I *am* to blame, even if it wasn't intentional. And I swear it wasn't. I wasn't jealous of him or —"

"Rafe!" She could scarcely believe the load he'd carried all these years. "Rafe, stop it. You can't take on that kind of guilt. Surely you understand that. You can't be serious that no one ever reassured you that it wasn't your fault?"

He shook his head. "No one — not Ma, not my father, not the men who took Ma in the ambulance. When I was a little older, I had a sense that . . . that what I did wasn't so . . . unusual. I mean, I was a kid. But no adult ever confirmed that for me. I even went to a counselor once, when I was eighteen, and she just wanted to know" — he raised his voice in a falsetto — " 'So how did that make you feel?' But you'd think when I said it made me feel *guilty,* that she might have offered some . . . consolation."

"She must have? She had to!"

He kept shaking his head.

"Oh, Rafe. That's awful. Oh, she *should* have."

"Yeah, but . . . I don't know, you read all the time about kids who are heroes. Kids who deliver babies in elevators and lift cars off of people . . . stuff like that. So why couldn't *I* have been a hero? Why couldn't I have been a hero when my brother needed a hero?"

"Rafe. Stop. Those hero kids are one in a million. Why do you think they make the news?" Her voice rose an octave. "You were just being a kid. A normal kid. You responded exactly like ninety-nine out of a hundred ten-year-olds would have responded." She put an arm around him and stroked his back as if he were ten again. "And I'm saying it now and I want you to hear me! What happened to Robby was not your fault. Oh, Rafe . . . how could you have believed that all this time? It wasn't your fault, Rafe. I'm so sorry no one ever said those words to you."

He said nothing, but he reached over his shoulder and gripped her hand against his back as if it were a lifeline.

After a few minutes — in a silence that felt holy — she dared to speak. "You know, someone also said — and it was *not* you-know-who — that you will know the truth, and the truth will set you free."

He smiled. "Yeah, I know that one. I guess I just need to start living it."

She took his hand. "Please, Rafe. Know that you can *always* tell me the truth. The whole truth. I . . . don't want a relationship that is any other way."

"I don't either, Britt. I truly don't. But . . . it's a hard habit to get out of. Especially when the biggest lies are the ones you've told yourself."

"I understand. But can I have permission to call you on it when I see that you're buying into the lie?"

"Will you be gentle about it? Please?"

She laid her palm on the side of his cheek. "I promise."

"So, you're saying the whole thing with Phee scared you because it took you back to what happened with Robby?" Britt squeezed his hand and shifted in the car seat beside him. They'd been sitting here for almost an hour. The sun had slipped behind the row of trees bordering the group home's property, and he'd finally turned on the ignition to run the heater when he noticed she was shivering.

"Yes, that was part of it. A big part. But more, I think, because it took me back to a time when I felt utterly helpless." He was beyond ready to change the subject, but he wanted her to be the one to do it. She needed to feel like all her questions had been answered. Because she, with her simple words, had offered him an absolution that no one else — save God Himself — had been able to offer. And his heart felt lighter than it had since the night he'd given it to Christ as a searching college kid.

She nodded. "I can understand that, I guess. I felt helpless with Phee. Until you came on the line."

He held up a hand.

"I know, I know. You're not a hero. Blah blah blah."

He freed one hand and tweaked her nose. "I'm not. But I love you for thinking I am."

They both stilled, realizing the implications of what he'd said . . . *I love you* . . . It was true. He'd known for a while now. But he hadn't thought it fair to declare it when she hadn't met Robby yet. And when she didn't know the whole truth about Rafe Stuart.

But she'd met Robby now. And she knew everything. And she was still right here beside him, looking like she might feel the same about him. And he loved her even more for it.

He scooted closer, leaned across the console and stroked her face, then cradled it between his hands. "I didn't want it to be so . . . casual when I first said those words. I didn't want there to be any doubt. But it's true. I love you, Britt. I *love* you."

"Rafe . . . I love you too." Her voice was barely a whisper. But in that whisper, he heard everything he'd longed for from her since that day she'd approached him in the hospital to say thank you.

Their kiss now was different from the ones that had come before. Sweeter, more serious, even as it was wonderfully playful. A seal on a promise they were making in this unlikeliest of moments. A promise for the future. The kiss deepened, mutually, but stirring feelings in Rafe that he knew oughtn't yet be awakened. He gently pulled away. "I love you. And I need to take you home."

She nodded in a way that said she understood. He settled back behind the wheel and buckled up. She did the same. Once they were on the road out to the cottages, he took her hand across the console, stroking her thumb, stealing glances of her face in the darkness of the car.

"So . . . what are we going to do about it?" he asked.

"About?" Her tone said she thought she knew what he was asking but didn't want to risk guessing wrong.

"About the fact that we are in love and we can barely find a minute to see each other."

"I think we are going to become best friends with our phones and laptops. My dad had this saying — and *please* don't tell me it was a Mark Twain quote . . . but Daddy always says, absence makes the heart grow fonder. If what we have is real, Rafe, we'll take what we can get and we'll make the best of it until our circumstances change."

"I know you're right . . . your dad is right . . . but I don't have to like it."

"Would it . . . cause issues if I come with you when you visit Robby? Not all the time," she added quickly. "But like we did

today. Then we can steal some time together."

"And some kisses?"

"Yes. Definitely some kisses."

"You don't mind coming with me to see
him?"

"I'm guessing it will get easier. And if you
and I are going to be a thing, your brother
needs to get used to it."

Rafe laughed. "We *are* going to be a thing.
And he'll adjust."

"Now, I just need to meet your mom."
She grinned up at him.

He held his hand up like a stop sign.
"Let's take one day at a time, okay?"

"That's not . . . another secret is it?"

"No. I promise. There's more to tell about
my mom's situation, but I'm *not* hiding
anything from you. I just didn't want to
burden you with her problems."

"You can tell me when you're ready. But I
really would like to meet her, Rafe."

"I'll see what I can arrange. And don't
worry. Ma will love you."

"She won't be jealous?"

He couldn't tell if she was teasing or not.
"No. She's not like that. But I've got to say,
I'm not too crazy about having to share you
with everybody."

"I know. Me neither." She reached for his

hand and squeezed it again. "Deep breaths.
We can do this."

CHAPTER 27

Britt rang the doorbell, then let herself into Phee and Quinn's house as had become her routine. She rounded the corner into the kitchen to put away the groceries she'd brought and nearly jumped out of her skin to see Phee standing there, fully dressed, stirring something on the stove.

"What are you doing? Phee!" She rushed to her sister's side.

Phee beamed but quickly grabbed the handle of the oven door and leaned heavily against Britt. "I guess I'm not quite as steady on my feet as I thought."

"What are you doing out of bed anyway? Quinn is going to have your neck!"

"Don't be so sure about that." Britt whirled to see Quinn standing in the doorway between the kitchen and dining room. He wore the same goofy grin that Phee had greeted her with.

"You guys! What is going on?"

"I got a reprieve." Phee's eyes misted. "The placenta previa is resolving itself!"

"Seriously?" Britt looked between Phee and Quinn. "You . . . don't have to be in bed anymore?"

Phee sighed. "Dr. Hinsen still wants me in bed *most* of the time, but I get to try being up for a short time each day."

Quinn came to the stove and took the spoon from Phee's hand. "But not to cook. That was staged just for your benefit, Britt."

Phee laughed weakly. "Isn't it great?"

"So . . . everything just . . . resolved? On its own?"

Phee nodded. "Dr. Hinsen said it happens sometimes. I'm still having trouble believing it myself. But I haven't had any bleeding for several weeks, and he told told me at my last appointment that he thought it might be resolving. Yesterday, he saw a measurable difference. So" — she spread her arms wide — "ta-da! I may still have to have a C-section, but he said if it continues to resolve he might even let me try a normal delivery. Please, please pray for that, sis."

"Oh, I will! This is unbelievable!" Britt hugged her, then pulled away. "It's so weird to even see you out in this part of the house."

"I know. I feel like I'm walking around in

a foreign country."

Quinn set the pan of soup they'd been stirring in the sink. "Yeah, well, just wait till next week after we've moved."

"I can hardly wait!" But Phee looked exhausted just speaking the words.

Britt wasn't sure it was a great idea to try to move into the new house while Phee was on bed rest, but maybe this latest news was confirmation that Quinn knew just what would cheer his wife. The plan was for Britt to be on Phee-watch Saturday morning while Quinn, Luke, Jo, Mateo, and whatever other crew they could assemble loaded the house up — all but Phee's room. They'd get everything moved over, then set up the master bedroom, complete with a new bed that had already been delivered. Then they'd bring Phee over, and Britt would help her get settled while the rest of the crew set up furniture and unpacked boxes.

"It sure will be nice having you on the property again." Not to mention how much easier it would be for her.

Phee frowned. "I know it's been a pain for you and Jo to have to drive back and forth. I just hope you know that you guys have been a lifeline for us. I'm sorry it's been such a hassle."

"Stop it. Not another word." Britt shook

her finger. "You know we'd do anything for you guys — and this baby." She put a hand on Phee's belly and was pleased to realize that she meant every word. Somewhere along the way, the resentment she'd harbored had dried up. And she was pretty sure that a certain tall, blond, and handsome man was mostly responsible.

"I second everything Phee said." Quinn took his wife by the shoulders. "Now, I hate to put a damper on things, but the show's over and you've been up long enough, Mama. You'd better get yourself and our baby back to bed."

"I know, I know."

"I'll go straighten your bed." Britt started for the bedroom, but her cell phone buzzed in her pocket and she stopped in the middle of the hallway to answer it. "Hello, this is Britt." She listened to the near frantic voice on the other end of the line, trying not to roll her eyes. "I'll be there shortly, I promise."

She ended the call and turned to Phee and Quinn with a sigh. "Those guests I just checked in locked their keys inside the cottage and are wondering if *someone* could come and let them in."

Quinn shooed her off. "I can cover here. You go. Maybe we should revisit putting keypad locks on those doors?"

"Maybe. But I don't mind. Remember Jo's on for tomorrow, but I'll be back Friday."

"And then Saturday, right?"

"Of course. I won't forget." She hurried back to her car, in awe that things had changed so quickly — seemingly overnight — for Phee. It would still be a long two months before the baby was here — assuming Phee went full-term — but what a relief that she'd be able to get up and move around a little. And being in the new house would be fun for all of them. She imagined Phee bossing her and Jo around from her bed, instructing them where to hang pictures and how the furniture should be arranged in each room. For the first time, she could see a little light at the end of the tunnel. For all of them, of course, but especially for her and Rafe.

Her thoughts quickly turned — as they did almost constantly these days — to Rafe and the change their relationship had undergone since that night they'd told each other "I love you." They'd texted a dozen times a day since that night. And she'd read every text at least a dozen times after it pinged her phone.

She hadn't yet told her sisters about what

had happened between her and Rafe. Partly because she knew they were both pre-occupied with their own lives — and rightly so. They both had major things going on in their lives right now. And when she did tell them, she wanted them to fully celebrate with her.

But part of her reason for not wanting to tell them yet was that she cherished this secret they had between them — Rafe and her — that no one else in the world knew yet. It was precious beyond belief, and Britt didn't want the feeling ever to end.

When she rehearsed how she would tell her sisters, she knew it sounded sappy and a little bit high-school. Though she knew her sisters were deeply in love with the men they'd chosen, they were both more practical women than she was. And she wondered sometimes if they would even understand how deep this love she felt for Rafe was. When her daydreams went south, she imagined Phee, and Jo especially, might accuse her of feeling nothing more than "puppy love" for Rafe. But she knew differently.

She and Rafe had talked just last night on one of their too-rare phone conversations, how if they were married, at least they'd see each other every night and early every morning. Rafe had been the one to say it, but she'd thought it many times. And it thrilled her that he was thinking the same way. And yet, they both agreed they didn't want to rush things. They wanted to be sure that what they had was not only real — of which Britt had no doubt — but also part of God's plan for them.

"I almost wish I hadn't even said anything," Rafe had said. "About marriage, I mean."

"What do you mean?"

"Doesn't every girl dream of a big surprise, Instagram-worthy proposal?"

"Not this girl."

"Really?"

"No. I haven't posted anything on Instagram for weeks. Well, except for what I put on the Airbnb's account. And that's purely work stuff. Pretty pictures of the rooms and the property. Nothing personal."

"It looks good too. I found it the other night when work was slow. I could see your touches all over it. You and Melvin. And his fur."

She laughed. "Yeah, even people who say they couldn't stay in Near Cottage because of Melvin still love seeing him on the feed."

"He *is* pretty photogenic. I'd be jealous if he had a sexy voice like mine."

"I take it you've never heard him meow?"

she teased.

He lowered his voice and crooned, "I'm not the least bit threatened."

She smiled now, remembering the confidence in his tone. She could almost see him swagger. She missed him. Wished he could be there to help with the move Saturday. The day promised to be a party. But Rafe had to work. She'd never considered, until recently, the danger Rafe put himself in every day on duty. So much could happen while he responded to a car accident, a house fire, a break-in. When she'd said as much, he responded by telling her that he felt pretty safe in the sleepy town of Langhorne, "where the most exciting calls we receive are suspected 'break-ins' that end up being some ornery cat knocking over a turquoise vase."

Again, the memory made her smile. If she'd known that embarrassing day that one of those officers would end up being the love of her life . . .

She eased her Escape into the space beside their guests' large SUV. The woman — Kathy according to her Airbnb profile — was waiting in front of the cottage, jacketless, blowing on her hands to keep warm.

Britt jumped out and hurried toward her,

key at the ready. "I'm so sorry you had to wait."

"Oh goodness, it's not your fault. I can't believe I was so stupid to lock myself out."

"No problem. I didn't have to come far." She unlocked the door and pushed it open for the guest. "Do you want to double-check that the key is here before I leave?"

"Oh, that's okay. I know exactly where I left it. My boyfrien — er, *husband* — is waiting for me at the casino. I just ran back to get some more cash." She gave a nervous laugh. "Unlike yesterday, we're not having such a lucky day."

"Oh, dear . . ." Britt started to say she was sorry, but she couldn't muster much sympathy, especially given that right now, the stupid casino was the main reason she and Rafe had such limited time together.

"Yeah, tell me about it. We pawned my diamond nose ring this morning." She rubbed at the left side of her nose. "But, hey, there's always tomorrow. His luck eventually changes. I was tired of that ring anyway." Again that nervous laugh. "He'd just better not touch these earrings." She tugged at one of the diamond studs. "My grandmother gave me these, God rest her soul."

Britt bit her tongue and looked away

briefly. "Well . . . if you're sure then. Is there anything else you need before I go?"

"No, I think we're fine. Thanks again and sorry for the bother."

Britt could only nod over the knot of anger in her throat. They occasionally hosted guests who just came into town for a weekend of gambling and drinking, but this couple had been here since yesterday and were booked for three more days. She and her sisters were always grateful for multiple-day bookings, but they weren't crazy about renting to casino customers — or to unmarried couples for that matter. Britt had to laugh at Kathy's slipup. Still, the sisters had decided early on that they couldn't judge their guests. The Airbnb provided a place for people to sleep and shower, and what their guests did while they were in town — as long as it wasn't illegal — was really none of their business. As Daddy always said, "You can't legislate morality."

But she and her sisters had prayed for their future guests from the very beginning. And since Phee had been on bed rest, she'd made it her personal ministry to pray weekly for the guests who would come through their doors in the week ahead.

Britt knew she couldn't fix the problems of everyone who darkened the doors of their

Airbnb, but sometimes she *wished* she could. She backed her car around, shooting up a rather reluctant prayer for the couple staying in the cottage. How that woman could be so blind to her issues when, to Britt, they were as plain as . . . well, the nose ring on her face.

Replaying her conversations with Rafe about the trouble his mom had gotten into, thanks to gambling, Britt tightened her grip on the steering wheel, her jaw tense. She'd asked to meet Rafe's mom, but it wouldn't be easy to guard her tongue — and her temper — when that day came, because it made her furious to think what his mother's mistake had cost Rafe. And her.

She wasn't sure she would have been as forgiving as Rafe if it had been Daddy who'd wracked up a gambling debt — something she couldn't even fathom. *Forgive my judgmental heart, Lord.*

And yet, selfishly, she couldn't help but wonder if Rafe's mom's debts would follow them into marriage someday — if marriage was what God had in mind for her and Rafe.

Still, thoughts of a future that didn't include Rafe were too depressing to entertain.

They'd dreamed together about the future, and they'd talked around the edges of the possibility of marriage. Feeling as they did about each other, Britt couldn't imagine that marriage *wasn't* in God's plan for their lives. But incidents like this one raised tiny doubts.

CHAPTER 28

"The cake was good, Ma." Rafe pushed his plate away and patted his belly. "I'd have another piece if I didn't have to go to work. But maybe you could take one to Robby."

"He doesn't need cake. He was getting chubby last time I saw him. Those nurses have enough trouble getting him to cooperate. They don't need him twenty pounds heavier."

"Robby isn't in any danger of getting fat, Ma. He's just growing. And getting some muscle."

She frowned. "I don't care. I made the cake for you."

"Do you care if *I* take him a piece?"

She worried the edge of the tablecloth and refused to meet his gaze. "You do what you want. I don't care."

"Thanks, Ma." He straightened in his chair. "Listen, there's something I wanted to talk to you about."

That got her attention. She tipped her head and studied him.

"I've met someone." He plunged in. "A girl. Her name is Britt and I want you to meet her."

"A girl?"

"A woman, actually. Britt is twenty-four. She runs an Airbnb with her sisters."

"Air-what? I don't know what that is."

He explained it to her. "You've probably seen the signs to their place out on Poplar Brook Road."

"Not that I remember. Now, where did you meet this girl?"

He made a point of checking the time on his phone. "It's kind of a long story, and I need to leave for work in a few minutes, but I'll tell you next time I see you. I just wanted to see if we could find a time for you and Britt to meet. I was thinking I could take the two of you out for dinner some night?"

"No, that's too expensive. You've done enough for me. Let me make dinner." She hesitated. "But . . . it'll have to be after my next paycheck."

"I thought you just got one. The next one won't be until the end of February, right? I don't really want to wait that long." He shot his mom a telling grin. "This girl is pretty special."

To his shock, Ma burst into tears.

He stared at her. "What's wrong?"

"Oh, Rafe . . ." She pulled a napkin from the napkin holder in the middle of the table and dabbed at her eyes. "Here you've met a nice girl you want me to meet, but you must be so ashamed of me. I've made such a mess of things for you."

"Ma . . . Don't worry about it. We'll get it paid off. It may take a while but we'll —"

"No . . . You don't understand. It's never enough. Never. He says he needs the money right away. Before the end of the month."

"What? You just paid him, right?" That's what she'd told him. He'd deposited seven thousand dollars in her account and she told him she'd written the man a check.

"No, he says he needs the rest of the money before February first."

"*Who* says that?"

"The man I borrowed it from."

"He can't do that, Ma. You let me talk to him."

"No. And he said he *could* require me to pay it and . . . that they could throw me in jail if he doesn't get the money on time."

"You didn't have a contract with this man, right?" He kicked himself now that he hadn't handled the payment himself. But Ma already felt so humiliated by the debt that he hadn't had the heart to make her feel even worse. And back then, he hadn't begun to suspect that this was more than just a friend loaning a friend money, foolish though that was. But it was becoming clear that this was far beyond that. It had to be a scam.

"No, he was so sure I'd double the money at the casino that he said we didn't have time for that. A contract. But I promised I'd pay it back, Rafe. I gave him my word."

"I understand. And if it's legit, we'll honor that. But not on his terms. You've already paid him well over half of what you borrowed."

"Yes, but there is interest."

An exorbitant percentage of interest from what she'd told him. Something was fishy about the whole thing and he wanted her free of it. "Listen, Ma, you don't need to worry for another minute. If there was no contract, nobody can send you to jail."

"How can you be sure? He said it's a serious offense. If I don't pay it off by his deadline."

Blood pulsed in his ears and Rafe clenched his fists. "He's the one who ought to be in jail. He not only took advantage of you, Ma, he lied to you. And now he's making threats. *That's* illegal."

"But I owe him the money fair and square. It was my fault in the first place."

"What's this guy's name anyway? Is he still in town?" Rafe's blood was near boiling.

"He must be. He showed up here yesterday wanting me to write him a check for the full amount."

"You *didn't,* did you?"

"No, of course not. I told him I didn't have that kind of money in my account. But . . ." Ma hung her head. "I gave him five hundred dollars. Cash. The last of my paycheck."

"Ma! What were you thinking? Did you get a receipt? Do you have the canceled check from before?" Maybe he could track down the man.

"No." She started crying again. "There was no check. I'm sorry I told you that. I . . . I paid him cash. Like he asked. But, Rafe, he said he'd be back every day until the loan is paid off. I told him —"

Rafe scraped back his chair. It was all he could do to keep from hurling the thing through the window. "You paid him over seven thousand dollars in cash? Tell me where to find that piece of dirt. What's his name, Ma? He has no business coming here and threatening you!"

She stumbled to her feet and grabbed his arm. "You can't talk to him, Rafe."

"Why not? I can and I will. He has no right to threaten you like that, Ma. Now what is his name?"

"No! Please, Rafe! You can't!" The words came out on a sob.

He didn't think he'd seen his mother so scared since the night Robby was born. "Ma? What is going on? What aren't you telling me?"

She stuttered to get the words out. "He-He said he'd *kill* me if I didn't pay back the rest of the loan."

He put an arm around his mom, doing his best to calm down. "Ma, listen to me. That man has no authority to make a claim like that. And believe me, he is not going to kill you while you still owe him money. He's just trying to scare you into giving him every last dime. And that kind of threat is a crime. He's the one who should be arrested. And I intend to —"

"No. It's not just that, Rafe. He said —" She dissolved into sobs again, weeping uncontrollably.

Alarmed, he put an arm around her, led her back to her chair at the table, and helped her sit. "Tell me, Ma. What did he say?"

"He said he'd hurt *you*!"

"Me?" Rafe almost laughed. "How? I'm not too worried."

"I . . . I told him you were a police officer. He said if you —"

"Wait a minute . . . Why'd you tell him that?"

"I wanted to scare him. I thought he'd leave me alone if he thought my son could arrest him. I thought —"

"Ma, I want you to tell me this man's name right now. In fact . . ." He rose again and grabbed his jacket off the back of the chair, shrugging into it. "I think you should come with me down to the station and tell the chief everything you've just told me."

For the first time, Rafe felt hope that Ma might be able — *he* might be able — to get out from under this crushing debt. If the man had coerced Ma in the first place, and now he was threatening her if she didn't pay back the money in a completely unreasonable amount of time . . . "What is his name, Ma?"

"I can tell you but . . ." The tears started again.

"What is it?" He worked to keep his tone even.

"I don't think he told me the truth about anything. Not even his name. I've been looking on the Internet, trying to find out something about him, and there isn't anyone on there with that name."

"Tell me the name." It came out too gruffly. "Please, Ma. You've got to help me with this."

"It's Buck. Buck Obermueller. But there isn't anybody out there with that name. I've looked."

"Buck sounds like a nickname. Did he give you any other name? A real name?"

"No. Just Buck."

"Ma . . ." He put his face in his hands.

"I didn't even know his *last* name for the first week we dated." She hung her head like before and reached a hand to the back of her chair to steady herself.

"Dated? What do you mean?"

"Don't be ridiculous, son. You know what dating is. He was . . . my boyfriend." She frowned. "Not for long, thank God."

Rafe shook his head. He couldn't even think about his mom with a man. He could barely remember when Ma and his dad had been together. To think of her having a "boyfriend" just seemed . . . wrong. But he shoved that aside for now. Far more important things were at stake.

"I want you to come with me down to the station. This guy has crossed a line. He

330

needs to be stopped."

"Maybe we could have your girl over for supper tomorrow night. It wouldn't be anything fancy, but I have some leftover chicken and noodles in the —"

"Ma . . . Ma!" Rafe shook his head. She was in complete denial. "We'll worry about that later. We have more important things to deal with right now."

Britt closed her laptop and rubbed her eyes. She'd spent more than an hour on Airbnb bookings and business stuff, but at least most of the paperwork wouldn't have to be done again until the end of next month. Usually Joanna handled the paperwork, but Britt had agreed to take it over until after the wedding so Jo could concentrate on planning and preparation for her happy day.

Jo still hadn't discovered their little secret project that was taking shape down at the construction company's shop. She and Rafe had missed each other coming and going there the last few days, but the last time she'd been out there to help, everything was coming together nicely. Quinn and Luke had decided not to assemble things up in the clearing until next month, but it was supposed to stay cold for at least the coming week or two, so who knew when they'd be able to set everything up. The wedding wasn't until May, so they had plenty of time, but Luke hinted that he wanted to surprise Jo with the reveal the first day they had nice weather.

Smiling, Britt tucked the checkbook and ledgers into the desk drawer. Though she hated the business part of running an Airbnb more than any other task, she still found satisfaction in seeing the figures on paper — or the computer screen, as it usually was.

She wondered if Jo would even have time to resume the bookkeeping after she was married. Between her job and Mateo, she was going to be busy. The sisters had talked about eventually hiring a business manager. But for now, there was no way they could afford that.

At least they had enough bookings to keep the bills paid. That had been their prayer for many months, and like Phee had said, there was no reason to get greedy. They had a lovely place to live and a steady income. Britt hoped Mom somehow knew, from heaven, the joys and provision her little inheritance had provided the three of them.

She slipped on her jacket to walk down to the mailbox. Having their box at the end of the lane had given them a good excuse to get some exercise every day, though Jo often complained that the mail wasn't usually worth getting. And too often, one of them cheated and picked up the mail on the way home from town.

She was halfway down the lane when Rafe's tone pinged her phone. He was later than usual this evening, but she wasn't worried. Their phone calls and texts had been sweet and full of longing, but she didn't fret when he didn't have time to call.

She stopped in the lane and read his message.

"Hey, sorry. I'm not going to have time to call tonight."

She voiced her reply and watched the letters appear on the screen: "It's ok. Is everything all right?"

"Just please pray for Ma. Still dealing with junk from the stupid gambling debts."

She voice-texted back: "I'm so sorry. I'm praying. Will miss talking to you, but I understand. Let me know how things are when you can."

"I will."

A few seconds passed and then another message pinged. "I love you."

She stared at the screen, and a slow smile came as she texted back — with her fingers this time: "I love you too."

Though they'd spoken those words almost every time they'd talked since the first night they'd declared their love for each other, he'd never texted the words before. Seeing them in print on her phone warmed her heart. She stared at them for a long time, praying God wouldn't ask her to give up Rafe. Especially not for a reason that wasn't even his fault.

She prayed for his mom then, but it was hard to muster much compassion or sincerity. And she hated feeling that way toward the woman who'd given birth to the man she adored. Especially when she hadn't even met her.

CHAPTER 29

Still humming the last song the worship team had sung, Britt noticed the date on her dashboard and sang louder when she realized its significance. Phee's due date was exactly two months from today. There was a time that eight weeks would have seemed like an eternity, but having been through ten weeks of her prescribed bed rest already, eight more weeks seemed like a mere breath. And if Phee went into labor early as the doctor predicted, it was even less. The thought buoyed her, and she sang even louder.

She rounded the curve in the lane to see a blue SUV headed toward her — the couple who'd been staying in the cottage for the last five days. No doubt headed for the casino. The woman, Kathy, waved and smiled from the passenger seat. Ever since Britt had rescued her after Kathy locked her keys in the cottage, she'd been extra friendly whenever they saw each other across the yard or coming up the lane.

As the vehicles passed, Kathy's "husband" kept his eyes on the lane, seemingly unaware there was even another car on the road. Probably trying to figure out how he was going to coerce Kathy into pawning her grandmother's earrings.

According to Kathy's Airbnb profile, she was from Indiana. Britt guessed they were both in their early fifties. The guy's information wasn't on the reservation, but Britt had come to think of him as Mr. Clean. A big guy — probably six foot four, shaved head, and a gold loop in his left ear — he was a dead ringer. He was actually a nice-looking man, but after hearing that he'd pawned Kathy's diamond nose ring while his own earring remained firmly affixed to his ear, Britt had trouble seeing him as attractive in any way.

From her brief conversations with Kathy, it sounded like the couple's sole reason for coming to Cape Girardeau was to gamble. She would never understand how people found that entertaining. Maybe for people like Rafe's mom, it was more about hope. An empty hope, for sure. But still . . .

They were supposed to check out of the cottage before three today. Maybe they'd decided to leave early and had already checked out. Out of money, no doubt. Britt shook her head.

"Forgive me, Lord," she whispered, checking her thoughts. If she didn't get her judgmental attitude under control before she met Rafe's mother, she might accidentally say something she regretted.

She changed into sweats and grabbed a sandwich for lunch, wondering how Rafe's visit with Robby was going. He had to work tonight and tomorrow, but they were both hoping to be at the shop Tuesday night. They'd agreed to go get hot chocolate after, just the two of them, and she couldn't wait. It would be the first time they'd had more than a few minutes together since the night she'd met Robby.

She hoped Rafe didn't suddenly decide Tuesday would be a good time to meet his mom. As much as she wanted to get that over with, she didn't want to sacrifice the time alone with Rafe. They had precious little together as it was.

"Looking good, you two." Quinn waved across the shop to where Rafe and Britt were painting the benches that would go up to the clearing where Luke and Joanna's wedding would be. Rafe sneaked a peek at

Britt, wondering if she was thinking about her own wedding guests sitting on these benches someday.

He hadn't yet updated her on everything that had happened with Ma. He just hoped when he told her about the threats and that Ma had given the guy even more money, she wouldn't decide it wasn't worth it to get involved with him. Right now, he felt like he was keeping an important secret from her, and not the kind she'd be thrilled to learn about when he finally told her.

He'd been on edge most of the night, ruining their last chance to be together this week. But he didn't want to talk to her about Ma's situation in front of the whole family. And tonight, except for Phee and Joanna, who was on duty with Phee, the gang was all here.

Quinn and Luke had ordered pizza for everyone, and they'd sat on high stools around the big work table in the shop, with shop heaters blowing on them from every direction. While they ate, Quinn doled out instructions. They would just about wrap up what they could do here in the shop in another night or two. Then it was a matter of waiting until the weather was nice enough that they could go up to the clearing and install everything.

338

Luke had decided he wanted Joanna there for that. "I don't trust myself to remember exactly where she told me she wants everything."

"Yeah," Mateo piped up. "They're still working on their communication skills."

That cracked everyone up, and Mateo milked his moment in the spotlight for all it was worth. Rafe laughed along with the rest, but every time he was around Mateo, he couldn't help but think of Robby and how things could have been.

When they'd finished their pizza and helped clean up, Rafe and Britt said their goodbyes and headed to his car. "Where do you want to go?" Britt asked.

"I don't care. Wherever you want to. You're not hungry, are you?"

"Are you kidding? After all that pizza?"

"Well, how about I just take you home then?"

"I thought we were going for hot choc —" She narrowed her eyes at him. "Are you okay?"

"Yeah, why?"

"You've just been . . . I don't know . . . cool tonight. And I don't mean *cool* cool but cold. As in distant." She stopped walking and put a hand on his forearm. "Did I do something to upset you?"

Instantly chagrined that he'd made her feel for a minute that his mood was her fault, he pulled her to himself and held her. "No, Britt. Never." He nuzzled the top of her head with his chin, loving the smell of her hair, the feel of her in his arms. "You're the best part of my day. Every day."

"You mean every day I get to see you. Which isn't nearly often enough." She pouted. She leaned into him and held on tight.

"I'm sorry I was moody. I didn't mean to take it out on you. I've just got a lot on my mind."

"So talk to me."

"It's about Ma, mostly."

She pulled away and sought his eyes. "I've been wanting to ask you all night if there's anything new, but I didn't want to ask in front of everyone."

"I appreciate that." He shrugged. "There's really not much new. I went with Ma down to the station, and she gave a description and filed a complaint. But we're going on a description that fits probably half the guys in the casino on any given night. I feel almost guilty because my buddies at the station are spending extra hours watching her house, in case the guy makes good on his threats —"

"What kind of threats?"

"To kill her. To kill me."

"Rafe! What?"

His laughter was sharp. "They're idle threats. Like I told Ma, they need her alive to get the money from her."

"But Rafe! What if they're not?"

"Don't worry. Ma's been staying with me, which" — he gave a dry laugh — "might have something to do with my mood."

"That bad?"

"It's not Ma's fault. She's as antsy as I am to get her back in her own house. The chief really does believe the threats are idle. They see players like this guy work the casinos sometimes. They're just looking for somebody they can control. Sadly, Ma was an easy mark. She said he was her 'boyfriend' for a while. So I guess you were right."

"Oh no . . . I never meant it that way though."

"I know. What makes me sick is that she didn't even know the guy's name."

"At all? Even when they were . . . dating?"

Rafe shook his head. "He went by Buck Obermueller. At least that's what he told Ma. She thinks he was lying about every-thing now. Buck sounds like a nickname to me, and nobody by that name comes up in police records. But like I said, all they have to go on is a description, and it probably matches a dozen guys at the casino and a hundred in this town: Tall, bald, piercings, tattoos. The only good thing that's come —"

"Wait . . ." Britt held up a hand. "You said tall, bald? Like a shaved head?"

"I don't know if he shaved or was just bald. Why?"

"And a pierced ear?" Her voice rose. "A big gold hoop earring in his left ear?"

He cocked his head. "Why are you asking?"

"Rafe, there was a couple staying at the cottage last week, and that's what the guy looked like." Her brow furrowed. "I couldn't say about tattoos. I only ever saw him in their car. A blue SUV. But they were in town to gamble, and the woman he was with — the one who made their reservation — told me he'd made her pawn her diamond nose ring. They were from Indiana — well, at least the woman was. She said in the messages before they checked in that it would be her husband with her, but she slipped up and called him her boyfriend when we were talking once."

He frowned. "Did she ever say his name?"

"If she did, I don't remember. Buck

doesn't sound familiar." She gave a little laugh. "I always thought of him as Mr. Clean because he looked just like the guy on the cleaning bottles. He was nice looking, but kind of rude. Or maybe standoffish is a better term. He never would wave or even look my way if we met on the lane or in front of the cottages."

"How long ago was this?"

"Just a few days. They were booked there for almost a week. I can check the booking information and give you the exact date. And the woman's contact info. Her name was Kathy. I don't remember her last name. It started with an L, I think."

He shrugged. "It might not be anything. But it's worth checking out."

"Do you think your mom is safe?"

"I'm guessing she is, but I'm having her stay with me for a few days. I'm not taking any chances."

"I'm glad."

"She isn't going to sleep until that guy is put behind bars. Or at least run out of town."

She pulled up the app and searched for the info, but Rafe put a gentle hand on hers.

"You'd better check the company's policies. You probably have to go through a special process to share a guest's private info. The guys at the station will know. But if you just give it to me, not only could it get you in trouble, but it likely wouldn't be admissible in court either."

She put a hand to her mouth. "I didn't even think about that. I'm glad you told me before I forwarded the info." She scrolled through the hosting information for a few minutes. "Here it is . . ." She read from the site. "*Data Requests from Law Enforcement.* There's a form you can fill out to request information."

"Great. Can you send me that link?"

"That won't keep the information from being inadmissible?"

"As long as you're not sending me personal information about the woman. Just forwarding the link to a request form shouldn't raise any red flags."

He only hoped this whole mess didn't raise any red flags with the woman he was growing to love more than life itself.

CHAPTER 30

February

February

"Did you hear?" Quinn announced to the motley group gathered outside his house on moving day. "The groundhog saw his shadow last week." Judging by the frown on her brother-in-law's face, he didn't consider this good news.

Britt groaned, her breath forming a cloud in the chill air. "That means six more weeks of winter, right? Well, five now."

Rafe looked skeptical. "I wonder how often that actually pans out."

"Tell you in a minute . . ." Mateo pulled off his gloves and tapped his phone's keyboard. "Thirty-nine percent . . . What? Stupid groundhog is wrong more than he's right. I'm not listening to his prediction."

"Me neither, buddy." Luke put a hand on the back of the kid's neck. "But I predict that if you don't put that phone away and get to work, Quinn won't let you have any of those cookies he brought from the bakery."

Mateo rolled his eyes, but slid the phone back into the front pocket of his hoodie. "So what am I supposed to move?"

Britt hefted a box from a stack next to the front door and loaded it into Mateo's arms. "You can start by carrying this to the truck. And then come back for another one."

"Then wash, rinse, repeat," Quinn said.

"Huh?" Mateo wrinkled his nose. "I don't get it."

The adults laughed, and Luke steered the boy toward the rented moving truck. "It just means you keep coming back for boxes till we're done."

Britt blew on her hands, wishing she'd remembered to grab a pair of gloves, but though it was in the mid-thirties right now, it was supposed to be in the sixties by noon. Quinn and Phee didn't have much furniture, and he estimated they'd be finished unloading at the new house before noon. "Except for the most important thing."

"You'd better mean me." Through the open door, Phee's voice carried from inside the house.

"And *you'd* better not be out of that bed," Quinn hollered back.

"I'm fine."

Quinn gave Britt a pleading look. "Can you go talk to her? Where's Jo?"

"I'm on it. Jo's on her way. She's running a few minutes late." It was Jo's turn to be on Phee-watch and she'd been given the assignment of packing up the master bedroom — under Phee's supervision — while the rest of them loaded the truck.

Phee's spirits had been so much better since the doctor had relaxed her bed-rest rules two weeks ago. She continued to do well and the placenta previa seemed to have, indeed, resolved itself. Her doctor warned them Phee would likely still need a cesarean delivery, but the risks she'd faced earlier were much less now and her mood showed it. With the added excitement of the move, Phee had been positively cheerful the last few days.

Britt found her oldest sister in the dining room dusting the chairs. "Phee, those are just going to get dusty again in the truck. Would you please go get in bed? For your husband's sake?"

Phee affected a pout. "I feel like such a slacker with everybody else working their tails off."

"You have the most important job on earth: keeping that baby safe until it's time for her to come out."

"Or him!" Phee countered. The betting pool was heavy on predictions of a girl — especially since there were three Chandler sisters.

"Now, put down the dust rag, back away from the table, and get yourself in bed." Britt snatched the dust rag from her hand.

"Party pooper." But Phee did as she was asked and headed back to the bedroom.

When Britt was sure her sister was settled, she walked back through a house strewn with moving boxes and partially disassembled furniture. It might have been sad, seeing the house in such disarray, but Quinn and Phee had never planned to live here long-term. Quinn had built this house — with another girlfriend in mind — before he and Phee fell in love, and they'd begun building their house on the Poplar Brook Road property shortly after their wedding.

All Britt could think about was how much easier things would be having Phee right up the lane from her cabin. Phee's doctor — and Quinn — still wanted someone with her, or at least nearby, at all times, but Britt and Jo would be able to run back and forth between the cottage and cabins and get some smaller tasks done while they were on Phee-watch. It had been a long haul, but they were beginning the home stretch now.

And for Britt, that meant one thing: more time with Rafe Stuart.

In the guest room down the hall, Luke and Mateo were working on taking a bed apart. Britt stuck her head in the doorway. "Have you guys seen Rafe?"

Luke hooked a thumb in the direction of the front yard. "He was in the back of the truck last I saw him, supervising the loading."

"Okay. Thanks."

She'd been so happy it worked out for Rafe to be here for moving day, but she hoped they'd be able to find a few minutes alone once the moving was finished. Between his working overtime and her helping Quinn and Phee pack, they'd barely seen each other the past couple of weeks. She missed him. And they had a lot of catching up to do. About his mom and that whole mess and about their future. The closer they came to Phee's due date, the more Britt saw a little light at the end of the tunnel — especially now that she and her sisters would all be back on the property together.

It was hard seeing so little of Rafe. Her daydreams were full of scenarios where he lived here too. Where she saw him every day and woke up beside him every morning. She warmed at the thought and shoved a box into the truck a little harder than necessary, as if that could explain her pink cheeks to anyone who noticed. The truth was, she didn't know how Rafe felt about moving out here if they got married. He was committed to his EMT job, and living here would put him at least ten minutes farther from work.

But if they married and Rafe wanted her to move into town, how could she keep the inn running? With her sisters taking on other responsibilities — a baby and Mateo — it would fall to her to keep doing the bulk of the work. Was that even what she wanted? With Quinn and Phee building their house here, they were all kind of locked into keeping the inn up and running.

Had she been trapped by circumstances once again? Would she always be the one who had to make the sacrifice for what she really wanted and step into a role simply because she was needed?

She brushed the troubling thoughts away, not wanting to ruin a rare day with Rafe. But they niggled at her the rest of the morning. Along with what she knew was the more important question: what *did* she want out of life? And why hadn't she been able to figure that out by now?

By eleven o'clock, they had everything

moved except Phee. The guys put together the new bed in the master bedroom, and Britt and Jo made it up with freshly laundered sheets and then hung sheer white curtains at the windows for privacy. Phee would no doubt choose something different for the room eventually, but for now, the space looked bright and airy.

Mary, Phee's former boss from the flower shop in Langhorne, had sent a cheery bouquet of pink and blue flowers for the occasion. Britt could picture a crib and changing table in the alcove off the bedroom. Phee would be ecstatic to have a new point of view and new inspiration being in their forever house.

Quinn stuck his head in the door. "Shall I go get her? Is everything ready for — Whoa!" His gaze swept the room. "This looks great, guys! I can't wait for Phee to see it!"

"Then go get her!" Britt shooed him off, and she and Jo bustled to put the finishing touches on the room.

Pulling back the curtains, she spotted Rafe with Luke and Mateo, breaking down the huge cardboard boxes. They were in animated conversation, and her heart swelled to see Rafe here at the property fitting in as if he'd always been part of their family.

Please, Lord, could that be part of Your plan?

Rafe hauled another load of cardboard boxes to the waiting truck and loaded them inside. Having promised Robby he'd visit, he'd been afraid he might have to cut out early, but apparently the saying was true: Many hands make light work. He chuckled to himself, wondering if that quote might be from you-know-who. He'd google it later and try it out on Britt if it was.

He looked toward the house, wondering how things were going with her. He'd seen Quinn drive up earlier and help Phylicia out of the car. He assumed that's where Britt was, but he hoped for a chance to talk to her alone before he had to leave. This text-messages-and-stolen-kisses relationship was not going to cut it. He needed some serious time with her.

At one o'clock, with the empty moving boxes loaded for recycling, Phee happily ensconced in her new house, and the moving crew gathered on the lane between the cabins and the new house, Quinn declared they were finished. "We've got pizza coming for anyone who can stay."

"Count me in!" Mateo crowed, then

quickly looked to Luke to make sure it was okay.

"You bet," Luke said. "We're in."

Rafe shook his head. "Thanks for offering, but I need to run. My brother is expecting me this afternoon."

"Sure appreciate your help today, Rafe." Quinn stepped forward and the two shook hands.

"Happy to help." He took a step back and caught Britt's eye.

The smile she gave him said she was longing for time alone as much as he was. He waited until the group began to meander toward Quinn and Phee's house for pizza, then pulled Britt aside. He put himself between her and the dispersing group, shielding her from view. He stroked her cheek. "I miss you."

"I miss you too. You sure you can't stay for pizza?"

"I'm sorry. I need to go see Robby." He hesitated, looking down at the gravel. "You wouldn't want to go with me, would you?"

"You wouldn't care? *Robby* wouldn't care?"

He gave a low chuckle. "I make *no* promises about Robby, but I'd love to have you go with me."

She ran a hand through her hair. "Could I

353

have five minutes to clean up a little?"

"Sure. But you look fine to me." He touched her face again. "More than fine."

"I'll be right back." She started for the cottage, then turned back. "Do you need some water or anything?"

He waved her off. "Thanks. I'm good."

"Don't leave without me."

"I'll be right here." He pointed to the spot where he stood. Didn't she know that he never wanted to do anything without her ever again?

CHAPTER 31

Britt brushed her teeth and quickly changed into a clean blouse. Melvin appeared in the doorway of her bedroom and meowed up at her. Suddenly, wheels started turning and excitement rose inside her as an idea formed. "Wait right here, buddy . . ."

She hurried outside to where Rafe was waiting.

"That was quick."

"Well, I had an idea. This might be off the wall, but hear me out."

"I'm listening." But his demeanor said he was skeptical before even hearing her suggestion.

"Remember last time we visited, and Robby said he wanted a cat?"

Rafe nodded, obviously not tracking.

"What if we took Melvin with us to visit? Do you think the home would allow that?"

"Hmm . . . Well, family members bring pets all the time, so I know it's *allowed.*"

His smile said he was pleased but that the idea had never crossed his mind. He thought for a minute before continuing. "I'm just not sure how Robby would react."

"Maybe he wouldn't understand that Melvin is only visiting? I'd feel awful if he thought we were bringing him a . . . *permanent* cat. But Melvin can't stay." She cringed. "Sorry. Maybe it wasn't such a good idea."

Rafe laughed at that. "Actually, I think it might be. You never know about Robby, but the nice thing is, even if he pitches a fit, he has a short memory. He'd get over it in a hurry. But do you think *Melvin's* up for this?"

She waved a hand. "Oh, Melvin's always up for anything that involves riding in a car."

Rafe scratched his head. "I thought cats hated riding in cars."

"In case you hadn't noticed, Melvin is not your stereotypical cat."

"Let's give it a shot then." He hesitated. "If things go south, can we put him back in his carrier? I don't want to have to cut our visit short . . ."

"Oh, of course. He'll be fine in the carrier."

Excited her plan had met with favor, Britt ran in and got the cat, placed him in the carrier, and loaded it in the back seat of Rafe's car. When she climbed into the passenger seat beside him, he pointed at her shirt, amusement making his eyes spark. "You've got fur."

She laughed and started to pick at the little wisp of cat hair stuck to her chest, then decided to leave it there. "I think Robby might like me better with fur."

Rafe looked at her for a long minute. "Do you know how much I love you right now?"

"I think I might." She leaned across the console for a kiss. "Now quit staring at me and drive this car."

On the drive to the home, he updated her on his mom's situation. "There aren't any leads on the guy. Not surprising with so little to go on. But she's been told to go to the police if he contacts her, and under no circumstances is she to pay him any more money."

"That must be so scary. And frustrating."

"More the latter for me. But yeah, I know Ma's been plenty scared. And sadly, this doesn't necessarily mean she's free of the debt, but at least it offers her — us — a little reprieve."

"How's it going with her staying at your place?"

He cleared his throat pointedly. "Let's just

say it's probably a good thing I'm working long hours right now. But I happen to know Ma's been going back to her house for most of each day."

"Is that safe?"

"I have friends on the force keeping an eye on the house. Ma's the only one who's shown up there. No sign of the guy who threatened her — there or in the casinos."

"Well, I'm glad they're keeping an eye on her."

"I just wish she didn't need someone keeping an eye on her." He blew out a sigh. "Our families are so different, Britt. I'm not sure you get that."

"What do you mean?" She thought she knew, and she wasn't sure she wanted to go there.

"Just being with your family, helping Quinn and Phee move . . . I saw what it could be like. Family. I never really had that after my dad left. It probably sounds strange, but I feel more like part of your family than my own. In fact" — he tossed her a sheepish grin — "if we ever broke up, I'd be as sad to lose your family as I would you."

"That's a huge compliment, Rafe. But, um . . . you're not planning on breaking up any time soon, are you?"

"Hopefully never." He patted her knee. "I just want you to know what you're getting into. Right now, the package I have to offer includes one halfway decent looking guy with a sexy voice . . ." He wriggled his eyebrows, trying, she knew, to lighten the moment. But his eyes held sadness as he continued. "It also includes an absent dad, a needy mom, a brother who will never grow up . . . It's not much, Britt. It's not much."

She thought about what Mom had said. *You don't just marry the man, you marry his family too.* And while she knew it was true in many ways, she now knew that sometimes the man was worth it. Rafe was so very worth every difficulty his family might bring their way. And not only had he risen above what had happened to his family, but he'd stood in the gap for Robby's sake. And if that wasn't redemption, she didn't know what was.

She opened her mouth to try to put that all into words that would soothe his fears, but something stopped her. The issues Rafe's mom was embroiled in *would* affect them. Already had, in fact. Was she willing to accept that without blame? Could she love Rafe's mom like he did — even if the gambling issues were ongoing — and not lay blame?

As if he sensed her misgivings, with one hand still on the steering wheel, he reached over to put a gentle finger over her lips. "You know, I spent so many years feeling completely unqualified to ever raise a family of my own."

"Oh, Rafe. We're all just a bunch of imperfect humans stumbling around, trying to find our way."

"No. That's not totally true. Don't ever belittle how blessed you are to have had parents that loved you and taught you and stayed together even when things were hard. There's something to that. There just is . . . and I don't have that."

"You're right. I didn't mean to make light of it."

He gave a wry grin. "And you still haven't met Ma. We really shouldn't be having this conversation until that happens." Apology shadowed his expression and he sighed. "I'm not ashamed of her. I hope it doesn't sound like that. But Britt, she's *nothing* like the mom you Chandler sisters apparently grew up with. And watching *your* family? I've learned so much. Hearing you talk about your mom, I feel like I knew her. And she was . . . *royalty* in your eyes."

Britt smiled softly, remembering, and

wishing so badly that Rafe could have known Mom. "She really was. She was one in a million. I wish you could have known her."

"Me too." He reached across the console and squeezed her hand. "And then there's Quinn and Luke. Not saying I'm jealous of those dudes, but man, that's a lot to measure up to."

"Nobody's measuring you up, Rafe. But if they were, you'd have nothing to worry about. And you didn't know Quinn and Luke when they first started dating my sisters. They weren't perfect. Still aren't. Pretty close to it, I must admit. But not perfect."

He smiled. "As long as you give me room to improve."

"And you, me."

"Okay. Deal." He sealed it with a kiss. "Now let's go give my brother a cat."

She held up a finger in warning. "A *temporary* cat!"

With Melvin in the carrier, they made their way down to Robby's room but found it empty. He wasn't in the day room either, but Rafe had let them know he was coming, so he had to be here somewhere.

"Why don't you wait here, and I'll go

check at the front desk."

"Sure." She looked around the room where a ragtag group of residents lounged in front of the TV, then gave Rafe a sheepish look. "Just . . . don't be too long, okay?"

"I promise."

At the front desk, an aide checked the schedule for him. "Oh, I see. He had a doctor's appointment today. Just a checkup. There were two or three who had checkups today, but they should be back by two thirty or three."

"Did they not get the message that I was coming?"

The aide shrugged. "I really don't know. I don't see it noted here. Who did you talk to?"

"It doesn't matter." Rafe shook his head in frustration. "I guess we'll come back later."

He went back to the day room and stopped in his tracks. Britt sat on the vinyl sofa with her back to him, Melvin standing in her lap. Paul and Gregory sat on either side of her, scooched as close as they could get without also being in her lap. Paul held Melvin's face between his thick hands and rubbed noses with the cat. Gregory had the other end, stroking poor Melvin's tail again and again. With her back to him, he couldn't see Britt's expression, but although the cat looked supremely happy, he suspected Britt wasn't quite so much.

He took a step, intending to rescue her.

But hearing her voice, he stopped.

"He sure is soft, isn't he?" Britt looked from Paul to Gregory.

"He is soft," Gregory said. "And he is black."

Paul opened his hands to inspect Melvin. "No, he's white too."

"But he is also black."

Britt laughed. Not a strained, polite laugh, but her genuine, full-throated giggle that Rafe loved.

"You're both right," she said. "Black-and-white cats like Melvin are called tuxedo cats. Do you know why?"

"Because they are black and white." Gregory bobbed his chin as if that settled it.

"Well, that's part of it. Do you know what a tuxedo suit is? Those fancy black-and-white suits men sometimes wear?" Britt sounded like a third grade Sunday school teacher explaining a Bible story.

"A monkey suit!" Paul exclaimed.

Britt laughed again. "Exactly!" She turned to Gregory. "Some people call them monkey suits. And doesn't Melvin kind of look like he's wearing one of those suits?"

Paul gave a wheezy laugh. "Melbin has a monkey suit!"

Gregory scratched his head, then inspected Melvin's tail again. "He is not a monkey. He is a cat."

"You're right. Oh —" Britt held a finger to her lips. "Shhh . . . Listen, guys. Do you hear that?" She tipped her head toward Melvin.

From across the room Rafe could hear the cat purring.

"He's running!" Paul shouted.

"He is not. He is standing still," Gregory corrected.

Britt smiled at Paul. "It *does* sound like his motor is running, doesn't it?"

"Yeah, see there!" Paul shot daggers at Gregory.

"Cats do not have motors." Gregory scooted away from Britt and folded his arms, pouting.

"This cat *does* have a motor." Paul emphasized his point with a sharp nod. "Melbin has a motor."

Rafe had seen these tiffs escalate, so as much as he loved watching Britt interact with them, he decided it was time to intervene.

"Hey guys! Paul, Gregory, how's it going? I see you met Melvin."

"Melvin is a cat."

"He sure is, Gregory." He winked at Britt, who did not look at all like she needed rescuing.

She beamed up at him. Melvin jumped off her lap, and Britt took the opportunity to extricate herself from the sofa.

"We probably should be going, guys." She scooped Melvin into her arms.

"We'll be back later, after Robby gets home," Rafe said, knowing it would make the leaving easier for these two.

"Is that Robby's cat?" Paul asked.

"No. It's Britt's cat."

"*I'm* Britt," she said.

"Hi, Britt." Paul waved, looking suddenly shy.

"Hi, Britt. Melvin is a cat," Gregory said gruffly.

Britt backed away with Melvin in her arms, and Rafe put an arm around her, steering her toward the entrance. When they were out of earshot, he pulled her close and kissed her cheek. "You are amazing."

She looked askance at him. "Why?"

"The way you handled those guys."

"How long were you standing there?"

"Long enough to know that you are amazing."

Britt grimaced. "It was touch and go for a

minute, but I think Melvin kind of broke the ice. I just kept wishing Robby was there."

"We'll come back. And you'll still be amazing."

"I don't know about amazing, but . . . ." She tipped her head, studying him. "I'm feeling kind of *brave.* What would you think about taking Melvin to meet your mom?"

CHAPTER 32

"Meet Ma? Today?"

Britt had to laugh at the incredulous expression on Rafe's face. "Yes, today. I mean, I don't want to impose, but we could take her out for coffee or something . . . while we wait for Robby to get back."

"I think . . . I like that idea. Are you *sure*?"

"Yes. Let's get it over with." She giggled. "You're sure she won't mind us bringing a cat into her house?"

"Remember she's staying with me."

"Oh." Britt had never been to Rafe's apartment. "You okay with that? Did you make your bed this morning?"

He laughed. "Haha. As a matter of fact, I didn't. I'm guessing Ma will want us to meet at her place. But I'm fine with whatever. The worst she could do is kick us out."

"Rafe!"

He pulled her in for a reassuring hug. "It'll be fine. In fact, I'll give her a call right now."

He smirked. "Give her time to put on her lipstick and earrings."

"Rafe! Be nice."

"I'm kidding. I love my mom. I want you to love her too."

"I'll love her because she gave birth to the man *I* love." That much was true, but she prayed she could offer his mother forgiveness.

Twenty minutes later, Britt wasn't sure what had gotten into her, and she was feeling far less brave as they pulled into the driveway at his mother's house. Rafe had called that one, and Ma had asked them to give her fifteen minutes to get her house "put straight."

Rafe got out and went around to open her door. Wordlessly, they went to the back and got Melvin out of his carrier. Britt held the cat as if he were a life preserver.

Rafe rang the doorbell and waited with his arm around her. She feared it was to protect her.

But when his mother opened the door and saw Melvin, Britt's fears dissolved.

"Oh, my goodness!" Mrs. Stuart started to reach for the cat, but just as quickly pulled away, looking at Britt. "Do you mind if I pet him?"

"Of course not. This is Melvin. He'll take

all the attention he can get."

"He is just the cutest." She stroked Melvin's silky coat and baby-talked him.

Britt watched with fascination, seeing where Rafe got his blue eyes and straw-colored hair. She even heard some of Rafe's inflections in his mother's voice.

Melvin leaned into her with his whole weight and wriggled in Britt's arms.

"He's trying to come to you, Mrs. Stuart. Is that okay?"

"Oh, please . . . call me Becky. And yes. I'd love to hold him." Rafe's mom looked to her again for permission.

"Of course! I'm warning you though, he weighs a ton." Britt sensed the woman was scrutinizing her. But hey, turnabout was fair play.

Mrs. Stuart — *Becky* — took Melvin into her arms and cuddled him like a long lost friend. She shot Rafe a scolding look. "Well, don't just stand there! Invite your girl in." She turned to Britt and shook her head as if her son was hopeless. "Welcome, Britt."

"Thank you. It's so nice to finally meet you. I hope this isn't too last minute."

"Not at all. My Rafe knows he's always welcome. And any friend of his is a friend of mine." She nuzzled Melvin with her chin.

"Especially if he's as cute as this handsome fellow."

The house had a faintly musty smell, probably from being closed up for the past few days. Becky led the way into a small living room that held a formal sofa and matching loveseat and chair. The furniture looked new, but the rest of the room was decorated with a mishmash of older furniture and what Mom would have called knickknacks. Some of them appeared to be a child's school projects — Rafe's, no doubt — and Britt wanted so badly to inspect them.

But his mother gestured for her to take a seat on the sofa. "Rafe, why don't you pour coffee for us? It's freshly brewed."

"I'm on it." Halfway to the kitchen, Rafe tossed Britt a look over his mother's head that said he couldn't be happier with the way things were going. Apparently, Melvin had worked his magic.

"You have your hands full." Britt motioned toward Melvin happily ensconced in the woman's arms. "Can I do anything to help?"

"You just sit right there and make yourself at home. Rafe knows his way around the kitchen." She stroked Melvin and called into the kitchen, "There are cupcakes on the counter, son. You can plate those up."

"I'm on it, Ma."

Britt exchanged a knowing smile with his mother and realized that she wasn't nervous at all anymore. It struck her that Rafe's mom had probably been as nervous as she was about this meeting. But Melvin had played his role flawlessly.

"So how old is ol' Melvin here?" Becky stroked a work-worn hand over his fur again, and Melvin arched his back to take full advantage of the massage.

"We're really not sure. He was my mom's cat, and she got him from a shelter. They told her he was still a kitten because he was so playful, but our family has had him for over ten years and he's still as playful as ever. And definitely not a kitten."

As if to prove Britt's point, Melvin hopped down from Becky's lap and did a figure-eight dance around her feet. She laughed and rewarded him with a scratch under the chin.

"Here we go." Rafe appeared with two plates bearing fancy bakery cupcakes and forks. He handed one to each of them. "I'll be right back with coffee."

"I apologize for not baking anything . . . homemade, I mean."

"Oh, we didn't expect you to fix anything. Especially since we came on such short notice."

"It's just that when you cook for a living, it's the last thing you want to do when you get home."

"Rafe said you cook for a daycare center? I can't imagine cooking for that many people."

"It's really no big deal. I think the worst of it is seeing half the food thrown away. Kids are so picky these days. And then every kid seems to have a different allergy. Or a mother who insists he eat vegan —" Her eyes grew wide. "I'm sorry. I hope you're not vegan . . ."

Britt laughed. "Oh, I'm a full-fledged carnivore, and I was raised in a family where if you didn't eat what was set before you, you didn't eat, period."

She heard Rafe rattling around in the kitchen and wondered if he could hear their conversation. And if he could, what did he think about it?

"Well, good for your mama. She raised you right, as I see it. Do your folks live in town?"

"No. My mom passed away a year ago. Cancer. And Daddy lives in Florida now."

Becky's eyes brimmed. "I'm so sorry for your loss. Both of them. I know how hard it was on Rafe when his daddy moved out. You have that in common, I guess."

Britt wanted to defend her dad. It wasn't the same thing at all, but she couldn't think of a way to do so without risking offending, so she just nodded.

"Did I hear my name being bandied about?" Rafe appeared with two steaming mugs of coffee and set one on each of the end tables near them.

"Oh, Rafe. Not those awful mugs. Why didn't you use the good china?"

Britt laughed. "Probably because he knew he'd have to refill a teacup five times for me."

"That's exactly right." He thanked her with a grin. "But I'll take this one and pour you a new cup in the china, Ma."

She shook her head as if he was hopeless. "It's fine. I just don't want your girl to think we're a bunch of hillbillies."

"Well, Ma, we kind of *are* a bunch of hillbillies."

Britt could literally see his tongue in his cheek, and it was all she could do not to laugh.

But judging by his mother's expression, she wasn't humored. "Now, you stop that." She turned to Britt with a roll of her eyes. "In case you haven't figured it out yet, this one's a tease."

She gave her warmest smile. "It's one of

my favorite things about him."

"So, you've met my Robby?" She said it with such apprehension.

"I have. We tried to see him again. Earlier today. But I guess he was out at —" She stopped, not sure if she should mention the doctor's appointment. Rafe had said his mom wasn't very involved in Robby's care. "We're going to try to catch him later. We thought he'd like to meet Melvin."

"Oh! He would just love that. That boy always wanted a cat. Rafe too. But it just wouldn't have worked with our life . . . and the home only recently started allowing pets." She stared off, as if remembering something from long ago.

Britt grinned at Rafe, who was snarfing his cupcake and slurping coffee. "You wanted a cat? You never mentioned that."

"I don't remember. Did I, Ma?"

"Well, of course you did. Wouldn't shut up about it."

"Hmm. I guess I don't remember."

Britt smiled to herself, relishing the conversation she and Rafe would have once they left here. She already felt like she'd learned so much about him and the family he grew up in. They were different from her family, for sure. But however broken, they were still a family. And she loved seeing this side of him.

They made small talk for a while, Melvin back in Becky's lap, no doubt leaving clumps of fur behind.

Britt caught Rafe glancing at his phone several times and knew he was antsy to get to Robby's before he had to start his shift.

After a few more minutes of small talk, he turned to Britt. "We probably ought to get going."

"Oh, so soon." His mother looked genuinely disappointed.

"Sorry to eat and run, Ma, but I have to work tonight. I won't be home till late. You've got your key, right?"

"I do, but I think I might just stay here tonight."

"Ma . . . I don't think that's a good idea."

She gave a furtive glance in Britt's direction, then sighed and looked her in the eye. "I suppose Rafe's told you about my . . . troubles."

Britt wasn't sure how to answer. "He's told me . . . a little. I'm so sorry."

"Well . . ." She made a clicking sound with her tongue. "I have no one to blame but myself. I'm —" Her voice broke. "I'm sorry if it's caused trouble for you. You and Rafe, I mean."

Britt threw him a desperate look, hoping

he'd field this one. He didn't, but Melvin came to the rescue, hopping down from Becky's lap and making a beeline for the kitchen.

"Melvin!" Britt started after him, offering a hurried apology as the cat darted into the kitchen. "Melvin! Get back here."

Scooping up the cat, she first stole a glance at the tidy, somewhat kitschy kitchen and pictured Rafe standing at the counter plating cupcakes and pouring coffee. It warmed her heart.

She lugged Melvin back into the living room and apologized again.

"That sweet kitty is welcome anywhere in my house." Becky rose and came close to scratch him under the chin. "I'd give just about anything to see how Robby reacts to you," she told Melvin.

"Why don't you come with us!" The words were out before Britt had a chance to think about the implications. She looked to Rafe, hoping he wouldn't have to backpedal on her behalf.

"Are you sure?" Becky looked so hopeful it almost broke Britt's heart.

"Of course, Ma. Come with us. Bring your things, and I can take you back to my place before I go to work."

"If you're sure."

He didn't give her a chance to argue. "We'll take Melvin and get him in his carrier, and you come on out when you're ready."

Britt stacked their mugs and plates and carried them to the kitchen, thinking it might give Rafe a chance to change plans if needed. But when she returned, his mother was gathering her purse and coat.

"Can I help you carry anything?" Britt asked.

"Oh no. I don't have much. Just let me get the lights turned off. I'll be right out." She was turning lights *off,* but her countenance had brightened by ten shades.

Rafe held the door and Britt carried Melvin to the car. While he opened the back of the car where the carrier was, she ventured, "I hope it's okay that I invited her. You're not upset, are you?"

He didn't reply, but when Melvin was secured in the carrier, he straightened, took her face in his hands, and kissed her soundly.

"What was that for?"

"I don't know what magic you've worked, woman, but don't ever stop."

CHAPTER 33

"Man!" Rafe shook his head slowly. "If you'd told me forty-eight flying monkeys in red jackets would land on my car driving down I-55, I would have believed you sooner than what actually happened today."

Britt laughed, thrilled herself with how the day had gone. "The only thing that could make the day even better is if you didn't have to work tonight."

"But alas, I do." He kissed her across the console, then checked his phone. "And I'd better get you home right now or I'll be late."

They'd gone through a drive-through for burgers since neither of them had eaten since the cupcakes at his mom's. But what a day it had been!

"I still can't believe Ma jumped at the chance to go see Robby with us."

"When was the last time she saw him?"

"I really don't know. But for the last few

years, she's gone maybe once a month. If that. And it hasn't gone well. Robby always seems to sense that she's there . . . begrudgingly."

"Well, neither one of them seemed begrudging today."

"I still can't get over it. Ma and Robby laughing together." He shook his head in wonderment and threw her a smile, but she didn't miss the sheen of unshed tears in his eyes.

"I'm telling you, it's Melvin." She glanced behind them where the cat carrier sat in the back seat.

"Well, that cat ought to win the Nobel Peace Prize then."

"I like your mom. You're a lot like her."

He looked surprised. "Really? How?"

"Just little things . . . mannerisms. The way you say certain things."

"Well, she *loved* you."

"How do you know?" But she was pleased, and she'd felt it too.

"First of all, I don't think I ever brought home a girl who was invited to call Ma 'Becky' within the first two minutes." He chuckled over a bite of his burger. "Not that I brought that many girls home to meet her."

"I was gonna say!" She laughed, feeling

such a weight lifted. She'd met Rafe's mom, things had gone great with Robby, who loved Melvin — and who did pitch a little fit when they put Melvin back in the carrier to leave. But they promised to bring the cat back soon. And it had been Becky who comforted Robby and patiently explained why they had to take Melvin home.

Best of all, Britt had gotten a little time with Rafe. Not nearly enough, but it would get her through till the next time.

At her cabin, he put the car in park and turned to her. "I really have to run."

"I know." She reached to stroke his cheek. "I'll see you . . . next time."

"Which will be?"

"Probably not till Valentine's Day." They'd planned to move everything out of Quinn's workshop and haul it up to the clearing in preparation for a big reveal for Joanna's wedding venue as soon as the weather was nice enough. "You didn't forget, did you?"

"Who would let me forget?"

She grinned. "Not me."

"Not you or Quinn or Luke. Shoot, even Mateo reminded me."

"Hey, this is a big deal."

"I get that. You're sure you don't mind spending our first Valentine's Day together with your entire family?"

"I don't mind. *This* year. But next year . . ." She pointed between them. "Just you and me, baby. Nobody else."

"I'll put it on my calendar." He glanced at the clock on the dashboard. "Hey, I *really* need to go." He wove his fingers through the hair at the nape of her neck and pulled her in for a kiss. "Good night, you magical woman, you."

"Cut it out, you goofball." But she kissed him long and sweet and decided she'd wear the label proudly after today.

"I'll call you." He kissed her again.

"You'd better." She pried herself from his arms and opened the car door.

"I will."

"See you Valentine's Day." She leaned across for another kiss.

"Get out of this car before you make me late and I lose my job and have to move into a homeless shelter — or in with my mom —"

"Get out of here, you nut." Laughing, she climbed out and went around to retrieve Melvin in his carrier. But she stopped at Rafe's rolled-down window for one last kiss. "Be careful."

"You know me."

"Exactly. *Be careful.*"

He gave a little salute and backed away.

381

But she stood, heart full, in front of the cabin in the cold and watched until his taillights disappeared around the curve in the lane.

Britt was about to close her laptop when a message pinged simultaneously on her computer and her phone. From Airbnb. Probably just something about a change in privacy policy or some other legal thing. She really ought to be more careful reading those things before she clicked Accept.

She opened the Airbnb app. A new reservation. Good. Things had been a little sparse this month, which wasn't unusual in winter. Southeast Missouri wasn't exactly a vacation destination in February. They'd run a Valentine's special and hadn't gotten nearly the response they'd hoped for. Little wonder, since they'd grossly neglected the marketing end of the Airbnb after Phee went on bed rest.

She glanced at the clock and decided to take care of this reservation before she went over to Phee's. She clicked to open the message and took in a breath. It was Kathy. Mr. Clean's Kathy. Kathy Landon, according to her profile.

Not sure what to do, she quickly tapped out a text to Rafe: "Just got a reservation request from Mr. Clean's 'wife' for this weekend. For TWO guests! Should I accept the booking?"

A few minutes went by before his reply came back: "The detective here talked to her and got nothing. But go ahead and book. If he shows up with her again, maybe they can question HIM. When's the reservation for?"

"Two nights. Feb 14–15."

"Valentine's Day?"

"Yep. We're running a special."

"Definitely book it."

"Will do."

"But don't you talk to either of them alone. I'll see if one of the guys from the station can be there when they check in."

"Okay. I'll try to pin them down on their arrival time Wednesday."

"Great. Sure would love to get Ma back in her house. ;)"

Britt laughed at the winky face that followed. And couldn't help but feel a little excited at the prospect of being a small part of resolving Rafe's mom's issues. Oh, how wonderful it would be if they could put this behind them. And put this guy behind bars, if he was indeed the same guy who'd scammed Becky.

Rafe had told her when they talked on the

phone last night that he'd had some hard conversations with his mom while she was staying at his place. He felt confident she wasn't *addicted* to gambling. Apparently, she'd seen an ad in a tourism brochure and, on a whim, took a chance. Mr. Clean — or someone like him — had picked up on her lucky streak and taken advantage of a wad of cash. And when that was gone, he'd made her a loan with an exorbitant interest rate. After meeting Becky, Britt could understand better how she'd have been flattered by the attention and wooed by the prospect of the things her winnings could buy.

How many others — women especially — fell victim to this kind of flattery, then got caught up in a web of deceit that eventually led to a bona fide gambling addiction? She prayed Rafe was right and that his mom hadn't fallen that far.

She clicked to finalize the booking and sent their usual friendly welcome message. Along with a prayer that this might, indeed, be the end of Becky Stuart's woes.

CHAPTER 34

Quinn crossed the shop floor and reached to shake Rafe's hand. "Hey, man. Sure glad you could make it."

"Wouldn't have missed it." Rafe shot him a wry smile. "Especially since Britt threatened me with death if I did."

Quinn laughed. "Those sisters do have a way with words, don't they?"

Luke came to greet him with Mateo trailing behind. They'd had to wait till the kids got out of school today to start loading. And now they'd be racing to finish in daylight. But the weather was good, and Rafe worked back-to-back shifts the rest of the month, so it was now or never.

"You up for this?" Luke asked.

Rafe laughed, nodding. "Ready as I'll ever be. You guys are going to have to tell me what you need. Since I've never been up in the clearing, I'm not quite catching the vision."

"Oh, you'll catch it once you're there. Piece of cake."

Rafe perused the huge shop floor where everything they'd been building for the past month was stacked for loading. He stood by while Quinn and Luke discussed which order they should load in, and once they started carrying stuff out to the truck, the work went quickly.

"So, do you think Joanna suspects anything?" Quinn asked Luke as they tied down the first batch of benches that would serve as permanent seating up in the clearing.

"If she does, she's a pretty good actress." Luke tousled Mateo's hair. "And speaking of good actors, this guy hasn't spilled the beans yet."

"Yeah, but we've told her a couple of whoppers trying to keep it secret." Mateo narrowed his eyes at Luke. "And if I get in trouble with Jo, it's *your* fault."

"Don't you worry, buddy, I'll take the fall for you. Generally speaking, lies about good surprises don't get punished."

"They better not." But his stern look quickly turned to a grin.

"Hey, Rafe . . ." Quinn motioned for him to follow him to the loading dock. "Give me a hand with these floor sections, would you? Luke, this won't take long, so if you and

Mateo can get the rest of the benches all moved over here, we'll be ready for them shortly."

They all sprang into action and by four o'clock, they were packed into the cab of the moving truck headed out to the property.

"So where is Jo now?" Rafe had his doubts about pulling this off as a complete surprise. Surely somebody would slip between now and whenever the weather was nice enough to do a reveal.

"It's her turn on Phee-watch," Luke said.

Quinn gave him a conspiratorial look. "I told Phee to be extra needy today . . . just in case Jo got any ideas about stepping outside."

"This is gonna be epic." Mateo beamed. "I betcha she'll cry when she finally sees it. What do you bet, Luke?"

"We'll be betting on the same team then."

Quinn smirked. "I bet they *all* cry."

"Then count me out." Mateo shook his head in disgust. "Why do girls hafta cry when they're happy? That makes no sense."

"Just don't ever tell *them* that, buddy. If you know what's good for you." But Luke looked sympathetic.

Mateo cocked his head to one side. "You think Britt will cry, Rafe?"

Rafe thought for a minute, trying to picture Britt crying over a wedding venue. "I don't think she will."

Quinn and Luke groaned in unison. "Oh, man . . ."

Luke punched his shoulder. "You haven't been around these parts long, have you?"

Quinn laughed.

"No. I stand by that. Britt's not really that sappy." He held up a hand, feigning a wince at Quinn and Luke. "No judgment on your women or anything."

That made them laugh louder.

"Want to take any bets?" Luke stuck out his hand.

Rafe shook his head and refused to shake on it. "I'm not a betting man." He wondered if these guys knew about his mom. If they did, they didn't let on. For which he was grateful. "But if I *were* a betting man, I'd still say Britt will be dry-eyed."

Good-natured jeering ensued until Rafe finally held up a hand in surrender.

"We'll see. I admit, you two have the upper hand. You've known her longer than I have." He turned to Mateo. "What do *you* think, pal?"

Mateo let out a laugh. "I'm betting crybabies all around."

Quinn and Luke high-fived the kid like

he'd just won a Super Bowl ring.

Rafe pretended to be defeated, but the truth was, he felt like he was being initiated into a fraternity he desperately wanted to belong to.

However, he just might have to have a little talk with Britt later tonight about her "expected" behavior whenever the reveal happened.

"And hey, buster . . ." Quinn winked. "Don't you go paying off Britt to stay dry-eyed or anything."

Rafe's jaw dropped. "What — How'd you . . . ?"

Luke slapped his knee, cracking up, and the three of them heaped more derision on Rafe. Funny though, it didn't feel like derision. It felt like he'd just passed muster. He was starting to think this tight-knit family stuff might not be a bad thing after all.

As the sun lowered, Rafe turned a three-sixty in the middle of the clearing above the cabins. The space was everything Britt had described it to be. Well, at least judging by the twenty-five minutes of daylight they had left before the sun sank behind the trees. A lacework of branches formed a canopy over a space that looked a little like a natural amphitheater.

Lights shone from the cottage and cabins

below, and Quinn and Phee's new house was lit up like a Christmas tree. The view from up here was incredible, and Rafe wondered if Britt was watching from her cabin.

He looked up at the strings of lights woven through the branches overhead and wished they could turn them on, but Luke had warned that Joanna would notice if the lights suddenly came on.

As it was, they'd crawled up a muddy road on the backside of the hill at ten miles an hour so as not to make any noise. Quinn's construction crew had cut the rough trail along the edge of the woods last week — after making sure Luke had Joanna safely out of town for an "impromptu" date.

"We'll eventually pave the road if the venue takes off," Luke told him. For now, it served the purpose of getting everything up into the clearing without going through the lane by the cabins.

Rafe had to admit he was intimidated by everything Luke was doing for his fiancé. The guy would be a tough act to follow.

"We're just lucky there's no leaves on the trees. You think it's dark now, it's practically pitch black up here in the summertime when there's no moon." He gave Mateo a playful shove. "Mateo can tell you all about that, can't you, bud."

The boy scoffed at Luke, before turning to Rafe. "Let's just say I wouldn't recommend you run away from home up here at night."

"Really? That sounds like a good story." Rafe smiled, hoping to encourage the telling of the story.

But Mateo just rolled his eyes. "Not all that good, actually."

"Well, it does have a happy ending." Luke laughed and gave Rafe a look over the boy's head that said *I'll tell you later.*

Rafe acknowledged him with a nod. He liked these guys. Wouldn't mind calling them brothers-in-law someday. And Mateo was a great kid. Unlike Rafe remembered himself being at that age.

His phone buzzed in his pocket, and his pulse edged up a notch. It was Britt. "I need to take this, guys."

"If you need to go, Rafe, I can take you back down any time."

"Oh no. I'm not on call at work. This'll just take a sec."

"KL is on her way. Guessing ten minutes out." Britt's text quickened his pulse even more. Kathy Landon, the so-called "wife" of Mr. Clean, was supposed to be checking in to the cottage tonight. Britt had texted

391

earlier that her guest was running a little late but had asked to please hold the booking.

He tapped a reply. "Do I need to come down? If Mr. C is with her do NOT talk to them alone."

"No need. One of your buddies is here from the force. Eddie?"

"Great. He's a good guy. BTW, the clearing is amazing."

"You're up there now? Good job going stealth. I can't see a thing up there."

"Good. Mission accomplished. Love you."

He started to pocket his phone, then quickly texted: "Hey, do Q and L know about my mom?"

An overlong pause before her reply came: "Yes. Both of them. Just the basics. I hope that's okay."

"Of course. They're good guys too." He typed a smiley face, then slipped his phone back in his pocket.

In the dusky light, Luke and Mateo unloaded benches and started setting them up. They'd decided not to set them permanently until Joanna gave her approval. But the dance floor location wasn't negotiable, so it would get permanently installed tonight.

Rafe had been germinating an idea and

had run it by Quinn and Luke to an enthu-
siastic response. Even as his palms grew
sweaty at the prospect of pulling off his
scheme, he smiled thinking what Britt's reaction would be.

Just as quickly, his thoughts turned back
to what was going on down at the cottage.
He kept one eye on the lane below them
while helping Quinn line up the squares on
the sections of checkerboard that made up
the dance floor. It took some work to get
the ground leveled underneath, but when it
was all assembled, the floor looked even bigger out here than it had in the shop. And
Britt would be thrilled to know that the
checkerboard design they'd painted had
lined up perfectly.

Rafe was tempted to try out a few dance
steps on the floor, but the guys had razzed
him enough for his predictions about Britt
staying dry-eyed. He wasn't about to invite
more of the same.

Quinn rose and stepped back to inspect
their work. "I think we can call it a night,
fellas. Good work." He ran a hand through
his hair. "Luke, you have everything you
need for the rest of the evening?" He cast a
glance at Mateo, who didn't know about
this part of the plan, which had been

hatched at the shop during the last work night.

Luke nodded. "I'm good."

Quinn frowned and shook his head slowly. "Man, it's going to kill me to have to keep this a secret for a few more weeks."

"Why can't we show it to Jo now? Tonight!" Mateo bounced on his heels at the prospect.

But Luke shook his head. "Then Phee wouldn't be able to come, buddy. That wouldn't be fair."

"But can't she ride in the truck and come up the way we did? The back way?" Mateo looked so hopeful that Rafe hoped the answer was yes.

But Quinn put the idea to rest. "We did think about that, buddy, but it's just too bumpy and muddy. We can't risk it for the baby."

"Don't worry," Luke said, speaking to Quinn as much as Mateo, Rafe thought. "It'll all happen soon enough. And Jo will be just as excited in a few weeks as she would be tonight. Maybe more, because she won't have to wait so long for our wedding then."

Quinn smiled. "Which will be here before you know —"

"What the heck?" Mateo shouted, then

clapped a hand over his mouth as if he hadn't meant that word to escape. But his focus had turned in the direction of the cottages, and he dashed to the edge of the clearing without waiting to see if he was in trouble.

They all followed his line of vision and ran after him as a parade of four police cars rolled up the lane to the cottage, all with red and blue lights strobing.

"What is going on?" Quinn's eyes grew wide, then darted to his house where Phee was. He looked poised to take off down the side of the hill.

But Rafe put a hand on his shoulder. "Hey, I think I know what this is. And I'm pretty sure everybody's okay down there. But hang on . . . Let me check." He started to dial Britt, but her ringtone sounded before he could finish.

"Rafe! Are you seeing this?"

"We are. You guys are all okay?"

"We're fine."

"For sure?"

"Totally. I'm over at Phee's with Jo. But Eddie sent me over here and told us all to stay inside. We're watching out the window, and they just took the guy out of the cottage in handcuffs!"

"Are you serious?" Hope rose inside him.

"It must have been him then. What about *her*? Kathy?"

"She's a little shaken." Britt's voice quavered. "I'm a little shaken myself, to tell you the truth."

"Yeah. You sound like it." He chuckled, but quickly turned serious again. "But you're all okay? You're sure?"

"We're totally fine. And Kathy's going home tonight. To Indiana."

"Okay. I need to let Quinn and Luke know what's going on. Mateo too." He chuckled. "He's pretty pumped. We have a bird's-eye view from up here."

Britt gave a shaky laugh. "I'm a little jealous. I just hope they can convict him."

"You and me both." His mind reeled with what that could mean for Ma — and for him personally. "I'll see you in a little while. Don't forget in all the excitement that it *is* Valentine's Day."

"Don't you worry. I haven't forgotten."

CHAPTER 35

The kitchen island at Quinn and Phee's house held a Valentine's dessert spread that would have made Joanna Gaines proud. Britt and Jo had put it together while the guys completed their mission up in the clearing. Britt didn't think Jo suspected anything, but she was on pins and needles nevertheless. Of course, maybe that had more to do with the fact that she'd get to spend Valentine's evening with Rafe. Never mind the whole family would be here. She'd take what she could get when it came to time with that man.

The guys had arranged to arrive one at a time, so as not to arouse suspicion. Quinn was the first to get there, and Rafe followed a few minutes later. His face lit when he saw Britt, but when he saw the food on the island, he whistled low under his breath and winked at her. "Now *that's* a sight for sore eyes."

Laughing, Britt tugged on his arm, so happy to be with him again. "I know you're famished, but we have to wait till Luke and Mateo get here." She took his hand and squeezed it.

"Did you come straight from work, Rafe?" Jo eyed him with genuine curiosity, and Britt prayed he'd come up with a story that meshed with hers.

He didn't miss a beat. And even avoided telling a lie. "Oh, don't worry about me. I can wait. Britt said you had some excitement here earlier."

Nice deflection. She squeezed his hand again.

Just then, Phee appeared from the bedroom hallway. "I'll say we did! I hope they stop that guy."

"Me too. Most excitement we've had around here in a while." Jo clucked her tongue, then shot Britt an annoyed look. "And Rafe, you do *not* need to wait to eat. You go right ahead and help yourself. Luke will understand. Besides, if you wait till Mateo gets here, there might not be anything left. I swear that boy eats like two grown men."

Rafe laughed. "That's what Ma used to say about me when I was that age. Growing is apparently hard work. And thanks, Jo, but

I can wait. For a little while anyway . . ." He cleared his throat and then looked at Quinn. "I hope none of this . . . the police cars and everything . . . reflects badly on business for you guys."

Quinn shook his head. "I doubt anyone will even know they took him out here. The girlfriend was the only guest here at the time."

"Maybe we shouldn't mention it to Mateo though. That might be too good a story for him to sit on."

Rafe squeezed Britt's hand so hard it hurt. She squeezed back and hoped Luke had warned Mateo not to say anything about having a ringside seat to the arrest. Poor kid was having to "sit on" an awful lot of secrets lately. Britt hoped it wouldn't be long before they could take Jo up to the clearing and end the suspense. But given the wintry weather forecast for the rest of the month, that didn't seem likely. At least they wouldn't have to worry about Jo deciding to take a hike up into the clearing.

Rafe let go of her hand and turned back to Quinn. "Well, I feel bad it had to happen here, but I'm afraid he would have gotten away otherwise."

"Don't think another thing of it, Rafe." Phee patted his shoulder. "I just hope this is the end of that whole mess for your mom."

Britt could have hugged her whole family right then. They'd each done everything possible to make Rafe feel welcomed and accepted. But she could tell Rafe was feeling a little uncomfortable about the whole thing. Turning to Joanna, she changed the subject. "What time did Luke think they'd get here?"

The doorbell answered her question, and Jo hurried to answer it.

A few minutes later, they were all gathered around the big table in Phee and Quinn's dining room with pretty Valentine paper plates overflowing with finger sandwiches, chips and dip, and three kinds of cookies. Britt had left a plate with an assortment of cookies in the cottage for Kathy, too, but she doubted the woman had taken them with her in all the excitement. Britt made a note to send those home with Rafe tonight.

After the table had been cleared and the kitchen cleaned up, Luke put his hands on Mateo's shoulders. "Well, I hate to break up the party, but this kid has school tomorrow."

"Awww . . . Do we hafta go yet? I promise I'll get up without griping when the alarm goes off."

Phee feigned a yawn. "It's about my bedtime too."

Britt was grateful, wanting at least a little time alone with Rafe before he had to go too. She knew he hadn't slept since starting the late shift last night. Life would have been about perfect right now if not for the crazy timing that prevented them from being together.

The thought made her catch her breath. And realize that it was true. She loved her life. Loved living out here in the country, loved running the Airbnb. Why was she so hung up on finding what it was she was created to do? Was there any reason this life couldn't be exactly what God had planned for her?

Rafe reached for his jacket on the back of his chair, and afraid he was leaving, she went to him. "Hey, if you'll stop by the cottage I'll send some cookies home with you."

"Well, I can't turn *that* down." He thanked the sisters for the meal and waited while Britt slipped into her coat.

Everyone left at once, and Britt and Rafe walked hand in hand to the cottage. A fingernail moon hung in a deep blue sky, and the night was so quiet she could hear them breathing as one. She unlocked the cottage and went to get the cookies while he waited on the screened porch. As she'd expected, the cookies were on the counter where she'd left them, still in their cellophane gift wrapping. "I know you're exhausted, and I won't try to keep you, much as I'd like to, but I did want to send these home with you."

"I'm glad we got to spend this evening together. Even if it probably wasn't the most romantic Valentine's Day you've ever had."

She looked up at him, longing growing inside her. "At the risk of sounding like a loser, I don't have a scrapbook full of romantic Valentine's Day memories."

"Ha, that makes two of us. So maybe this *was* the most romantic Valentine's Day you've ever had? In that case, you're welcome."

She giggled. "And you're funny."

He pulled her close. "You seemed kind of quiet tonight. Everything okay?"

"Was I? Quiet?"

"A little. Are you upset about the police descending on your place? I didn't really think through how that might affect you guys. I'm sorry if it —"

"No, Rafe. Not at all. Everyone meant it tonight when they said it was no big deal. I just hope it's the end of this mess for your poor mom."

402

"Yeah, me too. We'll see."

"It's a small miracle that Mateo kept his mouth shut."

A slow smile came to his mouth. "Yeah, that was pretty impressive on his part." The smile faded. "You're sure something's not bothering you?"

She paused, not sure if she was ready to talk to him about the thoughts that had come to her this evening. But they were probably the reason he'd thought she was upset about something. And she wanted to hear what he thought about her "revelation."

"If . . . if I was quiet tonight, it's probably because something occurred to me . . . watching my family — and seeing you there with them."

"Oh?"

"I realized that . . . I'm happy, Rafe. So happy. Just the way things are."

"And that was a revelation? You always seem happy. It's one of the things I love most about you."

"What I mean is . . ." She looked up at the crescent moon, trying to put words to her thoughts that would make sense to him. "You know how I've been wondering what I'm supposed to do with my life?"

He nodded.

"Tonight I just realized . . . I'm already doing it. Living the life I've been given. Just as it is. And I'm so happy. But isn't that too easy? Aren't we supposed to struggle — at least a little — to figure out what we were created to do?"

"I've never heard that was a prerequisite."

"But didn't you? Struggle, I mean?"

He thought for a minute. "I don't think the struggle was in deciding what to do with my life. The things that made me land on being a first responder were the struggle. No doubt about that. But that happened long before I was even old enough to think about what I wanted to be when I grew up. Deciding what to do with my life wasn't a struggle. I just kind of *knew.*"

"I hadn't thought about it that way. But I didn't know, Rafe."

"It seems like your struggle is that you think just because you've been thrust into nursing roles, you're 'doomed' " — he chalked quote marks in the air with his fingers — "to make nursing a career."

It was good to hear him affirm that. "I guess just because God gives us a gift, we don't have to make a career of it."

"Exactly. And isn't it possible that God placed you right where you are at just the right time so you could use those gifts?

Helping your family when your mom was sick? Helping your sister? But just for a time. It doesn't mean that's what you're obligated to do — to be — for the rest of your life."

She let Rafe's words sink in. "I do love my life. Even the 'nurse' part." She tossed him a grin. "I love it a lot more now that you're in it," she admitted.

"Well, of course. That goes without saying."

She patted his cheek. "And now that Phee is close to her delivery," she admitted, "I can see an end to the nursing part, which . . . I don't know if I'm gifted at that or not, but it's *not* what I want to do with my life. That I *do* know."

"Why not? I mean, nothing wrong with that, but I think you *are* gifted that way. You're compassionate and gentle, and you're always willing to put your own needs aside when someone else needs you."

"No, Rafe, I'm just a good faker. But sometimes — often, actually — I resent it." She shrugged. "Sorry to ruin your good impression of me."

He patted her hand. "It would take a lot more than an admission to being human to ruin my good impression of you."

"Well, thank you for that. I think . . ." She

rubbed her face, trying to clarify her thoughts. "I think mostly the whole nursing thing is just too stressful. I don't want to be responsible for someone else's life. Always feeling like if I make one wrong move, it could change someone's life forever. It was bad with Mom, but this thing with Phee . . . worrying that I might miss an important sign that she was in labor or the baby was in distress . . . It's just too hard."

He nodded silently and she gave a little gasp. "Oh, Rafe. That must be how you feel all the time in your job. I'm so thoughtless!"

"No, you're not. And honestly, yes, I understand the responsibility part, but it's not stressful for me. Well, in the moment, sure. But it's different for me. I'm coming on the scene after the worst has already happened. And that part *wasn't* my fault. Not anymore."

He stared straight ahead, drifting to that faraway place he often did. And she knew he was thinking about Robby. And wishing he could go back and change everything that had happened.

She reached for his hand and squeezed it. She'd learned that it was better not to say anything in moments like this. But just to be there. It really *hadn't* been his fault, and she thought Rafe knew that as truth, though he couldn't change it. And that was the great sadness of his life. She sent up a prayer that somehow, someday, God could redeem that sadness.

CHAPTER 36

"But it's barely eight o'clock. You just got
here." With one eye on the radar map on
the TV in Quinn and Phee's kitchen, Britt
gave Rafe her best pout.

"Sorry, love, but you know we're going to
have a gazillion calls tonight —"

"Say that again. Love . . ." She smiled up
at him, basking in the endearment they'd
begun to use with each other since Valentine's Day. Two weeks ago now. And they'd
seen each other exactly once during that
time. But they'd texted and talked on the
phone in the rare times they both had free,
and she didn't think she'd ever tire of hearing him call her "love."

"Luv." Now he made his voice harsh and
bucked out his teeth, trying, she knew, to
tease her out of her pout.

It worked, and she laughed. But that
didn't change the deep disappointment she
felt that the one night they finally both had

free had turned out to bring a blizzard. And of course, being the selfless, faithful worker he was, Rafe was going in to work.

They had yet to post their status as a couple on Facebook. Or anywhere else for that matter. Her book club friends only knew that she was dating someone, but she hadn't given them any details. She'd called Daddy and tried to prepare him that things were getting serious with Rafe. Jo and Phee knew, of course, but Britt rather liked keeping the whole incredible experience to herself. For now anyway.

Rafe went to the coat closet where Phee had hung his parka earlier. He pulled out the heavy coat and laid it over a chair. "Is your sister awake? I'll go tell her goodbye."

"Let me check. She's been having a lot of Braxton Hicks contractions this week. She says she feels fine and the baby is active and everything, but it seems like she's spent more time in bed than usual." She looked at the clock. "I'll be glad when Quinn gets home."

"When is that?" Her brother-in-law was in St. Louis at a builders convention.

"Tonight or tomorrow. He's waiting to see what the weather does." She looked toward the window where flurries swirled in the darkness beyond. "I've got to say, it's making me a little nervous."

He nodded, taking his gloves and hat from the pockets of his coat.

"I'll go tell Phee you're leaving."

She hurried back to the bedroom and peeked in on her sister. Phee was sitting up in bed with a novel open, but judging by her bookmark, it didn't look like she'd made any progress since the last time Britt had looked in on her. "Rafe is leaving."

"So soon? He just got here."

"I know. But he thinks he'll probably get called in. The roads are icing over."

"I wondered about that. I hope Quinn can get home."

"Me too. Rafe wanted to come and say goodbye."

"Oh sure." Phee scooted up in the bed and straightened the covers over her legs. "Tell him to come on in."

Britt went to the door and called him, and a few seconds later, he poked his head in the doorway, bundled up, hat and all.

Britt stood behind him, not wanting to miss a kiss before he left.

He waved at Phee. "I just wanted to say goodbye. Thanks for the hospitality."

"Bye, Rafe. I wish you didn't have to go out in this." Phee glanced over at the window.

"You and me both, but I probably ought to get to the station. People don't have brains enough to stay off the roads in weather like this. We're likely to have a lot of calls."

"Well, look who's talking," Britt teased. "Here *you* go out onto the roads."

"That's different. I know what I'm doing."

He waved at Phee again, and he and Britt walked to the front door together. She stepped out onto the portico with him but shivered and took a step back. The wind had picked up and a freezing drizzle came steadily down.

"Please be careful."

"I will." He gave her a quick, wholly unsatisfying kiss before tromping to his car through the three or so inches of snow that had gathered on the lawn. She reminded herself that this was Rafe's work and she would — if they ended up together — likely always compete with it for his attention in the years to come.

And she would worry about him every minute he was on duty. She closed the door and watched until his car disappeared around the curve in the lane. Judging by how slowly he drove, it was icy underneath that snow.

She locked the door and went to see if Phee wanted to watch a movie.

"I might start one, but I'm not sure I can stay awake. These stupid Braxton Hicks contractions are wearing me out."

A tiny alarm went off inside her. "Do they hurt?"

"No, not *hurt* exactly. They're just annoying." She eyed Britt and gave her a strained smile. "Don't worry. They're normal at this stage. I've been having more of them for a few days now. Supposedly they're like 'practice' contractions."

Relief went through her. "Well, you pick the movie. I'll go make some popcorn."

"No, *you* pick the movie. You're the one who'll see the whole thing. Except" — Phee smiled — "please don't make me watch *Sense and Sensibility* again. I've practically got that thing memorized."

Britt laughed. "Fine. I'll watch it later in the privacy of my own room. It's just *so* romantic."

She went to make popcorn and fix hot chocolate, but while the corn was popping, the doorbell rang.

"You expecting anyone, Phee?" she hollered.

No reply. She went to the window and pulled back the curtain. Rafe's car sat in front of the house in the same spot where he'd parked before.

She opened the door when she saw him coming up the walk. "Well, that was quick. You don't have to work?" The prospect delighted her. Especially since Phee seemed to be in bed for the night.

"You were right. I guess I'm one of those idiots I told you about." He gave her a sheepish look and stamped his feet on the porch. "I didn't get a mile out before I came this close to landing in the ditch. Twice. I called the station, and they told me to stay put. If you don't mind, I think I'd better hunker down here and wait until the worst of it is over. Nobody is getting out in this."

"Of course. Get in here. It's cold!" She pulled him inside.

"Yes, get in here before you freeze to death." Phee peered at them from the hallway.

"I thought you were asleep."

"Almost. I'm going to brush my teeth and go to bed." She grinned. "You two be good."

"Scout's honor." He gave a little salute, then looked apologetic. "Sorry if I woke you. The chief said they'll get the graders out in full force once it stops snowing, but it's coming down faster than they can scoop it right now. According to the weather service this isn't supposed to amount to much, so it shouldn't be long before I can get out."

"Well, you're welcome here as long as you need to be." Phee gave a little wave. "You guys find whatever you want to eat."

He turned to Phee. "I don't know if Quinn was planning to drive home tonight, but he won't make it far once he hits Cape Girardeau County. They've already closed the interstate up by Perryville."

Worry lines creased Phee's brow. "Let me call him." She went back to the bedroom and came back a few minutes later. "He and his foreman were headed home but started hearing about the weather down here, so they're trying to find a hotel for the night."

"Wow." Britt looked to Rafe as if for confirmation. "Is it really that bad?"

"It's crazy out there. I've never seen anything like it."

"Who'd ever think we'd have a *blizzard* this late in the year?"

"Oh, I've heard the older guys at the station talk about major snowstorms in April. The nice thing is they can't last too long."

"I sure hope not." Britt could see the worry in Phee's eyes.

"You need to get back in bed, sis. You know Quinn will be careful."

"I'm going, I'm going. You kids have fun."

Rafe looked over at the silent television. "Do you mind if we leave the weather on?"

"Of course not." Phee went to turn up the volume, then handed him the remote. "I hate thinking of anyone being out in this weather."

"I know," Rafe agreed. "I'd offer to shovel your walk, but it'd be covered over as fast as I could scrape it off."

"You two just enjoy the time together." She rubbed at her lower back with both hands. "I'd probably better get back in that blankety-blank bed."

"You sure you're feeling okay?" Britt studied her, a little worried by the deepening furrows on her sister's forehead.

"I'm fine." She hesitated. "It's just Braxton Hicks. I've probably been pushing it a little with my time out of bed though."

"Then get yourself back *in* that bed," Britt scolded. "Can I bring you some tea?"

"No. I'm good, thanks." She walked back to the bedroom with the cute waddle she'd developed as the baby grew.

"I'll help you get settled." Britt started after her.

But Phee shook her head, her tone uncharacteristically cranky. "Don't be ridiculous. I think I'm capable of getting myself in bed."

She disappeared into the hallway.

Britt hung Rafe's coat back in the closet. "I hope it snows twenty inches. I kind of like being snowed in. With you."

The smile he gave her said he wasn't torn up about the prospect either. When they were alone, Rafe turned to Britt. "Is she okay?"

She nodded. "I think she's just sick and tired of being in bed. And probably worried about Quinn being on the road too."

"I'm going to call the station again and find out what's up there."

"Can I make you some hot chocolate?"

"Mmm. That sounds good." He met her eyes as if seeing her for the first time tonight. "It kind of feels like we're school kids who got a snow day, doesn't it?"

She laughed. "It does! And I love it."

He picked up his phone, and she went to put a pan of milk on to heat. Turning the flame to low, she went back to the bedroom to check on Phee one more time. "Hey, sis, we're making cocoa. Do you —"

Phee sat on the side of the bed, eyes wide. "Britt . . . I think maybe my water just broke."

"What?" She rushed to her sister's side. "Are you sure?"

"Either that or I just peed the bed." A

416

strangled laugh came from her throat.

"Do you feel okay? I mean . . . are you having more contractions or —" She didn't have a clue what to ask. But this couldn't be good.

"I think I need to call Dr. Hinsen."

"Yes. Absolutely."

Phee picked up her phone, but her hands were trembling like Jell-O. She laughed again, but it sounded closer to panic than glee.

"It's going to be okay, sis. Maybe you *did* just pee."

"Well, that's embarrassing."

"Hey, you're pregnant. You can get away with about anything. Better pee than your water breaking."

"I know." Phee cringed. "But don't tell Rafe."

"Right." Britt shot her a wry smile. "Like I was going to run out and tattle on you."

Phee pulled her phone closer and scrolled through the numbers.

Britt took it from her. "Here, let me call."

She found Dr. Hinsen's after-hours number and entered it, then handed the phone back to her sister.

Phee started to say something, then held up a hand, as apparently someone answered. She explained what was going on and

417

listened for a long time, but she seemed calmer after she hung up. "The nurse said to empty my bladder and then lie flat for thirty minutes and see if there's any further 'leakage.' " She chalked quote marks in the air.

"Do you want to take a quick shower?"

Phee nodded. "Yes. Maybe I should."

Britt helped her into the master bath and got the water running. When Phee was safely seated under running water on the shower bench they'd bought when she first went on bed rest, Britt went to get fresh sheets for Phee's bed.

"Everything okay?" Rafe tapped on the partially open door.

"Come in. But hey, first, could you go turn off the fire under the milk on the stove?"

"Sure."

"And then could you help me with these sheets?"

"Be right back."

When he returned, she had the fitted sheet on and went to the far side of the bed. He helped her spread the flat sheet and tucked in his corners, helping her remake the bed.

"What's going on? You look worried."

"Phee thinks her water might have broken."

"Whoa . . . Is she sure?" His voice was almost a whisper.

"She called her doctor's answering service, and they just want her to lie down for a while and see if she loses any more fluid." She motioned toward the bathroom. "Let me get her settled in bed and I'll be right out."

"Okay. Holler if you need anything." He nodded, but Britt thought there was an edge of panic in his voice.

CHAPTER 37

Rafe called the station. With the phone at his ear, he gave Britt what he hoped was a reassuring smile and waited for someone to pick up. It took every last nerve to keep his voice steady as he spoke to the dispatcher. He would not let on how terrified he was. To Britt or to the dispatcher. But the truth was, he wished now that he'd forged ahead and tried to get to work so he wouldn't be stuck here with Phee threatening to go into labor. If she wasn't already.

Of course, he still might have gotten the call if she needed transport. But this . . . this was his greatest fear come to life!

When he hung up, he relayed the news. "Well, the good news is they're not calling in any extra help. They told me to stay put."

She eyed him. "And the bad news?"

"Nobody could get in if they wanted to. Thankfully, it's just the usual few cars in the ditch, and they're handling it. But if

420

Phee could possibly help it" — he tried for a smile he wasn't feeling — "she might want to hold off on having that baby tonight."

Britt's hand went to her mouth. "Is it really that bad?"

He nodded. "*Nothing's* getting through. The roads are icy and impassable. We've had six and a half inches already and no sign of it letting up."

"What happened to the three to four inches they were predicting?"

"Apparently this front decided to park right over Cape Girardeau County and stay a while. Patty — the dispatcher — said they're putting chains on a couple of the emergency vehicles in case they need to get through, but right now everybody is just hunkered down, waiting. It's even worse up in Perry County."

She shook her head, her eyes holding the same apprehension he was feeling. "Let me go check on Phee again."

She went around the corner into the bedroom. He could hear the sisters' voices mingling, low and intense, but he couldn't make out what they were saying. He grabbed the remote and turned up the volume on a new weather bulletin. It was more of the same with no end in sight. He shot up a prayer. *Please, God.* That was about all he could get out. But he trusted the Lord knew exactly what he was asking.

"Rafe!" Britt's strident cry came from the hallway.

He tossed the remote down and raced back toward Phee's room. "Britt?"

She met him in the hallway just outside the bedroom door, keeping her voice low. "She's having contractions, Rafe. Real ones. Not just the Braxton Hicks."

"How do you know?"

She nodded. "I can feel how rock hard her belly is getting with each one. I don't know if we were timing them right . . . and they're pretty irregular but . . . they're not very far apart."

"Are you sure?" he said again. But he was recalling things from the training films, and he didn't like the implications.

She nodded. "What are we going to do?" Her eyes were wide with unspoken fear.

"I think maybe, given her history, we need to call for an ambulance."

"But . . . they can't get through, can they?"

"They'll have chains on one of the vehicles soon. It might be slow going, but they should be able to get through." He wished he believed that, but remembering the road conditions just a mile up the road from here — and almost an hour ago — he had serious doubts.

Phee cried out from the bedroom, a strangled animal sound that was as familiar to Rafe as his dreams. *His memories.*

"She's in trouble, Britt! Call 911!"

She looked at him as if he were a stranger. "How do you —"

"Tell them to hurry!"

He burst into the bedroom to find Phee red-faced and panting heavily.

"They just keep coming! Contract —" She clutched the blankets with one hand, the other tensed over her belly. She winced in pain, almost writhing.

"We're getting help, Phee. Britt's calling now. It's going to be okay." His voice came out surprisingly calm, but he wished he could take his own words to heart.

He heard Britt in the hallway talking on the phone. Thank the Lord they still had power. Apparently, the lines were holding up under the ice.

After a minute, Britt came in, phone in hand.

He met her at the door, keeping his voice low. "Are they on their way?"

She nodded and whispered, "They said it might be a while though."

She went to her sister's side, knelt by the bed, and put a hand on Phee's forehead.

But out of Phee's line of vision, she shot him a look of sheer desperation. "It's going to be okay, Phee. We've got an ambulance on the way."

"Oh good . . ." Her voice trembled. "I think this is the real thing, sis."

Britt nodded. "I think you might be right. We're finally going to get to meet this precious girl."

Phee grabbed for Britt's hand. "Dr. Hinsen wanted me to make it till March."

Britt laughed. "I think you'll make it. Tomorrow is March 1."

"They say first labors are longer but . . . I don't know how much more I can take. It's . . . pretty bad, Britt. And . . . I was supposed to have a C-section."

"I know. It'll be okay." Britt shot Rafe a look that begged for help.

"Oh! Here comes another one." Phee put a hand to her mouth, but a cry of pain escaped.

"You can do this, Phee. You're doing great." Britt looked scared, but her voice remained calm and soothing.

Rafe watched the sisters together. And he prayed. Hard. He also googled "emergency childbirth" on his phone. What he found was sobering. But it served as a refresher course too. Okay . . . If he had to, he could do this. *Yeah, just keep telling yourself that, Stuart.*

He paced the hallway, feeling completely helpless. This whole thing was too much like . . . with Robby.

But he couldn't just do nothing! *Not this time.*

He checked the time. Twenty-five minutes had passed since Britt had called the ambulance. He dialed the station.

Patty, the dispatcher he'd spoken with earlier, answered. "They're on their way, Rafe, but it's slow going. They're practically having to plow a new path. How's your expectant mama doing?"

"Her contractions are pretty close together."

"How close? First-time labors usually take a while."

"The contractions are coming every four or five minutes."

"Hmm. When did her water break?"

He looked at his phone again. "A little over an hour ago, I'd say. Around nine o'clock maybe."

"Okay." Patty sounded relieved, even dismissive. "You've got some time. If they get any closer, let me know."

"So you can do what?" He hadn't meant it to come out so gruffly.

"Believe it or not, I've talked more than one baby into this world." She chuckled. "Not counting my own."

"You've seriously talked people through a delivery? Over the phone?"

"I have. One mama delivered her own baby with me on the other end." Pride filled her voice.

"Well, that's good. Because if that ambulance doesn't get here pretty quick, you're going to be talking me through delivering this one." *Or talking me off a ledge.*

"If it comes to that, you'll do just fine, Rafe. Just keep your head. You can do this."

"I'll try. There are some complicating factors though." He explained about the placenta previa and how Phee had been on bed rest. "It resolved a few weeks ago, but her doctor was still anticipating a possible C-section."

"I'll tell the crew to hustle butt."

"Thanks, Patty." He hung up and took a deep breath before going to check on Phee again.

Britt met him at the door, eyes wider than before, if that was possible. "Rafe, she was feeling like she needed to *push* on that last contraction. It's too soon to push, isn't it? Where *is* that ambulance?"

He told her what Patty had said about the

crew. "She said she'd talk us through this . . . if we have to deliver this baby. But I think you should call Phee's doctor. There might be something we need to know, given the placenta previa."

"Yes, Dr. Hinsen was still planning for the possibility of a cesarean delivery."

"I told Patty that. I've been studying up on childbirth for the last ten minutes" — he gave a dry laugh and rolled his eyes — "but I don't think I'm quite ready to perform a cesarean."

"I'll call Dr. Hinsen." Britt went for her phone on Phee's nightstand. But before she could reach for it, Phee grabbed her arm, another contraction starting.

The sounds she was making were exactly . . . *exactly* like the ones Ma had made when Robby was born. Rafe rushed to the side of the bed and knelt beside Britt. "Phee, if you can help it *don't* push. Not yet. The ambulance is on the way, but it's going to be —"

"I *have* to push. I can't . . . stop!" An unearthly sound came from her throat. She arched her back and groaned with what was unmistakably pushing.

Britt dropped to her knees beside the bed and cradled her sister's head until the contraction ended.

427

"Okay . . ." Rafe looked at her hard and made his voice firm. "We are going to deliver a baby."

"Rafe!" Britt's eyes were wild with terror.

"Where would I find clean towels?"

"Under the sink in the bathroom." She pointed, her words tumbling over each other.

"You help Phee get undressed. We need to check if she's dilated." He wasn't sure where the instructions were coming from, except that he finally felt like he was *doing* something.

He scrubbed his hands in the bathroom sink and returned with a stack of fresh towels. Phee was pushing again, harder than before. The sounds she was making carried him back to the night of Robby's birth. He fought his way back.

"The baby's head is *right* there, Rafe! I can see it!" Britt sounded more in awe than scared now.

But his adrenaline was off the charts.

"There it is again. Rafe, I can see the baby's head!"

"Okay. Okay . . . Let's see what we have." Rafe recognized that he was in a fight or flight response now, like he often experienced when he worked the scene of an accident. He knelt beside the bed and gently

428

lifted the sheet. "Britt, get my phone out of my pocket and call Patty. I just washed my hands and I don't want to touch anything. It'll be the last number I called."

Britt took his phone from his back pocket, then scooted on her knees toward the head of the bed to make more room for him. Her phone still lay on the nightstand, but the call to Dr. Hinsen had apparently gone to voice mail.

"Nine-one-one dispatcher." Britt tapped the speaker button and held the phone closer to Rafe.

"Patty, talk to me. We've got a baby on the way!" For Phee and Britt's sake, he worked to keep his voice steady, but he also wanted Patty to hear the urgency in it.

"You do? That was fast. Talk to me."

"We can see the head. The baby's crowning."

"Oh . . . Wow." The dispatcher seemed to take a minute to collect herself.

He knew the feeling.

"Okay," she said. "Tell me what we've got. Better yet, let me FaceTime you. It'll help if I can see things there. Is Mama okay with that?"

"Mama's fine with that." Britt answered for her sister.

"Just don't put it on YouTube," Phee

groaned.

That made the three of them laugh, but another contraction interrupted, and they quickly sobered. Britt disconnected, and almost immediately, Patty's FaceTime call came.

"Okay, let me see what Rafe is seeing."

Britt took the phone to the end of the bed but kept her gaze on her sister's face.

"Oh," Patty exclaimed. "That little one is in a hurry! Boy or girl?"

"We don't know yet," Britt supplied.

"Well, it looks like you're going to find out pretty quickly here. Can you bring me in a little closer?"

Britt moved the phone closer.

"Ah, okay. Everything's looking good. Has she started pushing?"

Patty's voice felt like a lifeline, and for the first time, Rafe thought he understood the things Britt had said about *his* voice that night he'd talked her through while they waited for the ambulance. "She's been pushing for a while now. Uncontrollable."

"Okay. That likely means she's ready. From how much head we're seeing, I think she's fully dilated." Patty's matter-of-fact manner gave him comfort.

"Yes, I think she is." He'd expected it to be awkward with Britt's sister, but he was in medical mode now, and all he saw was that the baby's head was definitely crowning. There was some blood, but it didn't appear excessive, and she didn't appear to be tearing.

"Okay, Phee." He looked over the sheet, waiting for her to meet his gaze. He forced a smile. "Your baby is almost here. The next time you feel the urge to push, go ahead and push." Almost immediately, she began that distinctive, plaintive wail.

The warnings about Phee's condition, placenta previa, sounded in the back of his mind, but there was no stopping this birth now. He prayed desperately that the condition truly had resolved itself and there wouldn't be any repercussions.

"Here it comes, Phee." Britt put her face close to her sister's, tears wetting both their cheeks. "Push, Phee. You're almost there, sis . . . Come on, little baby!"

"Oh! There you go! Almost." Rafe repositioned himself and adjusted the towels under Phee's hips. The baby's head came farther, then retracted. "You're almost there, Phee. Go ahead and push on this next contraction."

"It's starting. It's starting!" Phee sounded panicked, but she trained her gaze on Britt until her eyes squeezed shut with the effort of pushing.

A short reprieve and another contraction started. They seemed to come one after the other with almost no time to rest in between.

Another wave began and Phee bore down hard. All at once the baby emerged in a gush of water and blood. "He's here! He's out! It's a boy!"

Rafe quickly cocooned the tiny boy in a warm towel. In a state of awe, he looked at the little red body lying on the bed, arms waving in the air. But then they stilled, and a dreadful silence shrouded the room.

In that moment, all the fears that had bound him up carried him back to that awful, fateful night of Robby's birth.

"A boy?" Phee tried to sit up and see. "We had a boy? I don't hear him. Britt? Is he okay? Rafe? Is he okay, Britt?" Panic crawled into her voice.

"Where are we, guys?" Patty's voice came from the phone. "Everything okay there?"

Britt seemed to realize she'd lowered the phone in her haste to see the infant, and she aimed the camera at the baby.

"I don't hear him." Patty's voice seemed strained. "You may need to clear his airway."

Rafe's thoughts were once again dragged back to that awful day, and his strength leached from him. *Please, God* . . .

But fight-or-flight kicked in again, and remembering something from one of the articles he'd skimmed, Rafe gathered the baby, towel and all, into his arms and put his little finger in the infant's mouth, sweeping it gently.

Before he could finish, the baby coughed weakly, then sucked in a huge breath and let it out in a lusty squall.

Rafe almost cheered, feeling as though he'd just climbed Mount Everest. "He's fine. He's great. And he's got a set of lungs on him, this one."

He would have slumped in relief if he hadn't been higher than a kite on adrenaline.

CHAPTER 38

March

"And watch her closely for excessive bleeding." Rafe spoke to the young EMT with confidence as he apprised them of Phee's condition and helped them bundle up her and the baby. While Rafe had evaluated the newborn with Patty's help, Phee delivered the placenta without complications. Now, after letting her have some time to cuddle and nurse the baby, they were transferring mom and infant onto the gurney for transport to the hospital

Seeing him in full-on EMT mode, Britt's heart swelled with pride. It still seemed unbelievable to think that he had delivered her new little nephew! Everything had happened in a blur after that. Under Patty's direction, Rafe had cut the baby's cord and assisted in evaluating the infant for Apgar scores. The precious little guy had aced the "test" with a score of nine, and you would

434

have thought Rafe was personally responsible.

Well, in Britt's eyes, he was. Despite his initial apprehension, which only Britt had noticed, Rafe had risen to the occasion and kept them all calm with his matter-of-fact attitude and his professional management of Phee's delivery.

Though Phee had wanted to stay at home, Rafe — and Patty too — strongly recommended they go to the hospital so both could be checked out under better conditions and be near medical care should any complications develop before this winter storm was over.

"You still couldn't get hold of Quinn?" Worry lines criss-crossed Phee's forehead, even as she smiled down at her newborn son.

"Here . . ." Britt tapped her phone. "Let me try him again." It was after midnight now and she'd been trying, without success, to reach Quinn since the baby took his first breath. She tried once more with Face-Time. The app rang once, twice, then suddenly, there Quinn was, bundled in winter cap and hooded parka and standing in a dark, snowy parking lot somewhere.

Britt winked at Phee over the phone. "Hey, Quinn. Sorry to call so late."

"No worries. We just got back to the hotel. Been helping people dig out from this crazy storm. How are you guys faring there? Still have power?"

"Oh, we have power."

"Wait." Quinn looked at his watch and an edge came to his voice. "It's midnight. You're up awfully late. Everything okay there?"

She couldn't hide the smile. "Everything's just fine here. You want to talk to Phee?"

"If she's up. Don't wake her though."

"Oh, she's up all right." She turned the phone on Phee, coming close so he wouldn't miss that a *baby* was the reason for all the emergency gear visible on his screen.

"What?"

Phee's laughter was music. "Hey, babe. We've been a little busy tonight."

"What — Is that . . . ? *What* is going on?"

Phee laughed harder. "I'd introduce you, but I don't know his name yet. Thought you might want to weigh in on that one last time before we decide for sure."

"*His* name? We had a boy? What in the world? But . . . you're at home?"

"Yeah, well, this little guy decided he didn't want to wait around for the ambulance, so he just came on out to play."

"A boy! But . . . he's okay? *You're* okay?"

"Couldn't be better. And no C-section for me." Her voice broke. "Rafe Stuart delivered our son. And thank the Lord he was here!" The story poured out of Phee with Quinn muttering "You're kidding" at least a dozen times before thanking Rafe profusely and asking for his version of the story.

From her perch on the window seat beside the bed, Britt watched Rafe recount their adventure, feeling so proud of him and his role in this amazing story. The enthusiasm in his voice said he was practically floating on air. She was too.

"Wow. This is all just so unbelievable." Quinn's astonishment was clear, even in the fuzzy FaceTime image. "I . . . I think I need to sit down for a minute."

They all laughed, and Britt and Rafe called out their congratulations, then slipped out to the hallway to give Quinn and Phee a little privacy. The two EMTs who'd made the run in the snow followed them out of the room.

"You guys can wait in the front room," Rafe told the men. "We'll let you know when they're ready to go."

"You're sure it's safe to take them out in this?" Britt cringed to think what might happen if the ambulance slipped off the road.

But the younger of the two reassured her. "The snow has let up a little, and we'll just follow our own tracks back. Don't worry, we forged a trail on the way in. And we'll take it slow."

Rafe put an arm around her. "They'll be fine."

Britt relaxed against his strong shoulder, trusting his judgment.

The EMTs shook Rafe's hand in turn on their way to the living room.

"Way to go, man."

"Yeah, pretty cool," the younger guy said. "You'll probably make the news, you know?"

Rafe waved his comment away. "I don't want any of that. Just doing my job."

But Britt didn't miss the triumph in his demeanor.

When they were alone, she kissed his cheek. "You were so awesome in there! Oh, Rafe, I don't know what I would have done if you hadn't been here! If you hadn't come back —"

"You would have done what you needed to."

She shook her head adamantly. "No, I would have totally freaked out."

He tossed his head. "Well, don't think I wasn't freaking out a little myself."

"What? You were cool as a cucumber. It was like you deliver babies every day." Even as she said it, she knew he was remembering Robby's birth.

But he just smiled, then scoffed. "I'm going to say this was my first *and* last delivery. Not sure I'd survive another night like this."

"Me neither. But it was amazing."

His gaze captured hers, and he gave her a spontaneous hug. "It *was* pretty amazing, wasn't it? Suddenly there's this . . . this new *person* in the room. Just like that."

She shook her head, overwhelmed by the awe of it.

When Rafe didn't speak for a few moments, she looked up to see that his cheeks were wet with tears. "Rafe? Are you okay?"

He nodded, still overcome with emotion. Finally, he swallowed hard and when he spoke, his gaze was faraway. "You just can't know what a . . . *redeeming* thing that was."

"You mean because of Robby?"

He nodded again.

She reached up to wipe his cheeks with her palms. "I'm so glad. Oh, Rafe, I'm so glad." Only two weeks ago she'd whispered a prayer for him, asking God for that very thing. With that very word: *Redeem.* He had answered in amazing ways.

■ ■ ■ ■

Rafe didn't think he'd ever been in such a noisy hospital room. He half expected a nurse to appear at any moment and shut down the party that was going on in Phee's room. Looking radiant with the baby in her arms, she was on her phone, FaceTiming with her dad to introduce the first Chandler grandson. The rest of the family looked on. Even Mateo had been allowed into the room since he was twelve — and since the start of school had been delayed by two hours because of last night's snow.

Rafe stood behind Britt, watching from a distance, but feeling more like he belonged than he ever had in his life. He smiled as Phee relayed everything that had happened last night to her father.

But when she turned the phone's camera on Rafe, he took a step back and held up his hands. "No, no . . ."

Britt gave him a playful shove. "Get up there and take credit where credit's due!"

Turner Chandler nodded at him, and Rafe gave an awkward wave. "Nice to meet you, sir. Congratulations."

"Rafe? Sounds like you're the hero in this story."

440

Rafe shook his head. "Oh, no sir. That would be your daughter. She was a champ." He put an arm around Britt. "This one too. I had lots of help."

"Well, I'm glad you were there. We owe you our thanks. I look forward to shaking your hand in person one of these days."

"Yes, sir. Me too."

Phee beamed at him and turned the camera back on the baby. "Did anyone tell you, Dad? We named him William Turner Mitchell. After you."

"I heard that." He sounded pleased. "I like how you got Turner in there!"

"I think we'll call him Will." Phee looked up at Quinn as if to get his approval.

He nodded and stroked the sleeping baby's head.

After they hung up, Quinn took the sleeping baby from Phee and laid him in the bassinet. Jo and Luke said their goodbyes, despite Mateo's protests.

"You don't want to be late for school, bud," Luke said.

"Wanna bet?" He pouted.

Phee laughed. "You come out and see us after we get home and you can hold him."

"Really?"

"Of course." Quinn walked with them to the door of Phee's room. "Hey, you guys be careful on the roads."

"I'd better get going too." Rafe motioned toward the baby. "You've got a keeper there."

"You must be exhausted, Rafe." Phee reached out to touch his arm. "Go home and get some rest. And thank you again." Her voice broke.

Quinn echoed her words. "We can't thank you enough, man." He clapped Rafe's shoulder.

"I'll walk down with you." Britt went to the other side of Phee's bed and leaned over the bassinet. "Just let me tell this little guy goodbye. *Will.* I love it. Sounds like a little prince." She cooed at the sleeping baby and tweaked his toes through the blankets. "You caused some pretty major excitement, buddy. I hope that's not going to become a habit."

Phee laughed. "You've got that right! I think he's already caused quite enough trouble."

"Enough for a lifetime." Quinn turned to Britt. "Do you want to hold him?"

"Oh, can I?" She turned to Rafe. "Can you wait for just a couple minutes?"

"Sure."

He watched her reach into the bassinet and scoop up the baby as if she held newborns every day. She cradled him in her arms and whispered something he couldn't catch. But seeing her like that, so smitten and . . . *maternal,* he fell just a little bit deeper in love in that moment. And saw what he hoped was a glimpse of their future.

Still, the weight of his situation hung over everything. Britt didn't know yet that just before he'd arrived at the hospital, he'd gotten a call from a friend on the police force. Apparently, Buck Obermueller had made bail and they'd released him. There would be a trial, but it might be months from now. And with the guy on the loose and having everything to gain by seeing to it that no witnesses testified against him, Rafe couldn't let Ma move back home yet.

He and Ma were getting along fine. It wasn't that. In fact, their work schedules meant they were rarely home at the same time. And he did appreciate the meals she left in the fridge for him each day — though the bathroom scales weren't quite so happy about it. Still, it was unsettling to have Ma's situation up in the air. And it was still a possibility that she'd have to pay back the "loan" she'd agreed to. Which meant *he'd* be paying that money back. Money he didn't have to spare. Especially if he wanted to make a life with Britt Chandler.

He wouldn't tell Britt yet. He would not
ruin the joy of this day for her. But she'd
have to know soon.

CHAPTER 39

Wednesday dawned cold and clear, and by afternoon when they gathered up at the clearing, the sky was the soft lavender blue color that Mom always called periwinkle. They'd all started out at Quinn and Phee's house for hot chocolate under the guise of seeing baby Will on his one-week-old birthday. Jo protested when Luke suggested they go up to the clearing, since Phee had so recently given birth and Will was too tiny to be out in the cold for long. But Mateo begged, Phee insisted, and Quinn offered to stay behind with her. All of which were part of the plan for Jo's surprise reveal.

"Just FaceTime us when you get up there, would you?" Phee's voice held longing, but the longing was overshadowed by the love in her eyes as she looked down on her nursing baby, his face concealed by a blue blanket. "I can't even remember what the clearing looks like in the winter."

"Me neither," Jo said. "I haven't been up there since this guy" — she patted Luke's chest — "carried me in that stupid boot I had to wear forever after I broke my foot."

"Yes, and look how that ended up," Quinn said.

"Ended pretty well." Smiling, Jo held up the engagement ring Luke had given her when he proposed that night. "And I don't know how we're going to pull it off, but there *will* be a wedding up there in two short months. Even if people have to sit on blankets on the ground."

Britt could hardly stand it, knowing the surprise that awaited her sister at the top of those stairs. She didn't dare catch Phee's eye or their expressions would give it all away for sure. Either that, or she'd start crying because Phee was getting left out. She knew it had to kill Quinn not to get to see Jo's reaction to this project he and Luke had orchestrated and pulled off amazingly.

But at least they'd have it on video. And Quinn and Phee could watch in real time via FaceTime.

"Well, quit talkin' about it and let's *go*!" Mateo jumped up and down, as excited as the rest of them. It was a small miracle he hadn't spilled the beans yet. Of course they weren't up to the clearing yet. Britt exchanged looks with Rafe, and his wry expression said he was thinking the same thing.

She'd barely had a chance to talk to Rafe about the arrest that had been made two weeks ago right here on their property. Rafe's mom had identified Robertson Obermueller — Buck — as the man who'd made threats to her, and Kathy Landon had corroborated Becky's account, even mentioning that Buck had tried to pawn an expensive pair of earrings without her permission. No doubt the ones her grandmother had given her. For Kathy's sake, Britt hoped "tried" meant he hadn't been successful.

Britt had relayed what she knew to her family, and they'd all agreed to keep the details of the story under wraps both for the sake of Rafe's mom and so there wouldn't be any negative publicity for The Cottages on Poplar Brook Road.

By all appearances, the bottom line for Rafe and his mom was that they wouldn't be responsible for the money Buck Obermeuller had scammed from Becky. Rafe said the police chief thought there was even a chance his mother might get back, as restitution, some of the money she'd paid him.

"Okay, everybody ready?" Luke seemed pleased to take the lead in Quinn's absence, walking faster than necessary to the foot of the stairway that led up to the clearing. It was already getting dark, and he carried a huge flashlight, but he put his free arm around Jo.

Britt could almost feel the electricity in the air. Her sister was going to flip out when she saw the finished venue, almost exactly as she'd sketched it out.

Mateo ran ahead, according to plan, and flipped on the lights at the breaker box.

Jo shot Luke a questioning glance when the lights came on. "How did he reach the switch? Has he gotten that tall?"

"No, there's a ladder up there."

"There is? How do you know?"

"I was up there . . . a while back."

"When?"

Luke pulled her close and feigned an annoyed look. "Are you going to talk or walk?"

"What? You goofball." But Jo turned back and continued up the stairs.

"Hurry up, guys!" Mateo's voice wafted down from above them.

"Hold your horses," Luke shouted back. "Some of us are old."

Britt laughed. "Speak for yourself, Luke." She looked back toward Phee and Quinn's house, wondering if they could hear the chatter.

"Who's going to call Phee?" Luke asked, all innocence.

"I will," Jo said.

"No, let me." Britt quickly connected by FaceTime to Phee's phone. "Here. I've already got her."

It was a little white lie, as Phee hadn't answered yet, but she'd be forgiven in about two minutes.

They reached the last few steps and Luke grabbed Jo and turned her away from the clearing. "Hang on a minute."

"What's wrong?" Confusion knit Jo's brow.

"Just shut up and close your eyes."

"What is going on? We're already engaged, you know. You don't get a do-over."

"Excuse me? I think I was pretty thorough the first time around." Luke laughed and went behind her, reaching around to cover her eyes with his hands.

The guys had added more strings of lights over the dance floor after they installed it last night, and Britt's breath caught as those twinkled to life now. This truly would be an amazing wedding venue.

"Okay, you can open —"

"Wait, wait, I don't have Phee on yet." She checked her phone.

"Hello?" Phee and Quinn appeared on the

screen, smiling.

Britt held a finger to her lips to let them know the reveal hadn't happened yet. "Look how pretty it is up here," she told them. She turned the phone so they could see Luke covering Jo's eyes.

"Ready?" Luke looked at Britt.

"Everybody's here."

"Okay." Still covering her eyes, he turned Jo to face the dance floor and the benches, lined up as neat as church pews. Luke had come up earlier and lit the same lanterns he'd used for his proposal and set them on every other bench. "Ready?"

"For what?" Jo grasped Luke's hands over hers. "I have no clue what is going on here."

He took his hands away from her eyes and watched her face with the look of a man completely smitten.

Britt ran ahead of them to capture Jo's expression for Phee's benefit.

Jo stared at the clearing, looked to Luke, then back at the clearing — then promptly burst into tears.

Mateo roared. "Told ya!"

Britt held up the phone so everyone could see that Phee was crying too. Her own heart was full, but she was too happy to cry.

Mateo laughed harder. "Two down!"

Quinn, Luke, and Rafe seemed to find

that inordinately funny. Must be an inside joke. She'd ask Rafe about it later.

When Jo could finally speak, she wandered through the venue exclaiming how perfect everything was. "This is . . . I don't even . . . When did this even happen? Oh, Luke!" Her voice rose an octave.

"The benches aren't tied down yet," Mateo informed her. "Luke wanted to be sure and communicate with you before they set them up permanent."

Jo laughed along with the rest. "Luke is a very wise man."

He pulled Jo close and whispered something for only her to hear. A brief wave of envy washed over Britt, but a moment later, the strains of Pachelbel's "Canon in D" filled the treetops. She didn't know about this part of the plan.

Everyone looked up toward the speakers, then immediately to Luke, whose freelance DJ status made him the likely suspect.

He produced a handheld mike from his coat pocket and went to speak into Britt's phone. "Quinn, Phee, this one's for you. We'll hold the dance floor. And don't worry, Phee. I picked a really short version and it's already halfway over, so you'd better get to dancing."

Phee's phone glitched and then focused

again as Quinn set it on the dresser. Britt held her phone high so they could all watch as Quinn danced with his wife in their bedroom — a slow waltz with the baby nestled between them in Phee's arms.

Britt sighed, her throat tight with emotion at the sweet scene. As the song came to an end, Quinn danced Phee over to her side of the bed and "dipped" her and little Will gently onto the pillows as the last note faded. Phee giggled, Quinn gave a little wave, and a few seconds later, their screen went dark.

They all laughed, and a chorus of *awwws* rose. But the music started up again, and Luke grabbed Jo's hand and led her to the dance floor. Luke knew her well and had chosen "Sunrise" by Nora Jones. They drew applause and whistles dancing an endearing cross between the foxtrot and the bolero. Mateo even got in on the action when Jo whirled and pulled him onto the stage.

Britt FaceTimed Phee back, and before she turned her camera on the dance floor, she caught a glimpse of her oldest sister and Quinn sitting side by side on their bed, baby between them, laughing and clapping to the music. They must have been able to hear it at the house. It was almost like having them up here in the clearing.

Britt couldn't remember when she'd had so much fun. Or when her heart had been so full. But she kept stealing glances at Rafe, wondering if he realized that they were almost certainly next up on the dance floor.

They'd never danced together. She didn't even know if he liked to dance. Or knew how. For Quinn and Luke's sake, she prayed he'd be a good sport. But he just stood there watching the dance floor, avoiding looking at her, hands in his pockets, looking more than a little apprehensive.

Luke and Jo ended out of breath but laughing and aglow with love.

Luke pointed at her and Rafe in turn and beckoned them to the dance floor.

She looked at Rafe, trying to measure his enthusiasm and wanting to give him an out if he needed one. "We don't even . . . have a song yet."

But Rafe grinned at her and grabbed her hand, pulling her onto the dance floor. "Oh yes we do."

She laughed as the music began and she recognized the introduction to Brad Paisley's "Today," the song that had been playing in the coffee shop that night he'd first kissed her.

Rafe took her in his arms and cradled her head against his chest. An easy, slow dance that filled her with emotion. When their song ended, she pulled away, laughing, and started off the floor. But Rafe pulled her back.

She looked to Luke to see if more music was coming, but everyone had slipped into the shadows, leaving them alone on the stage. She looked back at Rafe and whispered, "Not only do you have a sexy voice, but you're a pretty good dancer too. Who knew?"

His goofy bow in response made her laugh.

"Oh, Rafe, this night was so much fun! I'm so glad you were here to share it."

"It *was* fun. I'm kind of sad the house and the venue are both finished. Now I won't have an excuse to come out here anymore."

"What do you mean no excuse? *Excuse* me? What am I?"

"*You* are adorable." He said it low enough that no one else could hear. But he kissed her in front of them all.

Mateo made gagging noises and hollered, "Ewww, you guys are worse than Luke and Jo."

The kid clearly enjoyed the laughter that followed.

But Rafe wasn't laughing when he took a

knee in the middle of the dance floor. Britt gasped. "Rafe? What is this?" Suddenly she knew exactly what it was, and like Joanna before her, she burst into tears.

"Haha! I win!" Mateo crowed. "She's cryin' like a baby!"

Rafe cracked up, but Luke shushed Mateo and pulled the boy back into the shadows.

She narrowed her eyes. "What's that about?"

"I'll tell you later. Right now I have a very important question to ask you."

Snared between laughter and tears, she could hardly breathe. She bent to meet his gaze. "Oh, Rafe. Are you serious? Is this . . . the big Instagram-worthy proposal?"

He looked up at her with that crooked little half grin she loved so much. "It might be. If you'd shut up long enough to let me ask the question."

Trembling, not daring to believe what was happening, she made a motion of zipping her lips. Then she dropped to her own knees in front of him.

"I wanted to tell you something I read the other day. I might have kind of" — a slow grin came — "memorized it. It goes like this: 'Life is short, break the rules. Forgive quickly, kiss slowly . . .' " He leaned in to demonstrate before continuing. " 'Love truly . . .' " His voice — that beautiful voice — hitched ever so slightly.

"Oh, Rafe . . . I love you so much."

"Don't you want to hear the rest of it?" He kissed her again, his composure regained.

She beamed. "I *know* the rest of it. '. . . never regret anything that makes you smile.' "

"Hey!" He tweaked her nose. "That would be *you,* sweet woman. But quit stealing my material!"

She tried to look appropriately sheepish. "Sorry, but I kind of like your material."

"Oh yeah?" He pulled her close and whispered in her ear. "Here's another one: 'To get the full value of joy you must have someone to divide it with.' "

Britt pulled away and studied him for a minute. "Did *he* really say that, or are you just making things up now?"

He laughed softly and pulled her close. "He said it first, but I'm saying it now. To you."

"Oh, Rafe . . ."

He put his other knee down on a gray square on the dance floor in the clearing, bowing with her, and it dawned on her that this glorious space in God's creation was about to become the venue for a third Chandler sister's proposal. Oh what a story they'd have to tell. Not just her and Rafe, but all of them! And the children who came after them.

Rafe waved a hand in front of her. "Hey, you. Did I lose you?"

"Just . . . daydreaming a little."

He rolled his eyes. "Now pay attention. This is important."

She waited, savoring every blessed second.

He took her hand and held it to his chest, and she could feel the strong rhythm of his life beneath her palm.

"Britt Chandler, you have given me so much joy since the day you first became my friend. Would you be my someone to divide that joy with? For the rest of our lives?"

Heart full to overflowing, she whispered through tears. "Yes. The biggest *yes* you've ever heard."

"I don't have a ring. I wanted to wait until —"

"I don't care about a ring. It's you I want, Rafe. Only you."

"Did she say yes?" Mateo shouted across the clearing. "She did!" Rafe shouted back, his smile as wide as the Mississippi. "A *big* yes!"

His laughter was drowned out by the cheers of her family. *Their* family.

CHAPTER 40

Britt was stuffing clean sheets into the dryer, daydreaming for the thousandth time about Rafe's sweet proposal, when her phone trilled. She didn't recognize the number but didn't have the luxury of ignoring her phone when it could be an Airbnb guest. Ironically, though the ad they'd run for Valentine's Day had garnered only one booking — Kathy Landon's — they'd had guests almost every night since, and several of them had mentioned seeing the Valentine's ad — and, of course, hoped to use the discount code, despite its being expired. Grateful for the business, Britt and her sisters had decided to honor the special price through March.

She tapped Accept. "Good morning. The Cottages on Poplar Brook Road. This is Britt."

"Oh. It *is* you. I wasn't sure if this was the right number . . . Oh! I guess I should tell you who this is. It's Becky Stuart, Rafe's mom."

"Oh, hi, Becky."

"I heard some news about you." There was a smile in her voice.

Britt gave a nervous laugh. "You did, huh?" She guessed Rafe's mom meant their engagement. Rafe had asked if he could tell his mom, but Britt hadn't heard whether he had or not yet.

"I just called to say congratulations. I'm so happy for him. Well, for you both, of course."

Good. He'd told her. "Thank you, Becky. We're really excited."

"I would like to take you out for coffee. To celebrate. Are you free tomorrow morning?" The invitation sounded well rehearsed.

But wow. Nothing like short notice. "Tomorrow? What time were you thinking? I thought Rafe had to work tomorrow."

"I don't mean with Rafe. Just you and me. I don't have to work Saturdays, so you just tell me what time is best for you."

"Okay . . ." She glanced at her calendar. "We have Airbnb guests coming tonight, but they won't check out until noon tomorrow, so maybe nine o'clock? Is that too early?"

"Not at all. Do you have a favorite place?"

She thought briefly about inviting Becky

out to the cottages, but it was too short notice and with guests here . . . "How about Coffee's On in Langhorne?" Maybe she'd tell Rafe's mom what a special role that place had played in her and Rafe's story. How they'd found their song that night.

"I know the place. Would you like me to pick you up?"

"That's sweet of you, but I'll just meet you there. I have some errands to run after."

"Oh. Okay then. I'll see you there."

"Thank you, Becky. I'll look forward to it." It struck her after she'd hung up that Becky might have been hinting for an excuse to see Melvin. But she wasn't inclined to change their plans now. She felt honored at Becky's invitation but a little uneasy that Rafe wouldn't be there to steer the conversation.

She texted him: "Your mom just invited me to coffee! Just the two of us."

She added a smiley face and hit Send. Rafe was at work, so she wasn't surprised when she didn't get a reply right away.

But a couple of hours later, he texted back: "Cool. When?"

"Tomorrow. At Coffee's On."

"Are you going?"

"Well, duh. Of course, I'm going."

"I love you."

"Love you more."

She waited for a few minutes, but that was all. It must be a busy day at the station. She spent the rest of the morning cleaning the cottage and making up the beds, then baking scones to have waiting in a pretty basket on the counter.

Since her talk with Rafe on Valentine's night, she'd found a new freedom in doing these mundane tasks. She loved her work, loved making the cottage and cabins special for guests. Loved thinking about their delight at finding homemade scones in a tidy kitchen that smelled of cinnamon and vanilla. *These* were the gifts she felt she was created to use. They weren't anything as noble as being a nurse, but hadn't she just read in her Bible last night, "If the whole body were an eye, where would the sense of hearing be? If the whole body were an ear, where would the sense of smell be?"

She might not be as important as an eye or an ear, but if God had made her to be a pinky finger or a little toe, she would be completely happy in that.

Britt's phone rang at seven thirty Saturday morning. Becky Stuart's name appeared, now that Britt had added her to her contacts. "Hello, Becky."

"Good morning. I hope I'm not calling too early. Listen, slight change of plans. I got inspired last night and tried out a new coffee cake recipe. Why don't you come to my house for coffee this morning instead?"

"Oh? Are you sure? Your house on Stanton, you mean? Not Rafe's apartment?"

"Oh, not Rafe's. I'm still staying there with him, but I needed to come home and water the plants anyway, so I thought I could entertain this morning."

"Okay. Sure. Can I bring anything?" She hoped she hadn't walked into that one.

But Becky didn't mention Melvin. Or even hint. "No, just bring yourself. And an appetite."

She laughed. "That won't be a problem. Thanks again. I'll see you in a little while."

She finished getting ready, checked the Airbnb messages, and headed for Becky's. Rafe had sounded really pleased to learn they were having coffee together, and Britt regretted that she hadn't thought of the idea first. She was anxious to talk to Becky and get a better feel, in person, for how the woman was feeling about her son's engagement.

She parked in the driveway where Rafe had parked that day they'd brought Melvin here. She locked the car and went to ring

463

the doorbell.

Becky answered almost immediately. "Come in, come in. My, don't you look pretty."

"Thank you." She inhaled deeply. "It smells wonderful in here." Cinnamon and vanilla . . . just like the cottage had smelled when she was baking her cinnamon scones yesterday.

"Oh, that's my coffee cake. Or maybe you're smelling the coffee brewing? Red Banner. If you've never tried their —"

"Oh, we serve their coffee at the cottages! Isn't it wonderful?"

"It's the best!" Becky beamed, and Britt sensed she had nothing but good intentions toward her. Suddenly, it seemed like the morning was going to be just fine. She felt the tension leave her shoulders.

Becky motioned her into the kitchen. While Britt looked on, she sliced the fragrant coffee cake and put slices on two plates, then poured coffee into mugs. "I remember Rafe said you like a mug instead of cup and saucer."

"Oh, goodness. Either one is fine. If you'd rather have a cup and saucer, don't let me stop —"

The doorbell interrupted her and Becky looked puzzled. "Now who could that be?

I'm not expecting anyone." She dried her hands on a dish towel. "I'm so sorry. I'll be right back."

Britt heard her go to the door, but then silence. When Becky returned a few minutes later, her face was ashen. She went to the sink and rinsed the knife and serving spatula she'd used, taking her time drying them with her back to Britt.

"Is . . . everything okay?"

Becky sighed and turned to face her. "Yes, but let's just stay here in the kitchen for a few minutes. I don't really want to talk to . . . who's at the door."

"What's wrong? Becky? You look scared."

The doorbell rang again. And again.

"It's Buck. That idiot! I don't know how he knew I was here, but I don't want to talk to him."

"No, of course not. You shouldn't have to."

Becky tensed at the sound of the screen door opening. Then someone pounded on the front door. Loudly.

"Good grief. He's going to break the glass!" Britt suddenly felt more frightened than annoyed.

"*Shhh.* He'll go away if we ignore him. Let's just try to enjoy our coffee." She took a sip from the mug she'd just poured, but then set it down and looked at Britt with tears welling. "I'm so sorry. I wanted this to be a special —"

"I know you're in there, Becky!" More pounding on the door. "Open this door!"

"Becky, I think we need to call 911!"

"No! Not . . . yet. I don't want to cause Rafe more trouble than I already have."

"Becky! Open this door before I bust it down!" The deep voice bellowed loud enough to rouse any neighbors who happened to be home.

Britt ran to the living room and rifled through her purse for her phone, but when she looked up, the man was peering in the window beside the front door, hands cupped around his eyes. The sheer curtains kept her from seeing him clearly and she hoped he couldn't see her.

Heart hammering, she raced back to the kitchen. "He's looking in your windows! I'm sorry, but I'm calling the police!"

"Yes. Yes, maybe you should." Becky sounded terrified. "I'm calling Rafe."

"Yes! Call him! Hurry!" She felt paralyzed. How far would this man go to get into the house? And how had he known that Becky was here? Had he been following her? Or had he seen Britt's car in the driveway and thought it was Becky's?

It seemed like forever before someone answered, but finally a woman's voice came over the phone. "Nine-one-one, what's your emergency?" The dispatcher's question thrust her back to the day she'd found Phee on the floor of the new house.

For a minute she struggled to find her voice. But the fear in Becky's eyes motivated her. "Someone is trying to break into my friend's house! It's on Stanton Street, but . . ." She touched Becky's arm. "What's your house number?"

"Four-fifty-five Stanton."

Britt relayed the address to the dispatcher. "The man is Buck Obermueller. He was arrested this past Wednesday. I don't know if he escaped from jail or if they let him go, but he's here at Becky Stuart's house and he's making threats!"

"We have an officer on the way, ma'am. How many people are in the house?"

"Just two of us. Becky Stuart and me."

"Are you safe inside the house?"

"Yes, for now." She switched the phone to speaker and held it so Becky could hear. "The doors are locked. But he's threatening to break the front door down."

"Okay. Stay on the phone with me, but get to a safe location in the house. Somewhere that he can't see you. Can you spell

467

the suspect's name, please?"

She did so while Becky took her arm and led the way down the hall to a small bedroom. Becky locked the bedroom door, then led the way to a tiny bathroom in the far corner of the room. She locked that door behind them as well, then pulled the blinds over the single, narrow window.

Becky was crying now, apologizing over and over. "I didn't dream he'd come here. Not after they took him in." Her phone hung limply in her hand, and it didn't look like she'd tried to dial Rafe.

Britt couldn't hang up on the dispatcher. "Did you try to call Rafe?" she asked gently.

"Oh, I think so? No." She punched at her phone's glass with trembling fingers.

But Rafe's image appeared, and then his voice, loud enough for Britt to hear. "Hey, Ma. What's up?"

"Oh, Rafe, I'm so sorry!"

"Ma? What's wrong?"

"Can I talk to him?" Britt whispered. She muted the dispatcher but left her on speaker.

Becky thrust the phone at her, squeezing her eyes shut.

"Rafe, it's me. We're at your mom's house. Buck is trying to get in!"

"What? Don't open the door!"

"No. We didn't. We're locked in the bath-room. The little one off the bedroom. I'm talking to a dispatcher on my phone. But Rafe, he's threatening to break down the door." She fought to keep her voice steady, for Rafe's sake as much as Becky's.

"Stay right where you are. I'm on my way."

"Nine-one-one said the police are on their way too."

"I haven't gotten called on that, but I'm on my way. You stay where you are!"

"We will. We're both okay."

"Ms. Chandler? Britt?" The dispatcher's voice made her and Becky both jump. "Are you there?"

She unmuted the phone. "Yes, I'm here. We're still locked in the bathroom."

"Okay. The police are approaching the house right now. Stay inside until I give you the all clear."

"Okay. We will."

"Stay on the line with me."

"Yes, I will."

Sirens sounded outside and again, Britt was carried to that night in November when emergency vehicles had swarmed Quinn and Phee's house. She reached for Becky's hand and squeezed it, trying to reassure the trembling woman. "Do you hear that? The police are here."

Muffled shouts reached them in the bathroom, the police shouting for Buck to stand down, Buck's grumbling compliance, and finally quiet.

Not daring to move, Britt looked into Becky's eyes, wondering if the fear and uncertainty she saw there was reflected in her own eyes. Footsteps sounded in the hallway, and then Rafe's voice — that strong, clear, beautiful voice — spoke her name. "Britt? Ma? It's me. You can open the door. It's safe to come out now."

What comfort those words gave her. Almost as if her life passed in front of her, a parade of events played in her mind. Difficult times, yes, but a series of events that only magnified God's goodness through all the trials. Mom's death had crushed them, but it had ultimately led to their happy life in the cottages. And it had brought Quinn into Phee's life. And because of Phee's difficult pregnancy, Rafe had come into Britt's life. And then in a glorious full circle, as only God could do full circles, the delivery of Phee's baby had brought redemption for Rafe's deepest sadness. How could she ever *not* trust God's amazing hand?

She rose and, pulling Becky up behind her, unlocked the bathroom door and then went to the bedroom door and unlocked it too. Slowly opening it, she breathed a sigh of relief seeing Rafe standing there in the hallway. She let Becky go to him first. He put an arm around his mom's shoulders and let her sob.

But his eyes were on Britt. And what she saw in their blue depths — the tenderness, the deep relief, the *love* — she would carry with her as long as she lived.

CHAPTER 41

May

Britt stepped back and took in the full-length view of her sister. "Oh, Jo! You've never looked more beautiful!" The truth was, ever since the night Rafe had asked Britt to marry him, the whole world had never looked more beautiful. But this was Jo's day, and Britt was determined to honor that fact.

Jo smoothed her finger-waved hair beneath a short ivory veil. "You don't think the veil is too much?" She looked in the arched mirror propped against the wall of Far Cottage, which served as their dressing room, just as it had for Phee's wedding a mere eleven months ago. Eleven months that seemed like a lifetime.

"No!" Britt and Phee said at once, and Britt carefully adjusted the rose-shaped fascinator and its birdcage netting veil that reached just to the bridge of Jo's nose. The veil had first been worn by Luke's grandmother and added the perfect complement to her sleek tea-length ivory silk gown — and served as her "something old" as well.

"You look perfect. Absolutely perfect." Phee's voice broke and she dabbed at a tear in the corner of her eye. "Shoot! I don't want to ruin my mascara! Did you guys feel this emotional at *my* wedding? Why don't I remember?"

"There might have been a few happy tears." Britt reached to tweak the little-boy toes peeking out of the bouncer on the floor. The baby had already kicked off one bootie, but so far, the tiny black bow tie stayed firmly clipped to his white onesie. He was precious beyond words. "You're just emotional because you know how soon it'll be Will here who's getting married."

"That's right," Jo said.

Phee's tears turned to a look of shock. "There will be no talk of Will's *wedding* any time soon. What are you two *thinking?*"

Laughing, Jo caught Britt's eye. "I'll tell you what *will* be here before we know it: *your* wedding, Britt."

Britt swallowed the lump lodged in her throat. "I'm still trying to wrap my head around how we all ended up with such amazing guys in such a short time. Mom wouldn't believe it!"

"No . . ." A faraway look came to Phee's eyes. "She would believe it. I think she'd say, 'Well, what did you expect? I prayed for those amazing men starting the day you were each born.' "

Britt fought tears and murmured her agreement. "If heaven has a balcony, I think Mom is looking down right now, praying for each one of us." She turned back to fiddle with Jo's veil again, not wanting the moment to turn maudlin. "Luke knows to fold this part up before the kiss, right?"

"Don't worry." Jo brushed a finger over the fragile netting. "We've been practicing."

"Yeah, I bet you have." Britt grinned.

"Oh Jo, I'm so happy for you!" Phee's tears started again. "I'm so happy for all of us. Look how blessed we are!"

Yesterday morning, Quinn had stayed with the baby while the three sisters went up to the clearing to string up the rag garland they'd made for Phee's wedding. The cream and white garland had special meaning since it was made from linen curtains Mom sewed for the bedroom the three of them shared as girls.

Britt and her sweet sisters had laughed and joked as they frolicked like children in the clearing, weaving the garland through the branches of the trees overhead. Britt had spent hours adding new paper hearts — pale blue to match Joanna's color scheme — to replace the tattered white ones from Phee's wedding.

And while she worked, Britt had plotted how, for her and Rafe's wedding, new paper hearts would be filled with quotes from a certain Missouri bard. It would be her surprise for the man who'd won her heart with those crazy Mark Twain quotes. She smiled again, imagining Rafe's expression when he discovered what the writing on those hearts held.

But that was for another day, probably after autumn turned the leaves to gold. *Today* was Jo's day, and for the first time in a long while, Britt had been able to celebrate her sisters' joy — both of them — without jealousy and without feeling like her own life was "less than."

It wasn't just that she had her own wedding to look forward to, though there certainly was that. But somehow, finding her place to belong — in using her talents and gifts, but more importantly being with Rafe — had made her realize some important truths. He'd helped her talk things through and understand that just because her life had been shaped by circumstances rather than her own conscious choices didn't mean that God wasn't blessing the details of her life.

The truth was, she couldn't have been happier than she was now, doing exactly what she'd been doing since the day they bought the property. Why had it taken her so long to realize that finding her wings meant embracing life the way it was? In all its beauty, but in all its difficulty too. And recognizing that she had placed her life in God's hands, and it was He who allowed and orchestrated every moment. She'd simply had to learn to *embrace* what she'd already been given. She had a feeling that task would be much easier now that she'd found someone whose desire was to help her fly high. Someone to divide the joy in the journey with her. *Oh, thank You, Lord. You've been so very good to me. And I am so grateful.*

She and Rafe hadn't set a date for their wedding yet, but with Buck Obermeuller behind bars and Becky safely back in her house, and with little Will safely in the world, she and Rafe had found more hours to spend together. They both agreed that sooner was better than later where a wedding was concerned, and they'd bandied about "Rafetember" or "Brittober" as possible dates.

She smiled at the thought, then bent to peer through the window of the cabin. The new leaves on the trees hid the clearing from view, but the sun streamed through the branches bright and warm. "It's going to be a perfect day," she declared.

And it was. The forecast was for a high of seventy-five degrees, and there were still enough daffodils and grape hyacinths blooming to dot the floor of the woods with color. As if that wasn't enough, the dogwoods had bloomed late this year and still wore a smattering of pink and white to add to the whimsy.

A knock came at the door and the sisters squealed in unison. Britt looked at the clock. Five till four. "It's time, Jo! Ready or not."

Jo shivered, but her voice was clear and steady when she said, "I'm ready."

Britt went to answer the door, opening it just a crack in case it was Luke. Jo was adamant about not letting him see her in her dress before the ceremony.

Their dad stood there in a tux, looking handsome and tanned from the Florida sun and younger than he had the last time he was home. He'd flown in from Orlando on Wednesday night and the sisters had loved having him at the cottage, doting on him, but also taking advantage of having his wisdom and advice where the property was concerned. Britt and her sisters agreed that Daddy seemed to be thriving in his new life. It was hard having him so far away, but it appeared God was working in their father's life too. And she couldn't be sad about that. She turned back to her sisters. "Can Daddy come in?"

"Of course!" Jo grabbed her bouquet and struck a bridal pose, and Britt flung open the door.

His hand went to his heart. "How did I get such beautiful daughters? Oh, I wish your mother could see you all! Jo, you are a vision!"

"Don't make me cry, Dad!"

He shook his head. "Okay then, you look like something the dog dragged in."

"Dad! Daddy!" But they all laughed and tears were averted. For now, at least.

"It's time to go up." He crooked his left arm and extended it to Jo the way they'd practiced at rehearsal last night. "Are you ready?"

"You guys go ahead." Phee bent to straighten the blanket over the baby, and Will rewarded her with a toothless smile. "I'll be out as soon as Mary comes for Will."

Phee's former boss at the flower shop had offered to babysit during the ceremony.

"Have you been up to the clearing, Daddy? Are the men standing up front already?" Britt prayed she wouldn't swoon seeing Rafe in a tux. He'd been so honored when Luke asked him to stand up with him as a groomsman along with Quinn and Mateo.

"I peeked at the top of the stairs before I came down here. The guys were headed that way."

Another knock at the door brought Mary. After Phee gave the woman quick instructions about bottles and diapers, Jo took a deep breath. "Okay, sisters. Let's get me married!"

Though the sun shone brightly above the leafy dome of the clearing at exactly four p.m., it was dim beneath the canopy of trees. Daddy led the way as Britt and her sisters climbed the rustic stairs up to the clearing. At Jo's instruction, the twinkle lights had already been turned on, and when their eyes adjusted, they gave a collective gasp at the enchanting effect.

The four of them exchanged quick hugs, then taking a deep breath, Phee, Jo's matron of honor, started her slow march to the front, disappearing from sight over the rise of the hill. Britt counted to ten as they'd rehearsed, then lifting the hem of her dress slightly to clear the spongy floor of the woods, she followed her sister. The matching dresses she and Phee wore were peachy-orange fluffs of chiffon, and she felt ultra-feminine with the skirt brushing her legs as she walked.

As she climbed the rise to the aisle that ran between the two groupings of chairs filled with guests, Bach's "Air on the G String" wafted through the space. She found the song heart-achingly beautiful, and the birds overhead seemed to sing in key with the musicians. Jo's day would be perfect. Absolutely perfect.

Tears threatened and Britt prayed they wouldn't materialize. This was the happiest of days! Still she couldn't help but think of Mom, and of how — even though Luke and Mateo were a blessed addition to her family — life would never be quite the same after this day. *Please Lord, don't let me cry!*

Her silent prayer was answered in her very next step. She reached the top of the rise and spotted Quinn smiling at Phee with such love in his eyes. Continuing her slow walk, Britt panned the altar area. Next to Luke, Mateo stood straight and tall with a fresh haircut that made him look like a young man instead of a boy. But from the moment her gaze reached the end of the line and her eyes locked with Rafe's, her only thoughts were for him.

He did his best to keep a serious expression, but his eyes danced for her. And she knew his thoughts were one with her own: soon, very soon, it would be *their* day.

Britt took her place beside Phee and forced herself to look away from Rafe, to turn to face their guests and watch her sister make the most important walk of her life.

The music faded and then the strains of "Canon in D" swelled, and the friends and family who'd gathered in this place with them rose to their feet, and all eyes turned on Joanna, radiant on Daddy's arm, her eyes trained on Luke's.

Britt sent up a silent prayer for her sweet sister, but her fickle thoughts couldn't help but revel in this prelude to the not-so-distant day that it would be *her* on Daddy's arm, walking this same rain-soaked aisle in this glorious woodland chapel to join the man God had brought into her life in a story they would no doubt tell to their children and their children's children. Perhaps for all eternity. Because their love story, like those of her sisters, was one that only God could have written. And one that only God knew the ending to.

Daddy gave Joanna into Luke's hands and went to be seated. The guests took their seats and the wedding party turned to face Pastor Franklin, but not before Britt cast one more longing glance Rafe's way. The look he gave her in return held all the promises she could ever desire, all the love she could ever contain.

Like Mom and Daddy before them, they would cling tight to God and take the good along with the trials, knowing that with His help, the trials would only draw them closer to the One who'd started it all.

A NOTE FROM DEB

Dear Reader,

As an author, I find it so difficult to write the final pages of the final book in a series. My characters become like dear friends and it's hard to say goodbye! I hope you felt the same as you read this third and final book in the Chandler Sisters series. Thank you for choosing to read my books. I don't think readers ever fully understand how much we authors treasure you and value your opinion. In fact, you are the very reason I write!

When I set out to write a series about three sisters, I couldn't help but think of my own sisters. As I said in my dedication, Vicky, Kim, and Beverly were the first friends I knew, and while Kim has been in heaven for many years now (tragically killed in a car accident as a twenty-one-year-old newlywed), Vicky and Bev remain my dearest friends. We've been blessed to live in the same town for most of the past six years, and my sisters would be in my top-five list for any road trip or girls' night out.

I knew writing about sisters might be fraught with tension as I did my best to *not* make my Chandler sisters too much like my real-life sisters. I was not succesful! Let's just say that any lovely and winsome qualities in Phylicia, Joanna, and Britt Chandler came straight from my own sisters. And any of the annoying or frustrating qualities of the Chandler sisters are purely inventions of my imagination. (Or perhaps those traits spring from my own personality? After all, I *was* the bossy eldest.)

All jesting aside, I hope these novels ultimately show sisterhood in the beautiful, loving light I've known to shine on it. Those we shared our childhood home with understand and know us like no one else can. And — hopefully — they love us despite our many flaws. In short, sisters are a gift from God and a blessing beyond words. (And brothers too! My dear, long-suffering brother, Brad, managed to grow up unscathed, despite being the lone brother of *four* sisters. Poor guy!)

I love that social media allows me to keep in touch with you, dear readers! If you don't already follow me on Instagram, Twitter, the blog I write along with several author friends, or my Facebook Readers Page, I'd love to meet you there! You can find links to all those connection points and more on my website at www.deborahraney.com.

As I wrap up this final novel in the series, my deepest thanks go out to the many people who made these books possible. My agent, Steve Laube, as well as Catherine DeVries, Steve Barclift, and the team at Kregel, especially my editors, Janyre Tromp and Cheryl Molin.

I owe more than I can express to my beloved critique partner, friend, and favorite author, Tamera Alexander, along with others who read my manuscripts and offered suggestions and solutions — especially my dear friend Terry Stucky and my sister Vicky Miller.

I'm so grateful for the encouragement and love of my family. Perhaps I *could* still write a book without the support of our four kids and their families, my amazing dad, my wonderful mother-in-law, and so many other family members and friends — but I sure wouldn't want to! You all make the journey an absolute delight!

As always, thank you, Ken Raney, the love of my life, for making life such a glorious adventure! Thank you for pushing me to be my best, for encouraging me to step out of my comfort zone, and for your unwavering support over the years.

And most of all, thank You, Lord Jesus Christ, for the immeasurable blessings You have bestowed, along with just enough challenges to produce perseverance, character, and hope.

Deborah Raney
January 20, 2020

486

BOOK CLUB
DISCUSSION GUIDE

Spoiler Alert: These discussion questions contain spoilers that may give away certain elements of the plot.

1. In *Finding Wings,* Britt, the youngest of the three Chandler sisters, feels that because of her place in the birth order, she sometimes gets the short end of the stick and is left with the tasks no one else wants to do. Have you ever felt that way in your family or at your place of employment? How did you feel about that and what, if anything, were you able to do to remedy the problem?

2. The three sisters have grown very close since their mother's death and their father's move out of state. The sisters have chosen to live on the same property and to run a business together. What do you see as the blessings of such an arrange-

ment? What might the pitfalls be? Do you think this dynamic changes once the sisters' love interests come into the story?

3. Some of Britt's feelings of being left out revolve around the fact that her sisters have found the men they want to marry, share their lives, and start families with. If you are a youngest among siblings, was it difficult for you to see your siblings achieve life goals that you were years from realizing? On the opposite end of the time line, if you're an oldest child, were you ever jealous that your younger siblings enjoyed the freedom of youth while you had reached a time of taking on responsibilities with family or work? Maybe things weren't typical for your birth order and you achieved something before an older sibling or enjoyed freedoms your younger siblings didn't have. How did these things affect your relationships with siblings or other family members?

4. Britt feels that she's been saddled with more than her share of caring for infirm family members. How did you feel about Britt's attitude? Do you think she was justified in feeling the way she did? Sometimes, because of a person's availability or

proximity or stage of life, that does seem to happen. Have you ever been in that position? How did that make you feel?

5. Did you feel that Rafe was right to take on his mother's debt, given how she acquired that debt? Do you think Britt had a healthy attitude toward the issues that Rafe's mom was dealing with?

6. What do you think about Britt's late mother's statement, "You marry the family, not just the man"? If you've been married, did you find this statement to be true? Why or why not?

7. Phylicia had to go on bed rest fairly early in her pregnancy. Have you ever been bedfast or homebound (maybe during the COVID-19 pandemic)? What were some of the challenges you faced, and how did you handle those challenges? What did you learn from the experience?

8. What conclusion did Britt draw (with help from her sisters and especially Rafe) about finding her wings and launching into the world? Have you had a similar experience? Have your thoughts about

"finding wings" changed as you've grown older? Why or why not?

9. What did Rafe and Britt learn about their faith in God through the trials and challenges they faced? Read Romans 5:1–8. Have you seen those Scripture verses played out in your own life?

10. If you've read all three of the Chandler Sisters novels, which was your favorite story and why? Do you prefer reading series to stand-alone novels? What are the reasons for your preference?

ABOUT THE AUTHOR

Deborah Raney dreamed of writing a book since the summer she read Laura Ingalls Wilder's Little House books and discovered that a Kansas farm girl could, indeed, grow up to be a writer. Her thirty-five-plus books have garnered multiple industry awards including the RITA® Award, HOLT Medallion, National Readers' Choice Award, and Carol Award, and have three times been Christy Award finalists. Her first novel, *A Vow to Cherish,* shed light on the ravages of Alzheimer's disease and inspired the highly acclaimed World Wide Pictures film of the same title. *A Vow to Cherish* continues to be a tool for Alzheimer's families and caregivers. Deborah is on faculty for several national writers' conferences and serves on the executive board of the 2,600-member American Christian Fiction Writers organization. She is a recent transplant to Missouri with her husband, Ken Raney, having moved from their native Kansas to be closer to kids and grandkids. They love road trips, Friday garage sale dates, and breakfast on the screened porch overlooking their wooded backyard. Visit Deb on the web at www.deborahraney.com.

The employees of Thorndike Press hope you have enjoyed this Large Print book. All our Thorndike, Wheeler, and Kennebec Large Print titles are designed for easy reading, and all our books are made to last. Other Thorndike Press Large Print books are available at your library, through selected bookstores, or directly from us.

For information about titles, please call:
(800) 223-1244

or visit our website at:
gale.com/thorndike

To share your comments, please write:
Publisher
Thorndike Press
10 Water St., Suite 310
Waterville, ME 04901